The Storm
War's End: Book 1

Christine D. Shuck

Table of Contents

"*We overstayed our welcome. We bullied, we pushed, we invaded...and when we were done, when the world had felt our presence in every corner of it, felt our hand on their backs, shoving our way into every aspect of their lives, faiths, even their very existence...we were hated. God, were we hated. In retrospect I can feel no real surprise for what happened next. Our time had come. For our hypocrisy, for our crimes, we each paid such a terribly high price. The world we had known, the nation that our parents had been told to be proud of, a place of fast food and 'freedom fries', home of the consumer, center of capitalism, world leader, it all ceased to exist. It was a slow, painful end, an extended death rattle, as we slowly tore ourselves apart, and then allowed others to finish off what remained.*

What was left in the wreckage of the world that was? We were. And this is our story, my story, and the story of us all. We have survived. We have found a way to live on...in a world where ghosts haunt us and memories whisper in our ears. Life goes on, one day at a time, and by the skin of our teeth and the force of our will, we will continue. What else can we do?" - **Jess's journal**

On "Black Monday" - the long-faltering United States economy collapsed into complete chaos. In the past few years state after state had found themselves out of money and out of options. The federal government stopped promising bailouts and instead preached "state independence" and "more autonomy." Road projects and other public works were halted and hundreds of thousands of state and even federal employees were left holding worthless checks their banks no longer honored.

Abroad, things moved quickly as well. Quietly, without fanfare or publicity, American troops had been withdrawn from the Middle East and Korean conflicts. In some places they left under cover of night, a stark gaping hole left in their absence. Iraq and Afghanistan dissolved into civil war within days of being abandoned, while their neighbors looked on and tried to decide how to fortify their borders and contain the violence while also finding a way to profit from the conflicts.

Where had it all begun? Some said it had begun with OPEC no longer honoring the decades-long agreement to set prices and sell their oil based on American currency. Others claimed it had ended with China demanding payment in yen, not United States currency on the billions in debt it was owed by the United States. Still others pointed far back to the strategies put into place after World War II that transformed the United States into an economic and political world power and consumer nation.

However, it had begun, it was all now crashing down in ruin. The United States had overextended itself and the future of its citizens, financially, and politically in the hearts and minds of people throughout the world. From the not-so-benign 'foreign policy', to the endless wars waged in the Middle East, our country, once hailed as a world leader, had become a mindless bully. We were the tyrant, the monster at the door. Where there had once been handfuls of money to seemingly any country that asked, now there was only debt and abandonment.

The militias that had gone underground or been forcibly disbanded in the mid 1990's came back with ferocious fervor. Perhaps they had never really left. But everyone from the Luddites to the Neo-Nazi to small bands of survivalists was forming, each seeking to put their own unique vision of how the world should work into action. And with those thousands of voices clamoring for different methods, different approaches – combined with the financial collapse from within, abandonment by the rest of the world and foreign banks screaming for payment – all of these things brought one of the most powerful nations in the world to its knees. It heaved a great sigh and quickly began to come apart at the seams. The federal system went first, then the states, breaking into chunks of territories, areas full of in-fighting and instability. Among the military factions, abandoned by their government, rose a particularly dangerous and powerful network of soldiers in the West. They called themselves the Western Front.

Comprised of units from Fort Pendleton and Fort Irwin and picking up odd assortments of the militaristic militias along the way, the Western Front began to tear its way through Nevada and Colorado. Their numbers ebbed and flowed, but as more and more of the basic infrastructure of the country broke down, their power in numbers and weaponry increased. They began to turn their eyes to the east and rumors spread that they would soon be on the move.

Jess was twelve years old on Black Monday, and Christopher was fifteen. But they both remembered that day, just as their parents before them had remembered the fall of the Twin Towers or the day that President Reagan was shot. Mom had lost her job two months before after the latest layoffs, and Dad headed home after sitting around for half the day. No business, no customers, no one out on the streets. As if a death knell had been sounded, those who were still employed, those who still had jobs and places to go to suddenly found themselves at home, wondering what would happen next. That evening they watched the television in dull shock as the President held a press conference to announce that all debts, foreign and private, were to be held null and void. The British, who were heavily invested in American banks, were already threatening embargoes. The Chinese had been rioting for weeks over the trade/import issues, and their government was making threats that continued to grow in clarity and intensity.

The world seemed to be falling apart. Jess's parents said little, and in the months and years that followed, they simply tightened their belts, planted gardens, began raising chickens for eggs and meat, and found ways to get by on less. As the infrastructure continued to collapse, utilities and out of area supplies faltered. First there were the brownouts, just a lull in the electrical flow that rarely even caused the computers to reboot. Later there were blackouts, first for a few minutes and finally hours and even days at a time. The price of natural gas spiked so high that Jess's father Michael, installed a woodburning stove in the living room against the west wall. It was a prized antique, but it was also an honest-to-goodness working stove and Jess's mother Tess experimented with it regularly, churning out loaves of bread that slowly transformed from inedible black carbon, to uneven half black half browned to beautiful, perfect loaves over a course of a few months. "The pioneers did it," she said proudly, "and I can too!"

But the real Black Monday, the one that came on November 4th, was the one that tore apart Jess' world. And when it was over, when the Western Front troops tore through the small town of Belton, with barely a hiccup of resistance from its terrified residents, destroying any who even dared fight back, Jess learned what real loss felt like.

In the camps, miles to the South, weeks of marching later, and hours of standing in line at gunpoint, she found herself thrust into a tent. There was a long folding table, three men seated behind it, with several checklists on the battered folding table in front of them.

"Name?" The first man asked, barely looking up.

"Jessica Aaronson." She replied. The second man ran his finger down the lists, "Age?" he asked, bored.

"15."

"Parents?" he asked.

"Daniel and Tess Aaronson." He scanned further, finding nothing. "Any other relatives?"

"My brother, Christopher Aaronson." She tried to stay calm. There were so many people here, so many places they might be. She had been just a few miles away at the store buying flour and haggling with the store owner, Michael Banks, over the price of apples when the troops came barreling in. Hearing the shots and the tank he had pulled a weapon from a hidden place behind the counter. They had shot him on sight when they saw the rifle in his hands. His blood still stained her shirt. For three days she had tried desperately to search for her family as armed men kept the bedraggled, exhausted groups of prisoners under close watch.

The second man found nothing in his lists. He shook his head at the third, who had been eyeing Jess in a way that made her skin crawl.

She shivered, it had rained earlier while she stood in line, and she was wet and cold, filthy, and too terrified to even care that she had eaten little more than a handful of food in the past few days. Where were Mom and Dad? And Chris? Where the hell was everyone? Belton was not a big town, but it wasn't that small either. She had only seen one neighbor she recognized, Mrs. Dillon from down the street.

The third man smiled wide at her discomfort. It was an evil smile, full of malice and Jess shivered again in her damp shirt, "Well, she's available for assignment then." He wrote her name down on his list, and checked the 'Troop Entertainment' box and turned to one of the guards, "Take her to Tent Five." As the trooper took her by the arm and led her away, she could hear him call to her, "I'll be by later to see how you've settled in." He laughed then, and it wasn't a pleasant sound, then barked at the man next in line to step forward.

Her feet slipped in the mud and the trooper kept a firm grip on her arm, practically dragging her along. Mrs. Dillon was there in the line outside, "Did you find your parents, dear?"

Jess was in near tears, "No, Mrs. Dillon. They're taking me to Tent 5; please see if you can find Chris or my Mom or Dad, please!" She broke into tears then, partially from the painful grip the soldier had on her arm, partly from absolute terror, what the hell was Tent 5?

Behind her, Mrs. Dillon stood stock still, her usually impeccably groomed gray hair in disarray. Strands of gray stuck out from her bun wildly waving in the late fall wind. A young boy, clad in an oversized, stained blue and red Western Front uniform stood nearby, smirking as he watched the girl being dragged away. The old woman turned to him, and took a hold of his sleeve; he was barely fifteen if even that, she shook him slightly and demanded "Where are they taking her?"

"Lemme go, lady!" he wiggled, and one of the guards stationed nearby leveled his rifle and yelled at her to get back in line.

"Where are they taking her?" she persisted, "What's Tent 5?"

"That's the whores' tent, lady. She's gonna be 'tainment for the men."

Her grip loosened and her eyes widened in horror. He grinned at her maliciously, showing a mouth full of tobacco-stained and twisted teeth.

His tongue darted out to lick his chapped lips, "She gonna 'git it good too." He pulled free of her hand and took the opportunity to give the shocked old woman a hard shove, "Now 'git back in line."

Then the boy spit a long brown stain in the dirt, marking the old woman's shoe with tobacco juice as he walked away. She just stood there, trembling, tears of pity trickling down her lined face. A small, thin, ugly girl behind her in line leaned close and whispered,

"Welcome to hell."

Mrs. Dillon didn't have long to wait. A mere ten minutes later and it was her turn before the three seated men.

"Name?"

"Esther Dillon."

"Age?"

Her lip quivered, "I'm sixty-eight years old."

"Family?"

"Only my husband, Murray, and he died last year."

The second man didn't even bother to look up, but the third man did. And with a cold smile he simply scribbled her name, checked the 'Range Disposal' box and nodded to the guard. "Take her to the range."

The old woman went quietly, most of them did, and if anyone had been paying attention, which they weren't, they would have heard the single shot ring out a few minutes later. She was the tenth one that morning.

"There are those who prey on fear. It isn't war that makes them evil; they were already brutal and sadistic by nature. War simply gives them some level of freedom to do as they will, to act on their deepest, darkest desires." – **Jess's journal**

Tent Five was large—larger than any of the other tents in this muddy hell. It sat apart from the others and the only way in or out was ringed with wire. The main entrance flap was pulled aside, it was dark inside, and men were entering and leaving. A handful turned to assess the new piece of ass being hauled in.

Jess had tripped twice, slipping in the mud and it caked the front of her jeans, her free arm, and part of her shirt since the soldier had not even paused, just dragged her along until she managed to regain her footing and trot unevenly next to him. Her arm felt like it was on fire and she knew there would be bruises from his relentless iron grip.

Abruptly, just inside the tent flap they came to a halt. The tent was a rabbit warren of halls and partitioned rooms. Jess could hear a woman screaming, no, at least two, and the unmistakable sounds of sex. *Oh God. Oh God, oh God, oh God.* Her heart began to pound faster, she stood stock still, listening to the sounds and realizing...knowing what kind of a place Tent 5 was.

The soldier holding her arm felt her stiffen beside him, looked over at her and saw the spark of fear, then understanding in her eyes. She hadn't known before, but she knew now, oh yes, she knew now. He waited a moment, even loosened his grip slightly...this was the fun part.

Seconds ticked by, three, four, and on the fifth second, she pulled hard and jabbed left with her elbow, backpedaling to make a run for it. Her elbow jab missed, he was prepared for it, as he kicked her legs out from under her with one ruthlessly efficient maneuver. He sneered down at her; the girl was stupid; she took him for a recruit, which was her first mistake. Her second had been trying to hit him and that earned her a strong punch which he delivered to her nose before her body had even hit the ground. Her head thudded on the ground and she went limp. It was disappointing to see her lose consciousness so quickly, he preferred his victims to be a little more sporting. How easily she was subdued.

What he was not prepared for was the knife that had mysteriously appeared in her hand. His knife! Her eyes snapped open and she slashed the back of his right knee, cutting deep as he fell to the ground. Bitch! She turned onto her belly, scrambling from him, stumbling to her feet, blood streaming from her nose from his punch, and ran...straight into the arms of two soldiers heading into the tent.

This time, when they knocked her to the ground she stayed there, until the wounded soldier could lever himself close enough to attempt to choke her with his hands.

The other men laughed as they pulled him off of her, "You'll get your chance to get her back, Robbie you dumb bastard, just as soon as you get patched up!"

And with that, the medics arrived and helped him limp away, and Jess lay on the ground, afraid to get up, bleeding from her nose and mouth now, and listening to his furious howls as they headed for the hospital tent. One of the soldiers kicked her in the ribs, fast, hard, and she gasped in pain.

"That's for Robbie. Now you stay there until we say you can move, bitch." She could only see his boots, but Jess could swear she heard him grinning.

A third set of feet approached from deep inside the tent. "Who do we have here, Cooper dear?" the voice was neither male nor female, it defied placement and made Jess want to look up and see, she hurt too much, though, and was afraid the bastard standing over her would give her another kick.

Cooper was tall with jet black hair and pale blue eyes, "A new whore for you Carmen," he replied, "And she's a feisty one." He reached down and hauled her to her feet effortlessly. Her head pounded in pain as Jess looked up to see that Carmen still defied description, man, woman—the creature was sexless. And from the expression on 'her' face, utterly heartless as well.

"Hmmm...rather dirty, aren't you? Didn't your mummy and daddy teach you not to roll around in the mud?" Carmen looked down his/her nose, vaguely amused. "Strip her clothes off, Cooper."

The soldier holding her grinned, and pulled her closer against him, taking the opportunity to grope her breast, squeezing it painfully. The second man unsheathed a long hunting knife. Jess knew it was hopeless to fight, if she struggled, she doubted they would stop from cutting her with the vicious thing. They made short work of it; Lieutenant Cooper looked disappointed at her lack of struggle. They took it all off, and she knew they had won the first round. Without clothes she couldn't leave the tent. If she provoked them, they would rape her right here, maybe even beat her some more, maybe even kill her.

Stay alive. Wait for the moment. All this, ALL THIS will pass—she counseled herself silently—she held back the tears, and endured their taunts. They would grow bored, want someone more entertaining. *Wait. Wait. Wait for the moment.* And before she knew it, the Carmen creature was shoving her towards crude showers.

Her composure was brittle. It survived the ice-cold water being dunked over her head, the brush used to roughly scrape against her rapidly bruising skin, and Carmen's long nails cutting into her skin as she dragged her dripping down a short hall, through a curtain and into a room with a filthy bed in it. It did not survive, however, what happened next.

Carmen was strong, she/he shoved Jess to the bed and before she could fight back or jump up Carmen grabbed one wrist and secured Jess to the bed frame with a pair of handcuffs. Lieutenant Cooper was the first one through the door, brushing past and already pulling off his belt as Carmen exited and announced, "She's all yours, boys!"

And hours later, when the men had used her violently, laughed at her tears, and came inside her with satisfied grunts, one after another after another—she lay there in shock. She had blood on her thighs, bruises on her arms and legs, she ached from deep inside in her bones and wondered if Hell could possibly be worse.

*"There are moments when all of it is too much, too painful to remember. Yet then I look around at those who I love and realize I would not be here, with these people who I love and who love me, if those awful things had not happened to me. How do you reconcile that?" - **Jess's journal***

It was time to go.

Mom and Dad had not come. Chris had not either. No kind words from any familiar face, only the soldiers, young, old, smelling like they'd never had showers, hairy, smooth-skinned—all of them on her, using her.

After a while, her body had gotten used to it, even if her soul had not. The soldiers, who had laughed and delighted in her fear and pain, were now bored with her lack of response and chose other girls. The same men who sought out the newly caught girls or ones who never learned to deal with the abuse – these men were the worst. They took an evil joy out of it; while many of the others came only for the simple release of sex. Some of the men might even have been nice, one or two she even caught herself thinking that she would have dated them, been interested...but never in these circumstances.

She'd tried to be brave, but the first days had hurt so damn much. Some of them had laughed at her tears or, like that awful Lieutenant Cooper, found a perverse pleasure in her fear and pain. He had visited her day after day, taking his time to hurt her in new and unimaginable ways. Cooper was a regular at Tent 5. He seemed to prefer blue-eyed blonde girls and Carmen; the gravel-voiced, angular, androgynous 'director' of Tent 5 was eager to give him whatever he wanted.

After all, he was moving up in the ranks. Cooper had recently come to Granger's attention and been made second Lieutenant. Being nice to him and giving him what he wanted meant he would keep Carmen well supplied with coke, meth, whatever the Western Front troops managed to turn up on their raids.

Jess submitted to all of them, she did not resist, not at all, not after those first few days. Getting punched or kicked hurt like hell, so she did her best to avoid it. She let her eyes go dead and her body limp. As the days passed, most of her bruises faded and disappeared. They watched her close at first, especially that awful creature Carmen, waiting for her to try to escape again.

"Keep myself fed, so I'm strong. Find clothing. Find a weapon."

She ate everything they gave her, but slowly, so it would look like she did not have much of an appetite. That was not hard to fake, the food was terrible and some days she was sure she would die in this awful place. Many girls had, some due to abuse, but usually by their own hand. Twice in the last month they had pulled girls out in the morning, past the others, their bodies stiff and eyes fixed and staring, having figured out how to escape the camp by some ingenious method of suicide.

In a way, she envied them. It seemed easier somehow, instead of dealing with each day's new horrors. Just a month ago, as the camp had moved through a new area, devastating some new town and rounding up the residents. They sorted through them much as the residents of Belton, Jess's hometown, were sorted through.

One of them, a young teenage girl, had fought back. She had actually managed to kill one of her rapists, her hidden knife sinking home high in his leg, the femoral artery, and he had bled out in seconds. They had spent the next five days raping her. Afterwards they had cut her throat and left her naked body lying there on the icy ground as the camp moved on.

Twice the camp had moved, marched for days on end and she had watched carefully for an opportunity for escape. Two other girls had tried; bullets tore through them before they made it fifty yards. It was a good lesson - fail to escape, and you did not get another chance.

Jess stared with dead eyes at the landscape of the encampment as she slowly ate her food. Each day she would sit at the table from a different angle, studying the details without moving. She did this with little movement and no obvious curiosity. To anyone watching her it would appear as if she did not really notice her surroundings. Tent 5 was close to the center of the camp. So was the mess tent. The men's showers sat to the north, but they had seen little use since it had been far too cold. The latrines sat to the south this time. Thank goodness for that. In the last camp, a couple of idiots by the name of Easter and Burton had dug them to the west of camp and the wind had blown their foul stench over the entire camp for several miserable weeks until the camp moved on.

Jess knew what she needed to do. She didn't question it, didn't mull over it, one way or the other, she was going to live...or kill as many of the soldiers as she could before dying.

After weeks had become months, they had stopped watching her as closely. One of her 'visitors' had dropped a knife, a tiny Muela still in its sheath. He had never visited again, nor reported the loss, most likely because he had died in a raid two days later. The knife was small, and fit in Jess's hand as if it were made for it.

As she lay on the bed, listening to the stirrings of the camp around her in the pre-dawn darkness, Jess resolved that it would have to be at night, and soon. The moon was new and the darkness would help hide them.

Them...it was no longer just her that needed to escape. Her friend Erin was in Tent 5 as well. She knew which room Erin was in and how to get to her. She had almost let her composure slip when she had seen her best friend hauled in two months ago. Erin had been with her family, visiting friends in Clinton when the Western Front blasted through Belton. Jess had thought of her best friend often, hoped that she was safe and wished she had gone with her on the trip.

She had shown no reaction to Erin's calls to her, not even turned and looked in her direction. She had sat at one of the battered tables with several of the other girls, and continued to chew on the half burned, half raw meat, and Jess's long blond hair falling down in a tangled curtain around her face. She could feel several sets of eyes on her as Erin screamed her name.

Let them think she was catatonic. Let them think that she was so messed up inside that nothing could touch her anymore. Let them think of her as a piece of furniture. Furniture does not think, it does not scheme, and it sure as hell does not even *try* to escape. Furniture is there to be used and then ignored until it comes in handy again. How she hoped that is what they thought of her now. Because if they did, then they would not know what was happening until it was too late.

Her lack of response seemed to satisfy the guard. He was tasked with watching the handful of girls eat their meal. The other girls looked over at her, barely interested, one of them glassy-eyed from drugs she had begged off of the men. Jess had seen what the drugs did, and alternated between coveting them and hating seeing what they did to the others. It took some of the pain away, made them not care they were being violated every day, but they slowly transformed under the drugs' influence and the physical abuse. From what Jess could see, *they* were the walking dead, not her.

It had killed her to listen to Erin's screams later that morning. She would have given anything not to hear her friend's pain. She even prayed to an indifferent God to help her not hear. It made no difference, and somehow, she felt responsible. Somehow, she had to get them out of there, both of them.

The weather was cold, sometimes bitterly so. The nights had slipped down below freezing and Carmen forced to dole out clothing to keep the girls warm during the cold nights and days. Socks, but not shoes, were allotted. Jess had contrived to steal an extra sock here or somehow 'lose' a shirt. She slowly worked at the hole in the bottom of her mattress until it was open just enough to hide the extra clothing. Without shoes to protect their feet, they would need as many layers of socks as they could squirrel away. The extra clothing would help keep them warm on the chilly nights.

Fortunately, the clothing was the same as the Western Front uniforms, an oversight on the part of Jess's captors that might help her to be less conspicuous when she and Erin made a break for it. There was no way she would leave without her best friend. They would escape or die together; it was the least she could do.

The handcuffs had stopped Jess from escaping long ago. She had tried everything, bent paperclips, a nail, but nothing would budge the locking mechanism. The solution to that problem came in the form of a visit from Allen Banks.

Last evening, just before the camp settled in for the night, Allen had come to her room. Allen was a few years older, also from Belton; he had been in her brother's grade. He used to visit their house often since his grandparents lived just a few blocks away. During the long summer months, he made a regular appearance every four or five days.

He would arrive at the house, red and sweaty from pushing his grandpa's old-fashioned lawnmower over his grandparent's large lawn. Allen had always been a bit on the chunky side, and she barely recognized the slim brown-haired man who pushed aside the curtain flap and advanced toward the bed.

He came in, said nothing and neither had she, neither of their faces betraying any recognition. He climbed on top of her, and leaned in as if he were kissing her neck as he whispered in her ear, "Jessie, a big storm's rollin' in tomorrow, next day at the latest," he pressed something into her hand, "Get the hell out of here. Head west. Chris is *alive*. We will join you if we can, but they watch us even closer than they watch you. When the time comes, you *leave*, and don't you dare look back or wait for us. Got it?"

She gave a small shudder in response and he knew she had heard him. His lips brushed her cheek, hesitated for a long second, then pressed fiercely against hers for a moment. It startled her, just as much as the change in his tone did when he sat up and slapped her thigh, "This little bitch is the most borin' piece of shit I've had in a long time. Carmen! Get me something that don't lie here like some damn log!"

Two other men passing by the open flap laughed as Allen strode out to join them. Jess snuck a peek at the piece of metal in her hand – an honest to god handcuff key! She quickly shoved it out of sight. Later she hid the handcuff key in the hole in her mattress.

Chris was alive! She composed herself before her face gave her away. For the first time in months, she began to hope. Allen's kiss still burned on her lips. The key would set them free.

Each night, before Carmen went to sleep, she made the rounds and made sure each girl's handcuff was tight around one wrist and secured to the bed frame. By that time, the camp was dark and quiet with guards posted and the rest asleep. Jess waited in the dark, eyes wide open and staring, body tensed, until she was sure anyone nearby was sound asleep. She fit the key into the lock, released her sore, scabbed wrist from its captivity and crept quietly through a hallway to reconnoiter.

Two guards and a shift change every four hours. The entrance was the only way in or out of the tent. Unless...Jess thought of the knife she had squirreled away in her mattress. Would it be able to cut the tent fabric?

The hardest part of it all was putting the handcuffs back on that night and then lying down to face another day. If she were not ready, *completely* ready, it would mean failure. Failure meant death and Jess was not ready to die, not just yet.

It was now late March. Spring and warmer weather were just around the corner. The camp was settling in for the night. No electricity combined with cold nights meant that, after sundown, activity slowed to a crawl. Jess had heard Carmen comment to one of the guards that there was bad weather headed their way. "Looks like there's a hell of a storm brewing," she said, "it's coming in from the West fast and hard. We'd best get all the girls secure now before it hits." They turned away two soldiers who complained loudly until one soldier's hat blew off his head and he ran after it. The lone soldier, with no companion to back him up, sulked away.

Night came early with black storm clouds leading the way, blocking the weak afternoon sun. The wind was beginning to howl, tearing at the tents, forcing the soldiers to damp the campfires for fear of sparks. There was little visibility, and thunder boomed in the distance.

Jess closed her eyes, waiting for the sound of footsteps to die away and darkness to descend. If only they could get out and away before the light show rolled in. She waited, long moments, her ears straining for any man-made sound above the wind and patter of rain on the tents. The canvas buckled and shook. It was noisy, that was good, better to hide any sounds she and Erin might make.

At last, when she had satisfied her fears that Carmen and the guards had settled for the night, she slipped the tiny key out of the hole in the mattress and it into the handcuffs. "*One...two...three*" [click]

The handcuff came loose from her wrist. She sat up quietly, heart pounding, turned and reached for the other handcuff in the dark and quickly opened and removed it from the bed frame. It didn't seem like much of a weapon, but who knew when it might come in handy. She slipped it into the pocket of the shirt she had 'liberated', reached again into the hole in the mattress, pulled out the three pairs of socks and slipped them over her feet. Three tiny, stale rolls of bread followed the handcuffs into her pocket. Food was food, and this little bit was better than nothing.

Finally, she pulled the thin blanket off of the bed, taking a moment to fold and roll it into as small and easily transportable bundle as she could. As she stepped into the long corridor, Jess's heart was beating so hard that it pulsed in her ears. Outside the tent, the rain had increased its tempo, the wind howling mournfully. She trembled as she stood in the narrow corridor. She had watched, listened, and she knew exactly where Erin was. She had counted the steps herself when they escorted her to the showers and back. *"Just eighteen steps,"* she counseled, *"just eighteen steps, you can do this."* She forced herself to move forward, counting each step and knowing, even in the pitch blackness of the corridor, that if she reached out, her hand now extended directly into Erin's room.

Her eyes were straining for any light, but there was none, so Jess closed them and envisioned the cot and its placement and moved towards it from memory. *"Just one more step,"* and she felt the side of the bed against her left hip. Now for the tricky part – how to wake Erin without causing her to scream or make any noise that would wake the others?

She reached out with her left hand and felt for her friend in the dark, she touched hair and felt Erin rouse and begin to tense as she shook off the sleep and realized there was someone standing over her. Jess bent close, "Erie, it's me," she whispered, using her childhood nickname and hoping to God the storm was loud enough to ensure her voice didn't carry to any others.

Her friend began to shake and sob quietly, found Jess's hand and grabbed it tightly. They hugged each other, both crying. It had been so hard for her to ignore her friend, to pretend to not see her. Erin released a small sob, "Shh, it's okay, we're getting out of here tonight," Jess whispered in her friend's ear and patted her friend's back with her free arm. Once Erin had calmed down enough to let go of her hand, Jess quickly undid the handcuffs and freed her.

She sat on the edge of the bed and carefully removed a pair of socks, pushed them into Erin's hands to put on and stripped the bed of its two thin blankets. Then she crept over to the outer wall of the tent and waited for a loud gust of wind and accompanying thunder to begin stabbing the canvas with the little knife. It took a long time to tear a hole in the thick fabric despite the sharp blade, but the girls took turns as Jess explained in a whisper about Allen's visit and the idea of using the storm as cover for their escape.

The rain was now drumming down on the tent, causing various drips where there were holes or thin, worn areas in the thick canvas roof. The girls worked as quickly as they could, their wrists aching from the effort and their knees sore and cold from kneeling on the floor. They had to get out and as far away as possible so that their tracks were washed away by the rain.

Finally, the hole in the canvas was big enough to fit through. It would be a tight squeeze. Jess grabbed Erin's hand and pulled her close, gave her another quick hug, "You ready?" she could barely hear her friend whisper 'yes' over the now near-constant thunder, "Okay. Here is what we're going to do. Climb through the hole and then head towards the right, that's the closest cover, in the trees a few hundred yards away. Whatever happens, don't stop and don't let them take you, no matter what, okay?"

Erin simply hugged her back in response and Jess could feel her head nod in agreement. She grabbed the blankets, gave one to Erin and kept one for herself. She also handed Erin one of the sets of handcuffs, "Just in case," and then pushed her way through the hole.

The rain instantly drenched them both. It was intense now, and the lightning wasn't too far off in the distance. They needed to hurry. Erin followed; her blanket clutched tightly in her hands. A quick survey around them showed nothing in the blackness. For all that either of them knew a sentry could be standing next to them. Jess had a firm mental map of the camp; she had taken surreptitious glances each time the girls were marched to the mess tent for their two meager meals a day.

She looked around, squinting through the water that poured from the sky, heavier than a shower, and ice cold. Where would they find Chris and Allen, which tent were they in?

Allen's words rang in her ears, "*When the time comes, you* leave, *and don't look back or wait for us.*" Tears joined the rain on her face. "Oh God, Chris, what should I do?" Even Erin did not hear her words; they were lost in the violent downpour. She clutched at Jess's arm, too frightened and disoriented to leave without her. Jess had to make a decision.

She grabbed Erin with her free hand and pulled her close, pointing to the line of trees. At that moment the lightning came closer and lit up the sky to the west, showing the line of forest, the outlines of the tents and no one else in sight. They walked quickly. Jess fought the urge to run. They didn't have much time, but she feared falling on the uneven ground and twisting an ankle. If they hurt themselves now, they would be able to manage a full-out run later.

Every part of them was soaked by the heavy rain and they shook, adrenaline coursing through them. They neared the edge of the camp and Jess caught a flicker of light as a tent flap opened and a sentry stepped out holding a small penlight. She pulled Erin with her into the shadow of the tent, her heart beating fast and painful in her chest. The man was only a few steps away. He stood there in the rain, facing away from them, his head tilted to one side as if listening for something.

The rain pelted him, rivulets running down his raincoat, and still he stood there. The pale yellow of the flashlight flicked lazily around, dimly lighting various dark corners of the camp.

The girls clutched one another, hearts hammering in their chests, terrified the soldier might turn around. The lightning was now lighting up the sky above the camp. Finally, after what seemed like hours, instead of mere seconds, he grunted, turned the flashlight off and slipped back into the tent.

They crept past his tent and began to run towards the trees. Their focus was on safety, the cover of the trees, and they moved as fast as the thin socks on their feet would allow towards the line of forest in the distance. Once they reached the forest, their progress slowed, the dense, twisting floor of the forest slowing them considerably. At least they were out of sight of the camp now. Above, lightning flashed, striking a tree at one point just a few yards from them. Jess could feel her hair stand on end and her body thrum painfully as the current passed through the tree and into the ground around it. The simultaneous crack of thunder was ear-splitting.

If they hadn't been so busy trying to put as much distance between themselves and the camp, the girls would have laughed at the irony. Running straight into a storm, a lightning storm, and nothing around them but trees! But at least they could see their way through the darkness and rain, the light show ensured that.

Jess would look later at her feet, bruised and scraped and swollen, and wonder how she had not felt a thing as they sprinted through the twists of the forests, falling, getting back up, and simply running with no clear goal except to put as much distance between them and the soldiers' camp as possible.

The storm passed over them and moved east and they continued to head west. Slowly, the rain relented. Hours later, dawn lit the tops of the trees, slowly filtering down into the damp forest below. By now both of them were exhausted, filthy, scratched and bleeding. Fear had spurred them through the forest, deep into its core, but the light of the new day, cloudless and barely above freezing, seemed to leach all energy from them. Their run had slowed to a walk and finally to a slow stumble.

"I gotta stop Jess," Erin panted raggedly, "Do you think it's safe to stop for a little while?" Her hair was a mass of tangles, burrs, and twigs. Her face was scratched and there were countless scratches and even gashes on her legs, the blood smeared and dried, where she had fallen when running. Jess thought her friend looked like hell. But then again, she probably did too; she just didn't have a mirror to gaze into.

In front of them was a stream, high and rushing from the night's rain, willow trees on the opposite bank and solid ledges of limestone lining the east bank. A fallen tree had created a bridge across and there was a nook on the opposite bank covered with leaves and moss. It looked as appealing as the softest, satin covered bed the girls could imagine sleeping in. They both noticed it at the same time and nodded silently, too exhausted to waste their breath or energy on words—yes, it would suffice. They crossed over the stream to the soft, mossy nook.

They gulped fresh water which had pooled in a crook of a bowl-shaped rock near their feet. Jess marveled at the realization that they had somehow managed to keep hold of the blankets during their panicked escape. Jess pulled one blanket into a semblance of a large pillow and they both sank down against it lying close to each other and shivering in their damp clothes. The other blanket barely covered them. Minutes ticked by.

"Jessie? They killed my mom and dad." Erin began to shudder, "And then they shot Toby 'cause he tried to stop them from taking me." Jess put her arms around her friend and held her close as the tears fell.

"They're all gone, Jessie, they just killed them and then they took me...and I saw you..." her voice broke, "and I called to you and you didn't look at me, Jessie...not once."

Jess was crying now as well. "Oh Erie, I wanted to! I wanted to stop them, to run then, but I was scared to. I'm so sorry Erie, I'm so sorry!"

And they said no more; just hugged each other close and cried, until they were too exhausted to cry anymore. And then the two girls slept. It would be late afternoon before either of them stirred.

“*It is the question, the unknown ending, which bothers me the most. When I reflect on the luck of our escape that night from the Western Front's camp, that no one saw us or stopped us, I wonder how we did it when so many others failed. I marvel at how* lucky *Erin and I were, but the questions always haunt me. What happened to Chris? What about Allen? Did they manage to escape? Did they die trying? I hate not knowing. I keep thinking that somewhere, out there, my parents might still be alive. That Chris and Allen might still alive. Some part of me is scared too. I'm scared to* stop *thinking of them. I guess I'm afraid that if I don't keep them alive in my memories, it will be as if they never existed. And that consequently, a part of me will cease to exist as well.* – **Jess's Journal**

Allen was an only child, on the plump side for most of his eighteen years, with brown hair and kind brown eyes. He had never been outstanding in much of anything, but he was kind and considerate to family, friends, and strangers alike. His favorite person in the world was his grandfather, Thurman Banks, a soft-spoken man with a shock of white hair and brown eyes the same color as Allen's. After old Thurman hurt his knee one spring Allen had made it a habit to walk over to his grandparent's house and mow the yard with Grandpa's antique push mower. It took a while, but then he would cool off with a tall glass of blueberry lemonade, courtesy of Gram. Later he incorporated stopping by at Chris's house for a video game or a game of catch.

He would never be as good as Chris at either activity, but his friend was always happy to see him and Mrs. Aaronson would hug him hello and usher him in the front door. She would give him a gentle push towards the basement where Chris and his friend Toby McGowen were usually hanging out. Chris was good-looking, blond and blue eyed. He was the star quarterback on the team and there was talk of a football scholarship even in these bad times. Sometimes it seemed to Allen that Chris was everything that Allen was not - good looking, athletic, and popular. But Chris was also down to earth and personable. He looked out for everyone, and he had stuck up for Allen, defended him against snipes about his pudgy waist and poorly-defined biceps. He had been an honest and true friend since grade school.

Allen would stay for hours, sometimes for dinner, sometimes the night if it was a Saturday. Eventually the phone would ring and it would be Gramps calling to give him a ride home. On the nights he stayed for dinner he avoided looking at Chris's little sister Jess. Her blond hair fell in waves around her shoulders. Her eyes were straight-out-of-the-Crayola-box blue and, like her brother, she was unfailingly kind. She never played the bratty little sister and would often join them in the basement with her best friend Erin, Toby's sister. They would play endless video games or, in later years when the power had failed, they would go for hikes and picnics in the nearby woods and parks.

In a way, Allen had always been in love with Jess. She was cute, sweet, and didn't seem to notice that he wasn't as good-looking or athletic as the other guys. She gave him her friendship, and thanks to the sobering fact that she was too darned pretty for him to even dare to ask out, he nurtured his little crush quietly and didn't seek to make it any more than that. He didn't have the nerve to risk rejection and she was Chris's little sister after all. He was certain she was oblivious to his feelings, anyway.

Those endless summer nights in Belton seemed so impossibly far away. What he didn't want to remember were the last few hours he had spent in the town of his birth. The soldiers and guns, the fires set to homes, and everywhere people screaming. He still had nightmares of Mrs. Brown crying in the street over the lifeless body of her husband and one of the kids from a block up wailing for his parents.

He had seen his 10th grade Honors English teacher, Mrs. Grady, with half her face burned. She had run from her house as the flames licked up the walls and consumed her roof, only to be cut down in the street by a bullet. She had stood there after the shot rang out with a startled expression on her face, the red stain widened on her white blouse, and she had slowly crumpled to the ground.

Others had been shot when they tried to return to rescue pets, other family members, or possessions. Half of the town had seemed to be on fire and he didn't argue with the soldiers as they aimed their weapons at him. He put his arms up, submitted to them as they shoved him to the ground and did a rough search of his pockets for weapons. The soldier searching Allen found his wallet, pulled out the cash inside and punched him, hard, when he raised his head to object.

The wallet, now empty of cash, was thrown to one side, his hands were bound in front of him with zip-tie and he was shoved into a large group of terrified residents.

It was the stuff of nightmares, watching your home destroyed, not knowing whether your parents were alive or dead, and that most of what you loved, what you understood of the world, had been changed irredeemably. Jess's parents were among the same group of prisoners as Allen was. Mr. Aaronson stayed relatively calm, struggling to ease his wife's fears, and Mrs. Aaronson was nearly hysterical, worrying about Jess and Chris. She had sent Jess to the store and Chris had taken off early in the day to visit a friend, she didn't know where. The three of them had huddled together as they were marched from town, south on Y for miles. There were other groups of prisoners, mainly young men and women. The children were sometimes left behind, if they caused trouble for the soldiers. This included moving too slow or crying too loud. By the end of the second day, most of the adults had exhausted themselves trying to carry the children along and avoid a confrontation with the soldiers.

Already several older men and women had been shot when they fell behind. Rumors flew thick and fast. Someone reported that they had seen the soldiers set fire to the old folk's home and laugh as its aged residents tried to escape, taking potshots at them and those who ran to help. It was brutal, unbelievable, and Allen wondered at what had happened to the soldiers' humanity. They weren't in a foreign land, where the people looked different or spoke a different language. The soldiers were shooting people who looked like their mothers and fathers, their grandparents.

Allen was witness to both of the Aaronson's end on the third day. One of the soldiers, obviously in command of the others, had had enough of the stragglers. When the man pushed his jet-black hair away from his ice-blue eyes, Allen couldn't see a trace of humanity within. Lieutenant Cooper ordered the adults holding the children to put them down and for everyone to start marching. The children were exhausted, they literally couldn't walk any further, and as they fell behind Julie and then Michael both tried to break ranks and help them. The gap between the group of prisoners and the children was widening and the smaller ones began to wail in fear. Allen watched helplessly as the raven-haired, blue-eyed devil shot Jess and Chris's parents. He felt frozen in time and space and the world felt hollow. A skinny, foul-smelling soldier gave him a good shove with his rifle. To help them meant to join them in their fate and try as he might, he wasn't ready to die. He turned away from the bodies, away from the small children grouped there on the road, and allowed the soldiers to herd him away with the other prisoners.

As he marched away, Allen thought to himself, "*This is what war does to us. War takes the best part of us away and makes us into something else.*" He watched those with some speck of humanity left in them turn away as innocents were slaughtered.

The desire for survival is a strong one. And in the end, even kind-hearted Allen valued life more than the moral high ground. What Allen did in the next few days and weeks and months, what he did to survive, would haunt his dreams every night for the rest of his life.

How ironic that, in the months since the invasion of Belton and his own conscription, his weight had melted off, revealing a strikingly handsome profile beneath. Between the marches, the beatings and threats, and his conscription into this bastardized excuse for a 'company' he had lost the baby fat that had followed him so doggedly into adolescence and young adulthood. His arms and legs were now lean and muscled, his stomach tight and flat. The first time he saw his reflection he pulled back in surprise. A different man, a stranger with haunted and hollow eyes, stared back at him.

The army that he had been forced to join was no army, no company at all. They weren't soldiers, they were terrorists, thieves and thugs all rolled into one. To save his own pitiful life he had convinced them he wanted to join. Allen had kicked and beat the other 'recruits.' He had visited the women in the tents. He had shouted, "Yes, sir!" with the rest of them. He had done all of this in order to live another day.

He had located Chris and carefully found a way for them to meet and plan an escape. They were both still watched, Chris more than Allen, because he had resisted. Allen had found a way to get near him and talk. He picked a fight and lost and got latrine duty. He knew Chris was already there. Then he had punched Chris, yelled at him, talked trash, and after the initial shock, his friend wised up to the act and played along.

They kept getting themselves in just enough trouble to be assigned the dirty jobs no one else wanted. Then they called insults at each other so that everyone was sure they hated one another. He found ways to communicate important troop movements and other news to his friend. Allen was able to update Chris that Jess and her friend Erin were both in Tent 5.

When Chris first heard about it, he nearly screwed it up for both of them, he lost it so bad. The thought of Jess in that awful place had stopped him in his tracks and he'd grabbed Allen's shoulder in a painful grip. Allen had punched him hard, hard enough to knock his friend down on the ground with a thump. He hadn't said anything for a long time after that, just stared into the distance. Then he'd got up, dusted himself off, and pulled himself together.

Over time, through the bitter cold of winter, they found ways to meet. Sometimes they would find a way to speak while in line for slop, near the showers, or by picking a fight and getting latrine duty again.

Whatever it took, they had to escape, and take the girls with them. It was Chris who had managed to get the handcuff key. He passed it to Allen reluctantly. They had argued about this over and over. He wanted to go to Tent 5 and see Jess. Allen knew what would happen. Chris would lose it again and make a scene. He would fight to get her out, and they'd both end up dead. Jess needed *out* and Allen was going to move heaven and earth to make sure that happened.

Winter was ending and the weather would soon turn from chilly winds to wet, tumultuous rainstorms. He had seen the first green weeds and spring flowers emerging. There had been a patch of jonquils and tulips in the ruins of an old farm just half a day's walk from here. He was sent out as part of a raiding party mid-March and recognized that winter would be over soon, early even, if the increase in vegetation and greenery were any indication. It was his willing participation in that particular raid which relieved any lingering concerns about where his loyalties lay. This freed him to roam freely through camp, which was the next to final step needed towards putting their escape into motion.

The raid, which had included actions that plagued him with nightmares; was a success and he and the other soldiers were rewarded with a visit to Tent 5. He'd been there twice before, once after he'd kicked the crap out of Chris, punching him in the face while slipping the note he'd written to his friend into his front pocket while he lay stunned and bleeding on the ground. The other time was when he kept some poor newbie recruit in line and stopped him from trying a very poorly planned escape attempt. He'd made it look like the kid had been stealing extra rations instead of getting ready to run. He'd saved the kid's life, but doubted the kid even realized it. In any case, it hadn't really helped him that much. A few days later the boy had made another attempt, and this time no one had bothered to try and stop him. He was shot dead less than ten yards from the tree line.

Allen knew exactly where Jess was being kept, although before this he hadn't been to her room. Her screams, coming from the opposite end of the tent the first time he had visited the tent had given him nightmares. The thought of her being used in such a way twisted his guts in knots and he had restrained himself with difficulty from running in, killing that monster Cooper and attempting some stupid and doomed escape. It had been a solid month before he could return and even then, he wasn't sure he could see her like that, so he stayed on the other side and did not attempt contact. Now that spring was coming, with the possible cover of thunderstorms, they could all escape. Footprints couldn't be as easily tracked without snow and ice on the ground.

Allen took a deep breath as he entered the tent, his guts twisting at the sounds that came from this awful, soul-killing place. It had been nearly four months since he had seen her. He steeled himself for it and pushed aside her room flap and walked in. She was lying there, not handcuffed, thank god; they only did that at night now. She wore a faded red Western Front uniform shirt and she had a thin blanket covering the rest of her. Someone had just finished with her. Allen's bile rose in his throat as the soldier had swaggered past zipping up his pants. Allen ignored him and held himself back from doing great violence at that moment. It was all he could do not to turn around and grab the guy from behind in a sleeper hold. It would be righteous and satisfying to choke the life out of him.

She didn't recognize him until he had climbed on top of her and leaned in close. In that moment she stiffened. It had certainly happened before with some of the boys she had known in high school.

They were conscripts, here under the same circumstances as Allen. But as the months stretched out and the distance between Belton and this place grew, they slowly changed. The tent had seen a slow uptick in visits from conscripts. They avoided each other's gaze if they met in the corridors but shame didn't stop them from coming back.

Her body was warm and soft underneath him. She smelled, *damn,* she smelled like vanilla and musk. He whispered in her ear the plan and slipped her the handcuff key. He was embarrassed to realize he had a hard-on, although who would have blamed him? It was natural; she was beautiful and sweet, even now in this terrible place. She was everything he had ever wanted. Maybe after this was all over, when they escaped, with effort he banished the thought and hope of it from his mind. Back to *business*. It was time to act tough like he did with Chris in front of the others. He kissed her lightly on the cheek and took one great liberty – kissing her on the lips. Then he had slapped her thigh hard, talked shit, and got up and walked out of the room. It was the grand and dramatic exit, and it had its effect. Carmen, that monstrous and sexless creature, laughed and pointed him down the hall towards another open room.

As he walked away, his hand strayed to his lips, still feeling the softness of hers against his and he realized that the only thing that had stopped him from grabbing her and running like hell for the door was the image of Chris trying to do it and how it would look when he failed. He had done what he could. Now Jess would have to get her and Erin out at the right time. Cross their fingers, cross the toes, and a truckload of luck, and they all might make it out of there alive.

His pretty fantasy of them escaping hand in hand together was shot to hell when Chris refused to head west that fateful night. Instead he insisted on heading towards Tennessee. "The girls will need a head start, and plenty of time, I'm heading southeast, so hopefully the trackers will follow my trail.

There are three others who know we are planning something and want in on it."

Allen did not like the sound of this. Together, they had a better chance of survival. But three new guys he hadn't met and didn't know if he even trusted?

Alone, what would the girls do in the wilderness? How would they cover their tracks or survive? He asked all of these questions and more of Chris.

"Erin knows plenty of survival skills. Her parents were some kind of survival nuts and Toby knew so much he could practically teach the rest of us how to live off the land and survive during any season. The family went camping all the time. Jess has the key. So, she will get them out of there and Erin will keep them fed. Besides," he said, sounding far more confident then he felt, "we just need to do big circles and then get everyone back to Belton. Not everything burned, not everyone is dead."

Allen just shook his head. This was not what they had planned. "I'll head northwest, get back up to Highway 60; hopefully I'll meet them along the way to Springfield. Don't go far into Tennessee, double back, and we'll all join up again."

It was wishful thinking, this plan of theirs. Its success was contingent on so many variables, and each of them had to go just right for success to occur. Despite the horrors of the past few months, Allen and Chris were still young and idealistic. They had no idea just how badly the plan would go wrong.

In the violent storm that followed, the three other men were shot in the back before they ran past the outermost tent on the north. The girls made it out and took off west, straight into the storm. Allen watched as they disappeared into the trees. Their escape was successful, no one raised an alarm until one of the guards had gone looking for something sweet at three in the morning. When he realized Erin's bed was empty of anything but a strategically placed pillow, he had woken the entire camp. Chris had also run into the night without incident, heading southeast towards Tennessee. Allen had delayed leaving until he was sure no one was following the girls. He was caught the following day as he lay wrapped in a sodden blanket, having passed out under a fallen tree, exhausted from running.

The memory of Jess's body beneath his kept him focused when they interrogated him. He had said nothing when their fists smashed his nose and knocked out two of his teeth. But he had screamed, oh god how he had screamed, as Cooper's knife cut deep into his ankles, ensuring he would never, ever manage to escape again. Or ever really walk. But Allen knew his time was up. They had thrown the dice and while some had won to play another day, he was a dead man. He said as little as possible, grinding his teeth as Cooper cut on him, and finally screaming when the pain got to be too much. He told them nothing, nothing more than they already knew. They knew that Jess, Erin, Allen and Chris had all come from the same small town. In his heart he nourished the hope that their escape was certain now. It had been three days and no word.

Cooper leaned close, shoved the knife in all the way to the hilt and twisted it back and forth in the deserter's gut. He smiled as Allen's eyes glazed in agony. He figured he had about twenty minutes, maybe thirty, before the little crap died. He took his time, described how he had screwed the little whores, both of them, but especially the little blond one, every possible way, again and again. He promised the boy he would do it again, when he found them, over and over and over, until they were both dead. He was pissed off and frustrated. Kipling would have a cow when he found out that he had knifed this little weasel but at the moment he didn't care.

Allen knew he was dying. He felt removed from it all, as the pain seemed to fade away. He could smell her still. That sweet, fresh scent as he had laid against her in Tent 5 stayed with him. He cherished that memory, held it close and ignored the man standing over him.

It pissed Cooper off that the kid took almost 40 minutes to die. He'd never seen anyone hang on that long. But what pissed him off the most is that when the damn fool finally did die, he was *smiling*.

*"*I *don't know what I thought. I guess it was that, somehow, Chris and Allen would magically appear. As we walked, hiked, and limped in the days that followed, I looked for them, sure they would be just around the next tree. Every creak from a tree, every rustle of leaves, I would jump and look. In my mind there were only two outcomes – it would be my brother and friend, or it would be soldiers from the camp. In some ways, that feeling followed me all the way home and stayed with me there for years. If I could only turn quickly enough, there they would be."* – **Jess's Journal**

A high-pitched whine in Jess's ear woke her with a start. Her body ached, burned in places, and her feet were throbbing. Again, she heard the whine at her ear. It was a mosquito, damned early in the season and hungry for what little blood it could find. Jess slapped at it and then stared at the masses of scratches on her arms and legs. What a night it had been – they had been too busy running for their lives to even feel their injuries until now. Erin's eyes flickered open, pupils dilated in fear, her body tensed. She sat up, disoriented and looking around her wildly, "Wh—what? Where?"

"It's okay Erie, everything's okay. It's just a mosquito come to finish us off." Jess joked to her friend and was delighted to see her manage a weak smile in return. It felt so damn good to have her best friend in the world back. She hadn't had any bad dreams, and despite their bruises and scratches and swollen feet, she felt as if she and Erin were the two luckiest people in the world right now. And then her thoughts flashed to Allen and Chris. Had they gotten out? She imagined a reunion, and then all four of them setting off together and heading home to Belton. She scanned the trees and fear and bitterness resurged inside her – how could they possibly find each other when Jess had no idea *where* they were?

It was at this point that her stomach rumbled painfully, making its presence, and its yawning emptiness known. Jess looked around, nothing but trees and more trees and the now quiet, gurgling stream at their feet. Her heart plummeted, what in the hell could you eat in a forest?

The sun was slipping down, casting long shadows around them. They wouldn't get far in the dark, not without moonlight, and Jess had timed her escape with just that, and a convenient thunderstorm, in mind. She turned back to Erin who was now crouched by the stream digging her long fingers into the mud near the base of a plant that was growing in the shallow waters. A bulrush-like appendage at the top of the stem waved in protest as Erin tugged at the entire plant, pulling it out roots and all. In a few months the spear that was just now beginning to emerge would turn to a dark brown. For now, it was a creamy color, barely yellow, new growth responding to the slowly warming temperatures.

Jess just gaped at her friend and wondered if she had gone absolutely insane. "Uh, Erie? What are you..."?

Erin turned and shoved the entire plant into Jess's arms. "Clean all the mud off, will you? Take special care getting it off the roots and the inside of the plant. I'll be back."

And with no further explanation she walked off, headed away from the stream, towards a thick clump of trees. A few minutes later she was back, one pocket bulging, and her shirt held like an apron in front of her, various leaves and flowers sticking out.

"I saw some ferns, but no fiddleheads; I can't wait until we can pick them." Erin looked over at Jess who was standing there, looking confused, the cattail dripping mud down her arms. "You haven't washed that off yet, what are you waiting for? Aren't you hungry?" she laughed at Jess's confused expression, "You're holding part of our dinner there, and I'm starving." She gave her friend a small shove, "Rinse it off and I'll explain."

If her friend was losing her mind, she was acting particularly calm while doing it, so Jess complied, mystified at the thought of eating some mucky old weed. As she rubbed away mud and waited until the water ran clean, Erin reminisced about camping with her family over the years.

"You remember how my dad was, always into the survival stuff." She laughed as the tears sparkled in her eyes, "He used to put on some silly old movie, *Red Dawn*, and tell us to pay attention 'cause that's how the world would end." She shook her head at the thought, "I just thought he was full of it."

She finished rinsing off the cattail and was silent for a moment, reliving their loss before she shook off the memory and brought her thoughts back to the present.

"We can't eat the fiddleheads till they emerge in about two weeks and that's a damn shame. They're the best. We usually pick 'em, cook 'em and smother 'em in Cheez Whiz, dee-lish!" She rinsed the rest of the leaves and flowers free of any insects or clinging dirt.

Jess wasn't as sure about their dinner plans. "You sure this stuff won't make us sick? I mean, if it were food, wouldn't everyone eat it?" This earned a giggle from Erin who handed her a handful of something resembling giant clover leaves.

"It's wild, silly, not like a crop that there are tons and tons of. Eat this, its sorrel, high in Vitamin C." She stifled another giggle as Jess put the leaves into her mouth and bit down and made a face.

"It's sour!"

"Yeah, well, it's good for you, so eat it." Erin handed her some other leaves, "And I actually found a small patch of dandelion."

"I'm not eating some old weed!"

Erin's smile vanished, "If you want to survive you will. This is *food,* Jess, and it's all we've got. I picked up some acorns, but we need to roast them, and I don't think we should risk a fire yet. We need energy to keep moving and get out of this forest and as far away from those bastards as possible." Her face took on a haunted look, "You got us out of that awful place, now I'll keep us alive. Okay?"

Jess nodded; her friend really seemed to know her stuff. Really, when she thought about it, she was too hungry to care *what* it was. "Okay, Erie" and stuffed the leaves in her mouth. They weren't bad, they reminded her of the peppery taste of arugula. Her stomach seemed to growl a little less, so whether it was 'food' or not, at least one part of her didn't seem to know the difference.

Later, her hand fell to a lump in her pocket and she retrieved the three stale biscuits. They helped provide some substance to the greens they had eaten and she and Erin tore into them gratefully.

As they ate, the sun dipped below the trees and darkness fell swiftly. The girls finished their sparse meal and took the last few threads of light to wash their arms, legs and feet in the clear, bracingly cold water.

As the darkness enveloped them, they curled into their nest, wrapped their arms around each other, and pulled the blanket close. Within moments they were both sound asleep.

"*Courage is not the absence of fear, but rather the judgment that something else is more important than fear.*" – **Ambrose Redmoon**

Chris had run through the night, through the onslaught of rain and lightning. He kept running, heading south. He figured he'd made it at least ten miles. He'd stuck to the roads and figured he could dive out of sight in time if he saw lights. The roads had all been empty. The signs for Route VV had given way to Highway U and Chris saw that he was still heading south when the sun began to clear the clouds in the east. It was cold out and his jacket was still damp, despite the rain having ended hours ago. His pants were damp too, but the rest of him was dry and warm from running. After months of being run from one place to the next, along with all of the latrine digging duty he'd been assigned, his body was in perfect condition. But even he had his limits. It was time to stop, rest, and eat some of the food he'd managed to squirrel away in the past few days.

A stand of trees a few hundred yards from the road looked promising. Chris could see several evergreens. All of the deciduous trees were still bare, but he could create a nest at the base of the evergreens and be out of sight. He turned off the road, avoided patches of mud that would betray his presence, and climbed over a bent section of wire fencing. He could see a house in the far distance. It had smoke curling from the chimney, so it was occupied, but with only a Western Front uniform on him he figured his chances of getting shot were far more likely than an offer of food. Perhaps after he'd had some sleep and it was closer to dusk, he would re-consider his options.

He moved the lower branches of the largest evergreen, hacking at one or two in order to lay a bed of pine needles beneath him as cushion and for some relief from the cold, damp ground. The last few months had prepared him for making do with little. He remembered the first few weeks after the troops had stormed Belton. From the stress and fear as they were herded south, to the hard, cold ground he had shivered on each night, he had nearly been broken by sheer exhaustion. Eventually he had learned to sleep whenever he was given the chance, whatever the time of day, and in pretty much any conditions short of a firefight. He knew it would be ten minutes, tops, before he would be sound asleep. Around him birds were waking up and cheeping at each other. He pulled his pack closer to him, double-checked that his little nest was well hidden and closed his eyes.

He wondered where Jess and Erin were. God, he hoped they had escaped. Were soldiers looking for them? Tracking them? His family had never been what you would call religious; and their parents had never taken them to church on Sunday. But he figured he would dot his i's and cross his t's and pray anyway. He closed his eyes, *"Please God, let Jess and Erin have made it out of there."* Considering what they had escaped from, they needed divine intercession just to survive and not be re-captured. He kept his eyes closed and thought about all of them – him, Allen, Jess, Erin – all of them making it back home. How wonderful that would be. The daydream pulled him in and he succumbed to sleep.

It was the dog that woke him. It sniffed him cautiously, wagging its tail slowly. The sun was slipping down behind another bank of clouds and he could hear rumbling in the distance. More rain on its way. Chris figured that was good, it would keep the signs of his passing to a minimum. The dog sniffing him was a mutt, but she had a collar so, *oh no, this old mutt was definitely a male.* Chris wondered if he belonged to the occupants of the nearby house. He hadn't barked or given away his position, a fact for which Chris was profoundly grateful.

A moment later someone called out, far away, too far to hear a name, and the dog bounded away. Chris lay there, unmoving, certain it would lead its master back to his hiding place at any moment. The minutes ticked by and no one came and darkness fell early as the cloud cover moved in and the thunder rumbled louder.

He slowly emerged from his hiding spot as the last of the light faded. The house in the distance looked old and he hoped they had a root cellar or a smokehouse. Those were typically separate from the property and often had food stored in them. This late in spring, there wouldn't be much left, but he needed something besides the hard biscuits he had in his pack. Some part of him winced at the thought of stealing. That's what it was. But what would he do after the biscuits were gone? He needed clean water too, and wondered if the rainfall had washed things clean enough to risk drinking from puddles. There had been no creeks in sight that morning.

The wind had picked up and he could feel a few remaining damp spots on his pants. It wouldn't matter, if the thunder and the black clouds on the horizon were any indication, he would be soaked again in a few hours anyway. He walked slowly through the thigh high grass until he reached the edge of a large cornfield. Only stubble remained from last year's harvest. Soon it would be filled with green again. Planting would begin in earnest in less than two weeks.

His thoughts flashed to his family's garden in Belton. By late winter his mother would be busy setting down detailed instructions for the rest of the family on where to plant and what. He could see her sitting at the kitchen table, gardening books scattered around her for reference. She would have numbered all of the raised planters in the yard and marked them clearly. When Dad finished tilling up the dirt and removing the weeds Chris and Jess were always tasked with planting the seeds according to the diagrams she had painstakingly drawn during the last months. He smiled at the thought. She was forever muttering about companion planting and 'crop rotation' as she marked, scratched out and adjusted for new plants each year.

Before he had found Allen, he had still held out hope they were still alive. But Allen had said nothing when asked, just looked at the ground and shook his head. If Jess and Erin hadn't made it out...Chris's stomach roiled at the thought...then there would really be nothing left to return to.

Lost in thought he had walked the entire length of the field and was now nearly at the house. He could see it in flashes of lightning. It was old, as he had hoped, probably late 1800's. The windows on the first floor were boarded up and it looked as if one of the outbuildings had burned. The work of the Western Front soldiers, no doubt. He could see pale light from one of the upper windows. It flickered, so it had to be a candle or an oil lamp. Maybe even a fireplace, he remembered seeing smoke curling from a chimney this morning. Dangerous to do so, but the occupants were probably armed and the troops looked for better pickings in the cities or larger towns when possible, which is probably why whoever lived there had survived for this long without having their home burned with them still inside.

He scouted around carefully, hoping the dog wouldn't bark, and found the root cellar a few yards away from the back of the house. It was unlocked and he carefully eased the door up and slid in. It was dark as a tomb and he tripped on the uneven stone steps and nearly fell, rapping his shin sharply. It was dry, well-kept and only a little musty, despite having dirt walls. He reached into his pocket, pulled out a lighter and shook it. It was low but he needed some light. The tiny flame revealed a surprisingly large room and several shelves were still stocked with food. He saw a variety of home canned goods and grabbed for the first green thing he could find. Green beans by the look of it. He also pocketed three apples, a jar of pickled eggs and two potatoes. His finger began to burn painfully and he dropped the lighter and lost the light for a few panicked moments.

The rain had begun to drum down on the wooden cellar door as he rediscovered the lighter and took one more look around. On the lower shelf was a line of what looked like canned meat. He grabbed one and put it in his rucksack and headed for the door. It was enough to last him several meals and miles of walking. Survival was survival, but he didn't like the thought of taking from others. He hoped that he could repay them some day.

He held himself back from running as he headed back toward the road. It was stupid and dangerous to run on uneven ground. As it was, he twisted his ankles twice on the way back to the road and soaked one of his shoes completely through when he slipped into a puddle.

As soon as his feet hit blacktop he turned right and headed south at a slow jog. He had miles to go before he would feel safe about heading back east and finally north towards Belton and the girls. Again, he prayed for their escape. After a short break to eat, Chris followed the road, away from Belton, away from the camp, and into the storm.

*"Without Erin, my God, I don't know how I would have survived. No matter what happened, we knew we had each other, and it kept us going those first few months. Somehow, knowing someone else had been through it, knowing each other as we had all of our lives, it somehow gave us both the drive to wake up each morning and try. You can't imagine how hard it was, some days I wanted to just lie there and not move, not eat, just hide from myself and the world and being alive. Everything I knew had been taken from me - except for Erie - oh God, Erie, how I miss you so. Even now, all these years later - I think I will miss you forever." – **Jess's journal**

Jess woke to cold. Erin had managed to pull all of one blanket and most of the other completely off of her and as Jess awoke in the cold dawn, her stomach wrenched and heaved. She stumbled to the stream, which had slowed to a sedate pace and the meager contents of her stomach splashed out onto the rocks. "Jessie?" Erin's sleepy voice broke through the stomach-twisting heaves, "Are you okay?"

"Yeah...yeah...just...peachy," she managed between heaves. Her stomach stopped its awful twisting and she stood back up, dizzy and still a little nauseous. "I've had this damn stomach flu for the last couple of weeks." She groaned as her stomach twisted again and she didn't notice Erin's narrowed eyes and pinched gaze.

"How long have you been sick, Jess?" Erin's voice was clear of any sleepiness now, she sounded frightened.

"About...oh!" Jess listed back towards the stream and heaved again, "Oh man, this sucks! Um...going on," she bent and retched, "about three weeks now. Oh!!! Why?"

"When was your last period?" Erin persisted.

Jess looked at her oddly, "I dunno, a month, maybe two."

"When exactly?"

"How the hell should I know?"

"Well, do you think it's possible that..."

The fear clicked on inside of her. The pieces fell in place. Worse than the twisting of her stomach or how bad her feet ached. Just the thought of...

"NO! Damn it! I told you I've got the stomach flu. Jesus, Erie, lay off the twenty-questions already!" Jess nearly shouted it, her whole being in chaos. She couldn't be pregnant, not that way, oh god, oh god, oh god. The panic rose up inside her and she bent nearly in half and retched again. Nothing but bile now. Surreptitiously, her hand reached for her belly, seeking a telltale bulge. Nothing.

Jess looked at Erin who was staring back at her, concern and fear evident in her green eyes. That they both knew the truth was obvious, but Jess wasn't ready to accept it and Erin saw no point in pushing it.

In the end, it would be evident soon, one way or the other. A long, awkward silence passed between them.

Erin finally broke it by saying, "I'll try and find some food, okay?" She glanced over at her friend—Jess was hunched over on a large rock staring at the burbling stream. "Even if you need to wait for a while to eat it, you know, let your stomach settle down, it'll be good to have it on hand." She reached out and squeezed Jess's shoulder and walked away quietly, up the hill towards the west, looking for a good north-facing slope to find some fresh greens for them to eat.

Yesterday had been unseasonably warm, which had allowed them to sleep comfortably with little cover or shelter, but today was on target for early spring, chilly morning and cool temperatures. The lingering cold of the night made every body part feel stiff and each bruise and cut was magnified. Her feet were throbbing in pain, and Jess noticed the multitude of sticks and burrs wrapped in the dried mud encasing the thick socks. They needed shoes, and blankets, food and somewhere they could safely hide until the camp was struck and the troops moved farther south into Arkansas. She pulled at the mud on her sock and watched pieces crumble away.

She tried to remember when her last period had been and couldn't. It wasn't as if they had ever been regular. She couldn't think of one since, well, since before they had been taken. *Shit*. Again, her hand reached for her belly. Wait, it *wasn't* flat, there was little bump, firm, not soft. *Shit, shit, shit!*

And then Jess realized it didn't matter. They would die out here, in the middle of the woods, and the awful thing would die inside her. And that was good. It was nothing more than a parasite, an invader, like the soldiers. She almost smiled in satisfaction at the thought of it dying with her. But she sat there, her ass sore from the ground, body aching, her bruised and swollen feet on fire, and her smile turned down. It was replaced with an almost feral snarl. She felt the anger build inside of her. She wasn't ready to die. Not quite yet. Whatever tomorrow would bring; she was going to live, and to hell with them all.

A quiet voice interrupted her thoughts, "Jess? You okay?" Erin had returned while Jess had sat there deep in thought. Jess could see that her friend had more of that friggin' wood sorrel in her hands that had tasted so bitter, plus other green crap that looked just as unappetizing. Erin looked down at Jess with concern and fear.

"Huh? Oh, hey Erie. Yeah," her body sagged a little and she relaxed, the snarl vanishing from her face. It was replaced by a satisfied smile, "Y'know, I better learn more about some of those survival skills you learned from your family. And we have *got* to find some shoes to wear, these socks won't last long."

Before Erin could respond she continued, "And I've been thinking about those lakes we passed with the camp. You know the ones to the north? They'd have fish and we might be able to find a boat to help move us along and stay off the highway. If we get just a little more north, we could have a fire, maybe catch and cook somethin'. And you know, I've been thinking..."

Erin laughed and hugged her. Come what may, they had each other and relief at their newfound freedom washed over both girls. Some of the plants slipped from Erin's hands. Jess was okay, she was okay, and the rest would sort itself out in time. They would head north towards the lakes. It was a plan.

They ate the greens Erin had picked, and tried to choke down some more of the tuberous roots, but they tasted and smelled like the muck they had been pulled from. Both girls spat out the roots rather than lose what little food they had in their stomachs. The air was warming considerably, and the sun was steadily rising in the sky. It was time to get moving.

They had come from the east, and now they headed due north, following the creek as it steadily grew in width from the few feet in width where they had camped to over ten, even twenty feet wide in some places. They gathered plants as they walked, nibbling on them to keep their hunger at bay. There was plenty of wild onion. It grew everywhere and the girls figured it was a favorite of the deer, since they saw tracks wherever they saw onion and the tops of the green plant had obviously been nibbled.

The way wasn't easy, especially since their bruised feet felt every rock, and branch and bramble. There were no mile markers to tell them how far they traveled that day, but the amount of swearing seemed to increase steadily as the day wore on. Already the sun was beginning to sink in the sky, it wouldn't be long until sunset, and Erin stopped for the umpteenth time to pull a particularly painful twig from her now bedraggled and hole-ridden sock.

Jess was slightly ahead of her, stumbling along, exhausted and swearing, "Godawful trees and forest and freaking nature. What I would give for..." She stopped and stared ahead and across the creek to the east. "Oh my god...Oh my god...Erie! There's a house over there!" Her voice fell to a sharp whisper, suddenly associating a house with people, and the fear that it could be occupied.

It wasn't really a house, more of a hunting cabin. The girls could see it clearly as they made their way over the creek and through the ice-cold water which soaked their socks and numbed their legs all the way to their knees. Teeth chattering, they edged through the trees, looking around for signs of life. Their ears strained for any sound, but there was nothing but the wildlife.

Down a steep incline, and onto the creaky front porch, it took the girls a moment to find the courage to get past the simple doorknob lock with a few well-placed shoves. The doorframe splintered and the girls peered into the sparsely furnished, one room cabin. There was a kitchenette on the west wall with a tiny window that looked out onto the creek, and a small curtained-off section in the northwest corner turned out to be a crude bathroom. On the south wall to their left was a twin bed built into the wall, cupboards above and below it and a small table & chair next to it. On the same wall as the door was a couch that had seen better days and a curtained window above it.

Everything was covered with a thick layer of dust. After days of nothing but hard, cold dirt to sleep on, both Jess and Erin figured they had died and gone to heaven.

Some scouting outside in the rapidly fading light upstream revealed a scattered group of cabins, mostly hidden from view in the trees. The silence was overwhelming; none of the other cabins appeared occupied. Erin noticed that the cabin could have running water once the connecting pipe was lowered into the creek. The sharp decline from the creek to the cabin brought a solid stream of water directly through to the sink. Of course, there wasn't any electricity, but there was a propane stove, an oil lamp with a full bottle of oil, a generous supply of propane, and a treasure trove of canned foods in the cabinets. They also found two fishing poles, a .22 Rimfire rifle, and *four* boxes of ammunition. Erin closed her eyes in silent thanks at that find.

To their delight they also found a raincoat that was lined and warm, blankets, and even a pair of shoes. "Here Jess, you try these, they're definitely too small for me," Erin passed the shoes to her friend. The shoes were made of canvas and had several holes. "These shoes are damn near worn through," Jess observed, but she tried them on anyway, "Hey, they fit!"

Erin smiled at her, "Better than socks, even if they are full of holes! So, does this mean I get dibs on the bed tonight?"

Jess just nodded, poked her big left toe through a hole in the shoe and grinned. They shook out the blankets outside and used a worn-out dishtowel to dust most of the thick film of dust away. Judging by the expiration dates on the food and the thickness of the dust, whoever owned this cabin hadn't been there in a long time.

There was nothing to identify who had stayed in this place. The girls both wondered, was the owner still alive? Why had this cabin, as remote as it was, been abandoned?

If this cabin could talk, it would have told the girls about a writer and critic by the name of M.G. Wood, who had owned the cabin and two hundred and fifty acres of land that lay to the north and west. Wood had bought the large property shortly after the first real estate crash of 2008 and had great plans for it. There was plenty of room for a main lodge and a succession of small, simple cabins – a quiet and peaceful writing retreat.

The old man who had owned the property before Wood had built the series of cabins and rented them out during the warm months to hunt and fish. After his death of cancer in 2008, his distant relatives in Brooklyn, New York were all too happy to unload the property for a fraction of what it was worth. Any money, they decided, was better than no money and an ungodly number of trees and dirt. People actually *lived* in flyover country? Why?

The real estate slump had been followed by the Great Recession. In late 2012 the real estate 'bubble' become a gargantuan sinkhole as the Alte and Option Arm loans shot up to higher rates. And as the new owner struggled with their own financial troubles, dreams of artist's retreats faded and years passed as the cabin stood alone in the woods, a good fifteen miles from the nearest two-lane road.

That night Jess and Erin feasted on tuna and a large can of hominy. They ignored the expiration dates, most of the cans showed dates that were a year or more past, and the food tasted just fine to the girls, whose palates were no longer that discerning. After all, they had eaten next to nothing for the past three days. They drank flat, boiled water by lamplight. Erin had insisted on firing up the stove and boiling all the water before they drank it.

"Giardia, it'll give us the runs among other things," she said by way of explanation, "so it's a good idea to boil the water before we drink it." After the tiny scraps of wild plants, they had eaten over the past two days, and the army rations they had been eating for months before that, their dinner was almost too rich to eat. The light outside had completely faded as they licked the remains of the tuna juice from their fingers, sitting on the floor with the lamp turned down low between them.

It wasn't long before they turned it off completely, partly out of fear that someone would see the light, and partly out of the need to conserve their resources. And the night found them curled together on the narrow bed for both warmth and reassurance. The girls slept, barely stirring when the wind kicked up a notch and the rain moved in.

A Flight Interrupted

"*Memory is a way of holding on to the things you love, the things you are, the things you never want to lose.*" – **Kevin Arnold**

He was home. It was nippy inside, as if the stove's warmth could not push back the chill of the spring morning. Chris could smell the bread baking but the house was empty, and no one responded when he called out. The only noise was a truck rumbling by outside and men's voices talking quietly in the distance. Jess's room looked as if she had just jumped out of bed. The bed was unmade and there was a pair of dirty socks beside it. A note on the floor in their mother's handwriting read, "Jess honey, please go to town, take that load of apples and see what you can get of flour and sugar." Reading it, he knew then he was in a dream. Jess had gone to the store that day, the last day any of them had been together as a family. The last day any of them had been free.

He moved on to his room. It too looked just as he had left it and was far more of a mess than Jess's room could ever be. Dirty laundry, unmade bed, and his belongings were scattered about, a maze of clutter on the floor. He was surprised by it somehow.

"I was such a complete slob," Chris muttered to himself. He closed the door and headed for his parents' room. It was empty. The bed was made and his mother's pajamas were neatly folded near the pillow on her side of the bed.

"Perhaps everyone is outside," he thought and headed back through the kitchen to go into the backyard. The bread was baking in the oven and he could tell it was nearly time to pull it out. Over the years they had all developed a nose for it. Flour was short, so they ate every bit that came out of that oven. If they didn't want burned bread it was in everyone's interest to keep an eye (or nose) out.

He opened the sliding glass door and the sun blinded his eyes. He had little time to wonder how morning had turned to late afternoon and a pulsing ball of fire that hung in the west. Dreams held by no standards, they knew no scientific laws or rules of physics. His gaze was drawn to his parents standing there, arms raised in the air. His father looked sad, his mother was scared and crying. Michael Aaronson spoke softly, "Please Chris, don't shoot your mother. Shoot me." Chris looked down and realized the rifle in his hands pointed directly at Julie Aaronson's chest.

"It'll be okay, son. I know they told you to do it, just shoot me and let your mother go." But the rifle barked out one shot and he watched his mother fall to the ground, blood staining the front of her shirt. His father turned away from Chris, his face set in sorrow, and knelt by Julie Aaronson's body, hands to her chest. Her eyes were wide and staring, and there was a single teardrop on her left cheek. Chris's father didn't seem to notice the blood bubbling over his hands and soaking his clothes. He kissed his wife, then turned back to look at his son, "Oh son, what have you done?"

It was his scream that gave him away and brought the two soldiers to his hideaway. The dream faded and Chris opened his eyes to the sight of a rifle barrel and booted foot. He followed the boot up to a leg, up further to the chest and the scraggly beard and gap-toothed grin of Tim Easter. The bastard looked delighted to find him, "Hey there shithead, where'd you think you were headin'?" He twirled his rifle around and smashed the butt end hard into Chris's forehead. His head bounced once on the ground and before he blacked out, he heard Easter and another soldier laughing.

Pain. A slow drip making its way from his forehead, down the left side of his head and falling slowly, one drop at a time, from his cheek. It was dark out. But he could smell beans and feel a smidgeon of warmth from the campfire. Chris tried to move and couldn't. No surprise there, his arms and wrists were bound behind him. He could feel the bark of the tree rough against his back. Easter was practically growling at the other soldier, one Chris didn't recognize, "You best give me that jar, asshole," he snarled at the other man, "I found it and I'll be damned you gonna eat it all." From the looks of it, the two soldiers were about to come to blows over the jar of pickled eggs they had found in Chris's pack.

Tim Easter was a small man, no more than five foot six, if that. He was skinny, although recently he'd put on a little weight after his stash of meth had dried up. He was still stringy though, and he smelled bad.

Not just body odor, but that teeth rotting in your head kind of thing. He fingered the holster that held his knife, trying to decide if it was worth cutting the other soldier to get his share of the food back. Chris tried to get a better look at the other man, but when he moved his head pain lanced through him and he let out a small groan. This earned him the attention of both men. Through the haze of pain, he could see they were both grinning with sadistic delight. He didn't recognize the second soldier at all.

"All right! Our little runaway's waking up!" Easter crowed, looking ready to do more damage. He stood up, the pickled eggs forgotten and unsheathed his knife. "Y'know, Lieutenant Cooper said to bring you back, but he sure didn't say I had to do it all in one piece."

Chris sneered back at the little man, "Lieutenant Cooper is a psychopath, and you're just his sad little suck-up, Easter." It was stupid to trade insults when he was at such a clear disadvantage. The fist that smashed into his face loosened a tooth and broke his nose.

The second blow knocked him out for the second time that day.

As he slowly regained consciousness he noted that the jar of pickled eggs was empty. So were the beans. His stomach roiled and his head throbbed. Now he was bleeding from a cut below his right eye, copiously from his broken nose and the earlier cut on his forehead. Chris looked as bad as his head felt.

He spit a small glob of blood out of his mouth and focused his eyes on his two captors. Easter turned back at him, eager to hit him again.

He didn't like fair fights 'cause he never won them. This advantage was more his style, "Wake up and ready for more, you little fuckwad?" he sneered. When Chris didn't respond he just smiled more, "Your little sis, now she was always ready for more."

Chris tried to still his response, but his pulse quickened and he stiffened, it wasn't just his blood that was making him see red. Easter grinned over to the other soldier, "Burton, you ever have any of that sweet ass? The bitch was in the second room on the left, she was good at fucking."

Burton spoke up, "Oh, yeah, nice sweet ass. You could tell she liked every minute of it. Shame Coop killed her." Chris's fury at the two had been building to frenzy until the last remark. He stiffened against the bindings; unsure he had heard right. Easter was watching closely and he nodded.

"Yep, he strangled those stupid whores, both of 'em. Caught up to 'em the same night as the storm and made both of 'em pay for all the trouble they'd caused. Shame too, 'bout your sister, shit; she was good for at least a few more weeks of screwin'."

Chris lunged against his bindings and felt one of the bindings give just a little bit. He could hear a hoarse scream of pain, and then recognized that it had come from his throat. Not Jess, oh God, not Jess. He shouldn't have listened to Allen, he should have gone in there, died fighting, anything but let them try to escape on their own.

He howled in grief, "You're lying!" If Jess was dead then he was all alone, no family, no one to go home to.

Much to Easter's and Burton's disappointment, the news that his baby sister was dead, quickly turned Chris's initial anger and denial into shock and unresponsiveness. All of their taunts were met with silence.

He did not move when they kicked him or hit him and he said nothing at all.

Easter and Burton left him tied to the tree all that night, and didn't bother offering food or water.

They had also taken a great deal of pleasure recounting Allen Banks' fate to Chris. He had no idea that Allen was the only truth they told that night. All that Chris knew was that no one who had escaped that night had gotten very far. He was the only one left. Eventually they stopped talking trash and grew bored. As the fire settled into deep orange coals, the two soldiers wrapped themselves up in their blankets and fell asleep. They were undisciplined, good only for simple missions like fetch and retrieve or securing food and weapons; they didn't think to take turns staying awake to keep an eye on their prisoner.

As the two soldiers slept Chris worked on a section of the rope, sliding it up and down, up and down over the rough bark of the tree. It was close to dawn when the rope finally broke. He didn't run. He retrieved a knife discarded from dinner on the ground near the campfire. Then he quietly arranged the bindings so that they appeared intact.

Easter and Burton had been tasked with bringing him back to the camp. They would be heading back today. If he ran, they would chase him, and likely bring even more men with them. He couldn't risk it.

Some dark part of him wanted them dead anyway. That dark part relished the idea of spilling their blood and ridding the world of their filthy, stinking presence. So, he waited, eyes closed to slits, until Burton roused first. The man stretched and yawned and staggered off to the woods to piss, kicking at Easter when he passed him.

Easter cursed and sat up, looked over at Chris and decided to have himself even more fun. He threw his blanket off, stood up and swaggered over to the tree where Chris hunched and feigned sleep. He unzipped his pants and aimed the stream of urine straight at Chris's head. What happened next was so quick, so brutally final, that Easter didn't even have time to scream. As he fell to the ground, blood gushing from his genitals and then, a second later from his neck, he just looked confused. He died that way, on the ground, his simple little mind unable to understand how a man could move so fast when he was tied up.

A few minutes later, Burton's body joined Easter's. Chris stood there for a moment, looking down at the two lifeless bodies at his feet and feeling nothing but a red haze of pain inside and out. Monsters like these had killed Jess. Monsters like these had killed his parents, his friends, and everyone he loved. He dragged their bodies into the thicker forest, as far from the road as he could stand to drag them. He pulled brush, dead tree limbs and leaves over the bodies, returned to the campsite and tamped out the last of the smoldering coals. With luck, no one would find the bodies or the campsite for a long time, perhaps never.

He rinsed his hands and face as best he could in a small stream nearby. He had collected the revolver from Burton, and another knife from Easter. He gathered up all of the food that was left, which wasn't much, and stuffed it into a rucksack with a blanket. Burton's blanket had smelled slightly less rank than Easter's, but they were both wretched, stinking things. He picked the lesser of the two evils, hitched the rucksack onto his shoulder, stuck the revolver in his jacket pocket and headed for the small pickup truck they had been driving.

He'd drive it out of gas and then ditch it, it was limited to roads and he wanted to disappear, that meant going on foot and probably cross-country. But for now, he wanted some distance between the bodies and him. If they caught up to him again, they wouldn't bother trying to take him back. After what he'd done to the other two, they'd shoot him on sight and apologize to Cooper later.

The tank showed as half full. That was good luck, the first in days. Chris figured he could get a hundred, maybe even 150 miles from the truck before it ran out of fuel. As he steered the truck onto the road, Chris took a long look up the road he had come from before he turned and headed south. Home wasn't home anymore. Not without Mom or Dad or Jess. Home was gone and so was the life he had known. He didn't know where he would end up, but he couldn't go back, not ever.

The faded green pickup headed south, all alone on the road, as the rain started up again.

"*The cabin we found. It came at a moment when I think we were both just ready to sit down and call it quits. We were hungry, exhausted, and so tired of running. I can still see the sagging, moss-covered roof in my mind's eye. In that moment, and in the days that followed, it was nothing less than paradise. It was a place of quiet and of refuge. Our bodies slowly began to heal; our nightmares and fears quieted some. And in some ways, our hearts began to heal there too.*" – **Jess's journal**

Jess began her day by stretching and, as Erin kicked out in her sleep, falling with a solid, painful thump onto the hard wood floor. "Ow!" She inhaled dust and sneezed violently.

Erin shot up out of bed at the noise and cracked her head against a small shelf on the wall above. Dust and books rained down on her, "Ow! Aw, crap!"

Both girls glared at each other, Jess clutching her sore hip, and Erin her injured head, before they began to laugh. It was funny, in a 'Three Stooges' kind of way. They laughed, swore as their body parts hurt even more, and took a good look around. The daylight from the two small windows was weak; outside the rain had continued through the night. It was now morning and it showed no signs of stopping. It made a quiet thrum against the roof of the cabin. The trees, which were still barren of leaves, shook back and forth with the strong gusts of wind that rattled the windows. Jess could feel drafts each time it did. It was obvious that the cabin was meant only for summer use.

Without a fireplace or insulation, it was barely livable in the nippy spring nights. It certainly wouldn't be warm enough during a harsh winter. But for the moment, it was shelter and that was exactly what both girls needed.

There was one sizable leak above the kitchen sink and another directly above the toilet. The one above the toilet had managed to soak the floor all around and a small rivulet of water angled across the uneven floor and pooled in the center of the cabin near the oil lamp and the remains of their dinner from the night before.

Erin eyed the wet toilet, grimaced, "Damn it, I really need to go!"

She grabbed a bowl from the cabinet near the sink and pulled the curtain closed after her and cursed even more as she realized there was no toilet paper and that the toilet was bone-dry. Her bright idea of catching the drips with the bowl didn't work very well. The water simply splashed out of the bowl and showered her with small droplets which sprayed in every direction like a fine mist. She set it aside and let the roof drip onto her head, cussing and laughing simultaneously.

"Y'know. We might as well leave the lid open." She called out to Jess, "It's dripping right over the toilet, at least that way there'll be water in the bowl!" They ended up doing just that.

The small stove generated a little heat, but both girls were worried about making it last, so they turned it off as soon as the water had boiled and split a large can of stew between them. With breakfast out of the way, and the rain still coming down at a good clip, they had little they could do except explore the inside of the cabin. Erin didn't have any shoes to go mucking about in the rain with and Jess had no desire to explore outside by herself.

They went through all of the food – canned, dried and powdered, and estimated how much they had. They were lucky, whoever owned this cabin had stocked it very well. With both of them eating three meals apiece, they had about three weeks supply of food on hand, all the water they needed thanks to the creek, a rifle and ammunition, the ability to fish, and relatively dry shelter. For the moment, they were safer than they had been in a long time. Jess took note of the dates on the labels. All of the food had expired within the past eighteen months but none of the cans were bulging or damaged. It was probably safe to eat and the previous evening's meal had been edible enough. She wondered what had happened to the owners of this little cabin and why they had never returned to it.

"Erie, you know how to shoot, right?" Jess asked her friend after they finished planning out their meals for the rest of the day.

"Yeah, sort of." Erin replied, "I took this handgun shooting course when I was thirteen. My dad and Toby usually went hunting while I stayed home with Mom or came and saw you, so I don't know much about rifles." She pulled the rifle out of its box and began inspecting it.

"It can't be too much different. Let's see..." Erin began to mutter to herself. She found a tattered manual in the box and began to reference back and forth with it. Soon she was busy assembling components and digging into one of the boxes of ammunition.

While Erin lost herself in the task at hand, Jess kept busy by putting all of the food back away and then started up the stove. She boiled more water to make hot cocoa. The yearning for some hot, creamy chocolate running over her tongue was almost painful. The water was running clear and cold from the sink spigot. It was slow and had very little pressure. The fact that it was running at all meant that she didn't have to go out into the rain for it and that sounded more than okay to her.

The rain subsided and the bright rays of the sun were peeking through the clouds. When the water came to a boil, Jess carefully dissolved the contents of the packets into two freshly rinsed mugs. Erin had disassembled, reassembled, loaded and was now peering through the sights of the rifle as she aimed it towards a wall. "I've got it all figured out," she announced, and then sighed in pleasure as Jess handed her a steaming mug. "So, it's pretty straightforward," she paused and took a cautious sip of the hot chocolate, "Oh, damn, this is *good*." Her eyes rolled and she grinned at Jess over the rim of her cup and then noticed the sun for the first time. "Hey, the rain has stopped! Right on, we can go out and take a look around – maybe even do some target practice!"

"We aren't shooting that thing off until we are *sure* there isn't anyone around for miles." Jess interrupted firmly. "Sound like that carries, y'know." Erin looked deflated. "But you can show me what you were doing and hell, maybe we can try hunting something if the coast is clear."

The girls savored every last drop of their hot chocolate and then Erin pointed out and named each part of the rifle, referencing the manual every so often as she disassembled and reassembled it again for Jess's benefit. She took care to show her the safety and explained how to load the rifle and how to aim and then let Jess dry-fire it. Jess paid sharp attention. If anyone came near them, she figured she would fill them full of holes and *then* ask questions. At one point she swiveled the gun around, crossing in front of Erin. Her friend ducked, grabbed the rifle, and barked, "Don't *ever* point a firearm at anyone unless you mean to kill them."

Jess rolled her eyes at her friend, "Erie, ease up, it isn't even loaded!"

Erin just stared back and said, "Jess, always assume a gun is loaded. Always treat it like it is. Otherwise you'll end up shooting yourself or someone else. My dad knew someone who had owned guns for years.

He screwed up one day, thought his gun was empty, and shot himself in the foot. Dad always said his friend was lucky that all he ended up with was a hole in the foot and not the head for being so stupid. So, I mean it, treat it like it's always loaded."

Jess sobered and promised to be more careful and pulled on the raincoat. Erin grabbed a blanket for a little additional warmth and they both headed outside. The temperature was already rising as the skies continued to clear, and considering the sun was nearly overhead, it was also close to lunchtime. Neither of them was particularly hungry thanks to the hot chocolate, which gave the girls time to explore their surroundings.

To the west was a small shed, more of a lean-to really, and it was locked with a sturdy padlock that resisted their efforts to open it. They left it for another time when they could find some solid rock or lever to force it open with and then spotted the overgrown remains of a road. From the look of it, you couldn't even call it a road, merely two ruts carved out of the grass and underbrush and certainly not used anytime recent. Near the lean-to there was a ringed fire pit with two enormous stones situated near it, obviously used as seating. Green blades of grass were growing in the middle of the pit, and it looked as though an old bird's nest had fallen down into it from the trees above.

As far as the eye could see there were trees and underbrush, slowly turning from dead winter brown to green in the wet coolness of spring. None of the other cabins had anything stocked inside them, just bare furniture as thickly dust-covered as their cabin had been.

Neither of the girls had any interest in exploring too far. Erin didn't have shoes, and both girls' feet were still sore and swollen. They stopped often and listened for any sounds, anything that indicated the presence of other people, soldiers or otherwise, but all they heard were the birds, the wind and water rushing in the creek. They were utterly alone.

In the end, they spent six weeks at the cabin, recuperating, growing strong, and improving their survival skills. Jess discovered she was a pretty fair shot, and Erin became adept at fishing. They managed to supplement and extend the stock of food at the cabin with fresh, wild plants, and a good deal of fresh-caught fish and squirrel, rabbit, and even the lone wild turkey.

At first, the idea of dressing game that they killed was disgusting and off-putting. Jess found she was more nauseous then ever and Erin had to take over all of the gutting and dressing so that her friend could keep most of their hard-earned food down. It was now obvious that Jess was pregnant, but it was something that neither of them spoke of.

They didn't talk about Tent 5 or about their families or friends, and they rarely spoke of the future. But as their bodies healed, they fell into a quiet rhythm of survival—it was what they both needed, time to heal mentally and physically.

The days lengthened and grew warm. It was now mid-May and Jess's belly was well-rounded, quite pronounced due to her thin frame, and her breasts were full. She had begun to help with field dressing their kills after her nausea eased up, but now she could feel the thing inside her kick. God, how she hated it, this *parasite* that made her sick, shaped her body into something that was alien and awkward, and brought back memories she dearly wished to never re-visit. Each time they tried some new food, some wild plant or mushroom that Erin assured her was safe, Jess secretly hoped it would make her just sick enough for it to let go and disappear from her. That's how she pictured it too, simply dissolving away some evening like a bad dream. She said nothing to Erin of her feelings in this matter, although she was aware of her friend staring at her from time to time, on the verge of speaking of the taboo subject. She could barely stand to think of it herself. Better instead to simply survive and take one day at a time.

They had managed to break into the small lean-to and found it had served as a smokehouse at one time. Later use seemed to indicate that it was a catch-all for hunting and camping supplies. A gold mine for the girls who knew they would need to move on soon. They found a large tarp, miraculously whole despite the obvious signs of mice, an ax, rope, and a set of knives that Erin immediately claimed would be far better suited to cleaning game than the knives stocked in the cabin.

They cleared everything out of the smokehouse and decided to fire it up and smoke something. This resulted in some hilarious attempts at smoking and preserving the meat first from the turkey they killed (a pitifully scrawny specimen) to more successful forays in smoked rabbit and squirrel. Erin became so good at it that Jess had a hard time keeping up the supply of fresh game until they turned to also smoking the fresh-caught fish.

It was after a particularly large haul from the smokehouse that they found themselves dining on the last of the green beans. The propane stove would be too cumbersome to carry with them, and they were nearly out of propane anyway, despite their careful conservation, so Erin didn't object when Jess started it up and used it to heat not just the water, but a single can of sweetened condensed milk.

"It's time to move on, isn't it?" Jess said it aloud, even though she knew the answer already. Erin had been on a smoking and preserving kick, and with the supplies dwindling, it was time to leave. They had both known they couldn't stay here forever.

"We've got a long way to go," Erin said as way of an answer, "So I guess it's time we got started." There really wasn't anything more to say. The next day they packed everything they could comfortably carry, rigging it on a length of tarp between two sturdy poles with leather straps lined with fur at either end. The straps fit over their shoulders, one girl in front, the other in the back to balance the load. The fur lining would be warm in the hot weather, but soft against their skin.

Their supply of dried meat and fish would last for a while, a week or better, before they needed more food. And it was in this way that they started off, both barefoot, their feet hardened by walking without socks or shoes for many weeks now. Jess refused to take the worn-out sneakers—it wasn't fair that Erin had nothing and she did.

They stripped the cabin of nearly anything that they could use and reasonably transport with them. As they left, the girls closed the door behind them, silently grateful to the unknown owner who had helped them to survive. The woods closed in around them. They followed the ruts in the overgrown path and then turned back towards the creek. It was time to go home.

Welcome to Tennessee

*"*H*ell is yourself and the only redemption is when a person puts himself aside to feel deeply for another person."* – **Tennessee Williams**

The dark, unwelcoming barrel of the shotgun was the first thing his eyes focused on. The voice was the second. "Welcome to Tennessee, boy. Now get the heck out." The owner of the voice was male, with a thick drawl. He didn't sound particularly welcoming, but it was the shotgun that brought home the point with crystal clarity. Chris hurt, all over, and he was completely disoriented. For a moment, he could not remember where he was or how he had gotten to be on the ground, covered by a filthy blanket. He blinked and tried to focus on the man behind the gun. The rising sun flared behind him and all that Chris could make out was the man's outline.

"I know you can hear me, boy. So's you best cotton to what I just said. Get the heck back from whence you came. Now. Before others less kindly than me find you."

Someone who was less kindly than pointing a shotgun at him and telling him to get out? With a statement like that Chris had no interest in meeting any others. The old man jerked his blanket away, exposing the uniform below. "We don't take kindly to the West telling us how we should live. 'Sides, I've heard some damn messed up stuff comin' in whispers on the wind. You're lucky I don't shoot you right now, boy."

Chris shook his head. He showed his hands were empty of weapons and tried not to look at the shotgun barrel, because it was making him damn nervous.

"Sir, I was a conscript. They took our town, burned it to the ground, and killed most of us. I escaped and they are probably hunting me as we speak." He tried to meet the man's eyes, but the sun was so damned bright. "I've got a broken ankle and no gun at all; I lost it when I nearly drowned in this damned swamp."

As if on cue, the broken ankle began to throb mercilessly. He had hobbled for nearly a mile on it, practically screaming in pain each time he had to put pressure on it. The bones inside had scraped against each other in a way that would have made his skin crawl if he wasn't busy trying to not pass out.

"Lake."

"What?"

"It's a lake, boy. Reelfoot Lake. Formed when the New Madrid went ape crap 'bout 200 years ago. Don'tcha pay attention to your history, boy?"

Chris thought that it wasn't *his* history, he wasn't from Tennessee. Instead he simply replied, "Uh, I guess not, sir."

The man just let out a harrumph and stood there, not moving, just staring. Chris shifted uncomfortably and the bones grated together, he barely stopped himself from shrieking in agony. He tried to slowly sit up and lean towards the injured ankle but was pushed to the ground by the dark snout of the shotgun barrel. Rough hands went through his pockets, found the spare ammunition clip he hadn't managed to lose and relieved him of his knife as well. Once that was done, the stranger held out his hand to Chris and slowly pulled him to a sitting position.

"Let me see that ankle, boy," Chris could see that the man was old, seventies maybe, his hair was white through and through. "I was a medic a long-assed time ago now, but I ain't forgotten everything, just my granddaughters' names occasionally, and they usually forgive me for that." He pulled off Chris's boot, which did earn a scream of pain. Chris was desperately trying to clear the black spots in front of his vision as the old man ran his calloused hands lightly over the swollen ankle. "Yep, that's broken and sure, that is." He looked thoughtfully at Chris, looked him over, and looked him up and down.

"Okay, this is what I'm a'gonna do. I'm going to get you out of the open," he gestured to a stand of trees about 100 feet away. "And I'm a'gonna go back and get my girls out here to help get you to our place. Ain't no way you can walk that far and ain't no way an old fart like me is gonna be carrying a fine strapping lad like you over my shoulder."

With that he pulled Chris into a standing position and looped the boy's arm over his shoulders. A hundred feet felt like a hundred miles. The swelling and throbbing of his broken ankle had him sobbing in pain by the time they reached the break of trees.

The old man settled him slowly down against a tree. Chris's vision darkened and his head swam. "Don't you make a sound there, boy, not a peep. Like I said there's others won't give you the time of day, just shoot you when they see those colors. I'll bring back a shirt and jeans for you to wear. I'll be back in two licks." Chris barely registered the man's departure through the haze of pain. Eventually, he relaxed enough to doze lightly. It was a welcome respite from the throbbing fire that consumed his foot.

The murmur of voices snapped him back to consciousness. Two teenage girls walked with the old man. The old man had exchanged his shotgun for two long poles and a rucksack. The girls were both armed; their slim hips bulged, each wore a tiny revolver on one side and a sharp, long hunting knife on the other. They looked openly skeptical as they caught their first glimpse of Chris.

The older one, she had to be close to Jess's age, eyed his clothes, "Gramps, you said he was hurt, y'didn't mention he was the enemy."

"He ain't the enemy, girl."

"But he's wearing a Western Front uniform."

The old man looked irritated, "And he's explained why so's you better never mind." He bobbed his head towards Chris, "Boy, I brought you a change of clothes. You to take off those you got on and let us get 'em gone where no one else will go a'looking. Folks round here'd just as soon shoot you if they see those colors. After your good and dead they might think of askin' questions. So, skivvy on outta them and put on these." He tossed the rucksack and Chris caught it. He pulled off his shirt quickly and then looked distinctly uncomfortable.

The taller girl rolled her eyes, "Oh for Christ's sake, ain't nothing we ain't seen before."

"Carrie Lynn Perdue!" Her grandfather barked, "Don't you use the name of the Lord in vain!"

She was instantly meek, "Yes, Gramps, sorry." Her grandfather harrumphed and gestured for both the girls to turn away while Chris took off his pants. They rolled their eyes and grinned mischievously as they turned their backs.

It took him a fair bit of time to maneuver with his swollen ankle, which had doubled in size from the night before. By the time he had put on the pants and buttoned his shirt his head was swimming and he felt sick to his stomach. He closed his eyes and willed his stomach to settle. He was startled by the soft, warm hand that gently touched his forehead.

Both of the girls were tall, slender, and had long blond hair. The taller one, who the old man called Carrie, had emerald green eyes and her younger sister had that half blue, half brown, half something else that people usually just called hazel. Right now, a pair of the most amazing green eyes were staring into his and looking concerned. "Gramps, he's got a fever too."

"I ain't surprised about that. Let's get him on the gurney and get him back to the house. Liza, you take these and burn them down at the pits. Make sure no one sees and make sure they're burned to nothing. Then you hustle yourself back to the house right quick, y'hear?"

"Yessir," the girl chirped and disappeared into the woods with the bundle of clothes.

Chris slowly stood up with Carrie on one side and the old man on the other. They helped him hop to the stretcher; a sturdy piece of canvas attached to the two poles, and laid him down on it.

"I could try and walk," Chris said, his voice sounded embarrassingly feeble to his own ears. Carrie snorted, crouched down at one end, and gripped the poles.

"One, two, and three!" Carrie and her grandfather heaved him into the air and began to walk steadily.

It wasn't long before they were huffing and puffing from the exertion. It took several sets of walking and then sitting down and resting before they reached their destination. What Chris could see of it from his limited view was a decent sized farmhouse and several outbuildings. Several trees, on the outskirts of the property had been felled recently and Chris noticed that the view from the house was clear in all directions. It was a well-situated, defensible property. Anyone who tried to take the house would have zero cover for a good 100 yards in any direction. Unless you were suicidal or had a true hard-on for trouble, it would be advisable to find a better target.

Liza caught up to them, materializing at Chris's right shoulder and grabbing half of her grandfather's side of the stretcher. "Y'didn't blindfold him, Gramps. Y'shoulda."

The old man's breathing was labored. "When I need yer opinion, girl, I'll tell you what it is. You let me do the worryin' 'bout this fella. You burn those clothes down to ash?"

"Uhh...yessir." She tripped over a rock and lurched to the left, and the three of them all stumbled and nearly dropped him. Chris's damaged left ankle rapped hard against the undamaged right and he passed out.

"Other *things may change us, but we start and end with family"* – **Anthony Brandt**

Chris opened his eyes and frowned. The deer standing over him was still. It didn't move, it didn't blink, – and it didn't seem to even breathe. It took him several moments to realize it was only a head, a hunting trophy, mounted on the wall.

The past couple of days had been a blur of pain. They had set his ankle, he certainly remembered that. He wished he didn't. He distinctly remembered cursing and screaming, which was surely offensive to the old man and his scream had been embarrassingly effeminate. The pretty girl with the green eyes must have been greatly impressed with that.

After that had come waves of heat, then cold, and the ache from the damaged ankle, all in succession, as they battled the fever that had beset him. His fall into the swamp, the exposure to wet and cold, as well as the stress of the escape and no food in days had opened the door to a bad cold, complete with a racking cough, which had then turned to pneumonia. Today was his first lucid day in what seemed like forever.

He took a moment and looked around him at the room. Paneled walls all covered with furred trophies or pictures of hunters. He was lying on a worn, lumpy couch with a handmade quilt covering him snugly.

He could see it was made of plaid flannels, most likely old cast-off shirts. His stomach growled loudly. How long had it been since he had eaten? He dimly recalled Green Eyes, what was her name, spooning broth into his mouth. When had that been? Last night?

A lively young face appeared in his field of vision. Hazel eyes and pixie nose and damned if he could remember this one's name either. "You're awake!" She grinned at him and then turned and yelled over her shoulder, "Hey Carrie, tell Gramps that he's awake!"

It was Gramps that answered, "Stop your bellowing child, I'm right out here." From his position on the couch, Chris could see that this den opened into a short hall and a kitchen beyond. The old man set down the basket of eggs he had just brought in from outside and made his way slowly into the room. "So, you finally lucid, boy? You've been near to dead for six days."

Six days! Six days he could barely remember. His brain was still fuzzy from sleep as he tried to figure out how far he'd come and how long it had taken. Weeks? Months? He would later map it out and discover that he had traveled for nearly three hundred miles. He'd just kept going, kept running. It hadn't made sense, not then, and certainly not now. Who the hell ran towards Tennessee anyway? Yet here he was.

The old man was standing there, waiting for Chris to open his mouth and say something, anything, "Thank you sir, for not shooting me." What else could he say?

The old man laughed. He laughed until he choked and then bent double to recover. He grabbed Chris's shoulder for support and managed to wheeze, "Boy, you are something, you truly are.

You been gabbling on for days about Jess and Erin and Allen and I figure I know more 'bout you than you know yourself." He took Chris's hand in his and firmly shook it, "I'm Fenton Perdue, by the way. And I'd like to think I made the right choice in saving your sorry ass. But I'd sure like to hear how a Missouri boy ended up in this neck of the woods, sure and how I would."

The older girl, Carrie, had slid into the room. On her heels was a young boy, maybe five, maybe younger. His hair was blond and he had the same emerald green eyes. Carrie didn't look old enough to be his mother, but he leaned against her, eyes locked on Chris. Fenton followed Chris's gaze, "That's my grandson, Joseph, and a'course you already met Liza and Carrie. You remember that, right?"

"Yes sir, I remember." His stomach groaned loudly, and Liza giggled.

"Well, shoot, boy, I plumb forgot my manners." Fenton looked embarrassed, "You need to eat. You ain't had nothin' but broth for days." He motioned to the girls, "Help him on into the living room and we'll get some breakfast cooked up."

Chris sat up slowly, amazed at how weak he felt. As soon as he did, another part of his body made itself known. Damn, but he needed to piss.

"I uh, I think I can make it on my own," he said as the girls tried to take his arms and lift him up. "I uh, could I uh, use the facilities?" Liza snickered, and Carrie just rolled her eyes at her sister. She smiled at him, a nice smile, and held his arm firmly as he slowly stood up.

A wave of dizziness washed over him and black spots appeared before his eyes. As his vision cleared, he realized he was leaning heavily against the girl, his head had settled against hers and she was desperately trying to hold his weight. Her hair smelled of wood smoke and sage. He had never been near a woman that smelled so wonderful. No perfume in the world could compare.

He closed his eyes and sniffed again. "Um..." The uneasy tone in Carrie's voice snapped him out of it, as did the now screaming urgency to pee. He muttered an apology and took some of his weight back, battling the dizziness and the sharp protest from his damaged ankle and allowed her to guide him down a dark hall to the bathroom. There was a bucket of water inside, sitting next to the toilet. "We lost water pressure a few months ago, so just do what you need to and then I'll come in and flush it out with the bucket. Okay?"

"Yeah, okay. Thanks, Carrie." She vanished from the open door. The bathroom was very dim, it didn't have any exterior windows, and what light there was came from a bedroom off of the hall. The old man had mentioned breakfast, so it must be morning. He pulled the pants down and sat on the toilet, too exhausted to stand, and closed his eyes in relief. A few moments later she came in as he was wrestling with the bucket while trying to balance on one leg. "I said I'd do it."

"I know. I just..." his voice trailed off, he could barely stand, barely walk, felt as weak as a kitten and all he wanted to do was sniff her hair again. She just smelled, so...his vision blurred again. He needed food and he really need-ed to sit the hell back down.

"Liza! Gramps! Help!" he could hear Carrie's voice calling from far away and he came to with a start as he crashed to the ground, rapping his broken ankle sharply against the bathroom cabinet. Hands grabbed him on all sides, pulling and pushing him to a standing position. They shuffled awkwardly back down the hall with Carrie directing, "No Gramps, not back in the den, let's get him out to the living room. We can prop him up and feed him easier there."

Before long he was settled in what he was sure was the most comfortable recliner he had ever had the luxury of sitting in. "I don't see why he's gotta sit in my chair," Fenton grumbled.

"It'll be easier to set a table up for him here."

"But he's in my chair!"

"Oh Gramps, you'll live." And with that Carrie walked into the kitchen and began cracking eggs and turning the oven on to heat. "I'm fixing biscuits and gravy with eggs on the side." She announced, her hands busy, "Joseph, go grab us a jar of peaches and dish some up for...for..." "We don't even know your name."

"It's Chris. Chris Aaronson." He fell in love in that next moment. The moment the girl turned and smiled at him. Her teeth were perfect and her smile dazzled him. "Hi Chris," She turned back to her brother, "Get some of those peaches in a cup for Chris, Joseph. And stop gawping at him, he don't bite."

The little boy filled the bowl and Chris attacked the offered food, trembling weakly, as he tried to hold himself back from inhaling the peaches. Eggs replaced the peaches along with a cup of steaming black coffee. After that followed the biscuits and the gravy and Chris ate every scrap of the food they placed in front of him. He even ran a finger along the plate to catch the last bits of gravy and crumbs.

He looked up to see the entire family watching him. The old man was smiling. The little boy, Joseph, was staring; he'd never seen anyone eat so much so quickly. And the girls looked pleased, especially Carrie, when he licked his finger clean of gravy and thanked her.

"Now, boy," Fenton said.

"His name is Chris," Liza inserted.

"I know what the boy's name is, girl!" Fenton snapped, "Now, boy...I mean, Chris," He rolled his eyes at Liza, "We'd sure like to hear 'bout how you ended up in Tennessee."

Chris started at the beginning and told them how the Western Front had invaded Belton, shooting anyone who fought back, burning houses, taking the young and able. He explained how his sister and two of their friends had also been held in the camp, how they had planned an escape. He told them he had run southeast of the camp for more than twenty miles and thought he had escaped successfully and planned to turn north and circle around Springfield and head back towards Belton when two soldiers had caught him, beaten him and tied him up.

"I found out that my sister and everyone who had escaped that night had already been captured and that I was the last one left. They said Cooper was in charge now and that he had...he had..." He broke down then, unable to repeat the terrible soul-killing things the men reported that Cooper had done to Jess before he killed her and Erin and the rest.

"Everyone I know is dead. My parents, my sister, my friends." His eyes were dark holes of pain, "They were planning on taking me back to camp, but I managed to kill both of them. If I hadn't, they would have never stopped hunting me." He looked at them then, the girls had tears in their eyes, "After that I took the truck, drove it until it was out of gas and then I just started walking. I don't know what I expected to find, or where I was planning on going. I just...couldn't stay there. And I kept going until I fell into that swamp and lost my gun."

"Lake," Fenton corrected.

"Huh? Oh yeah, right. Lake. And that's when you found me."

Carrie asked softly, "And where would you go once you have healed up?"

Chris tried to imagine what tomorrow would bring and simply shrugged, "I've got nowhere in particular to go. My family is gone. I don't want to fight in another man's army, especially not one that killed everyone I loved. I just..." his voice trailed off, he hadn't really thought about what he wanted to do or where he would go.

He'd just kept walking and tried not to think about anything more than food, shelter and basic survival. A wave of exhaustion hit him then. The moving around for the first time in days, the massive amount of food he had just eaten, all of it hit him at once and he drooped.

"Boy, you are all done in. Close your eyes and get some shut-eye. We'll talk later." As Chris closed his eyes gratefully, the old man sighed and shook his head, "And a'course, he's in my chair."

The last thing Chris heard before he succumbed to sleep was Carrie, "Oh Gramps, you'll live."

"When Quincy found us, I knew he was gone. I knew it, and I mourned, for he was a good and kind man. At the time there seemed to be so few of them left.

She showed up alone, no mama and no brother. I can only guess at what happened after we left. Maybe we were tracked, maybe it was just bad luck, I'll never know. But my heart jumped when I saw her. I named her Quincy right there on that bridge, moments after we recognized her loping along, her nose to the ground, sussing out where we had trekked in the two weeks since we'd last seen her. I suppose I could have been more original, but I saw the sign on the bridge leading into the town of Quincy and figured it was fate. I am thankful she found us, she ended up saving my life more times than I can remember." – **Jess's journal**

"Clinton? Shee-it. You girls got one hell of a long walk ahead of you," the grizzled old man laughed, "sure you don't wanna stay here with me?" He winked at them.

It was a tense few hours since first meeting, but Arno Cooper, "Ever'one 'round here just calls me Coop," appeared relatively harmless. It helped that he hadn't been armed with a gun and they were, both girls ready to draw blood rather than pass the time of day. Being back on the road nearly three weeks now hadn't dulled them at all, they were jumpy and scared, so they knew he was there long before he was aware of them. He had been muttering to himself, picking burrs off of his shirt, slapping at the occasional mosquito and inspecting some traps along the same creek the girls had been following for the past three days.

Jess had seen him first and wanted to avoid him. She suggested tracking around in a broad circle, but the woods were thick with black locust trees, these nightmarish trees were loaded with sharp spines on their branches. They had stumbled into a dense thicket of the trees a week or so ago and been rewarded by several painful bloody wounds before they had managed to escape to open ground. Erin was far braver; she wanted to know where they were, and how far they had to go to get to Clinton.

Without a map, the next best thing was asking someone. They had both agreed to tell no one of their ultimate destination. If anyone was looking for them, or if the soldiers took a turn back northwest, they reasoned that it would be better for them to be heading for Clinton. After all, that was familiar enough country to get them the rest of the way home to Belton. And right at the moment they came to an agreement, the dog lying on the ground near the old man had woken up, let out a short bark and 'pointed' right at them.

It was early June and the day was already uncomfortably warm. If you looked a distance away you could see the waves of heat pulsing through the air. Old Coop, who turned out to be an experienced trapper, had managed to snare a skunk, two squirrels, and a large groundhog in his traps. The skunk's smell was overwhelming at first; the girls' eyes watered from their vantage point only a few yards away.

He had offered to share his bounty and their store of smoked fish had run out two days ago—by now their growling, empty stomachs were stronger and no doubt louder than their fear. So, they stood back and watched as he field-dressed the catch, started a small campfire and talked endlessly. In a way it was a comfort to hear another voice. He spoke of troop movements and then turned autobiographical.

"So, my Alice, she passed away a few months after Black Monday and my boy Scott joined up with uh, with the Army not long after." Blood dripped from his fingers as he skinned the skunk, "Haven't heard nuthin' in over two years from him, but we was never what you'd call close."

He waved a gore-covered finger at Erin, "Fetch us some water from the creek there, would ya' Missie?" A streak of blood smeared across his cheek as he wiped the sweat away. Erin warily took the indicated bucket and headed for stream, never looking away from the old man.

He slowed in his constant patter, took a long look at Jess and asked, "Them soldiers knock you up, girl?" Jess bristled, and said nothing. He took her silence for confirmation and said, "My Alice, she had herself an affair, got herself knocked up. The man was worthless, wouldn't stand by her and took the next Greyhound outta town after I came and err...*talked* to 'im. I coulda divorced her, but I didn't. I stuck by her and she birthed that child," he stopped and smiled crookedly at Jess, "We named her Tiffany and I swear to you I never loved a child more than I loved that little girl. Now my boy Scott, he was some five years older than his little sister. He was my own flesh and blood. But he and me, we were always strangers living in the same house."

Erin had returned and was listening quietly, the pail of water sloshing in her hands. He turned and gestured for her to put it near the campfire and Jess spoke for the first time, her finger slowly easing off of the large hunting knife near her side, "So what happened to her?"

The old man's hands stopped for a moment in their work. He stopped and looked up at Jess and said, "Same as what happened to you girls, 'ceptin my girl ain't never gonna come back." His grizzled and lined face twisted in pain and he looked down at the small bloody creature in his hands, "I heard she gave 'em hell. Got one of 'ems knives from 'em, sneaky-like and cut up one of the bastards nice and good. They killed her for it, after they were done using her, then dumped her like she was a piece of trash."

He took a deep breath, swatted at a hovering mosquito and continued, "I'd been tracking 'em since she went missing. See she'd been in town visiting a friend of hers the day they blew through. Three days later I found her body, and I found one of 'em who was too shot up to fight.

They'd left him behind too. Damn, when I was in the Service you didn't run off and leave your men, and y'sure didn't rape innocent young girls. Anyways, he told me everythin' afore he died." Cooper's eyes were red and blood-shot when he looked back up. "I'm just an old man. I wanted to kill 'em all, but a'stead I took her back home and buried her next to her mama. Thank God my Alice weren't alive to see what they did to her baby." He shook his head, bent back to skinning and repeated, "I'm just an old man. God forgive me, I'm just an old man."

Erin and Jess exchanged glances. It was a beautiful summer day, hot, even in the shade. Both the girls' skins were tanned and brown. In another space and time, you would think summer break from school, swimming pools, guys and even a party or two. Above them the clouds were white and fluffy with just a hint of gray. The rain would come tonight, like it had each evening before, and when it did it would sink blissfully into the earth and add to the humidity the following day.

How could it be so beautiful out when there was so much loss and heartache? The sun shone overhead and the birds sang. Life went on, and it seemed so impudent, as if life was laughing at their traumas and dismissing them as irrelevant. In the shade of the trees near the creek, with only the mosquitoes to harass them, they felt relatively safe. Here was a man who had lost someone. He hurt just as they hurt and what was to be done? What measure of justice would he ever receive? Cooper was just another lonely old man, his world crushed by events beyond his control in a world gone mad.

The old man led the way back up the creek to a small double-wide and a handful of outbuildings in various stages of disrepair. Several chickens clucked and scuttled about in a fenced section of the yard with a small chicken coop attached. The mobile home had seen better days. Two of the windows had been smashed and Coop had simply nailed plywood over them. He shrugged, "Ain't much in the way of supplies for fixin' the windows around here no more. So, I just did what I could. It leaks a little when it rains."

He had a solid patch of garden, filled with green beans, peas, and a multitude of other plants. "What I don't like, I just barter." He grinned, "I ain't terribly fond of watermelon, for instance, but my Alice always growed it and so I just kept it up. I got a neighbor up the way who is particularly skilled at bagging turkeys. I make sure he's got plenty of watermelon in the summer and he takes care to see I got me a turkey or two each winter. It all works out."

It was a quiet place. It wasn't fancy, but it was peaceful, and they reveled in the comfort of sleeping in an honest-to-god, full-sized bed that had room enough for both of them.

In the end, they would spend two weeks with old Coop in his small ramshackle mobile home a mile to the north of the creek where they had found him. They stayed in Tiffany's room, not willing to be separated, still not willing to trust even a beaten-down, grizzled old man. With his hospitality came changes of clothes and shoes in both girls' sizes, Scott's shoes had fit Erin and Tiffany's had fit Jess. Finally, they were able to have something different than the ragged remains of those hated Western Front uniforms. The uniforms were stained and dirty anyway, stiff from being worn day in and day out and only hand-washed and hung to dry when the days were warm enough to go without while they dried. They burned them at the first opportunity.

Tiffany had been both girls' size, but certainly not their taste—hers ran to sparkly, sequined tops and lots of pink. She must have been a real 'girly girl' in her clothing and decor. Perhaps that was what made it rather shocking for the girls to imagine her actually taking a knife and killing a man.

Jess found that Scott's spare clothes were more accommodating of her swelling belly and old Cooper assured her that they were welcome to any of the clothing they wanted from his children's rooms. They fished and stocked up on meat from Cooper's traps and ate fresh peas and strawberries which seemed to grow overnight in the raised beds behind the old man's trailer.

As the sun dipped down below the horizon on the twelfth day, both girls found themselves at ease with Cooper. Erin sat cross-legged on the ground in a pink crop top with 'Princess' emblazoned upon it in sequins, while Jess relaxed in a lawn chair in camouflage fatigues and a giant black Insane Clown Posse t-shirt. She winced as the baby rolled and kicked inside her, pressing sharply on her full (it always seemed full these days) bladder. She turned to her left, reached down and scratched behind the girl pup's ears. Cooper had just two of them left. The puppies were ten weeks old. They frolicked around the property, long legs and lean bodies, still awkward as they ran.

They cried out with piteous yaps when the old man would tie them up and take their mother away with him to go trapping. One of them, the girl pup, had taken a shine to Jess and kept seeking her out, butting her head against Jess's hand and insisted on following her everywhere. Her liquid brown eyes stared up at Jess and her tongue would frantically lick the air as Jess bent close and stroked the puppy's soft fur.

The pup's fur was brown with patches of white and she had huge, floppy ears that perked up with interest at the smallest sound from Jess. Each morning, the little pup was the first to greet Jess and she howled at night when Old Coop locked her up with the others in the dog run. How Jess wished she could take the pup with her, but it was impossible, they barely had enough food for themselves, much less a growing puppy.

She met Erin's gaze and nodded to her friend. They had talked about it the night before. It was time to move on. Cooper had just finished telling a funny joke and Erin's smile dropped, her face grew serious and her laughter was cut short. She cleared her throat, "We, uh, we need to get back on the road again, Coop." The old man fell silent, looked at the ground, and said nothing. Erin continued, "We've got to go home, y'know, to find out if anyone of our friends or family managed to stay alive."

Cooper looked like he was about to object, or try to talk them out of it. He opened his mouth to speak but the words never came out of his throat. He struggled silently for a moment, and tried to collect his thoughts before speaking. It was obvious to both of them how much he had enjoyed having them there and how desperately lonely the old man was.

When the words did come, his voice sounded rough and strained, "Well a'course y'all gotta go. I knew you'd be headin' on once y'got some rest in. Y'headin' out tomorra'?"

Jess's throat felt tight. Cooper was a decent man, the first either of them had seen in a long time. He was a little rough around the edges, but deep inside, there rested a good, kind soul. "Yeah, tomorrow."

The old man nodded, "Well, y'all need somethin' better 'n that rifle and one lonely box of ammo."

He got up and ducked into the trailer, rummaged inside a cabinet and returned with several boxes under his arm and sat back down in his weather-beaten wood chair. He tossed a box of shells to Erin, they were 22s, a full box of them. Erin grinned like she'd been handed gold. But Cooper wasn't done yet.

"Y'all need somethin' small and easy to conceal like this little lady." He reached into the box and pulled out a revolver, with inlaid wood in the handle and black steel. He handed it to Jess.

She ran her hands over it. It wasn't a new gun, but it had been well cared for. It smelled sharply of cleaning fluid and the wood felt as smooth as silk. He showed her how to pull it apart and pointed out the grip safety on the back strap. She looked up and saw Coop's eyes steady on her. "Smith and Wesson, Model 40 Centennial. She's small, easy to hide in your pocket, but I found a holster for her. I used to take my Tiffany target shooting with this little lady. She takes five rounds, and ya got 'bout 30 rounds of .38s left in that there box. You keep her with you at all times. Keep her loaded. Will ya do that Missie?"

Jess nodded, unable to speak, reminded suddenly of her dad. This man looked nothing like her dad, but he was a father through and through. You can tell that about some people. They are the people who change irrevocably when parenthood visits them. They never stop caring; never stop seeing their own children in stranger's faces. She struggled up from the lawn chair, leaned over and hugged the old man, and went inside the trailer. She suddenly felt exhausted and she didn't trust herself not to cry. She lay down in Tiffany's frilly pink bed and closed her eyes. Outside she could hear Erin and Coop talking, too quiet to be heard. By the time Erin joined her in bed, Jess was sound asleep.

Jess and Erin were both up with the dawn. They weren't surprised to see Old Coop awake as well. And he had already brewed up a large pot of his dwindling stash of coffee and baked some biscuits for them to eat and take on the road. They had packed extra changes of clothes and Erin was sporting hot pants and a crop top with 'Spoiled Rotten' spelled out in a rainbow of shiny letters across the front. She had the rifle slung across her back, and Jess had her shiny revolver in a holster strapped to her fatigues. The pups were tied up, the little female crying and lunging at her lead, trying to escape and join the girls. Jess knelt down and hugged the pup close, felt her warm body writhe against her and the dog's tiny tongue lick her desperately. Somehow the pup knew she was leaving.

The sun was out and it was time to go. Coop reached out and hugged Erin, "You stay safe now, y'hear me, girlie?" Erin smiled and thanked him and then it was Jess's turn. He hugged her, then reached out and put a rough, gnarled hand firmly on her rounded belly. She nearly jerked away, but the sad look in his eyes stopped her. "Jessie girl, listen to me now and humor an old man."

She stilled and looked back into his eyes. "This baby in you, it ain't done nothin'. It ain't asked to be here and it's as innocent as one of God's lambs." Even now, with it so obvious what was happening, she hated to think about it and tried to pull away, but Coop persisted, "I know you think this ain't what you want. An' I can't blame you girl if y'think you hate this creature inside you, but it's a blessin' and someday you'll see it that way."

He held her gaze with his and said, "Children's are blessin's. They are the gift God gives us to tell us the world ain't all pain and death and loneliness." His eyes blurred with tears, "I hold my children in my heart and think of them each day. So, you remember what I said when this child comes outta you. Will you remember that Jessie?"

His features blurred as the tears leaked from her eyes and ran down her face. For that moment she let them fall. She was so damned scared and he knew it, he understood it somehow, and she felt like curling up in his arms and never leaving this quiet place.

Instead, she nodded tearfully and hugged him, and managed to croak out, "Thanks." Tears blurring both of their vision, the girls set out along the creek, large new backpacks full of food and supplies slung to their backs. The old man stood there for a long time, long after they had disappeared from sight, before slowly turning away and returning to his lonely, empty home.

"I long, as does every human being, to be at home wherever I find myself." – Maya Angelou

Chris pulled the weeds from the raised beds of the kitchen garden and threw them towards the enclosure where the chickens clucked and jockeyed for position. They angled for the larger bits, pecked and squabbled over the choicer pieces. It reminded him painfully of home. Jess had done this for Mom in the family garden back in Belton.

They might have had a smaller plot of land, not a full-fledged farm with a pond and fields, but chickens are pretty much the same wherever you go. He closed his eyes, remembered her voice as she talked to the chickens, her wavy blond hair tied back in a ponytail and the chickens clucked back at her, bobbing their heads in time as she spoke. What she would say to them, he didn't know, but the sound of her voice, and the memory of it now, was bittersweet.

The sun was barely up, the house behind him was quiet, and he savored this moment of solitude. It would be another scorcher today. Already the air was uncomfortably hot and humid. His ankle still ached, but it had been set straight and he hoped it would heal completely given time. He had come down the back stairs too quickly and it had twanged a painful warning until he slowed down. He didn't have far to go. The raised beds were, after all, right off of the kitchen. Here the curled leaves of lettuce sprang in a dramatic show of greens and reds. The pole beans and green beans were growing well and there was room for more in a half-used bed. The soil was rich and loose, well-composted.

He thought of his mother, Julie, digging her hands deep into the soil. She would smile and dig, weed, plant and talk about the gardens for hours. How she had loved her gardens! The memory of her smiling face hurt him deep inside. He imagined his parents' last moments, as they tried desperately to stop the enemy soldiers from abandoning a group of small children on the road so many miles from home. It was just like her to speak up, to try and stop such a thing from happening, and for Dad to stand beside her no matter the personal cost.

He had wrung the details out of Allen. It had been hard to hear, harder still though to not know. His friend had looked haunted as he had recounted the Aaronson's end, as if he thought Chris would hold him responsible somehow or blame him for not interceding. If only he hadn't have taken that hike and gotten caught up in the first wave, he would have been with them when it all came down. Chris didn't blame Allen, not at all. Instead he blamed himself. He hadn't been there when they needed him most. And they had died there, miles from home, alone. They had deserved better than that.

He sat on the edge of a raised planter and looked over the greenery. Everywhere there was green and life growing. The beans snaked their way up the poles and the peas were fat and heavy, ready for picking. Plump, red strawberries hid under leaves and he picked a few and ate them. They were warm and juicy, the sweet tang bursting on his tongue when he bit into them. The plants were growing fast, but he would need to water today. He'd do that, and ask the old man if there was any more of the bean and squash seeds left to plant since there was still time to get them in and growing.

As he shifted, his ankle twanged again. He still favored it, but it was getting stronger by the day and his limp was barely noticeable.

He nearly jumped out of his skin when Carrie's voice sounded at his ear. It would be a long time before he would be able to react normally. He was still in combat mode, ready to run or fight at the drop of a hat. She patted his shoulder and smiled, "How's your ankle today?"

The wonderful scent of her, this combination of sage and wood smoke, washed over him, "I...uh...it's fine. Damn, but you scared the hell out of me."

"I'm sorry," her emerald-green eyes stared into his, twinkling in amusement. "I didn't mean to." She was close, way too close, and Fenton would damn near kill him if he so much as touched her. Of that he was sure. Carrie laid her hand on his cheek.

Chris was handsome, there was no denying it. Carrie stared at his deep blue eyes. The only imperfections were the scar on his forehead and a slightly bent nose. Both of the wounds had come from those soldiers.

In a way, it made him more handsome to her eyes. He had a way of look-ing at her that made her want to get closer. She was used to guys taking the lead with her. She'd done her share of making out, but nothing more. Going all the way was supposed to mean something and she figured she knew who that guy was. Chris seemed to really like her, but he still pulled away and she didn't know quite how to handle it. It sometimes seemed that he was avoid-ing being alone with her.

Chris had to stop this. Carrie was only sixteen and Fenton was protective of both girls. The old man was very, very protective. The two of them had been dancing around each other for weeks. She flirted with him constantly and he struggled with keeping the image of Fenton and his shotgun in the forefront of his memory. The old man wasn't going to cotton to Chris cozy-ing up to his precious granddaughter. There were limits to a man's hospitality after all.

He shook his head at her and gently removed her hand from his cheek. Carrie looked hurt and a little put out, but then she smiled and told hold of his hand, pulling him to his feet. "Come on, I want to show you something. If you think you could handle a little bit of a hike." His ankle twanged again in protest at the thought of going anywhere. And worse, he wasn't sure he should be alone with her. It was getting harder and harder to resist the im-pulse to kiss her. Against his better judgment, he let her pull him along. They walked out past the perimeter of the property, into the trees which quickly became thick woods.

The going was difficult and several times they stopped so that he could rest a moment. The heat of the morning was radically altered underneath the leafy canopy of trees and there was a cool breeze. "It's just a little ways further," Carrie pulled him up and they walked again, slowly edging their way down an embankment and crossing a lively creek. He could see tiny fish darting between the rocks and several dragonflies buzzed by with iridescent green and blue-hued wings. They crossed the creek, squeezed through a stand of trees and stopped in a small clearing. Wildflowers bloomed everywhere and he could see a chimney and the remains, mostly intact, of a small stone house. The roof sagged and it looked as if it had been deserted for a long time.

The clearing was a paradise of flowers, birds chirping, and the gurgle of the creek behind them. Carrie smiled at Chris, and stepped closer, "Do you like what you see?"

The scenery melted away, and all Chris could see were beautiful eyes and perfect skin and soft lips. He slipped his hand behind her head, ran his hands through her hair, and kissed her softly. The kiss went on and on, intensifying as her mouth opened to him and their tongues entwined. She pressed herself against him and his other hand slid slowly down her back, finding her shapely buttocks and pulling her up closer. His breathing had quickened and in his mind a war was being fought. Part of him wanted to stop this; because he was sure Fenton would come around the corner at any minute with the shotgun and shoot him dead for touching his precious granddaughter. The other part of him wanted to pull her to the ground, slip off her tight, sexy jeans and drive into her.

A few long, hot moments later and they had ended up on the ground, her shirt unbuttoned and a white, lacy bra covered her perky young breasts. He took a deep breath and sat up. Carrie looked hurt, "What's wrong?"

"Besides the fact that you are beautiful and sexy and I want to do far more than just kiss you?" Chris smiled, "I'm thinking that Fenton has got one damned scary shotgun."

Carrie's eyes lit up at hearing "beautiful and sexy" and looked disappointed at the mention of her grandfather. "Gramps is just being protective. Since our parents died, he's taken care of us. He doesn't think of me as a woman."

"You're not a woman, you're only sixteen," Chris reminded her gently, "And I'm nearly twenty."

"I'll be seventeen in less than a month, and you're nineteen not twenty," she retorted, bristling at his comment. "I know my mind and I'm not some silly little girl."

"No, no you're not." He kissed her again, long and slow. It was full of promise of things to come. "But I cannot have sex with you, Carrie. Not now. I like you. I like you a lot, damn it. I like your whole family, for that matter. I don't want to piss off Fenton and I don't want to rush things with you." He took her hand, looked down at the ground, "I've been thinking. I've been doing a lot of thinking and I want to stay. Here. With all of you Perdue's."

Her eyes sparkled at the next words, "And I'm thinking that I've never met anyone I thought smelled as wonderful as you, or who was as smart and funny and beautiful as you. I think that here is a good fit for me. I can help with the stuff Fenton is getting too old to do. We could make this farm work, and not just survive, but be *okay* here. Better than okay. But if I stay, then I gotta do this right between you and me. I gotta do it like Fenton expects me to and damn well court you and not have sex the first time we go off alone together."

She laughed at that. And she knew he was right, even if she didn't like it. "You really want to stay?"

"Yeah, I really do."

"Okay."

They returned to the house with a load of blueberries. The abandoned stone house was the original homestead on the property. The blueberry bushes were bountiful there and had grown wild after they had been left behind. They wrapped the blueberries in Chris's shirt since they didn't have a basket. When they returned, Fenton was sitting in a chair on the wide front porch, thoroughly cleaning his shotgun. He looked pissed. Carrie started to say something to her grandfather but Chris handed her the shirt full of blueberries and gave her a small shove towards the house. He limped over to Fenton and sat down, very aware of his own bare chest and the set look on the old man's face.

"Mr. Perdue." The old man harrumphed and said nothing. "My ankle is healing and, if you want, I can be on my way in a few more days with my thanks for your help and hospitality."

Chris took a deep breath, "But I'd like to stay, sir. I think I could be of use here. For one, I could get some of those blueberry bushes dug up and transplanted closer to the house. I know how to take care of chickens; raise vegetables and I can learn the rest. I've helped my dad with roofing and construction, and once my ankle is healed, I could fix that leak in the barn. If you'd want to keep me on, that is."

There was a long silence as the old man digested the offer and oiled the barrel of the shotgun. "I ain't blind y'know. I seen you two looking at each other. Whatcha plannin' on doin' 'bout that?"

The shotgun was currently in pieces. Chris figured he was relatively safe, "Sir, I'd like permission to court your granddaughter."

If he could have read Fenton Perdue's mind at the moment, he would have known instantly that his words and his attitude were perfect. Fenton was old-fashioned. He'd been raised by his grandparents after his father died in the war and his mother died in childbirth. His grandfather had instilled in him a sense of honor and chivalry that was long dead in the modern world.

The old man loved his grandchildren more than life itself. When their father had died in the Amtrak bombings just months before Joseph was born, Fenton had insisted the kids and their mother Amy move back to the family farm. She had been a tiny wisp of a woman who had given birth to Joseph three months to the day after they buried her husband. Just a few months later, Fenton had insisted she see a doctor.

She had been losing weight and was listless and slept round the clock. They'd had to put baby Joseph on formula because Amy just didn't have enough milk to sustain him. The doctor gave her a battery of tests, looked grim, and sent her to a specialist in Nashville. She was diagnosed with pancreatic cancer. She had died less than three months later. It had been just Fenton and the children ever since.

He stopped polishing the shotgun and looked over at Chris, met his eyes, searched them for deceit. He thought about how happy Carrie had looked in the last few weeks and how gentle Chris was with Joseph.

Even Liza seemed to appreciate his company, especially when she had discovered that they shared a love for science fiction. Chris had done a lot of reading those first two weeks while his ankle healed. There was no denying it; the boy was a good fit for their family.

Young love. I wonder if it will actually take. He thought about Molly, who had passed away over thirty years ago now. They'd met at a square dance when she was fifteen and he was eighteen going on nineteen.

Her daddy had been a doctor and her mama a nurse in the war. They wanted something more for their daughter than a life as a farmer's wife. But as the years had passed, they had seen how much the two were in love. Fenton had ended up being drafted and sent off to Vietnam as a medic. Thousands of miles from home he had watched men bleed out, spending the last moments of their lives in alien jungles, so far from their homes. So many lives lost, so many dreams dead with them, before he had returned home to his grandparent's farm, safe. After three years of courting, he had asked Molly's daddy for his blessing and the man had given it. They had married, built this enormous house after his grandparents died, and began practicing at making babies. Oh, how they had practiced! Both of them were only children and they wanted a big family. They dreamed of a passel of kids to fill the house's five large bedrooms and tumble through the gardens.

Fenton looked out over the land. It had been in his family for more than a century. And for the last five years he had wondered who would take it on next. Joseph? Carrie? Liza? Who would stay and work this land? The dreams he and Molly had had of a passel of little Perdues died the day of Isaac's birth. The birthing had been hard and the doctors said if they hadn't of taken everything out, she would've bled to death. So, they loved their son and loved each other for the rest of their time together. That time hadn't been nearly as long as Fenton would have liked. Molly had gotten breast cancer during Isaac's freshman year in high school and passed away less than a year later.

He looked again at Chris and realized the boy had been sitting there patiently, waiting for an answer. "Yes son, you can court my granddaughter. And heal up quick, 'cause I think the southwest corner of the house roof is needin' some repairs."

"Thank you, sir."

"Gramps."

"Sir?"

"Y' can call me Gramps. Everyone else does."

"Right...Gramps."

Fenton closed his eyes and listened as Chris got up slowly and limped inside the house. He heard the boy whisper to Carrie. She let out a happy squeal and gave him a loud kiss. Fenton smiled sadly. *I miss you, Molly.*

"**A** *damn smart man that I cain't 'member the name of right now said, 'There comes a time when you have to make a decision. Y'either lie down and get busy dying, or y'haul yer ass up and gits to fightin.'*" – ***Arno Cooper***

It had been a week and still the pup moped, barely touched her food and refused to play with her brother. At present, she was lying near Coop's feet staring at the bend in the road where she had seen the girls disappear from sight. Her brother was pulling on her ear with his sharp teeth and trying like hell to get her to play – but the girl pup wouldn't budge.

Coop saw the writing on the wall. The pup had given her heart to that Jessie, and there wasn't anything to be done about it except send her on her way. He smiled as he thought of it. This one was worth a lot. She had the right instincts to be one of the best hunting dogs he had ever bred. Lord knows he had been breeding them long enough to know. She was young, but damned smart.

Annie, the pups' dam, was the only one of Coop's dogs to survive when the troops blew through town. She had been out with Coop, checking lines and rooting out pheasants. Annie and the old man had returned to chaos – the rest of Coop's dogs dead, Tiffany missing, the trailer a jumbled mess and their entire stash of canned food gone. Except the beets, seems no one wanted the beets. Damn fools. Coop smiled at the thought, he *liked* beets.

A couple of months later Annie disappeared for a few days. Several weeks after she returned it became obvious, she was knocked up. Coop chuckled at the irony that for all his careful breeding, Annie had apparently found just the right mix of wild seed. All three of the pups she had borne in this litter were exceptional. One boy pup had been snatched up by the Walkers and Faen Brooks was coming for the last boy pup today.

Coop reached down and petted the little girl's ears. "I shoulda sent y'with her when they left." The pup whined sadly. "Hands down, girl, you're the best I got." The pup did not respond, just continued to stare down the road.

His rough hands slowly undid the collar from the pup's neck. Dozens of pups had worn this old leather collar, but none of them had been quite like this one. It seemed fitting somehow, considering what he was planning on doing. The pup looked up at him, tail slowly thumping. "Go on with yeh," he pointed towards the road, "You got a long road ahead of you if you're gonna catch up with 'em. So's you best get started." Annie gave her daughter one sharp bark of encouragement.

For the first time in over a week, the girl pup looked excited and alive. She looked up at Coop and back at her dam, then turned and ran towards the road. She stopped for a moment, stared back at the trailer and its inhabitants, wagged her tail, put her nose to the ground and then disappeared round the bend and on into the trees.

About an hour later, Faen Brooks showed up. He was a small man, with dark hair, pale blue eyes and sunburnt skin. He was Coop's cousin three times removed. Around these parts, if your family stayed around for long, and most did, eventually everyone was related to everyone else.

"Hey Coop, whatcha know?" The old man just grunted and pointed to Annie. She was lying on the ground a few yards away, not so patiently enduring her son's industrious attempts to get her to play. The boy pup tugged on one of her ears which earned him a short growl and quick snapping of teeth to show her displeasure.

"I need a full pack of jerky, any dried fruit you got," Coop replied, staring at his prize hounds, "and every box of ammo you can spare."

Faen looked pissed, "Now look here Coop, y'know we ain't got much, that's askin' an awful damn lot for one little pup that ain't even proven himself."

The old man didn't even look up. "That's for everythin', not just the pup."

"What the hell you talkin' bout, old timer, *what* everything?"

Coop looked over at the younger man, "The dogs, both of 'em. The trailer, the land, most of my traps, and whatever else you want."

The silence stretched on as Faen tried to stare Coop down.

One minute...

Two minutes...

Three...

He finally broke, "Godamnit Coop, no. This won't bring her back. Scott is still out there. What's he gonna do when he comes back from the Army? Find y'all gone with no one left?" Faen shook his head, "Think about how he'd feel, old man, with his whole family gone. He'd..."

The old man interrupted, "Scott didn't join the Army," he looked down at the ground, "That boy ain't got a home to come back to after what he done."

The younger man gaped at Coop in shock. No matter how bad Scott had acted up in years past, the old man had always shown him a patience and understanding that belied the crusty old-timer image that Coop had cultivated so well over the years.

Coop continued, "He joined 'em, the *Western Front*, he joined 'em *willingly*, and he was one of the bastards that tried to," his voice broke, "tried to...Tiffany was his *sister*, his own blood!" He sat for a moment, body shaking.

"I thought I could set it to rest, but I can't. I'm going to that camp, and I'm gonna finish him, and as many more as I can. That's just the way it is, Faen, so's you take Annie and that pup and you take good care of 'em, y'hear?"

Faen just stood there in shock, unable to form words; finally, he nodded, reached out a hand and grasped the old man's shoulder. "I'll take the dogs now, come back with a full pack for ya. Y'leaving first thing in the mornin'?"

"Yep."

"I'll bring it by at first light."

Faen's wife, Connie, went ballistic when she heard about Coop's plans the next day at breakfast. Faen had gone out at first light with a full pack of food and three boxes of shells that they really couldn't spare.

He given it all to Coop and watched the old man take U.S. 13, turn a bend and disappear from sight. Annie had gone crazy, pulling at the lead and trying like hell to break free. Faen calmed her down as best he could, she was a fine hound, but her heart belonged to Coop.

As he fought to keep the dog in line, his thoughts turned to his kids. Mick was turning twelve soon, Emmy was just six years old. Faen's stomach clenched at the thought of what this war could do to them in the years to come and wished the old man well.

He didn't tell her the truth about Coop's boy. That was something he just couldn't fathom. How could that boy join the Western Front? He'd always seemed a bit cold. The girls thought he was devilishly handsome, and Faen had to agree on the devilish part of it. Still, the idea that he had joined the Western Front – it was like suggesting you join the Union when you lived in the South, or like joining Al Qaeda after losing your family in the Twin Tower bombing. It was crazy!

Some part of him feared that if he said it aloud it would make it real. He may never have liked the boy, but damn, he wouldn't have expected this out of him. Besides, Connie had babysat Scott when she was a teenager and she'd always had a soft spot for the kid.

Faen just sat and stared at his scrambled eggs and let Connie rant about the stupidity of old men. When that didn't work, she pleaded with Faen to get on the road, catch up to Coop, and talk some sense into the old man, but her husband was unmoved. "He's got a right, Connie, he's gotta do this and I expect he'll be back. 'Member, he was some badass in 'Nam. I hear tell he had something like a hundred and fifty-eight kills. Shit, but that old man was legend back in the day."

Swearing earned him a small, annoyed smack on the back of his head from his wife. Only five-foot-tall, Connie was a spitfire and she didn't like swearing. God help Mick and Emmy if they let loose anything they had picked up in the schoolyard. She had thrashed Mick but good after he had uttered "Jesus Christ" within earshot. Connie was a deeply religious woman, and she did not cotton to profanity of any kind.

Faen knew the chances of the old man coming back weren't good, not at all, but if it calmed down Connie, well, she'd come around to an understanding of it later. That night she was so angry at Faen she made him sleep on the couch. Despite the fact that he could feel every spring and every lump in the aged thing, he slept well, feeling safe, well away from his angry, little wife.

By nightfall on the first day, Coop made it almost seven miles before he stopped and pitched a tent. By his reckoning, it would take two, maybe three days of hard walking before he reached the camp. In the end, it took him nearly a week and a half. He twisted his ankle crossing a river, two of the bridges had been torn out and his arthritis slowed him down considerably.

The last night of Coop's life found him camped without a fire. He didn't even set up the tent. He was so close that could hear men calling to each other in the enemy camp as he oiled hinges and sharpened the teeth of his snares and traps, all of them.

Coop's traps, snares and guns killed and maimed a lot of men early that morning. He had been a sniper in Vietnam, brought in on the tail end of the Tet Offensive. He had lost his cherry (in more ways than one) near Khe Sanh. Arno Cooper had been one of the best snipers the Army had ever had.

But time catches up to us all. Thirty-four minutes after the first shot had been fired; twenty-eight men lay dead. One of those twenty-eight was a good and honest man.

Captain Scott Cooper, stood over Old Coop's lifeless body, the Glock 40's barrel still smoking. There was not a trace of emotion in his handsome face, no recognition or acknowledgment of the man he had once called "Pops," in his pale blue eyes.

He ran a hand through his coal-black hair, removed a stray leaf and walked away from the old man's body without a backward glance.

"*War is the perfect excuse for all of my most beautiful dreams to finally come true. I've been waiting my whole life for this.*" – **Scott Cooper**
When the two girls had escaped into the storm, he had heard talk there was others connected to them. He asked the right questions, got a hold of one who hadn't managed to run fast enough, and got to use his favorite knife.

In the end that sniveling little deserter had told him little he didn't already know and begged for death. Five men had tried to desert the same night as the girls escaped under the cover of a violent thunderstorm, three were shot, the fourth, one Allen Banks, had made it almost to Highway 60 before they caught up with him and hamstrung him. The fifth had run southeast, towards Tennessee, and gotten away. That one was the blond girl's brother.

Scott seethed as he walked past the bodies of the men his father had killed and kicked one furiously. He was still pissed all these months later that he hadn't found the deserter or the two little whores right away. He had lost valuable time; there was no word from Easter or Burton, the two fools he had sent south after the brother. He had just sent another pair of men in search of the two whores after the last pair disappeared or deserted. He spat a fine stream of tobacco juice on the ground and walked back to his nice tent. It was the largest, and it had an actual honest-to-God bed in it. Right about now one of the new whores would be waiting there for him.

He liked breaking the new ones in; they were more interesting when they fought. He likened it to breaking a horse – you had to break their spirit, break them to the point that the stupid whores knew *you* were the one with the power.

The camp had just blown through another podunk town and picked up some new girls to replace those fool enough not to root out the bastards growing in them. He didn't waste time – when he heard of any whores who started showing he didn't even bother wasting a bullet, the knife worked just as well and it *felt* better.

The other men kept their distance now. They followed his orders and kept their mouths shut. No more Captain Kipling to give them orders, no more arguments about whether or not Tent 5 was 'within guidelines' – Cooper had used that favorite knife of his and taken care of the CO nearly two months ago. That damn politically correct little twit would not be rattling on about human rights anymore.

Kipling had been field-promoted after Granger had been taken out in a skirmish near Bolivar. Scott shook his head at the loss. Granger had been a mean S.O.B. who didn't give a crap about the Geneva Convention or what any other fool political monkeys thought.

He had set up Tent 5, coordinated the sorting of prisoners, and arranged for the range disposal of the old and weak. Under Granger's command this rattletrap group of fighters, once saddled with some stupid official military designation Cooper couldn't even remember now, had become a terrifying future for any unfortunate towns that lay in its path. Few survived the onslaught, and those that did were either conscripted or put to use in other ways.

Those too old or young to fight, work or whore were ended quickly and efficiently. No need to let survivors loose to warn others of troop movements or to get some stupid ideas to fight back later.

Granger had been a great man and Cooper had been his apt pupil. Then he had to up and die and that fool Kipling had taken over. Nearly shut things down around here. He was old school; he'd been with the regiment from when it still *was* a regiment and still in contact with the Western Front.

The long silence from HQ had rankled at Kipling, he'd complained to Granger that they needed to follow commands and find out what the hell had happened. But since the entire cell phone array had been destroyed, along with most of the power stations and other networks, they were back to the frigging Dark Ages. *"We might as well be fighting in the Civil fucking War."* Cooper had listened to the two go at it and wondered why Granger didn't just shoot the uppity little twerp.

The night Kipling ordered Cooper into his tent to tell him how things were going to change now that Granger was dead and that orders would be coming soon to stand down...that was when Cooper had had enough. He waited until the camp was quiet and then he put to use some of those skills his dad had so foolishly taught him. He snuck in and cut Captain Kipling's throat ear to ear. There hadn't been any voices saying "nay" when he told the men the next day that Kipling had put him in charge. He'd sent two men on the southern routes that night, and two on the road towards Belton, those runaway whores' hometown. "No one deserts and no whores get to leave," he said, surveying the mass of faces he had called to the camp meeting. "You leave here and it better damn well be in a body bag."

The following weeks would see several tests of that edict – in the end, no one survived stepping away from camp, unless they were under orders to go.

He was almost to his tent and he pulled on his belt, unbuckling it in anticipation. Inside of the dark tent he removed his ammo belt, placing it well within range. Most of his men were idiots just begging to be told what to do and where to march. The fact that he kept them fed, clothed, and well-laid did wonders, but he was no fool. There were some who still thought they were in the Army, and he knew that the way he had taken the reins of power in this crappy little corner of the world could be the same way they got rid of him. He was taking no chances. He kept a knife close by as well.

The girl was there, tied securely to the bed, her wrists and ankles already bleeding and raw from trying to free herself. Excellent, a fighter, he'd have himself a nice little ride. As it was, she started screaming and even attempted to bite him the minute he removed her gag. A solid punch to the mouth slowed her down and the second punch knocked her unconscious for a few precious seconds. He straddled her and waited patiently for her eyes to flicker open. "You can scream all you like," he said smiling down at her, "In fact, I like it."

His beautiful face turned hard and cruel and his hand lazily traced its way down her from her collarbone, past her breasts and towards her groin, "But if you try and bite me again, I'll break every bone in your face and make sure you choke to death on your own teeth." He smiled again and the girl began to sob, the devil himself couldn't have been more handsome or evil. "Great...let's get started then."

The girl's screams weren't the only ones in the camp that night, but they were certainly the loudest. Even heartless Carmen had paled slightly when she saw the girl delivered to Tent 5 the following morning. She had put her in a sectioned off area, an infirmary of sorts, to heal. No other man would have wanted her in the state she was in.

Little good that small kindness did. The ungrateful wretch managed to hang herself with a section of the shower curtain two days later when one of the fool guards had turned away for what he swore was just a moment. Her name was Lucinda Abernathy and she had turned fourteen years old one week earlier.

"*War does not determine who is right - only who is left.*" - **Bertrand Russell**

Easter stood in front of Chris, blood seeping from a scarf around his neck. In the past few months Easter had gone from a deathly white to a pale gray, then slowly darkening as he decayed further with each new dream. His skin had turned almost black now. "Your sister is dead because you failed, Aaronson," the corpse sneered, "You couldn't even pull off an escape. Banks, your sister, your parents, it's all on you. You couldn't even kill me right, 'cause here I am hauntin' your dreams all these months later."

Chris twisted away from Easter's grasping hands. The stench of the corpse filled his nose and made him want to retch. "You're just a dream. You're dead and you're just a dream, Easter." He shoved the corpse away from him and ran, trying to put distance between this remnant and himself, tried in vain to escape the dream.

He ran for what seemed like forever, but when he turned around there was Easter and behind him, Burton too. "Everything you touch will rot and die, Aaronson, just like me. You can't protect 'em, you'll only get that sweet little piece of ass raped and murdered, just like the rest. I could use a taste of that sweet little thing," the corpse taunted him. Chris screamed then, consumed with horror at the thought of Carrie at the hands of Easter or the likes of Cooper and all the rest.

"Chris! *Chris!* Wake up!" He came to in the dark, someone standing over him, a light in the doorway.

"Carrie girl, you stand back, child." He heard Fenton's voice from the doorway.

"But Gramps, I..." Chris realized the person standing over him was Carrie.

"No buts, girl, stand back," Fenton's gruff voice admonished, "The boy's havin' more than just a bad dream. You give him space now." He had pulled Carrie out of range, "Son, can you hear me?"

Chris was still shaking from the dream. The smell of rot and decay lingered in his nose. "Yessir." The old man came nearer and an oil lamp lit his way. He extended a hand to Chris, pulling him up from his huddle at the foot of the bed. How had he gotten there? He didn't even remember. He put a hand on Chris's shoulder, motioned to the others to leave and closed the bedroom door, giving the two men some privacy. He pushed Chris down onto the edge of the bed and settled into a chair close by.

Fenton's voice was uncharacteristically kind, "Son, what were you dreaming about?"

Chris shuddered and told him about the nightmares. "I keep having them. They aren't going away. And now...now they always bring up Carrie...I just...I'd do anything to protect her and Liza and Joseph and you."

"Son, I know that. I let you stay here and I feel that in you." Fenton reached over and clasped Chris's shoulder, "You did what you could for your family and their deaths are not your fault, son. They just aren't." The man's eyes welled with tears at the thought of the losses he had seen in the past few years, "We are your family now, Chris, and don't you forget that. I know you'll do right by us, too."

"But sir, what if..." His guts were still twisting over the thought of Carrie ever being hurt, "What if I'm bad luck? What if being near me gets people...hurt?"

Fenton grasped Chris's shoulder harder, "You are not to blame for the evils of war, son. God only knows why we have to suffer so, mebbe it'll make us all better men, but you gotta believe that the world can be better." He smiled crookedly, "Believin' is half the battle to makin' it happen." He let go of Chris and sat back in the chair, "Besides, you crap out on me and who's gonna get the back field plowed for the winter crops? Go back to sleep son, and don't let me catch my granddaughter visitin' you after hours. I reckon I can tell when two's been sharin' a bed or not."

With that he stood up and stretched, limbs creaking, and ambled to the door and on out of the room where the others were huddled in the hallway. "Back to bed all of you. And that'd best be your *own* beds if you know what's good for you!" The old man was mellowing a bit; he had chosen not to make too fine a point on the fact that Chris's bed had shown signs of two people, not one, recently sleeping in it.

A few minutes later a slight creak at the door had announced Carrie's presence. "Chris?" her voice sounded worried, "You okay?" He smiled in the darkness in her direction.

"Yeah babe, I'm okay." She slid onto the bed next to him. Despite the unrelenting muggy nights, Carrie would sneak into his bedroom each night and they would sleep spooned against each other. He felt her now, just inches away from him, and felt his body respond to her presence as it did each night. He'd managed to keep himself under control, despite the ever-increasing desire to consummate what they had only danced and teased around for months now. "You'd best go back to bed."

He could feel her disappointment and the hint of a pout, "Why can't I stay here with you? I'll make sure and be gone before Gramps wakes up."

"I think we've pushed our luck enough for tonight. 'Sides, we're going into town tomorrow. Let me get a shred of sleep and if I have any more of these damned nightmares, I'm not gonna be waking you up too." He found her lips and kissed them. Sure enough, they were pouting.

She returned his kiss enthusiastically, and Chris pulled her onto his lap and lifted her easily as he stood up, felt her long legs wrap around his waist. He walked to the doorway in this manner, which elicited a frustrated growl from Carrie as she realized he was putting her out of his room for the night. He was learning just how willful the Perdue women could be. One last long kiss and he set her down and slowly shut the door as she grumbled her way down the hall.

The nightmares stayed away, and he managed five blissful hours of sleep before being pounced on by a ball of energy just after dawn. "It's wake up time, Chris!" Joseph Perdue was bubbling over with excitement, "We're goin' to town today!" The three-year-old bounced on him over and over. He was a cute kid, which was the only reason Chris didn't strangle him after Joseph kneed him accidentally in the groin.

Liza appeared at the doorway. A smirk spread over her face as she took in the scene of Chris bent double and Joseph jumping on the bed blissfully unaware of the pain he had just inflicted. Joseph kept jumping, "Mornin' Liza!"

"Mornin' Joseph. Go get yourself dressed so we can go to town right after breakfast." She tried not to laugh at Chris's pained expression.

"Mornin' Chris, you coming into town with us? Or do you think you need to...um...*rest* some more?" Her lip was twitching.

"I'll be fine, thanks so much, Liza." Chris gave her a look that spoke volumes and she ran off to the kitchen, laughing merrily. He slid gingerly out of bed, concentrating on carefully easing his aching gonads into a pair of jeans. Fenton had kept him busy fixing everything from fencing to roofs and his skin had darkened to a light bronze in the hot summer sun. His chest was well developed too after months of hard work and he grinned as Carrie stopped by his doorway and let out a low, appreciative whistle.

Fenton came walking by then and harrumphed at his granddaughter, "Mind yourself, girl."

She winked and her face assumed an innocent expression, "I am, Gramps!" The old man moved down the hall, calling for his coffee. From the smell wafting from the kitchen, Liza had brewed it already and was now working on the rest of breakfast. The girls took turns prepping breakfast for the family, and Chris often lent a hand with lunch and dinner. Every meal they sat down as a family and ate together, no matter what project was underway. Fenton insisted on it.

Chris's family hadn't been much different, so it felt normal, reassuring.

The Perdue's would say grace, talk about their plans or projects for the day and enjoy the bounty of their hard work. Running the farm was full of challenges and the work seemed unending, but Chris had eaten better in the last few months then he had when he'd been conscripted.

Overall, the time spent with the Perdue's had been one of healing, physically and emotionally. He had been laid up until mid-April, but by mid-May he was working hard each day in the fields. By summer he had been agile enough to begin repairing the barn and re-shingling the roof of the farmhouse.

The girls had convinced Fenton to take down the various trophies and removed the worn sofa from the den. A full-size mattress and box springs which had belonged to their parents had been retrieved from the basement and the small closet held all of their father Isaac's old clothes. Chris was nearly the same size and the jeans and shirts fit relatively well, although his growing muscles made the shirts rather tight. Fenton had told Chris he was welcome to any of Isaac's clothes that could fit and it helped that they didn't have to explain purchases of men's clothing in town until they were good and ready.

He was nervous about the trip to town. Tiptonville wasn't a large place by any means. Chris hadn't thought his hometown was much of anything, but it had held tenfold the number of residents that Tiptonville boasted. Of course, that was before everything had gone to hell, who knew how many lived there now or in Tiptonville for that matter. He wasn't sure he was ready to meet the townsfolk or that they would buy the story he and the Perdue's had cooked up of him being a friend of the family.

Fenton had made it clear that Chris wasn't to ever speak of his participation, unwilling or not, in the Western Front. "There's some'd rather string you up from the nearest tree than get your story, they find that out, boyo." Fenton had warned him gruffly, "You keep your mouth shut and follow our lead."

They had had a near miss a week or so back when a couple of boys Carrie's age had stopped by the farm looking for work. Fenton hadn't told them "no" but instead said they should check back around harvest time. Chris had been off at the old farmstead digging up the smaller starts of blueberry bushes to transplant nearer the farmhouse.

Carrie hadn't been in favor of that, mainly because having the bushes closer to the house meant they couldn't run off with the excuse of picking blueberries. She had stalked away from him in a snit and been at the farmhouse and able to help Fenton run the boys off after basic pleasantries had been exchanged along with a promise to come to town soon.

Lost in his thoughts, Chris picked at his food. Liza looked offended, "What? Is there somethin' wrong with the eggs?"

"Wha...huh? The eggs? No, no, the eggs are fine." Chris looked down at his plate, still filled with food and shoveled a large bite in his mouth, chewed and swallowed. "I just, Gramps, you sure me coming into town is a good idea?"

"Son, it'll be fine." The old man reached over and squeezed Chris's shoulder, "You're a friend of the family and you visited us here 'bout five years back. Your family is gone, but you found our address in some papers, remembered us, and headed our way. You been here since late spring and been earnin' your keep working on our farm." He winked then, "No one's gonna believe an old codger like me would put up with you or take you in 'less you was who I said you was."

He turned towards little Joseph, "Now mind you, Joseph. Anyone asks you who young Chris here is and you just say he's a friend of the family. You remember that, right Joseph?" The boy nodded solemnly.

Fenton looked over at Carrie, "And you girl, don't you be hangin' on him or making them damn googly eyes. You made a list of what we need, right?"

Carrie looked offended and muttered under her breath before responding, "I got the list right here Gramps." She read it aloud and he had her add three items – buckshot, a 1982 Chevy pickup truck repair manual and propane.

"Don't know what we can get or what'll be available, but we'll ask 'bout 'em. Okay let's get going! We got a long trip ahead of us." The truck had refused to start the previous day and Chris had wished for the hundredth time that he had taken the basic automotive classes at school like his buddy Allen did. He had been the one to ask Fenton if he had a truck repair manual and the old man had looked embarrassed and shook his head no. Apparently Chris wasn't the only one who had skipped automotive class. "Football." The old man gruffly commented, "I was busy with football. That is, until I mashed my left knee the last game of the season. Still pains me."

So, they would do it the old-fashioned way and take a horse and buggy the three plus miles into town. The last time they had gone into town, while Chris was still laid up with his broken ankle, they had walked, and Fenton's left knee had swollen to twice its size. He couldn't walk without grunting in pain for weeks.

With Ichabod hitched and ready, they had climbed into the buggy and started off. The road was clear, with the exception of several abandoned vehicles that had been pulled off of the road. Chris thought that it looked as if there had been a conflict of some kind, but not recently. Two of the trucks were not only turned over, they had been set on fire. Fenton followed Chris's gaze as it lingered on the skeletons hanging from the burned-out trucks.

"Western Front," he said gruffly, "I told you we don't much cotton to the West trying to tell us how to live. Those boys are a warnin' to anyone else foolhardy enough to bother with us." Chris realized how dangerous admitting he had any association with the Western Front, unwilling or not, would be to all of them.

Two tall lookout posts sat on each side of the road right before they reached town. They were similar to the 'high hides' that deer hunters use, but were larger and probably better insulated for winter use. The rough wood was covered in corrugated metal sheets. Chris figured it was hotter than hell in those things. He could see the outline of a man inside and noticed the cold, dark snub of a rifle in the other lookout post. They had a great view from up there, and could sound the alarm long before anyone came within striking distance of town.

Fenton followed his gaze and waved towards the outposts. Chris did his best to look as unarmed and helpless as possible. Anyone with a decent set of binoculars would see that both the girls and the old man were armed, so he figured the snipers manning the outposts wouldn't shoot him or think he was holding them hostage. He was nervous nonetheless.

His focus on the high lookouts provided an excellent opportunity for the men stationed in the waist high grass to approach without his notice. He couldn't help flinching in response to the rifle that appeared to his right. "Hold up!" The man that held it eyed him suspiciously, "Ho there, Fenton."

The old man smiled down at the armed man, "Ho there, John. Like you to meet a friend of the family. This here's Chris Aaronson, hails from a ways from here." The armed man looked them over carefully, noting the relaxed looks on the rest of the family.

"Friend of the family?"

"Yup," Fenton nodded coolly, "The son of friends of Amy's. He came out here, what, five years ago a'visitin.'" He pursed his lips, "Nothin' left for him so's he sought us out, due t' his family bein' gone. He's been helping out on the farm these past two months. Came just in the nick of time for plantin' season."

John nodded, letting the barrel slide away from the group and backing away. He let out a shrill whistle to the sentries above and their guns disappeared. "Take care Fenton." He nodded at Chris, "Nice to meet you, Chris. You all go on through."

The buggy pulled away, passing the outposts and continued towards town. Chris heaved a sigh of relief and Carrie squeezed his arm. "That was John Carter, he's Carl's stepdad." She leaned close, and whispered "Liza and Carl like each other."

Fenton grunted, "I heard that."

"Oh Gramps!"

The first of the town buildings appeared at the crest of the hill. Chris looked around. Most of the buildings were intact, and there wasn't much to see. It was a tiny town, a fraction of the size of Belton.

Chris had thought Belton was small compared to the sprawling streets in Kansas City just a twenty-minute drive to the north, but this was like having a Main Street and nothing else. How had they made out so much better than Belton? Dumb luck?

The first sign of damage that Chris noticed was the crumpled water tower. Carrie followed his gaze, "They took out the water right away. I haven't had a decent shower since, thanks to those bastards."

Fenton growled at her choice of words, "Mind your tongue girl." He didn't say much more, after all, he missed regular showers too.

There was a café, but it looked deserted, most of the windows had boards over them. There was a large two-story brick building with white columns on the left side of the street. "That's the old bank," Fenton noted as they passed by, "Least it was until they built that fool building next to it." He cocked his thumb at the Regions bank sign, which was broken, and the building the sign belonged to was gutted.

Directly following the stately brick building was a narrow alley and then another fairly plain two-story brown brick building. At first glance it seemed to be nothing more than a dump for miscellaneous junk. But the buggy turned and headed towards it and Chris could see a rough hand-lettered sign in the window that read, "Tiptonville Trade Mart." Just inside the door was a tough-looking man with a rifle tucked against his shoulder. The guy looked him over suspiciously and rested a large hand on the Bowie strapped on his thigh.

Fenton handed Joseph down to Chris and carefully eased out of the buggy with a low groan. Riding in the buggy had been easier than walking, but the old man wasn't as flexible as he used to be. He handed the reins to Carrie and pointed to a bike rack twenty feet away.

There was a dappled pony already strapped there. She nodded and walked the horse and buggy over to it while the others headed towards the Trade Mart. At the entrance, Fenton put his arm across Chris's shoulders and nodded to the man. "Morning Wes, this here is Chris, a friend of the family. He's been with us these past two months, working the farm."

Wes's gaze never left Chris. His nod was brusque, "Where you hail from?"

"Northwest of here, sir."

"You've been in the forces, seen action, haven't you?"

Chris had been unprepared for such a direct question. "I, uh…"

Fenton interceded, "The boy has seen loss. He lost his family and then headed here because he had nowhere else to go. I think Wes that we can leave it at that."

Wes's eyes narrowed as he shifted his focus to Fenton, "Been reports of Western Front troops deserting, coming this way. Also been raids, south in Dyersburg. Bastards came into the outskirts and were forced back west." His eyes moved back to Chris, coldly assessing him, "Them soldiers been doing more than just shooting men, Perdue, they've been killing kids and older people, raping the women. I hear tell they ripped up parts of Missouri bad, and I also hear they ain't 'zactly following orders from the chain of command no more." He said all of this while trying to stare Chris down.

Chris just stared back, feeling more pissed by the minute. This guy figured he was from the west, and was coming to all the wrong conclusions. Carrie broke the impasse by returning from hitching the horse and grabbed Chris's and Fenton's sleeves, "Come *on*, I've got a list a mile long and we need to figure out what crops we brought in can be traded for. And it's gonna be hotter than he…" She gave a quick glance over at her grandfather, "heck…soon. We need to get unloaded and reloaded and I want to check out the local news before we have to head back home. You were going to look for the Chilton's manual, remember?" She said all of this in one quick tirade and then stood staring at Chris expectantly while ignoring Wes's glare.

After they moved past and away from Wes, Chris relaxed and let out a deep breath. Something told him that guy was going to be trouble. For the rest of the time they were there Chris felt like every move he made was being watched. Anytime he looked up and towards the direction of the entrance, he could see Wes staring at him.

They spent nearly an hour at the Trade Mart and Chris watched Liza and Carrie go to work negotiating the best trade they could for what crops they had brought in. He smiled as he watched the girls at work.

They were naturals, born to haggle and seemed to be experts at negotiating the best trade possible. His smile turned down when he thought of Jess, and how good she had been at it. He had turned his back to Wes and could feel the man's stare, right in the middle of his back. It made him wish he had a gun, or at the least a knife, but Fenton had worried that if he were armed, he would be shot by the sentries on the approach. After seeing the burned-out trucks, bodies and the sentry towers, he understood the old man's concerns. The citizens of Tiptonville were determined to keep the rest of their people alive and well...and keep the rest of the world at gunpoint.

They finished up at the Trade Mart and headed for another small store down the block. Inside it was filled with an eclectic mix of hardware, automotive and farm equipment parts. This store didn't have any armed guard at the front, only one ancient, white-haired old man at the back counter. "Mr. Liles!" Fenton called out, loudly, smiling like a kid.

The old man peered, squinting at them through thick glasses. Chris thought he must be the oldest man he had ever seen.

They moved closer, Fenton in the lead, and the old man grinned, showing nothing but toothless gums. "Young Fenton! How are you boy?" Hearing a man that he called Gramps referred to as a 'boy' was rather disconcerting.

"I'm fine, sir, just fine." Fenton took the old man's hand gently and gave it a firm shake. At one time, the man may have been larger, but now he seemed a frail wisp, with papery thin skin and several large dark bruises on his face and hands. He was alert, and looked over the group before him, quickly singling out Chris for his attention. "Hello, young man, and who might you be?"

Fenton pulled Chris over to him. "Chris, this here is Mr. Otis Liles. Mr. Liles taught me Biology in high school and he was the team's football coach as well. Mr. Liles kept me in line but good." Good sweet lord, the old man had to be ancient! "Mr. Liles, this young man is a friend of the family and he's been helping out on the farm for the past couple of months." Chris nodded and shook the old man's cool, bony hand carefully.

"Hello, Mr. Liles."

The old man beamed. "My boys never seem to forget me, though they are getting fewer and fewer each year." His smile dropped, "Especially with the troubles we've had lately. It's good to meet you, young man."

His attention turned to Carrie and Liza and down to little Joseph. "It's so good to see the three of you children growing up so well!" They all nodded and smiled at Mr. Liles. "So, what can I do for you Fenton, my boy?"

"Well, Mr. Liles, I guess I should have taken that Auto class from Mr. Elias." Fenton looked sheepish, "The truck has broken down and I need a Chilton's manual to see if I can fix it."

The next half hour involved a flurry of questions on the problem, including a lecture on how carburetors worked. Eventually the entire group was involved in finding the appropriate book, stashed in a dark corner with liberal amounts of dust and dirt, and then directed to various parts of the store for parts needed to fix the problem. In return, the old man accepted a small basket of eggs, a loaf of freshly-baked bread, and the promise of a future dinner at the farm. In spite of his fragile appearance, Otis Liles moved more spryly than Fenton did, despite Fenton being decades younger.

Their mission complete, Chris and the Perdue's said their goodbyes and headed for the door. Mr. Liles would be visiting them for dinner in three days, and Chris was eager to find out just how old the old man really was. As they made their way out of Mr. Liles store, waving goodbye and thanks, Chris glanced over and saw that Wes was standing there at the corner, watching and waiting for them. Chris could feel the tension building, this guy meant trouble, bad trouble.

Carrie whispered next to him, "Ignore him, Chris, he's a jerk." But Chris kept eye contact, he couldn't help it, this guy got his innards to jangling.

Fenton eyed Wes, nodded curtly to him, and gripped Chris's shoulder firmly. "Time we got back to the farm, son. Liza, go unhitch that horse." Wes was advancing toward them, his eyes drilling into Chris.

Chris stood his ground, returning the gaze steadily. Fenton's grip tightened. "Son, you go help Liza with Ichabod. That damn horse has been skittish since he smelled those burnt bodies outside of town. Go on with you now." He pushed Chris in the other direction and stepped toward Wes.

Wes stopped short of simply walking around the old man, but his gaze never left Chris, who had turned his back to Wes, Liza sidling up to him on one side, Joseph's hand firmly in his, as he walked towards the horse and buggy a few yards away.

He could hear Wes speaking to Fenton, sounding angry, and Fenton's calm and clear reply, "Wes Perkins, you may have served in the Gulf and know your way 'round a rifle, but you don't know nothin' 'bout people. That boy is nothing you need to worry about and he is what I've said he is, a friend of the family. You leave it at that, and don't make me raise my voice. I still remember your punk ass trying to bully the others in preschool and it looks as if you haven't changed a bit in thirty-five years of living."

Wes looked pissed, especially over being reminded of the fact that Fenton had known him when he was barely out of diapers. "You'd best get back to your post and worry about keeping this town safe, 'stead of worrying about things that aren't any of your business."

As he turned and marched away with Carrie towards the buggy, Wes called after him, "Well don't expect none of us to be coming down as far as your farm, old man. You're on your own way out there."

"That's the way I like it!" Fenton grumbled, muttering further comments that were neither friendly nor repeatable in mixed company.

Carrie would have smiled if she wasn't so scared for Chris. Wes was bad news. He'd come back from Iraq in 2006, rumors of a dishonorable discharge on the wind and slapped around his young wife so bad that one day she'd left town with their two kids and never come back.

When the fighting had broken out, he'd taken lead, and showed some of the other younger men in town some rather effective, lethal fighting strategies. It had kept most of the residents of Tiptonville and the surrounding area free of the death and destruction other small towns had suffered, but something about Wes Perkins wasn't quite right. No one spoke of it much now, but Wes wasn't someone you wanted near you in times of peace and only questionably in times of war.

They loaded up the buggy, climbed in and drove past Wes's hard stare.

"I'll be keeping an eye on you," he said, staring at Chris as the buggy drove away, back out of town. They passed the outposts silently, and breathed a collective sigh of relief after they had passed the burned-out trucks and cleared the town limits.

As the farm came into view, Carrie leaned over and hugged Chris tightly. "You're new in town, it will get better, I promise." Her touch was reassuring, and Chris relaxed into it, even if he didn't believe her words for one second.

"The first time we heard gunfire, my parents told me that it was nothing. We read by lamplight in the basement and pretended to be pioneers. It would have worked if they weren't so scared. But I remember the fear even though their features have faded from my memory. I pretended right along with them for Tina's sake, she was only three and I; I was the big brother after all.

By the third night of gunfire had gotten closer. The sirens, normally used to warn us off dangerous weather, were going off, warning all citizens of Clinton of an imminent invasion.

No one was pretending to be pioneers anymore. We were all just scared and edgy and Mom and Dad insisted we sleep inside the cupboard nook behind the false front. There was a shelter in the basement that we had made for all four of us with another hiding spot within the cupboard built inside and a false back inside of that. It was so small that only Tina and I could fit and it led into a crawlspace that smelled of mildew and dust. We were able to drag blankets and pillows through with us, and Tina was terrified and cried herself to sleep huddled against me. With the cement walls of the basement above and all around us, we could hear very little from outside our little nest. And that night, as Tina and I slept, the troops moved into the town, and quickly began smashing through the houses, street by street.

I think they knew what would happen. I have such a hard time forgiving them, that they would die and we should live. What kind of a world was left for two small children to exist in all alone?" - **David's journal**

David woke first. He eyes snapped open. He had been dreaming it was Christmas morning with presents all around the tree. The dream had frayed away, disrupted by screams. Now he heard nothing. There were no screams, no murmurs, no guns or explosions—not even the crunch of the gravel road outside. Tina slept curled against him, her breath warm and moist, his shirt was damp at the spot where her face pressed against his chest. Normally he would have shoved her away, called her a little baby. But at the moment he wasn't feeling so big himself. He felt small and alone. It was light out, he could see that much, but nothing else. He strained his ears to hear anything but the soft rhythm of Tina's breaths, in, out, occasionally sighing as she slept, whining to herself. A bad dream?

After several minutes he could hear the faint twittering of a bird, the crackle of gunfire far, far away. Were Mom and Dad still sleeping? Tina's breathing barely changed as he carefully shifted her off of him, covering her with a warm blanket like Mom always did before he slipped away, back through the hidey-hole into the hidden room. The room was empty, the door was open and, and he could see...*sky*?

David blinked, confused, and rubbed his eyes. Perhaps this was a dream.

He stepped through the wreckage of fallen timbers, small mountains of furniture mixed with plaster and wood and clothing. Open pipes dribbled water and he realized his feet were wet. He stumbled forward, earning a great painful gash on his leg from a protruding board. The silence was terrifying but hearing the noises he made reverberate through the mess of what had been his home was even more awful. His mind was devoid of any words to describe what he saw or name the overwhelming dread he felt. Mom and Dad weren't in the room. His home was destroyed. He was completely alone.

The boy stood and stared. His leg bled freely from the wound, but he took no notice, standing there immobile until he heard a high wail of fear behind him. He turned to see Tina's small tousled head peering from the false-front cupboard. Her eyes were black holes of terror. She looked just as confused and shell-shocked as he must have and her lower lip quivered.

"Mommy!" she wailed, ignoring David as he waded back to her and tried to help her out and up. "I want Mommy!" she wailed again before he could shush her. He slapped a hand over her mouth.

"Shhh! We'll find Mom and Dad, but you gotta be quiet! The bad guys might still be here!" he warned her. Although it seemed impossible that things could get worse, her eyes grew bigger at the thought. She quieted, screwing up her face at the dark mess of water and clinging to her brother, wrapping her arms and legs around him.

He lifted her up and tried to carry her, but the way was too cluttered and he tripped, spilling them both into the dirty water and plaster that lay throughout the basement.

To her credit, Tina made very little noise, despite her skinned knees. Her world had changed far too much and she was in the same state of shock that he was. By the time they managed to crawl and shove their way out of the debris to the other end of the basement they were both filthy and wet. The stairs leading up were broken in several places, but enough of the staircase was intact for them to slowly climb up and out.

Tina clung to her brother's back like a monkey, and then silently followed him after he set her down and pushed through the remnants of their home. Slowly, both children exited through what had been the living room and into the back yard.

It took just moments for the two children to find the lifeless bodies of their parents. They lay crumpled in the grass within feet of each other. Dad looked as if he had been trying to reach Mom. His arm was stretched out towards her. Their mother lay face up, eyes staring wide open and clouded and Dad was just an arm's length away on his stomach.

David sat down abruptly on the grass next to his mother. He reached forward hesitantly and touched her. Her skin was cold, rubbery, and he felt his stomach flop and his hands shook as he reached over and closed her lifeless, staring eyes.

Tina said nothing, just held his free hand and pressed her face into his shoulder. Her little body was shaking uncontrollably. He thought briefly that he should say something, tell her Mom and Dad were in heaven or something, but he couldn't make the words come. Not any words. What can a ten-year-old child say to his baby sister of three? Neither of them had words for the horror before them.

It would be hours before they left the bodies of their parents. And then it was only because of the gnawing pain in their stomachs. Life rudely continues on in the face of death, and bodies still need nourishment.

David dug through the wreckage until he found a snack pack of fruit cocktail, the kind with the pull-top lids. They both ate ravenously, silently, avoiding the sharp rim as the dipped their fingers in for the last little specks of syrup.

Tina stared up at him, absently licking a dribble of fruit cocktail syrup from the corner of her mouth. "I'll find us more food in a little while," he told her and walked over to the shed in the corner of the property.

It was still intact, rather incongruous when you looked at all of the devastated houses around it. On the inside of the door hung a shovel and David took it down from its hook and walked back to where his parents lay.

Digging a hole deep enough for both of them was amazingly hard.

David dug and dug and the patch widened, deepened until it was a few feet across and maybe half a foot in depth. His hands, back and shoulders hurt and he was dirty and horribly hungry. Tina had refused to leave his side and sat clinging to his leg, slowing his movements and exhausting him further. He stopped, rubbed his hands and straightened his back. Behind him, Tina sucked on her thumb noisily and whimpered for food.

"C'mon, Teen," he took her hand in his, "I'll find you somethin' to eat." They trudged past the remains of their home and on to the Connor's who lived down the street. The Connors had left a week ago, headed east towards family in Illinois, and Mr. Connor had come by and told Mom and Dad to help themselves to whatever they left behind. Most of it was probably still there in the hand-dug bomb shelter hidden behind shelves of books. It was a survival cache that they didn't have room to take with them when they ran when news of the advancing troops had spread.

The bomb shelter had been raided, the shelves of books that Mrs. Connor loved so much had been tossed willy-nilly to the ground, but no one had discovered the cache of foods concealed behind the bookshelves. David found canned meats, vegetables, ready-to-eat soups, even canned milk. A trip through the Connor's ruined house also yielded a hand-operated can opener. David wrestled with it, opening a can of milk, and one of the soups and greedily sucked down his share of both before his sister could have a chance to eat. The look on her face made him feel awful. Her lip trembled and he patted her hair clumsily and made sure she ate the rest of the soup and milk.

"Sorry 'Teen, I was awful hungry. Hey look, there's some of Miz Connor's homemade strawberry jam, ya want some?"

Tina perked up and minutes later was happily sucking strawberry jam off her fingers as David led her to a broken and dripping water pipe to wash up.

Tina's fine blond hair would soon become matted beyond all hope of redemption. David did his best to keep his sister's hands and face clean, but the rest of her took on a grayish grimy appearance in the days, weeks and finally months that followed.

In the end it had taken two full days to dig the single grave deep enough to bury their parents' bodies in and a full week for the blisters to heal. The stock of canned food at the Connor's had eventually run out. David expanded his searches to the other ruined houses around them. Twice they had hidden from troops marching through the area.

The uniforms were different, but a stranger was a stranger and the children were too frightened to test the foreign soldier's kindness. The men strode through the ruined stretches of houses, their machine guns hanging from their shoulders, searching for loot, for food or clean water, or anything else they took a fancy to. They robbed the dead, shot at any stray animal unfortunate enough to cross their paths, and drank bottles of alcohol (David had read the labels of the empty bottles discarded at their camp sites) before finally moving south towards more populated areas.

Spring had turned to high summer, but their hidey-hole stayed relatively cool. David made sure that they both drank from the broken water pipes and not the pond or the brackish water that collected in the drainage ditches. Only once had they made that mistake, and Tina had gotten so sick he was afraid she would die. She had run a fever, hot to the touch and glassy eyes for two days before slowly getting better. When the water pipes slowed to a trickle and finally petered out, David searched for new ones with Tina following silently behind wherever he went.

There was a pattern to the days now. Each morning he would wake first and then shake his sister awake. He would turn his back while she used the overflowing, stinking toilet in the house down the street, and take her to the nearest water source and make sure she washed her face and hands. They would eat canned food for breakfast, wash again and scout for supplies. They took it street by street, fanning out in ever-widening circles. The walks were taking longer and longer, and often they would stop at a familiar shelter and sleep for a while with the sun burning hot overhead. Tina was still little, so she needed more sleep. And David found it easy to nod off with his sister cuddled against him, even on the hottest day, her little body moist and heavy.

Later they would take what they had found and head back to the hidey-hole for dinner and to sleep. Sleep came with the setting sun. The few candles they had found were precious and the flashlights and batteries even more so. So, by the time the darkness fell completely, the two children were already well snuggled into their nest, lying close to each other for comfort. If their parents could see them now, David mused one night, they would both be smiling in surprise and pride at how good he was being with Tina. The only time they argued had been over what to eat, pickles or olives, for dinner one night. Other than that, he had been the best big brother he could be; better than his parents would have ever dreamed. Tina whimpered suddenly in her sleep and he pulled her closer and patted her matted hair until her breathing evened and her body relaxed once again.

Two More Makes Four

"*I've learned so many things in the past ten years. Things they didn't teach in school or even in the Boy Scouts. If the 'me that was' ever met the 'me that is' – would I even recognize myself? I know how to take a life. And I have done it to save me and mine. I know how to butcher game and livestock, raise food to eat, track deer, and break through ice in the winter to make sure I've got water to drink. I know lots of things – but most importantly I know that you don't have to be blood to be family. Jess, little Erin, Becka, Jacob – they're all my family, just as much as Tina is. Even Q2 is family. Even Lord Flea. I can't imagine life without them. I don't think I would want to.*" – **David's journal**

Jess and Erin moved steadily north, following first the Luc River, then Clinton Lake, and now some other unknown body of water. Their progress was far slower now that Jess's belly had swelled pushing against the oversized shirt and forcing her pants to swoop in under it.

They were held with a safety pin now that the button had popped off. She was so damned tired of walking. Worse yet, the awful thing inside kept kicking her. Worse yet, it kept her awake during the nights when they lay on the hard ground exhausted from another long day of walking.

Erin still insisted on boiling any of the water they found. There was usually dirt or sand in it now that the rains were less frequent and the water levels low in the creeks. The flat dull taste it had after being boiled tasted putrid to Jess, but she drank it anyway, despite the way her stomach roiled in protest. At least she could keep food down, that was an improvement over the spring, but now backaches and heartburn had set in.

The sun wasn't even beginning to dip down over the horizon when they reached the outskirts of Clinton. Erin insisted they stop at the ruins of a church. Quincy had been whining and nuzzling at Jess's hand for the past hour. She was only a few months old, but the young dog knew when her mistress tired.

"You've got circles under your eyes so bad it looks like you've been punched," Erin observed, giving Jess a gentle shove down on a nearby pew after lining it with a tattered and filthy blanket. "For crying out loud, just lay down for a little while, I'll scout for some food and water and make sure the area is safe. Quincy, you watch her close and make sure she rests." The dog whined softly in response.

Jess didn't argue, she was too exhausted. She sunk down on the pew and closed her eyes. Quincy licked her hand softly, whined again, and settled down on the ground keeping contact with Jess at all times. The pup was acting weird and had been all day. Jess's back hurt, her feet hurt, hell, just about everything hurt today. Last night had been sleepless; they had both listened to the gunfire in the distance wondering if it was headed their way.

So now when Jess closed her eyes, sleep came quickly, stealing across her and propelling her instantly into a dream. A nightmare really, it was always the same—men surrounding her and reaching for her. She pushed herself against the far wall, trying to escape, always trying to push them away as they crushed her beneath their sweating bodies.

It was the crunch of feet on broken glass and Quincy's short quick bark that woke her instantly, her heart pounding in fear. Half her mind was still in the nightmare. Instantly her hand found Lady, as she liked to call her gift from old Coop, she kept her eyes closed as she listened for the next step. She would die before she went back, of that she was determined. Another quiet crunch, this one only a few feet away and she launched herself upward despite her awkward, protruding belly.

Brandishing the revolver, she screamed wordlessly. The tiny child cowered before her, mouth open and stock still, a terrified expression on its grimy face. Quincy's body pressed firmly against Jess's legs and her tail thumped against the ground as she whined in excitement.

It was just a child. A little slip of a thing, no older than four years and maybe not even that. It had matted filthy hair that might have been a light ash brown if it were clean. To guess, Jess would have to say it was a girl, but with all of the grime it was difficult to tell. The child's eyes flicked away from Jess and focused on someone behind her and she spun to find a young boy, older, equally filthy, looking terrified and armed with a brick. He held it defensively, eyeing her with a wary, frightened stare.

Just then, Erin's voice rang out, "Whoa kid, drop the rock! We come in peace!" She had returned from scavenging and was standing in the broken doorway of the church with several cans tucked under one arm and a blessedly rare, unopened bottle of spring water in her hand.

Both children shifted on their feet, their attention turned to her and they prepared to bolt. Erin smiled winningly, "I found beef stew and green beans and even some sweet, condensed milk. Is anyone hungry?" The little one licked her lips at the mention of the milk and looked over at the older boy for direction. It was obvious to both of the girls that, except for each other, these two children were completely alone.

Jess took advantage of the girl's interest and spoke, "My name is Jess, and that's my friend Erin. What's your name?"

A grimy thumb had found its way into the girl's mouth and it muffled her words, "Deena."

The boy spoke up, "She's Tina, and I'm David."

Jess smiled at them and sat back down. They were only kids. She would be less threatening if she were sitting. Besides she was still tired.

She put the revolver away and gave the older boy a steady, reassuring look. He eyed her back warily. "We'll share what we've got with you if you're hungry."

The boy nodded and relaxed his hold on the brick, finally setting it down as Erin pulled a prized can opener out of their pack and opened the cans. Both children said nothing, just stared intently at the cans of food until they were opened and offered to them. And even after that there were only quiet smacks of satisfaction intermixed with loud gulps.

The little one, Tina, giggled as Quincy placed her paws on the girl's shoulders and licked her face ecstatically. The pup was unable to control her enthusiasm at meeting new friends, especially one of such a small size. Jess was amused to note see the dog's industrious tongue had cleared away a great deal of the grime.

Erin teased details from the boy, learning that he and his sister were alone, and had been for months now. Recently they had heard gunfire again and hidden from the soldiers moving through the area. "They shot the Tubman's dog Reggie," David noted solemnly, "we hid from everyone after seeing that."

Jess and Erin told the children an edited version of how they had been captured by soldiers and had finally managed to escape. "You did the right thing to hide," Jess assured them, "Those men are very dangerous."

Tina had finished licking the last of the condensed milk from the can and boldly climbed into Erin's lap, tucking herself against the teenager and playing with the collar of her shirt before slowly slipping into a light doze. David offered to show the girls the hidey-hole and Erin stood up, shifting the sleeping child to her shoulder. Tina was still young and used to regular naps. She wrapped her legs around Erin's waist and whined. Both the girls found themselves smiling; the tiny girl was adorable despite her grimy, tattered appearance.

It was only a few blocks to the hidey-hole, but Jess felt nauseous and dizzy by the time they arrived. Quincy was close to her side, so close that twice she nearly tripped over the pup.

"What is up with you, Quincy?" the dog merely whined and licked at her hand while trying to move closer.

Every day that passed she had moved slower and slower, and her belly grew bigger and bigger. It had made for miserably slow travel as well.

It disgusted her, the thing kicking and rolling inside her and the way her body felt like it didn't belong to her anymore. Had it ever? Since the soldiers had taken them, since that moment she had been dragged into Tent 5, her body had no longer been her own. She was tired of running, and tired of the thing inside her. Her stomach twisted again, cramping painfully, *"Great, not only am I friggin' tired, but now I'm going to be sick."*

By her side, Quincy whined softly and licked at Jess's hand. The pup had been glued to her side all day, quietly whining and butting Jess's hand with her wet nose. David pointed to a tiny, dirty hole in the middle of the ruins of a house and announced, "That's where Tina and I sleep."

There was no way to get down the staircase, unless you weighed less than 50 pounds, and the tiny hole he was pointing to was far too small for Jess or even Erin to fit through. A few yards away from the ruined house was an uneven mound of dirt. Erin followed Jess's gaze and took in the crude marker and heaps of dead flowers scattered over the hard earth. It had to be the kids' parents.

The sun dipped lower in the sky and the ominous beginnings of thunder rumbled in the distance. Jess stared at the dark gray storm clouds gathering. There wasn't any shelter to speak of; even the ruined church behind them had been missing its roof. Jess felt like screaming, crying and just plain collapsing on the ground in frustration and exhaustion. Things couldn't possibly get worse.

Or could they?

Jess felt a gush of fluid rush out of her, flowing down her pant legs and soaking her tattered pants and shoes. It wasn't a stomachache; it wasn't bad food... 'it' was coming.

Jacob's Birth

"*Jacob asked me today about his father. I didn't know what to say. I haven't told him the truth. I love him so much, so very, very much. I look at him and I know exactly who his father is. His face was so distinctive, and Jacob looks just like him except for the eyes. My sweet Jacob has my blue eyes, not his father's ice blue. Sometimes I tell myself I can't know for sure; it could have been any one of them. And it could have been...but it's not. Jacob got angry last Saturday; he was so angry I thought he was going to hit David who had been teasing him relentlessly. But the look on his face, it brought back awful memories. David said I turned as white as a ghost. How do I tell my son, who I love more than life itself, that his father is a monster? How do I tell him that if I ever see that bastard again, I'm going to kill him? So, I lied. I told him his daddy died before I got to know him very well.*" – **Jess's journal**

There was very little in the way of shelter with the roof of the house gone and rain fast approaching. Neither Erin nor Jess could fit through the small hidey-hole in the basement. But shelter here they must, there was too much activity to the south, troops were moving through. In addition to the thunder, they could now hear gunfire coming from the south.

Had they known that Clinton had become a battleground between several warring factions of groups, with names they had not even heard of, the girls would have avoided the ruined town. But there had been no way of knowing and now they were in the thick of it, with the baby coming, and soldiers to the south heading their way.

The storm was barreling in from the West, clouds black and menacing, lightning dancing through them and the accompanying thunder was growing in frequency. If they went east it would only follow them, and there was no known shelter that direction anyway. A few hours at most, and they would be caught in the heart of what was promising to be a violent summer storm.

Jess was relieved when Erin came back from checking out the shed, which she said would do in a pinch. The roof was intact and she smiled encouragingly at Jess who was sitting on the ground, pinch-faced and white-knuckled, clutching a clump of grass as another contraction hit, "C'mon, I'll get the packs and the kids can bring blankets and pillows."

Jess just nodded, the pain was getting bad and she was scared, god, she was so damned scared. What if something went wrong? What if she started hemorrhaging? Or what if the thing got stuck inside her? More than anything, though, she just wanted it out.

This thing had been growing inside her body, taking her food for its own, slowing her down, and making her vulnerable. She wished for the hundredth time she had been brave enough to kill it early on.

When her water had burst, she had looked at her wet pants and shoes and the small pool of fluid forming around her feet in numb shock.

This nightmare that was her life, with the desperation of day to day survival, she had found it surprisingly easy to ignore the expanding belly. Even the incessant kicks of the unwelcome creature that was inside her; how many times had she shrugged it off, worrying instead about how much further they could walk in a day, or how long the smoked meat would last before they needed more?

A shed it was, full of lawn equipment that Erin and David hastily pulled out and threw to one side. There was a momentary surprise as a family of rabbits burst from a hole beneath the structure and ran pell-mell into the brush. Quincy left Jess's side for the first time that day and dove after them. "Quincy!" Erin called in exasperation, but the pup ignored her then disappeared from view, eager to catch a rabbit for her mistress.

The grass was overgrown, high, and thick low-branched trees surrounded the shed. If they were lucky the roof would have no leaks and with evening coming it was a relatively safe place to hide from enemy eyes.

They quickly set about making a nest of sorts. They needed two, actually, one for the children in the far corner and one for Jess to have her baby in. Blankets, old clothes, and an armful of stained couch cushions were put to use.

Erin turned to David, "I'll need water, lots of it, take the bucket and fill it as full as you can." He left silently, Tina a step behind him, holding on to his shirttail with one grubby fist. They headed for the pipeline. When the water had stopped running months back after a particularly fierce firefight he had searched for days and finally found a broken pipe one block of demolished houses over. At first it had gushed water, but now it was down to a small, but steady trickle. It would take a while to fill the bucket.

Thunder rolled ominously, and Tina trotted to keep up until they reached the pipe. In the distance they could hear the chatter of machine guns, the troops were close, too close, and David wished he could just run back to the hidey-hole and forget about getting water or waiting for the baby to be born. He wondered if Jess would die, didn't having a baby sometimes kill the moms?

Back in the old days, back when there were covered wagons and no cars, women and babies died in childbirth. He'd read about it in a book, so it had to be true. It didn't seem right, having a baby here without a doctor. You were supposed to go to hospitals for things like that. He remembered when Mom had Tina just over three years ago. She was gone for days to the hospital; he had visited with his dad every day. His mom had looked so tired, but smiling and happy too. He had even held the squalling red bundle that was his sister. But the hospital was gone, nothing but a bombed-out shell. Besides, even if it hadn't been bombed, there weren't any doctors there. They had run away, died, or been captured long ago.

Tina tugged on his shirt and David jumped in surprise. He'd been standing there staring off into space while the bucket filled to the top, dribbled over and trickled onto his shoe. He hadn't even noticed he was so lost in thought. He hoisted the bucket, making his way back to Erin and Jess, slower now, the bucket heavy and sloshing from side to side.

As they neared the old shed, the rain began to fall, fat large drops that turned into a downpour the last twenty feet to the shed door. They could hear Jess's groans of pain as they pulled the door open. David hoped no one would come close enough to the shed to hear or find them, and again he wished he and Tina were in their hidey-hole.

Hours passed. The night had long descended along with the storm. The branches of the trees whipped in the wind outside the small structure, flailing themselves on the roof like grief-stricken mourners, despairing at what the world had become. A small leak was dripping in one corner, and the door rattled with each gust of wind.

Lightning flashed, lighting up the two small windows of the shed and the accompanying thunder shook the small building in tandem with Jess's screams. David and Tina were huddled in a corner, terrified, eyes big as saucers. The children were torn between wanting desperately to be back in their hidey-hole and staying with these two girls who had fed them and befriended them. And the screams were ear-splitting. If it weren't for the furious storm outside David would have pulled his sister to her feet and fled back to the only home he had known.

Instead he and Tina watched in horrified fascination, his sister rocking herself back and forth in his lap, sucking on her thumb and fully attached to his shirt like a small monkey to its mother. It wouldn't be long now.

"Oh *God*! Erin! It hurts, it hurts! Oh god, get this thing *out of me*!" Jess was sobbing in fear between the screams.

The baby was almost there, and the pressure and pain were unbearable. Surely, she was being ripped apart. She felt mind-numbing terror at the thought of bleeding to death and could only envision this creature inside her as some awful alien clawing its way out of her. Jess was losing her grip while Erin tried to make wordless sounds of support as she held Jess's hand and peered down between her friend's legs. A lightning flash lit up the shed and she saw...she saw...

"Jess! I can see it! I can see its head! Hold on sweetie! It's almost here!"

She reached for the cleanest sheet she could find; ready to catch the damn thing when it shot out. She imagined it would be rocket-powered by the sheer force of Jess's pushes. Jess hunched forward, her face screwed up and her mouth opened to let out the loudest scream yet.

Her body convulsed and the baby's head pushed out, hesitated for a short moment at the shoulders and then slowly slid out. It was all rather boneless and anticlimactic as Erin lifted it with shaking hands.

Blood and amniotic fluid had gushed out with it, and there was this weird white paste all over the thing. It didn't move, not a twitch. What *was* this nasty white shit all over the kid? It was...wait...she looked at the naked infant closely in the darkness...and aided by another flash of lightning she saw...a boy...it was a boy!

"It's a boy, Jess, you had a boy," she grinned, "Told ya you were carrying him low."

"Is it, is it...dead?" Jess asked with an almost hopeful tone to her voice.

It seemed for a moment to be the epitome of how awful life was, this creature who had occupied her, a product of the horror she and Erin had endured at the hands of the soldiers.

The noise of the storm seemed to subside, and there were several long seconds of silence. The baby didn't move. The door to the shed swung open and all four of the occupants looked up to see the deadly black nose of an AK-47 pointed directly at them.

The soldier swung his rifle at each in turn. The baby who had been so silent, so surely dead, let out a liquid gurgle, a burbling cough, and then...a thin wail of dissatisfaction. But no one looked at the baby; their eyes were riveted on this creature of death, with his deadly weapon pointed at them, standing stock-still in the doorway. Tall, blond, and as the lightning lit his face, rather good-looking. He stood for a moment, taking in the scene before him.

There were two young children huddled in a corner and two teenage girls frozen in fear at his feet. In the red-haired girl's arms was a tiny, squirming newborn. Another flash of lightning showed he was a boy.

The baby had obviously been born mere seconds ago; his umbilical cord was still attached. They all looked at him with undisguised terror.

Corporal Jacob Daniels, Sr. turned his gun to each in turn. A rifle was propped in the far corner of the shed. He stared at the newborn, and remembered the day his son had been born. The nurse had handed him his tiny son, wiped clean and wrapped in a soft blanket, and he had stood there in the Army hospital in Fort Hood, stunned at how tiny and fragile the child was.

Jacob Junior, in that happier time and place they had named him, later they called him JJ for short. A thousand images of his smiling face flickered through the Corporal's memories like a home movie. He had grown so quickly from a tiny infant to smiling toddler and finally into that precocious four-year-old who insisted he was going to grow up and be just like Daddy.

But Nancy hadn't wanted to be a military wife. She'd wanted more. She'd wanted to finish her Master's in Art History and who was he to hold her back? When the end had come, she had already moved to Austin and served him papers. He'd managed to come and visit and see them as often as he could on furlough. But it wasn't enough for little Jacob who would cry and beg his father not to leave at the end of the visit.

No one had ever been able to tell him exactly what happened to Nancy and JJ, but they had been too close, probably still asleep on that beautiful Saturday morning, when a small tactical nuke blew a crater into the northeast section of the city and annihilated anything within a twelve block radius of the Arts District and the University of Texas where Nancy was a student. He wanted to believe it had been quick, that his boy hadn't suffered, and that he hadn't died screaming like the scores of others they had showed on the enormous viewscreens in the Fort Hood Commons.

The children at his feet were holding their breaths, eyes wide, terrified.

They were all children, even the older two, who couldn't be out of their teens yet. What in the hell was he doing here? As if losing JJ wasn't enough. This war, it was killing them all, taking apart families and destroying lives. He could hear his men moving closer, calling over the radio for his status. Soon they would be close enough to see the shed and its occupants.

Inexplicably, almost unbelievably, he lowered his gun. His body sagged slightly, revealed exhaustion and...pain?

In a voice that was surprisingly soft, barely heard above the thunder and wind he said, "I had a son once. It seems...so...long ago. His name was Jacob." Then, without another word, he turned away, softly shutting the door behind him and disappeared into the raging storm.

The baby was still crying softly, as if he were politely asking to be put back in the warm world, and next to the steady heartbeat, that he had been evicted so rudely from. Erin sat numbly, as the baby wiggled, his umbilical cord still attached, looking at this alien creature in her arms that had somehow just saved them from certain death.

Tears began to stream from Jess's eyes and she held out her arms, "I want to see him."

Suddenly this thing was a child, a boy, something that was a part of her, not a piece of the monster who had raped her and put his seed in her. And as Erin gently passed the baby to her, she felt her heart stretch, as if the holes of so much loss were knitting together. Mom was gone. Dad was gone. Christopher was gone. Their memories, the loss she felt at their absence in her life were overwhelming. Gone, so many people she had loved and needed.

But this one, this small little crying, naked boy child, somehow, he filled those gaping holes and she felt her heart expanding in her chest.

She pulled him up closer to her, softly touching the baby beneath all the sticky paste and blood. His heart beat was strong; his face wrinkled and red. She barely noticed Erin pull out the small knife and sever the umbilical cord, or take a soft piece of cloth, dip it in water and begin to clean off the sticky paste and the blood that covered them both. When they were relatively clean, she set a blanket around Jess's shoulders and covered the infant with another.

Jess just looked in the baby's bright blue eyes and smiled. "Hi," she hesitated for a moment, "I guess I'm your mommy."

The baby's soft cries stilled, as he blinked once at her, his small hand fisted and waved as if to say hello back. They stared into each other's eyes for a long moment. Jess's mind raced with images of those long dead. Mom, Dad, Chris, Allen, people she had depended on and been devastated when they were torn from her. This child, this little baby needed her, he needed *her*.

And then, as if it were the most natural thing in the world, she pulled open her shirt and offered one breast to the tiny little mouth. And all four of them stared in fascination as the baby began to nurse.

Outside the storm raged on as a corporal called to his men, "Move north. There's nothing here but the dead."

And the troops marched on, with Corporal Jacob Daniels, Sr. leading them. He marched through the mud, past a row of bombed out houses. He barely noticed the crude grave markers, or the bodies lying in ditches far north of the small town. Instead, he remembered the laughter of a blond-haired little boy who had died far too young.

"I only knew Erin for a short time. At the time she seemed so much older, I guess I thought of her as an adult. Looking back, I realize that both Erin and Jess were barely five years older than me, still teenagers, essentially still kids themselves. War and loss took away so much of our childhood. Yet, somehow, Jess and Erin didn't just save Tina and me, they saved our childhood too. We still had to take on responsibilities and tasks that many adults hadn't had just a decade earlier, but they were both young and they knew how important it was to have fun. I remember smiling more in just a few weeks than I had in nearly a year." – David's journal

Erin closed the tattered, water-stained book with a thump; she had found it in the remains of the town's library. "Says here he's got jaundice, that's why he's all yellow."

Jess rubbed her eyes, yawned until her jaw cracked and jiggled the baby against her. He was asleep, and had been asleep for well over five hours now, but she was so worried about his lack of appetite and the further yellowing of his skin that *she* had not been able to sleep.

"Great," she could hear herself snapping, "So what the hell do we do?"

Erin's satisfied grin turned down at the edges. "Well, it says here he needs ultraviolet light. Some kind of incubator thingy that they have in hospitals...but the hospital is in ruins. And it probably needs electricity to run it, which we also don't have."

Jess felt a wave of despair wash over her. It felt like the whole world was aligned against her. Quincy whined and laid her head on Jess's leg.

She had come back before daybreak the morning after the storm a long scratch on her muzzle, a tiny limp, dead rabbit in her mouth. She seemed abjectly apologetic for running off the day before. She had barely left Jess's side in the two days since and was fascinated by the tiny human her mistress held so close.

Jess jiggled Jacob a little more forcefully; desperate to wake him and be sure he ate. It seemed he hadn't eaten much at all since he was born and she was beginning to be afraid he would just fade away. The sun was out and it was a beautiful day outside the shed. Tina had fallen asleep in the sun, her half-eaten peach in one hand and David had returned a few minutes before with fresh water to wash their dishes in.

"Great, just great! So, what do we do now?" The lack of sleep was making her nuts, so was the heat, and the kids and the...

"Just put him in the sun." David stood behind them, a bucket of water rested on the ground near his left foot, water still sloshing over one side. Somewhere in the wreckage of his house he had found shorts and they were ripped on one side of the waistband. He had also taken off his shoes and his bare feet were caked with mud.

Both of the girls turned and looked at the boy. They looked so confused he thought maybe they hadn't heard him the first time. "Just put him in the sun. Not for long, just a little while, a few minutes." They still stared at him and said nothing. "You said he needed ultraviolet light, right?"

Erin nodded slowly, "Yes...but..."

"But what? The sun has ultraviolet light. I read it in a book." He looked at them with the disdainful expression only an eleven-year-old child can pull off successfully. Erin and Jess continued to gape at him as he shrugged and took the tiny baby from Jess carefully. "Like this," he said speaking to the baby, "out here in the sun where it's nice and warm."

He gently laid the sleeping baby down and pulled the covers away from the baby's skin. The infant squirmed slightly in his sleep and was still again.

"But won't he get sunburned?" Jess felt stupid asking this of David, who was little more than a small boy in her eyes.

David rolled his eyes at her, "Of course he will...if you leave him out too long! Just a few minutes at a time. That ways he won't get too much sun, but at least he'll be less *yellow*."

Jess and Erin both looked at each other and then Erin shrugged, "Aw hell, what can it hurt?"

And so, they tried it, laying the infant out just a few minutes in the sun, wrapping him back up, and then doing it again twice more later in the day.

By the end of the next day, he seemed a little more alert, a lot hungrier and far less yellow. Sunlight seemed to have done the trick nicely.

But now they found themselves faced with another problem—diapers.

Every house they searched came up empty for them. They all felt far from safe in the town so a fire was out of the question. No fire meant no hot water and no way to clean themselves or their clothes.

Currently the infant was swaddled in strips of a sheet that had been relatively clean. Erin knew they would need to move on soon—and that meant supplies and diapers if they could find them.

She took David and headed back to the ruined library on the other side of town. It was located in a strip mall near some stores. It looked like Ground Zero for the firefight they had heard several days ago.

The bodies had been left to rot in the hot summer sun. The stench was overpowering as they approached the Big Lots store. Fifty yards from that was the collapsed west wall of the library. Erin pointed David towards the library, "I'll meet you there, but I need to check this out first, okay?"

David just nodded and backed away to the safety of the ruined books. Whenever a breeze blew over the bodies his stomach roiled in protest. He tried to breathe through his mouth so he didn't lose his breakfast.

Erin wrapped a cloth around her mouth and nose, took a few deep breaths and then entered the Big Lots. She avoided looking down as she stepped over one, two, and then a third body near the entrance. She brushed away the flies that swarmed around her and managed to make it down a main aisle before retching into a bin of throw rugs.

"Baby section, baby section," she murmured to herself trying desperately to not think about the smell or the bodies. She turned right and passed through the clothing and accessories section and took a sharp left.

Success! Many of the hooks were empty, but there were layette sets, onesies, tiny socks and hats, a lone pink blanket, and...diapers. Holy cow, actual diapers! Erin forgot about the awful smell from the corpses, ran back to the previous aisle and grabbed large bags to stuff the diapers into. She grabbed every package of diapers. They were all different sizes, but who cared, at least they were better than rags!

It took two trips to retrieve all of the baby-related items and she and David lugged the mess back to Jess with triumphant grins. At least now they had something to dress Jacob in. He was tiny, even the newborn sizes hung off of him with room to spare.

The next morning Erin and David returned to the ruined library. There they rummaged through the collapsed building, tossing books into two piles—ones that would help and ones that wouldn't. The system seemed to work pretty well. Many of the books were water-damaged and unusable, others had no bearing on their hopes for survival. Danielle Steele was definitely on the larger 'not helpful' pile.

Erin was at one end of the building, looking through what remained of home and garden topics, such as vegetable gardening and a book on how to raise chickens. David had burrowed into one corner and found some books on trails and wilderness camping and survival skills.

When the sun was directly overhead, they stopped, exhausted by the heat, found a tree and sat in the shade of it and Erin opened a can of beets she had been avoiding eating until she absolutely had to. David didn't look too impressed with the lunch menu, but he reached in and took a slice of the reddish-purple vegetable. A moment of silence passed and their hands connected as they both reached into the can at the same moment.

David grinned up at her, his lips and teeth stained red, and juice dribbling down his chin, "It isn't too bad, y'know?" She found herself agreeing. Who would have known that canned beets could taste so good?

"What's that you've got?" He asked pointing to a plain white book she had on the top of her stack of books.

Erin looked over at the book and held it up so the boy could read the title— "Wild Edibles of Missouri," Erin shrugged, "This canned food is catch as catch can. Who knows when we'll have it or when we won't? So, I figure we'll supplement with wild plants along the way. Jess and I ate plenty on the way here. Some of it isn't bad tasting at all. But I only know of some plants, not all of them, so this'll help."

David looked stunned at the idea, and began to look suspiciously at the greenery surrounding the ruined building. The grass was patchy, mostly weeds and high growth now that summer had come and there was no one left to even care about mowing.

"Like what? Do you mean like...*weeds*?" he asked, looking hard at the landscape, as if expecting them to tell him their secrets.

Erin smiled and obliged him by opening up and thumbing through the book. She murmured to herself for a moment and then said, "Dandelion. You can make tea with it, and you can put the leaves into a salad or cook them. And it says that dandelion leaves are very nutritious and is a liver cleanser. We ate them on the way here, but I didn't know about the liver cleansing part of it." She paged to the front of the book, scanned some of the pages and raised her eyebrows,

"Huh. Amaranth. Well, I'll be…I'm sure I've seen that along the way." She turned the book so that David could see a picture of the plant; the blooms were heavy with seed. "It says here that you can eat the seeds, shoots and leaves of the plant."

David looked around. Over in one corner there was a huge clump of dandelions and plenty of other unfamiliar plants he would have previously dismissed as simply being worthless weeds. He smiled,

"That's cool. Can I read that book too?" She grinned back and passed him the book.

By the end of the day they had a decent stack of books on a variety of subjects. It would have taken several trips to bring all of the books they had set aside back but David led the older girl to a trailer buried in the high grass down the street. It was small, the kind you hitch to the back of a car.

"It's kinda like a big wheelbarrow," he commented as he dumped an armful of books into it. It had sidewalls, about one foot high, that held the books with plenty of room to spare. Once they had loaded it up, they each grabbed a part of the chain looped around the handle and headed back towards the hidey-hole and shed.

Twice on their way back they saw other people rummaging through the rubble of houses. Erin looked over at David each time and asked, "Do you know them?" He just shook his head. "Best we keep going then." And they walked on, ignored by the survivors who seemed intent on salvaging any remnant of their lives that they could.

Erin and Jess knew they had to move on, and discussed it the fifth night following Jacob's birth as they lay under the bright full moon. David and Tina had retreated to their hidey-hole for the night, burrowing underground where they felt safest. "We need to move on," Erin began, "it isn't safe here."

Jess had been dozing with Jacob nestled in the crook of her left arm, steadily nursing at her breast. "Hmmm," she murmured sleepily, "it isn't safe anywhere." At the moment, here in their little bed of blankets, under the stars and moon, it felt safe enough, but she lay there and thought about home and became more alert. "We could try and go home. Maybe some managed to escape or hide out."

"Maybe."

The pause lengthened into minutes as they both lay there staring at the sky. Neither one of them wanted to voice the hope out loud—the persistent niggle in both of their brains that suggested that perhaps some of their family or friends had survived the enemy assault. What if in just saying it out loud they jinxed it? Hope was almost a painful weight, a yawning *need* for normalcy. This past week had been so beautiful, so peaceful after the fierce storm.

The sun had shone bright and full each day, the air thick and hot and full of the earthy smells of plants growing and blooming. The earth had continued to turn, despite the chaos in the land, and now the dog days of summer were at their peak. It was hard to believe that it was late August already. If it weren't for the shattered remains of houses all around them it would have been a normal summer day.

Jess spoke first, "We used to camp out in your backyard on nights like this."

Erin smiled in the moonlight, "Remember how Chris and Toby came over and scared us one night? I swear I peed my pants, I was so scared!"

Jess giggled, they had been about eight years old and their older brothers had snuck into the backyard wearing hockey masks. This after all four of the kids had watched a horror flick in the basement that night starring some bad guy named Jason who wore a hockey mask. "Remember how loud I screamed? Your mom and Dad thought we were being murdered! And then we were all in trouble for watching that awful movie!"

They both giggled like little girls at the memory and fell silent, lost in the memories of those that they had lost. Across the night sky a satellite moved steadily, the Big Dipper was clear and easy to see. Moments passed, and then they both spoke at once.

"I miss them so much."

"Let's go home."

A sigh and a deep breath, and Jess spoke again in the silence, "Yeah, let's go home."

"I asked Jess once why they didn't leave me and Tina there in Clinton. We were a liability, as was proved just a few short days later. I asked her why, and she just looked at me and said, 'We were family, even then, and family doesn't leave family.' I'd like to say that was the moment I fell in love with her. But truth be told, I'd been a goner for a lot longer than that. She never blamed me for what happened to Erin, not once. I wonder if I would have felt the same."
– David's journal

The morning dawned, the temperature rising quickly, making each of the small group wish desperately for the good old days of electricity and air-conditioning. Except Tina perhaps, who had no real memory of such luxuries. The sun wasn't even up above their heads and it was already miserably hot. The cicadas thrummed noisily, filling the air with rasping waves of sound.

Jacob whined fretfully at Jess's breast, suckling half-heartedly, his skin moist and slightly flushed. Erin had found a can of evaporated milk and handed it to the children to drink. Tina drank a lion's share of it before handing it to David who drained his portion in two huge gulps. A can of pears disappeared almost as quickly.

Erin had foisted Spam on Jess, along with a handful of dandelion greens. "I found out we can make tea out of the flowers if we find a safe place to have a fire." Jess simply raised an eyebrow and grimaced at the bitter taste of the leaves in her mouth. She balanced Jacob with one hand and tried rolling Spam inside of the leaves—that seemed to cut the bitterness substantially. Their eyes met over David and Tina's heads.

Erin spoke first, "We used to live north of here, you know." Tina was busy licking the inside of the pear can but David looked up and nodded. "And we've been talking about heading back there."

David froze, looked scared. "You're going to leave?" Tina had been oblivious to the conversation until the word 'leave' was uttered and she began to whimper, her eyes big and fearful.

"Well, Belton, that's the town we used to live in, has lots of houses and they aren't all bombed out like here," Erin said. She said it, hoping it was true, hoping she wouldn't return and be proved a liar.

"We want you to come with us" added Jess, "You can't stay here. There's not much food left, and the house is in pieces, no roof. What would you do when winter comes?" From the startled look on David's face it was obvious he hadn't thought that far ahead. "If my house is still there, my family might even still be alive, and we'd be safe," she went on.

For a moment she allowed herself to imagine the shock and surprise on her parent's and brother's faces when they saw Jacob. It would be a hard thing for them to accept—to know how he came to be. But they would look at him and see he was a baby, innocent, and besides, he had her eyes. In the end they would love him! She let the daydream carry her away for a moment before returning to reality and the work of convincing the two children to accompany them.

"Come with us."

Tina had stopped whimpering and now had a grubby, syrup-covered thumb stuck in her mouth. Her eyes were fastened on David, waiting for reassurance and direction. Erin and Jess watched as he looked back over his shoulder at the mounded grave of their parents. Grass had begun to grow on it, poking out of the piles of drying, limp flowers that Tina heaped on the mound each morning and night. The crude cross David had fastened out sticks and twine, listed to one side. It seemed wrong somehow to leave them here, but he knew the older girls were right.

He nodded. Jess smiled at him and hugged Tina close to her with her free arm. It was settled.

They didn't leave that day or the next—it would be five days before they were ready. It was still very soon after Jacob's birth and Jess was slow and tired easily. Belton was nearly sixty miles away. That wasn't much when you considered how far they had already come, but there were five of them now, not two, and the going would be slow.

"We need a plan on what to do if we run into any troops," Erin said later that day. They had stopped to rest in the shade after scouting nearby houses for rope and backpacks. The jackpot, a tent big enough to sleep all of them had been discovered in Mr. Pierson's shed. The Pierson's had a son close to David's age. Joey was a year younger, but they had played together regularly.

The Piersons hadn't run, like so many others did. The main house had burned, and David poked through the ruins a couple of weeks later and found skeletons. He didn't stop to puzzle it out, or figure out who had died there. It was just a jumble of horror in his memory. He'd run like the devil himself was after him and not returned.

David had pulled out the now tattered and worn book, "Wild Edibles of Missouri." He had been reading it obsessively since Erin showed it to him at the ruined library. The once pristine white cover was now grubby with dirt, beet juice, and God knows what else. The pages had been dog-eared and little slips of ragged paper tucked into the special sections. She gazed at him a moment and then shrugged and turned back to Jess. At this rate the kid was going to be an expert on edible plants.

Jess had leaned back against the tree; Jacob was sleeping contentedly against her side in a sling they had rigged from the remains of an old sheet. Her eyes were closed, sweat trickling down her face. "We could take Highway 7, then Highway 71 after we reach Harrisonville. That's the only way I know."

Her friend sighed in exasperation. Jess wasn't good for much these days. She was still weak and sore, and the baby woke up every couple of hours wanting food. Asking her for advice was rather pointless. If Jess had been any more exhausted, she would have probably volunteered to return to the enemy camp some 200 miles or more behind them. Erin rubbed her eyes; she wasn't getting much more sleep than Jess was.

Each time the baby cried at night she too was instantly awake, terrified someone would hear him. Now that they had thought of the sling he cried far less, especially during the day when the sling rocked him to and fro. He seemed comforted by that. She rubbed her eyes and desperately tried to think about crossing miles of grassy fields out in the open for anyone to see. She closed her eyes, stretched back in the grass and tried to will a solution into being.

David's words took her by surprise, "We need camouflage so we can't be seen."

"Huh?"

"You know, we need to look like the ground we're walking through and we should only travel at night or early in the morning when no one is out and around." Erin sat bolt upright and stared at the kid. For only being eleven years old, the kid was damn smart. He continued, ignoring her stare, "I read this book where it said that if you were goin' through forests than you wear green, and in desert you wear tan, 'cause it makes ya blend in. I can see pretty well in the dark, y'know, I could lead." He looked up then and studied her, "What? Did I say something wrong?"

Erin couldn't speak. She just stared at him and shook her head, "Damn kid, you are something else. C'mon, we sure have some work to do."

She turned to Jess who had fallen asleep, the baby cuddled against her chest and Tina's tangled head of hair resting against one leg. Quincy lay at her feet, tiny puppy paws twitching in time to some doggy dream. They looked kind of cute, in a ragged, half-starved, and filthy sort of way. For the tenth time that day she wished for a hot shower and handfuls of scented shampoo and conditioner.

"C'mon, they won't be going anywhere soon." And the two of them headed off to find spray paint.

*"*C*an you put a price on family? Can you put one on sacrifice? Tonight, my thoughts are on all of the ones who are gone...Mom...Dad...Chris...Erin. They say that, when someone dies, they don't truly die if you keep them in your heart. Those words seem so trite, so small and insignificant. War, death, knowing what gunfire sounds like and how it feels to be so damned hungry you think you're gonna die. Those things seem real to me. They aren't some stupid platitude that no one really understands. Not anymore, at least." – Jess's journal*

When Jess opened her eyes, the sun was sinking. A red-orange ball of heat occupying the horizon to the west. She was disoriented, her mind still foggy with sleep and the heat of the day. A handful of wilted dandelions thrust in her face did not help matters.

She jerked back and focused on Tina's grubby face smiling proudly, "I found dinna." She waved the dandelions, still sporting a clump of dirt and several terrified ants which were running pell-mell back and forth across the leaves trying to escape their doom. "See Yess, I found dinna."

Jess couldn't help but smile at the child. Grubby face and hopelessly tangled hair notwithstanding, she was an adorable child. "Oh sweetie, you did, you found dinner! Thank you, Tina!" She took the wilted greens from the tiny, nearly black fist and looked around for the others.

On a level patch of land Erin and David had erected the big tent they had found and were at one edge of it, obviously exchanging heated words. "What are they doing?" She asked it aloud, but hadn't really directed it towards the little girl.

"Dey's arguing," the little girl replied apprehensively, "Brother wants big stripes and Erin made small stripes and den dey started yellin.'" Her face took on a knowing expression, "Dey's need a nap."

As she finished, David walked away from Erin, huffing and mad. He stomped over and sat down nearby, practically shaking with anger. His face was red and he looked close to tears.

Before Jess could utter a word, Jacob woke with a wail of hunger. She busied herself with adjusting layers. She shifted the infant so that his tiny mouth could reach her breast and he greedily began to nurse. She winced, her breasts were sore and painful still—when would her boobs get used to feeding this little guy?

Erin came over and flopped onto the ground near Jess and the baby.

"Good lord, strip me naked and tie me to a friggin' anthill. I give up."

She snuck a peek at David who was looking the other way, shoulders stiff and back hunched, desperately trying not to let the tears show. "I think that we are all hungry and need to eat. And as for you, kid, I'm sorry I didn't listen, 'cause you're probably right about the damn stripes too. You're right about damn near everything else these days."

David let out a small but audible sniffle, "Kid, I'm sorry, okay? We'll do it your way, all right?"

"My name's not *kid*, it's *David*. I'm named after my dad," the boy's voice cracked with emotion despite his best efforts to sound dignified. He was tired, exhausted and hungry, and worn out from the late summer heat. He was, after all, only eleven.

Tina cuddled up to him and patted his hand, "So-kay, brother, s'okay." She looked over at Erin reproachfully, "You was swearin', that's not nice."

Jess grinned at Erin, "She's right, y'know. Be nice or we *will* strip you naked and tie you to an anthill!" Her smile belied the threat and it seemed contagious. Before long even David was smiling tentatively through his tears.

Erin looked defensive, and then apologized again, "I am sorry, David. Let's stop for now and rustle up some grub for everyone, okay?"

The boy wiped his eyes and nose with the back of his hand and just nodded, still unable to speak. He reached for their small stash of canned goods and located a can opener. The group dined on cold pork and beans, some surprisingly tasty Vienna sausages, one for each of them, and a large jar of spiced peaches. Out of politeness they each tried a wilted dandelion flower, after removing the ants, and praised Tina loudly for her efforts. The little girl beamed with pride.

As the last of the light died, Erin and David went back to the tent and finished the painting. The tent was now camouflaged for the forest and the two returned speculating on how they could camouflage it for the plains that they would also be crossing through.

Their plans were interrupted by the sounds of sporadic gunfire. Both Erin and Jess's eyes turned to the distance – the shots were coming from the southeast. *Shit!* Their eyes turned to the tent and recognized it would be akin to a flashing beacon that someone was around. They needed to be hidden...*now*. In what seemed like seconds the tent was down. While the girls disassembled, David and Tina ran and gathered personal items, hiding them, and doing their best to erase the evidence of their presence from the grassy lawn. The basement of the children's ruined house seemed more than attractive at the moment, despite the dangerous descent over the broken stairs. Jess and Erin had learned the trick of it in the last two weeks – hug the wall and hope to God the supports didn't break loose. With little words and black terror in Jess and Erin's eyes, they made their way into the dark, cluttered basement. It was dark outside by now, thank God, and that would hide them better than anything else.

Jacob had woken and began to wail as Jess made her way to the bottom of the stairs.

"Jesus Jess, shut him the hell up!" Erin hissed, "They're almost on top of us!"

She shoved her friend into a dark corner and pulled the remains of a bookcase over as a cover of sorts, then ran to the opposite end of the basement looking for another dark spot to hide. Tina had already crawled into the depths of the hidey-hole and David's feet disappeared behind her. The gunfire was loud now and they heard the men yelling to one another as they moved down the deserted street.

Jess patted him, made soft shushing noises and tried to get him to nurse. The baby would have none of it. Jacob began to wail louder, picking up on her fear and broadcasting it. It was as if she were standing with a megaphone advertising their position. She was terrified of being discovered. It didn't matter that these men couldn't possibly be from the camp that she and Erin had escaped from. They had guns and they were soldiers. None of the kids needed to know anything more than that. Their survival was dependent on their adeptness at hiding and scrounging. In this, all four were clearly on the same page.

Jess would later learn of the absolute chaos the Western Front had devolved into. There were no organized attacks, no common enemy to fight against, there were simply the ones with guns and the ones without and a lot of hungry, desperate people on both sides. The 'troops' the children hid from that night were nothing more than a leaderless group of thugs who, after losing their commander and three-quarters of their complement in a skirmish five miles to the southeast were trying to make their way around a larger group of equally starving and desperate men to the north. None of it really mattered, because in two weeks' time every one of the men currently terrifying the kids would be dead...after they made the error of engaging a group far larger in size.

Jess knew none of this. She only knew that Jacob was picking up on her terror and that his cries would end them all if she didn't do something fast. Despite her pounding heart and the fear that shot through her like knives, urging her to run in blind panic, she took one deep calming breath and then another and another. Slowly she willed her body to relax and allowed a sense of peace to envelope her.

One hand cupped Jacob's head and she hummed silently and steadily. She closed her eyes and remembered the weeks spent healing in that quiet cabin in the woods. She pictured that peaceful week spent with old Coop and the days of the journey along the way to Clinton. The other hand gently held Quincy's muzzle closed. Life wasn't all pain and fear and death. She knew that. She thought of her parents, of Chris and Erin and her childhood and smiled at the memories they still brought her.

She hummed softly to the infant in her arms, whispering in his ear. "I love you Jacob, I love you so much."

The infant stilled, turned his head and rooted for her breast, whimpering softly now, responding to her change in mood. The pup whined softly; her little body occasionally flinched at the loud explosions of sound. Jess wondered what the little mutt thought of it all.

The men passed, exchanging calls, rummaging in the ruined house above, shooting at shadows. They moved on. When it was quiet, Erin gathered up a blanket and found her way back to Jess who was half asleep. Jacob snored gently, moist and warm against her. Erin caressed his tiny head, which was silky soft. She murmured apologies to her friend.

"Sorry Jessie, I didn't mean it; I know he couldn't help being scared."

"S'okay, Erie. It all came out all right." Jess replied, "But I think we better head east for a bit. Those guys went north and we don't want to run into them anytime soon."

The children didn't emerge from their hidey-hole, except for David poking his head out and whispering good night to Erin, who bedded down close by. A night on a cement floor was a small price to pay for their narrow escape.

"It was my fault. I still remember it, when I'm alone with my thoughts, I think about how I was the one responsible for what happened that awful day. It was the first time I've killed anyone. The first time I had held a gun in my hands, pointed it at any living creature and pulled the trigger. It didn't look like it does in the movies. There is this anticlimactic moment when the body falls and you wonder if they are really dead. You walk up, the sound of the gunshot still ringing in your ears and you see it. There is that look in someone's eyes as they lie there dying and there's nothing you can do. You just stand and watch what was a person become empty, as if someone walked out and left the house, door hanging open, with all of the familiar furnishings, but no one inside to greet you." – **David's journal**

The day dawned hot and muggy. Jess woke first, and smelled then felt the wet coming from the bundled baby. The diaper had leaked, soaked through his wrap and into her clothes. "Ugh!" He'd crapped too, by the smell of it. The sun was barely brightening the sky and as she moved, he woke and began to fuss.

Her movements woke Erin who blearily made her way up the half-smashed stairs. As Erin emerged to ground level she looked around for any signs of the soldiers. The area looked clear. Quincy followed, nimbly climbing the rickety stairs and squatting to relieve herself before returning down the stairs to Jess's side.

Jacob's thin wail of distress began to build as Jess set him down and searched for clean clothing in the packs a few feet away. She had just pulled on a relatively clean shirt when David, followed by his little sister, emerged from their hidey-hole.

Erin called down, "Looks all clear. I think they headed north, let's get some food and eat it quick. I think we should head east, and soon. Who knows who might come up the road next?"

Jess couldn't help but agree. She started to strap Lady to her waist and hesitated, looking over at David. He had been eyeing firearms with more interest in the past few days. They made eye contact, "Would you like to carry it?" she asked him. His eyes widened and he grinned.

"This isn't a toy, y'know. The second you don't respect it, you're dead. This is a machine made for killing." He stared up at her and nodded silently. "I'm just loaning it to you. It's hard to handle with the baby and all."

She showed him how to carry it, even found a way to attach the holster to a piece of rope he could use as a belt and gave him a push up the stairs to Erin. "Ask her to show you how to use it."

They took care of their basic needs, ate a little breakfast and were ready to go by mid-morning. The tent they had taken such pains with the day before had been torn in their haste to dismantle and hide it before the soldiers discovered them. A large hole in it made it useless at keeping out rain or wind and it was at the worst of spots, part of the support structure for the tent stuck through. It had been rendered useless.

Instead they would pull the little trailer Erin and David had found. It had good solid tires on it, but it wouldn't be good for extreme terrain and neither of the girls liked the idea of it leaving tracks as they went through muddy areas. It was useful for now and they decided that if it became impractical, they could always carry their belongings on their backs.

Jess and Erin exchanged looks above the heads of the younger ones.

The looks were solemn – if they brought these kids with them, they were responsible for them, it meant they had to be cared for, fed, and sheltered. Once they left, they were committed to protecting David and Tina's lives just as much as they would their own. They wouldn't back out now, but it suddenly dawned on them just how much responsibility they were taking on. A few weeks ago, they had been responsible for each other – just two lives. Now, with the birth of Jacob, and meeting David and Tina, the task of surviving had become far more complicated. There was an unspoken question and challenge hovering there in the air between them for a moment, then a sort of release. They were committed and it was time to go.

Tina cried for the first few blocks and then stopped. She was young, in a few years she would have few if any memories of her parents to cherish.

David said nothing, but he cried silently all the way out of town and well into the empty fields.

He silently mourned his parents and the battered home they had left behind until the flowers and plants they were walking through distracted him. As they moved through the fields, he began to pay attention to everything growing around him.

Here was chicory, the leaves could be added to soup and salad and the roots ground into coffee. He wrinkled his nose at that, his dad had always drunk coffee black and with no sugar. Here was wild carrot. It didn't taste good raw, the book said, but it would be okay if cooked in a soup. A while ago they had passed several clumps of wild onions and he had stopped long enough to pick them. The tall plants with yellow sunflowers were everywhere.

David recognized them from a sketch in the book as Jerusalem artichoke. Their tubers, whatever those were, were edible. He paused for a moment and Tina stumbled to a halt behind him as he realized that he was *surrounded* by food. After months of fearing the canned food would run out and that he and Tina would starve to death, this was a revelation of epic proportions.

They quickly abandoned the little trailer. It had been fantastic on paved roads, the surface it was designed for, but when it came to heaving it over fences, it was too much. Jess couldn't handle much with the baby and if she handed him to one of the children he immediately began to wail. That left Erin to somehow wrestle it over a fence with two vertically challenged, and noticeably weaker children helping her. The first day was spent making little progress in terms of distance. Finally, they stopped, divided and reduced their belongings into a transportable system between the four.

The only incident came on the second afternoon as they passed by a small stream. David casually reached out and uprooted some plant with an umbel of white flowers and began to clean off the root. Erin looked over, did a double-take, and snatched it from his hand before he could take a bite.

Before he could think to say anything more than a startled, "Hey" she had examined it intensely, thrown it to one side and pulled him over to the stream.

"Wash. Now. Anywhere you touched that plant." She instructed, tight-lipped and frightened.

"Why? It was wild carrot, Queen-somethin' lace, that's food. I know it isn't supposed to be good raw, but I figured I'd try a bite anyway." He argued, confused and angry.

"No. That was water hemlock. Look closer." She pulled him over to the discarded plant, jabbing her finger fiercely at the areas of the plant, "See? Smooth stem, not hairy like wild carrot. And see how it is mottled? And almost purple-colored, not green?" The boy stopped looking defensive and his face assumed a look of terrified wonder.

"The leaves are lance-shaped, not feathery. This plant would have killed you if you had eaten any of it. Horribly and painfully, I might add." Her fierce look gave Jess a full-body shiver.

David washed thoroughly in the muddy, shallow stream. He did it silently and no one said anything. Jess and Tina were somewhat afraid to, and Erin tried to calm down. How close that had been! If he had eaten just a bite, just one bite. She looked down and realized her hands were shaking. Erin closed her eyes and tried to breathe calmly.

When she opened them, David was standing there, hands still moist from the stream, with a determined look on his face, "Show me again, Erin. So, I'll know and remember."

Knowledge would keep them alive, nourish them, and protect them from harm. He would learn this and never forget. She showed him again the characteristics and he watched and listened with an intensity that impressed both girls. Even Tina watched and learned. The rest of the day was spent identifying plants as they walked. They found lamb's quarters and gathered it for adding to soup later on, as well as plenty of wild carrot that reappeared in the meadows they walked through and were easy to pull up and gnaw as they walked. The book was right, raw wild carrot didn't taste good at all.

"We need a shovel," David pointed at the tall Jerusalem Artichokes, "A little one that we can use to dig up the *tubers*." He liked that word.

When David had broken down and asked what tubers were, Erin had not laughed as he expected her to. Instead she had explained that they were the thick underground parts of a plant that were edible.

"Like potatoes or, well Jerusalem Artichoke looks more like ginger root actually. Have you ever seen fresh ginger root?" He shook his head, absorbed her explanation, looked again at the tall plants and wished he could start digging.

Two days of walking did not get them far. Not with a newborn and a small child. David could handle the day-long walks, but Tina stumbled behind, moving slower and slower until they were forced to stop every hour or so. Jacob was even more demanding. The gentle rocking motion of the sling helped him to sleep, but still woke every two to three hours for feedings. She learned to nurse as she walked, but his constant waking at night exhausted her. Each time Tina slowed down, Jess stopped and sat down too. Their progress was agonizingly slow.

It was a testament to how long all of them had survived that they did not complain or argue. They simply did what they could and took every opportunity they could to rest. Late in afternoon on the fourth day Tina simply sat down on the ground and refused to move an inch farther. There wasn't much argument from anyone except Erin who was worried about camping out in the open. It helped ease her mind to see that the grass and weeds were tall; she even hiked a ways back and said that from her vantage point she couldn't even see the small group once she got very far.

"Unless anyone saw us stop here, we should be fine." They munched on the last of a box of crackers. David and Erin took turns peering through binoculars at an old farmhouse in the far distance.

David said, "I just want to hike over there and see if there is anything we could use. Like a shovel." He was still obsessed with the tubers and was eager to get a chance to dig them up.

Tina was already fast asleep, curled up in a dirty little bundle near Jess's feet and Erin and Jess were finishing off a can of green beans. It wasn't much, but it was enough to quiet their stomachs.

Quincy nuzzled Jess and whined softly, as if asking permission, "Oh go on with you. Catch us a rabbit or a squirrel, okay?"

The little dog was fast, damned fast, and she managed to keep herself well fed on birds and rodents. Every couple of days she would flush a rabbit and bring it back to the girls, her tail wagging madly. She would lay it at their feet, neck neatly broken, not a mark on its fur. They didn't feel bad for the soft little bunny – food was food and rabbit turned into pretty good rabbit stew. Quincy wagged her tail and disappeared into the tall grass.

Jess waved a hand at him, "Go ahead kid. Sorry, I mean, *David*. Just keep your eyes open, all right?"

David jumped up, adjusted the cord around his waist that held the revolver and dashed into the field, eager to explore the farmhouse. He quickly disappeared from view. Erin pulled her lank hair out of the ponytail holder and grimaced over the twigs and knots running through it. "God, what I would give for a shower. Think that place has got any running water?"

Jess just shrugged. She was too tired to think. Jacob fussed at her breast and she patted his back rhythmically until he settled down and began to nurse steadily. In the months and years that would follow this day Jess would wake screaming. She would wonder over and over why she didn't stop Erin or David. Her exhaustion, coupled with lack of preparedness from Erin and the curiosity of youth from David would be their undoing on that hot, fall day. Jess didn't see what was coming, didn't recognize that they had all cheated death, for far too long. She said nothing as Erin stretched, grimaced over her grimy state, and set the .22 Rimfire on the ground next to Jess. "I'm going to go with him and just see what's over there. I'll be back soon."

She disappeared into the overgrown field of grass and the tattered remnants of last year's corn. Tina turned over, rubbed her face against Jess's leg and burrowed closer. The heavy curtain of sleep began to steal over Jess as Jacob's lips fell from her breast and his breathing deepened into sleep. Moments ticked by.

It was still light when Jess heard the scream. The sun had slipped below the horizon, and there was little light left in the sky. From this distance it was wordless, impossible to be sure what she had heard, but she was sure it was Erin. Quincy had just returned with a large rabbit in her jaws, its furry legs were still kicking. The dog turned in the direction of the farmhouse, dropped the rabbit onto the ground and began to growl steadily.

It was enough to wake Tina as well and she jerked to a sitting position and looked around in confusion for her brother.

"Tina, listen to me. Take the baby and be very quiet." Jess pointed to a tree in the distance, "Go to that tree and wait for us to find you. I'm going to go find your brother and Erin."

The little girl nodded and Jess quickly wrapped her son in a sling around Tina, praying the little girl wouldn't trip and fall. "Take it slow, okay? And be very quiet!"

"Quincy," she turned to the dog, "Stay with Tina. Stay, girl!" The dog let out a mournful whine and looked agitated, but she obeyed.

She grabbed the rifle, gave the little girl a small push in the right direction and then turned and ran, keeping as low as she could, towards the old farmhouse. Whatever the trouble was, she was headed straight for it.

She was within thirty feet of the farmhouse when the first shot rang out. Another ten feet out when the second shot came and then she was inside, no hesitation, bullet in the chamber, finger on the trigger and the adrenaline pumping through her.

There were four people in the main room – two soldiers, Erin, and David. One man was already dead on the ground, Erin was down and clutching at her chest. A stain of red quickly spread from beneath her hands. The second man was aiming his pistol at David, but he was distracted by Jess bursting in. She took it in quickly, aimed at the man and pulled the trigger, chambered another round and shot again. Two dark holes appeared in his chest and he stared down at them in surprise. The soldier stood there unmoving for one long moment, then collapsed to the ground and did not move.

Jess skidded on her knees to her friend's side. She grabbed Erin's free hand, her mind racing with thoughts of bandages and stopping the massive flow of blood. *Oh God, there was so much blood.*

Her friend attempted to speak. Erin's mouth opened, choked on the blood now surging through her esophagus. Blood sprayed from her mouth, spattering Jess. She tried again to speak, gasped, and then breathed no more. She died there, her eyes wide open and staring, her hand limp in Jess's grasp.

Jess began to scream.

*"*R*emember to be gentle with yourself and others. We are all children of chance and none can say why some fields will blossom while others lay brown beneath the August sun. Care for those around you. Look past your differences. Their dreams are no less than yours, their choices no more easily made. And give, give in any way you can, of whatever you possess. To give is to love. To withhold is to wither. Care less for your harvest than for how it is shared and your life will have meaning and your heart will have peace."* – **Kent Nerburn**

Fine-boned fingers covered his eyes, the smell of freshly turned dirt and the mint she had been picking filled his nose, "Guess who?"

Chris smiled, "Hey Liza. Making mint tea?"

Carrie's sister let out a disappointed sniff, "You knew it was me!"

"Of course. You smell different than Carrie." He didn't tell her that Carrie had this indescribable scent, this earthy combination of sage and wood smoke that was almost drug-like. It pulled him in and made him want to get closer, wrap his arms around her and never let go. Liza smelled good too, but she smelled of childhood and cinnamon. He couldn't explain it any better than that.

In the past few weeks Liza's attitude toward him, and towards her sister, had begun to alter. She kept seeking him out when the others were busy with tasks. And whenever Carrie and he were together, she picked fights and argued with her sister endlessly.

It had taken him a while, but he had come to suspect that Liza had a crush. She would be fourteen in just a few months and she was acting as if Carrie was more a rival than a sister. Carrie was confused by the behavior, commenting to Chris in private that they had always been close and rarely fought like other siblings. "I just don't know what's with Liza these days, everything I say or do is wrong," Carrie nibbled her thumbnail, "It's almost as if she is dying to pick a fight with me. But why?"

Chris had caught Liza spying on them twice now. They still hadn't gone all the way, but they were getting close, and he was worried that things were coming to a head. He had to deal with it, somehow. He looked up at Liza, who was staring down at him with a confused, half-hopeful smile. *Crap.* He set down the basket of tomatoes he had been picking. It was nearly full, the red and orange fruits firm and beautiful, promising to explode with juice the instant they were cut into. He figured he had three more baskets to pick before he would be done for the day.

"Liza, we need to talk."

She grinned happily, "Did you finish 'Voyage from Yesteryear' already? I just left it by your door two days ago."

He shook his head and her expression turned from excited to guarded, "No, I haven't finished reading it yet. But it's good," he smiled at her, "I had a hard time putting it down this morning and getting to work."

He pointed to the raised planters and the tomato cages, "Help me pick more?"

"Sure."

As they fell into a rhythm, he got up the courage to say what was on his mind. "Y'know Liza, you are a very pretty girl." He saw her hand pause; almost drop the tomato she was holding. "I know you like me. And really, I'm flattered, I am." He met her eyes then, she looked afraid, "But I..."

"You're in love with Carrie."

"Yeah, I am. I want to marry her." Her chin dropped to her chest and he thought he saw a small tear fall to the ground. "Liza, I'm sorry. I know that doesn't make it any better, but I really am. 'Cause you are a really cool chick, and you love sci-fi, which totally kicks ass," that elicited a small wet giggle, "I want us to be friends and, if your granddad doesn't shoot me first, someday I'd like to be your brother."

Liza looked up at him, her eyes wet with tears, "I...oh...why do you have to be so damn nice, Chris? Couldn't you just say, buzz off kid, you're sister's way hotter than you?"

It was his turn to look away. He hated to see the kid cry. "Sorry Liza, that's just how I'm wired, I guess. And besides, you aren't a kid, anymore, and you are hot. Or did you miss the way Carl Owens stared at you all last week?"

He didn't dare tell her how much she reminded him of Jess when she was a high school freshman. It was painful to look at her sometimes.

Just thinking about Jess now, imagining how she had died, made him want to scream. He hadn't protected her, but he would protect Carrie and Liza, Joseph and Fenton with his dying breath. He couldn't bring back what he had lost, but he could make sure he didn't lose anything more. Lost in his thoughts he was surprised when Liza wrapped her arms around him. He hugged her back, hoping he was doing the right thing, and she kissed him lightly on the cheek. Before he could react, she had bounded away, heading for some quiet corner to compose herself.

He visibly jumped when Carrie's voice spoke from behind him, "So, that was what was going on these past few weeks?" Chris whirled around to face her, "That's why she's been so pissy! She likes you?" She seemed blown away by this fact.

He smiled at her, "Is it so hard to believe?"

"Well, no." She stood there with a peculiar smile on her face.

"Well, then what are you smiling about?" He was feeling a bit defensive. After all, he'd tried to be nice about it and the kid had still run off crying.

"I'm thinking that you are really, really sweet." Carrie stepped forward, put a hand on each side of his face, and kissed him softly. "You saw it when I didn't. You made her feel cared for, even if she couldn't have you. Thank you for that."

"You aren't pissed because I hugged her and she kissed me?"

He couldn't believe his good luck. A beautiful, sexy girl who wasn't crazy with jealousy? She shook her head wordlessly and kissed him again, this time with promise and intent. He kissed her back, ran his hands down her back and slid his hands over her short shorts. The kiss was intense, passionate.

Unfortunately, it was cut short by a shout for help from Fenton. The shout came from the barn where Fenton had been tinkering with the truck for the past week now. The carburetor had been a relatively easy fix, but the huge dent that Liza had put into the front fender when she ran it into a fence while learning to drive had caused significant damage. The Chilton's manual they had found in town was getting its fair share of use as Fenton paged through it, uttering long-winded complaints about the dangers of teenage drivers.

His yell brought everyone running. This was a good thing, since he seemed determined to bleed to death from a large gash on his forehead. Blood streaked down his face and Liza beat the rest of them to the barn, arriving at her grandfather's side first. Her face still showed signs of tears, but no one noticed. Chris pulled off his shirt and used it to apply pressure to the wound.

"Jesus, Gramps," Carrie helped her grandfather to a seated position on an old tire, "what happened?"

Fenton gave her an irritated look, "Young lady, you keep using the Lord's name in vain and I'll wash your mouth out with soap. By damn, I can't even see out of this eye!"

His right eye was covered in blood, which had alarmed Chris until he realized it was merely flowing from the wound above.

"I managed to walk into the shelf over there."

He gestured at a shelf that had been mounted on the wall and stacked with boxes of screws. It was now hanging precariously from one end and all of the screws were in a jumble of broken boxes on the floor.

Liza examined the wound, "Head wounds bleed a lot, but this *is* a deep gash. Good one, Gramps." He grimaced at her.

"We had better clean it up and put in some stitches." Liza spent time studying medical texts when she wasn't reading science fiction. It made sense for at least one person to know medicine, especially in these times, and Fenton and Carrie had both encouraged her studies by trading eggs and live chicks for two medical textbooks. Liza had begun studying in earnest the year after her mother's death. She had helped Fenton set Chris's ankle when he had first arrived and even corrected his technique when they wrapped and then splinted it. Currently she was working her way through a thick manual on obstetrics. Chris had seen one of the pictures and felt his stomach roil. Definitely not his cup of tea.

"Can you make Gramps better, Sis?" Joseph asked. The kid looked scared.

Liz paused in her examination to smile at her little brother, "I sure can, Joseph, Gramps is going to be just fine. Let's get him back to the house and then we'll fix him up better than ever." She turned back to Fenton and the three of them hoisted him to his feet

In the end, the 'couple of' stitches had been ten, perfect little sutures. Fenton insisted on several healthy swigs from a full bottle of Jack Daniels hidden deep on a high shelf. Chris retrieved it and smiled. He could see ten other bottles of hard liquor, all unopened. He figured old Fenton had put them up there about three years ago, about the time the girls and their mother had arrived, and hadn't touched them since.

"That there needle is gonna hurt," Fenton had given as way of explanation, "I plan on making it hurt less." He had still had a few choice things to say during the procedure.

Carrie started canning the tomatoes Chris already picked. He picked the rest while she worked over the stove blanching, peeling, and preparing the tomatoes. This task lasted late into the night. They lit a gas lamp to see by and kept working on the pile of tomatoes.

As they worked, they listened to Fenton sing, quite drunkenly now that nearly half the bottle of whiskey was gone. When in his cups, Fenton seemed overly fond of Elvis Presley. The tomatoes were all canned; jars lined every piece of available countertop.

Joseph was curled in a small ball on the couch and Fenton was launching into the *fifth* rendition of "You Ain't Nothing but a Hound Dog" when Liza took the bottle out of his hand and handed it to Chris.

She rolled her eyes at him, suppressing a smile, and nodded to the high shelf. She and Carrie each took a side and gently pulled Fenton to his feet. They guided him slowly up the stairs to his room.

Chris returned the bottle to the shelf, and took a moment to look over what else was up there. The old man had quite a selection.

The warm hand that ran up his leg quickly changed his focus. The thought that came next was shocking in its simplicity. "*What are you waiting for?*"

He climbed down from the counter and turned to face Carrie. The moon had risen in the sky and the light from it poured in the kitchen window. He leaned over, blew out the lamp and pulled her close. She felt the change in him and responded in kind; shivering slightly as his lips found her neck and worked their way up to her right ear. He whispered in it, "Let's go for a walk." He felt rather than saw her nod.

He grabbed several blankets, spread one over little Joseph and the other two he tucked under his arm. Quietly they slipped out of the door, closing it quietly behind them.

Hand in hand they walked. They didn't discuss it, and their feet carried them unerringly to the old farmstead. It was their special place. They had been slipping away for make-out sessions there as often as possible in the last few months. He carefully spread the blanket out and they lay down, side by side. The stars were incredibly bright and beautiful. It was warm and all around them the night pulsed with life, thousands of tiny creatures attending to their nocturnal activities. They took notice of the two humans in their midst and shied away, creating a bubble of space around the couple.

As they watched a satellite slowly make its way across the sky Chris wondered if the space station was still up there, and if there were any astronauts inside. If there were, and if the rest of the world was in as bad of shape as the U.S. was, they were nothing but frozen skeletons by now.

He pushed those thoughts out of his mind and thought instead of how amazing Carrie smelled, even with the scent of tomatoes clinging to her. He reached down and took her hand in his. It felt tiny and fragile in comparison with his, but he knew that was an illusion. Carrie was a strong woman, in mind and spirit. She knew her mind and she fought for what she wanted. Here he had a future, a family and love.

He pulled her close and leaned in for a kiss. It heated and went on and on as their pulses quickened. Their clothing fell in a heap and the lovemaking was as gentle as he could make it for her. In the end he collapsed beside her, burrowed his face into her neck and kissed her moist skin.

All of these months of playing, of dancing about and teasing, and they had finally gone and done it. At least he knew Fenton wasn't busy cleaning his shotgun right now. The minutes ticked by and Chris pulled part of the thin blanket over them. He could hear Carrie's breathing settle and even out.

"Carrie?"

"Mm?"

He jostled her, "Wake up."

"I'm awake."

He pulled himself to one elbow and looked into her face. He could see it clearly in the moonlight. Her eyes were open and she had a satisfied, almost smug smile. He reached out and smoothed a lock of hair back behind her left ear. "I love you Carrie Lynn Perdue. Will you marry me?"

She smiled even wider, put her hands on both sides of his face. "I love you too, Christopher Michael Aaronson. And yes, I will marry you."

What followed was a good deal more of what had just occurred. It continued, with little sleep through most of that night. The sun was just beginning to peek over the horizon as the two lovers slipped back inside the house.

"*Seeing her there, I knew she was gone. The blood pooled from her back, mixing with the blood of those two animals. Even in death they contaminated and sickened everything they touched. David was shaking and crying and still he tried to do right by her, reaching forward, closing her staring eyes. He said I screamed over and over and over until he brought me Jacob and thrust him into my arms. But I don't remember screaming at all, I only remember thinking how deafening the silence was. We buried her the next morning, out back, in a small, overgrown garden, near a clump of iris. I remember there was a creek nearby. David found a large limestone slab and shoved it at the head of the mound. We didn't bury the others. To hell with them.*" – Jess's Journal

The first sound that David heard through his tortured and ringing eardrums were Jess's screams. They were wordless, horrifying keens of despair as she clutched Erin's hand and rocked back and forth. Blood covered both of them and pooled on the floor. He dropped the revolver he had been clutching, watched it slide from nerveless fingers.

Oh God, he had actually killed one of them. But he'd been too late. The second one, the dark-haired greasy one, had gotten a shot off, straight into Erin before Jess had come running and dropped him with two quick shots. Erin's eyes were open still, staring, and she had a slightly bewildered look on her face.

For a moment he had wondered if there was a chance, she would be okay, that she would recover, and then he saw the wound and the blood that poured from it, and from her mouth and nose. Tears came then, as he stared at her, watched her try to speak, choke and weakly spit out a mouthful of blood. Her head fell back against the wood floor, her eyes glazed and he knew she was gone.

That's when Jess had begun to scream, and sit seemed as if the screams grew louder with each passing moment. He reached over, his fingers trembling, and closed Erin's eyes. Mom's had been like that, but clouded, and he could still picture their faces. On the ground, bodies cold and stiff, life gone. He was too shell-shocked, terrified by what he had done and how this had gone so wrong to think any longer. He just sat and cried while Jess screamed over and over and over.

Minutes, what seemed like hours, went by and the shadows had darkened, night was almost upon them. He came to his senses, got up, and walked out of the farmhouse and into the field to find Tina and the baby. He didn't have to go far.

Jacob's shrieks of hunger and fear were like a beacon. He found Jacob and Tina huddled near a fallen tree, the baby howled for milk and Tina just shook in complete terror. He hugged her to him and took Jacob into his arms. The baby's face was bright red from screaming. No amount of shushing or cooing would help. He could still hear Jess keening in the farmhouse. Erin was dead. Why had he wanted to explore the shed and farmhouse, why?

Quincy had stayed with them all the way back to the farmhouse. She whined in response to the sounds of Jess's obvious distress. But her mistress had told her to stay with Tina, and young as she was, the pup followed orders. Tina kept a death grip on his shirttail as he trudged back to the house with Jacob shrieking the entire way. Maybe if he could get the baby in Jess's arms she'd calm down and feed him.

Anything but that awful sound she kept making. Tina stopped in her tracks at the sight of the bodies and refused to enter the front door. Her tiny body shivered with fear. He had to pull loose from her grasp in order to get to Jess and thrust Jacob into her arms.

The baby's screams triggered the mothering instinct and she could feel her breasts fill painfully in response. Somehow Jess let go of her friend's limp and lifeless hand and stood up. She couldn't stay in this room. She made her way to the front porch, her shrieks turned to deep, racking sobs and finally to a half-hearted humming as she tried to calm her screaming son.

Out of the room, it didn't seem real. Erin couldn't be gone. Not after all they had been through. They had survived the troops taking their town. They had survived Tent 5 and the months afterwards in the cabin in the woods. They had made the long trek to Clinton and avoided the soldiers and the gunfire. And now, on their way home, to die like this? It couldn't be. Night had descended and there were few stars, just inky shadows.

David reappeared with Tina, dragging most of their supplies and equipment, and his voice was cracked, wounded, when he spoke, "There's a big tree, not too far away. We could stay there for tonight, Jess. It's away from the house, in case others come. What do you think?"

When Jess answered she could barely manage a whisper from her raw throat, "Yeah. Okay, lead the way."

It wasn't far to walk. They stumbled in the dark to the tree, pulled their blankets close to each other and lay down on the hard ground. Jess felt the boy snuggle his back into hers, Tina wrapped in his arms and Jacob in hers. There was some comfort to feeling him wedged against her and needing reassurance. Quincy curled against her legs, whining softly.

"We'll bury her in the morning and move on, in case there's more of 'em."

Out of the dark came his response, "'Kay."

*"**I** love the warm months. When the memories come, when my heart breaks just thinking of those I have lost, I go out into the garden. I pull up grass and weeds and train the vines. I dig deep in the rich earth. It brings me comfort and soothes the hurt. Each year is a miracle, each day and week and month that passes is a song of triumph. We rise again, we survive, and I can feel life in each handful of dirt I move."* **– Jess's Journal**

Jess lay on a pad from the porch swing, a thin blanket over her. Jacob was cuddled close. He was asleep, having fussed and cried a good part of the night. She wasn't much better off. Her dreams had been bloody and violent.

The world seemed full of death and despair, despite the sun and the birds chirping. Signs of life and growth surrounded her. It felt like a slap in the face. How dare the world be so beautiful, right here, when only a few hundred feet away Erin's lifeless body lay? She had managed to dig down several feet before the sun climbed high in the sky. She collapsed on the ground to rest and nursed Jacob.

David had scrounged a late breakfast, discovering several woody radishes and asparagus stalks in the old garden and supplementing them with a precious can of beef stew. Jess hadn't been hungry, but she sat up and ate what David handed her. The food tasted like sawdust. Erin was gone, but no matter how much that hurt, she wasn't, and three young lives depended on her now. They needed her to stay strong.

She swallowed mechanically, and sipped from the cup of tea David had passed to her. It was hot and he must have used the farmhouse stove. It probably ran on propane, this far out in the country. The kitchen was accessible without going through the front entry and living room where the soldier's bodies lay, flies buzzing around them. There were mint leaves floating in the tea.

As she peered down into the cup, David said, "I found some plants out in the garden. A big patch of mint, so I put 'em in a cup and boiled some water." Jess raised her eyebrows and sipped again. "It's just those leaves and nothin' else, but I like it. I picked a lot and put 'em in one of the packs."

He looked away, back at the partially-dug hole and the sheet-draped body nearby. "I'll dig for a while."

He didn't want to tell her yet, but he knew he would have to soon. Before he had heated up the water in the kitchen he had gone through both soldier's pockets. It had taken every bit of nerve he could manage. Hands shaking, he had collected weapons, gone through their packs and found extra ammunition and some cans of food. He had also found something else, something that changed everything and made him want to run screaming back to Clinton with Tina's hand clutched in his. As much as he wished for the safe comfort of his hidey-hole, he knew Erin and Jess had been right. They couldn't survive the winter there. So instead of running he held his tongue and dug deeply into the earth.

The grave was dug by the time the sun was directly overhead in the sky. Jess had done two more stints, with David helping. She dug into the earth and cried, stopped, and then dug some more. Eventually it was deep enough and she hugged her friend to her, pulled her body into the open grave and then slowly climbed out. After that came the hardest part. She shoveled the dirt over Erin and slowly buried her friend deep in the ground. Quincy had let out a long, sad howl when the dirt began to cover Erin's body. Then the pup had sunk down on the ground, tail curled up underneath her and ears flat and whined. By the time they had finished shoveling the dirt into place; Jess was shaking with exhaustion and grief. She had no more tears left in her and her head pounded in agony. A few feet away, Tina fanned Jacob as he slept and watched the process without speaking. She hadn't spoken a word all day.

Tears streaked and mingled with the dirt on David's face as he pulled over a large rock. Despite his young age, the boy was strong. He shrugged off an offer of help from Jess. "I got it." He heaved again and managed to set it up right at the head of the grave. Jess she felt a wave of pain and loss crash over her. After all they had been through; to lose Erin now seemed to be more than she could bear.

Jess searched for the words to a familiar prayer. Her parents hadn't been religious, they had never gone to church, but it seemed like there were special words you were supposed to say during moments like that. David and Tina both looked up at her expectantly. She dug in her memories and finally remembered the Lord's Prayer.

"Our father who art in heaven," the words were reassuring somehow, although she couldn't have explained why. Perhaps certain words, when said in the right sequence, had power.

"Hallowed be thy name. Thy kingdom come; thy will be done…"

Could it be that they had power to bring peace, heal wounds, or renew hope? David's voice chimed in and Tina tried to as well, but she didn't know the words. "On earth as it is in heaven," When they finished, the silence stretched for several long moments. Jess cleared her throat.

"Erie, it doesn't seem right leaving you here. I promise I'll come back and put a better marker here as soon as I can." She stopped, took a deep breath, "You saved my life too many times to count and I will miss you forever. Please forgive me for not being quicker. I love you so much. I'm so sorry."

It didn't seem enough. It felt unfinished somehow. So, she searched her memories and smiled as the tears slipped down her cheeks. The words flowed, as she spoke to the memory of her friend and their childhood adventures. She recalled all of the good memories, all the beauty and laughter they had shared. It took a while for Jess to say goodbye to a friend she had grown up with.

When she was done, she placed her son in his sling, picked up what she could carry of their packs, turned toward the east and began to walk. David and Tina followed close behind and Quincy ran ahead. None of them said anything for a long time.

"*When David showed me the paper, I panicked. What if there were more men out there looking for us? I'll never know how many they sent, or why they felt it was so important to get us back. All I knew was that the note listed descriptions of Erin and me, along with the names of our family and friends. They knew where we came from. And months after we escaped, they were still looking for us. Going home was suddenly a walk in the wrong direction.*" – **Jess's journal**

David hesitated for several hours, then finally, when they stopped to rest and eat a bit of food, he got up the courage to show Jess the note he had discovered on one of the bodies. The paper had been folded several times and was well-worn. But Jess and Erin's names had both been on it, along with a physical description of each girl, and the town of Belton as their expected destination. The soldiers had been looking for *them*. He didn't know why and that scared him.

"I found this on one of the soldiers," he handed the paper to her and watched her read it. The color drained from her face. "Do you think there might be others?"

Jess said nothing in response. She stared at the paper for a long time, reading and rereading the few words until she had the note, even the shape of the letter formations firmly fixed in her mind.

They finished eating and Jacob fussed in the wrap. Jess changed his diaper, wrapped him back against her, and began walking without a word to David or Tina. Soon after, east turned to due south as they discovered the first of scores of bodies. There had been fighting here recently, a few days at most, and the smell from the corpses was sickening. Tina whimpered in fear and hid her face in her brother's shirt as they skirted around the dead. Quincy's tail stayed permanently tucked between her legs and she walked as close as possible to Jess, her ears flattened, her body tense.

Jess wondered if the bodies belonged to some of the troops who had passed through Clinton recently. It seemed safer to head south for now. As they turned south, the northwestern edge of Harry Truman Lake appeared and due to the inability to head east unless they wanted to swim, they hugged the lake edge and continued south, away from Belton, yet again.

It was sunset when they made camp on a bluff overlooking the reservoir. Decades ago, the U.S. Corps of Engineers had purposely flooded sections of the low-lying valley, creating Truman Lake. In the distance, tips of dead, drowned trees poked up from the middle of the water. Even the top of a chimney could be seen. It was an old homestead that had long been abandoned and then submerged when the waters flooded the valley.

They didn't dare build a fire. The highway, probably Highway 7 from Jess's quick review of the map they had found in a broken-down truck, was also within view. What they could see of the highway, someone on the highway could likely also see of them. No reason to take chances.

Again, Jess forced herself to eat. There wasn't much, and because they couldn't build a fire, she let Quincy eat the rabbit she had flushed out and caught shortly before they stopped for the night. The young dog eagerly tore into her meal.

They slept huddled close that night. It was warm, not oppressively so, but warm enough. Still, they needed to feel safe, needed to hear the breath of another living person and feel their presence close. Life was so fleeting, so painfully short at times; they needed each other more than ever before. So, they slept, deeply, without dreams or nightmares on that bluff, legs and arms intertwined, bodies curled close.

Keeping the small band together and safe overrode Jess's desire to head home. They continued south the next day, keeping the water's edge within sight at all times. It was late and almost time to stop for dinner and camp for the night when David commented on the strange tree. It was bent, twice, at nearly perfect right angles, "This tree is weird."

Weird or not, it was a reasonable place to stop. The sun would soon be setting and it was time to scrounge for food. Quincy had disappeared into the brush to the west, probably hunting for a rabbit or squirrel. They heard her give one short, quick bark. David had been picking from bushes and digging up little plants all along the way. All of his studies of the now filthy, dog-eared and ragged book were paying off. He could easily identify plantain, cat-tail, wild onion, fiddlehead ferns, oxalis and a host of other edible plants. As they walked, he would suddenly stop and dig something up and stick it into his pack.

The long-bladed shovel he found at the farmhouse had become his walking stick and was never far from his reach. Tina had begun to help as well, and when they stopped for any length of time, both children would forage a little, always within sight, and pick up what plants they could to supplement the dwindling supply of canned food.

As Jess began to search through the cans for dinner, David continued to study the strangely formed tree with interest. It was such a specific deformity. And there was nothing in sight that indicated why it would be shaped that way. "It's like it's *pointing* to something," David commented, unable to stop staring at the tree.

An unexpected voice answered, "It *is* pointing at something. That, young man, is what the Osage call a *thong* tree."

The owner of the voice was a bright-eyed old woman, who leaned on a walking stick and blended seamlessly into the trees twenty feet away. A rifle was strapped to her back and her dark eyes sparkled beneath a crown of white hair pulled into a loose bun. Wisps of her hair hung freely. She was slim, dressed in a simple t-shirt and jeans with solid, no-nonsense hiking boots on her feet. Quincy squirmed in excitement at her feet; apparently, she had found a person instead of the usual rabbit or squirrel.

David jumped in response and the rest of them froze in place. But it was hard to be afraid of one little old woman, especially with Quincy's relaxed canine confidence in the stranger. Jess scanned the rest of the woods surrounding them and saw no one. When her gaze returned to the old woman she saw long, deep lines etched in her face. It was hard to keep her guard up; the old woman looked friendly and had reached down to scratch Quincy behind the ears. The dog leaned a floppy-eared head against the woman's jeans.

Jess spoke first, "Uh, hi."

David spoke as well, "Why's it called a thong tree and who're the Oh Sage?"

The old woman laughed then and the lines in her face deepened as she did. The children relaxed for the first time in a long time. Here was someone who was not a threat.

"Well I'm Osage, Little One, and the rest is better explained a short walk from here." She glanced up at the sky, "Rain is coming." She turned and began walking west, away from the lake's edge, stopping only briefly to glance back and crook a bony finger at the group. "Come this way then."

Quincy bounded after her, and a moment later, so did Jess and the kids, lugging the packs they had recently shed from their backs. It was odd, she hadn't even introduced herself, yet the little group followed her wordlessly.

Through the clearing and into the deep woods they walked. A winding path, with several sharp zigs and zags, was barely visible unless you knew what to look for. It eventually led to the base of a wide-mouthed, low-ceilinged cave. Seconds after they followed the old woman inside of the cave, the skies outside darkened, rumbled ominously, and then opened up and began to pour rain.

Thanks to the rain and clouds, the inside of the cave appeared dim. After bending slightly to pass under an overhanging rock, the ceiling raised above Jess's head. It was about twelve feet high in this main outer chamber. Ahead of them it closed down again to a dimly lit opening in the back. There appeared to be some kind of light source on the other side. They kept to the path on the left and avoided the deep holes dug on the right-hand side. It appeared to be an archaeological dig site in process. Pickets and string sectioned off areas in meter squares, delineating one section from the next. Signs labeled each square and in some of the sections there were spearheads or pot shards laid out, in the exact position they had been discovered and excavated.

Jess and the children followed the old woman back through this outer chamber, through the small man-height opening. Jess could see that the light source, judging from the water dripping down on one edge was a natural skylight that reached all the way up through the cave ceiling. This inner chamber was immense, and there were several other smaller dig sites at regular intervals throughout. It was obvious that the old woman lived here as well. There was a section with a table, several chairs and some stacks of boxes and containers all situated away from the falling water, but close to the 'skylight.' The rain came in and pooled in a lagoon the size of the front chamber, then flowed away along a small rocky stream toward the pitch-black rear of the cave.

The old woman stopped near the campfire located across from her living area. She stirred the embers and gently placed another log on to burn. A spit held three blackened lumps above the crackling fire. It was difficult to tell, but Jess guessed it was probably squirrel.

She spoke then, as she moved from the fire to the supplies nearby, "Not much meat for all of you, but I wasn't really expecting company. I can cook up some ramen and I'm sure I've got some other goodies in here to add to it." She opened boxes and handed a saucepan to David, "Fill it up with rainwater there and put it on the fire, *Min'-dse*." She smiled and her teeth were white and perfect, "My name is Dr. Madeleine Falling Water, but you can call me Madge. Let's get some dinner and then we'll have story time."

Jess wasn't sure what to think of the old woman or of story time but at that moment Jacob signaled he was awake, hungry, and ready for a change by wailing loud and long. She pulled him out of her wrap, where he had been hidden from sight, and Madge moved faster than it seemed possible for a woman her age.

Before Jess could object, Jacob was lifted from her arms with a cry of joy and a barrage of words in a strange, guttural language. Oddly the baby stopped crying immediately and stared at the old woman intensely, watching and listening to everything she said.

She unwrapped his coverings, clucked over his wet and bulging diaper, and immediately set him on a coat on the cave floor and changed him, reaching impatiently for the clean diaper which Jess found and handed to her after a bit of scrambling. Madge then swept him up in her arms and spoke rapidly in the foreign language to the infant, cooing and kissing, and then handing him back to Jess to nurse.

She pointed a slender, bony finger at Tina, "Little one, *Ni'-da-wi*, go out to the front of the cave and pick as many dandelions as you can find." She gave the little girl a soft push back towards the entrance to the cave and pulled Jess by her free hand to a chair set apart from the others in one corner. "Here child, sit here and give your son his dinner."

Jess sat in the chair and let out a small groan of pleasure. It was a canvas sling, suspended on a wooden frame, and then lined with soft furs. It felt delicious. She arranged her wraps, offered Jacob her breast and settled back bliss-fully content in the most comfortable seat she had sat in since the week at old Cooper's place. Her eyes closed and she slowly drifted towards sleep as the others moved about the cave preparing dinner.

Jess was startled awake by a steaming cup of tea thrust under her nose a half hour later. The tea was followed by a hearty bowl of ramen noodles, thick with dandelion greens, and small bits of savory squirrel meat floating in it. They ate in shifts, for there were only two bowls. The light from the natural skylight had dimmed and disappeared as night fell. The fire was built up, and they made little niches of blankets or backpacks to curl up against and stare at the old woman. She had promised them a story, after all. She reached over and plucked Jacob from Jess's arms, cuddling and cooing at him and began to speak.

"One day, the chief of the Quiet Earth people was hunting in the forest. He was looking for a symbol to give life to his people. He came upon the tracks of a giant deer and he became very excited.

'Grandfather Deer,' he said, 'surely you will show yourself to me. You will be the symbol of my people.'

He followed the tracks. His eyes were on nothing else as he followed those tracks, and he ran fast through the forest. Suddenly, he ran right into a huge spider web that stretched between the trees, across the trail. When he got up, he was terribly angry. He struck at the spider who was sitting at the edge of the web. But the spider jumped out of reach. Then the spider spoke.

'Grandson,' the spider said, 'why do you run through the woods looking at nothing but the ground?'

The chief felt foolish, but he answered. 'I was following the tracks of a great deer,' the chief said. 'I am seeking a symbol of strength for my people.'

'I can be such a symbol,' said the spider.

'How can you be a symbol of strength?' said the chief. 'You are small and weak, and I didn't even see you as I followed the great Deer.'

'Grandson,' said the spider, 'look upon me. I am patient. I watch and I wait. Then all things come to me. If your people learn this, they will be strong indeed.'

The chief saw that this was so. And so the spider became one of the symbols of the people."

Madge looked around. Tina was nearly asleep, curled in a ball near the old woman's feet. David was staring attentively and Jess was nearly asleep herself. She smiled at David, "What did you think of the story?"

He didn't smile, instead he looked sad. David thought of the old farmhouse and the blood and of Erin. In his memory, so fresh and raw, he could still hear Jess's screams as she held her friend's hand.

"I should have watched and waited more, but I didn't and then Erin died." The old woman nodded slowly. Jess opened her eyes, stared at David and Madge, but said nothing. She wondered where this was going.

The old woman's voice was kind and matter of fact, "This happens. Many have died this past year and even more will die in the months and years to come. You are young, you are *Min'-dse*, the bow. You bend, and you learn and grow strong. You stay alive, someday you will be *Ku'-rux*, the bear," she smiled at him, then made a fierce face and growled playfully, her wrinkled hands imitating the claws of the bear.

"You will be a fierce warrior. But you must first learn patience, to watch and wait for the right moment; this will make you a strong man someday."

Madge nodded then at Jess and stroked Jacob's sleeping cheek, "You too are young, but you and your family have seen much hardship, will you tell me your story?"

David interjected, "We aren't family. Jess and Erin found Tina and me in Clinton. Our parents are dead. And Erin is dead now too. The soldiers killed her."

The old woman stared at David for a moment, "*Min'-dse*, you are all family now. In the past, my people warred with other tribes. When too many of the warriors died, my tribe would go out and take people from other tribes to adopt and bring into the tribe so that our numbers did not dwindle and be gone forever from this world. You have found each other, bonded together in a common need, and this means that you are family."

She reached down and stroked Tina's hair.

"But it is late and you are all tired. Let us share more stories tomorrow, when our bodies are well-rested."

She pulled herself upright and brought Jacob back to Jess, watching approvingly as Jess carefully folded the infant back into the sling without waking him. She showed them a sleeping chamber that branched off to the left of the large inner chamber. They were surprised to see that the sleeping chamber had six cots in it.

Only one cot had blankets, and it was obviously Madge's cot. Jess and David looked at each other in the flickering lantern light. It felt as if they had hit the jackpot. First, they had eaten a hot, satisfying dinner and now they each had an actual bed to sleep in. They smiled for the first time in days.

Madge bustled about and reached into a box and pulled out blankets for each of them. David went back and woke up Tina and held her hand as she stumbled sleepily into the small dark chamber. Madge had lain down on her cot, and hummed some wordless song for a few minutes, lulling them into sleep. All that could be heard after that was the occasional pop or spit from the fire and the soft splashing of rain.

*"*T*here was something about Madge that spoke security, knowledge, and peace. She knew so much, instantly cared for us and pulled us into her world. We were safe, loved, and protected. I learned more about the ancient people who had occupied this land, and how relevant their lives and knowledge were to us right now, then I ever imagined possible. Somehow too, she helped me find some peace with Erin's death and my part in it. She was a mother, favorite aunt, and revered grandmother all rolled into one. Madge reminded me that family is not always who we are born with, but who we choose to love. She helped me to see how much we all belonged together." – **David's Journal***

The fire crackled merrily, flames licking over the newly added wood. The skylight in the cave showed that dawn had barely arrived, the light was still gray and indistinct when Jess awoke to the sounds of Madge bustling about. She was muttering to herself and had a list and pen in hand. When she looked over and saw Jess's eyes open, she smiled at her, "There is much to do today, child, so much to do. We must make this place into a refuge for you and yours. Winter will be coming soon."

Jess wasn't sure what to say in response. Winter? Stay in a *cave* for a full winter? A nice meal and a night's stay, that was fine, but a full *winter*? She wondered if the old woman was stable. Perhaps she was suffering from dementia or was just old and crazy. With all that had happened, it was a wonder they weren't all crazy. The memory of Erin's empty staring eyes flashed through her mind. And the bodies, so many bodies to the north. How would they ever survive to get past the fighting?

Were there others out there looking for them? As her mind tumbled through its fears and concerns, she began to waver. Perhaps a winter here wasn't such a bad idea. Her thoughts were interrupted by David yawning and stretching at her feet. His eyes widened in momentary fear as he looked around, his sleep-fogged brain not remembering the night before for one short moment.

As the others woke, Jacob kicked and grumbled a moment before letting out a wail of hunger and discomfort. He was wet again and Jess realized they were almost out of diapers.

Madge eyed the dwindling stack of diapers her and added to her list, "We'll need grass and rabbit skin for *Mi'-da-in-ga*, wood for bowls, at least two deer." David had already made his way to her side, reading over the list.

"Who's Meedah, Meedah…" He stumbled over the word.

"*Mi'-da-in-ga*," Madge replied, stressing each syllable, "It means Playful Sun."

"Okay," David looked confused, "Who is that?"

"The little one, the boy. You call him Jacob, yes?" Jess nodded, "Well he needs diapers, and there's no Pampers factory around here. So, we must get sweet grass and rabbit skin for his wraps."

David and Jess exchanged raised eyebrows. In the coming months they would find Madge to be an enormous wealth of information, support, and love. Throughout their stay, however, she would insist on calling them by strange names they had difficulty pronouncing. No matter how often they referred to each other by their given names, she would always respond with a correction. It was her one idiosyncrasy and one that they soon came to accept.

When Tina crossed her legs and looked nervously about, Madge led the children out of the cave and made a sharp turn to the left. The path through the trees was narrow and less than a hundred feet away there was a small opening in the trees. An outhouse sat squarely in the middle of it. Despite its function, it did not emit a smell. Inside the rough-hewn walls was a toilet seat mounted over a bucket filled with sawdust. Beside it was a barrel piled high with clean sawdust. Madge instructed Tina to throw a handful of sawdust down when she had finished and cover any waste.

A few yards from the outhouse there was an outdoor shower. The shower could be used by first pumping water through a small pump from the local stream to a water tower nestled high in the trees. They would do this first thing in the morning and the black walls of the water tower pulled in heat and warmed the water quite efficiently during the warm months. It was usually enough for two showers if they took short ones.

After everyone had had a chance to use the outhouse, Madge directed them back to the cave, stopping only to cut down several swaths of milk thistle along the way. She carried them gingerly, her worn hands encased in thick gloves to avoid being pierced by the thorns.

Breakfast was dandelion tea and thick oatmeal sweetened with some wild berries that David had collected the day before. Madge had stripped the leaves and flowers off of the milk thistle and set them to boiling in a pot over the fire. As they sipped the last of their tea and handed the bowls around, Madge told them about her work as an anthropologist and explained that the cave site was an archaeological dig from the Middle Woodland era (200 B.C. to 450 A.D.).

"I headed a team of five up until a year and a half ago. Things just went from bad to worse in Kansas City, where I was based, and when everything fell apart, I headed up here after the first big thaw in the spring. I was hoping that some of the team might make it back here, but so far no one has. My children are long grown and gone overseas. I haven't heard from any of them for more than a year." Her dark eyes shimmered, "I've been alone here until you children came along."

Quincy quietly gnawed on a small pile of rabbit bones at Jess's feet and then licked the bowls clean after everyone had finished eating.

The next hour was spent sharing their histories with Madge, including the loss of Erin just a few days past. Jess passed Madge the note describing Jess and Erin and listing Belton as their hometown and probably destination.

"We were planning on heading for Belton but with all the fighting...and this note David found on one of the soldiers...I just don't know what to do." Jess confessed, tears in her eyes, "I want to go home, but I'm trying to keep us *out* of danger."

Madge read the note and said nothing for a few minutes. "I haven't seen hide nor hair of another living soul in over four months until you children showed up. And I'm pretty sure that's likely to continue. This cave is not on any of the common maps; it isn't obvious or noticeable from the water line. And the nearest road is a hard-going seven-mile hike from here. It was most certainly used in the past for shelter by my ancestors. That was a long time ago, but I think we could do so again and make it work, even in winter. In the spring you could move on if you liked."

She paused and smiled at them each in turn, "I'm not saying it won't be hard. But if my people lived on this land for centuries, I know we can manage to do it for a few months. I've been fine here all summer and I had packed enough for a team of six, so there are plenty of food stores plus the natural resources nearby. I've been a student of the old ways since I was as young as *Min'-dse* here."

She nodded towards David. "Some hard work and preparation and we will be fine. In the spring, once your trail has grown cold and your pursuers have given up, then you will be free to return to your home in Belton."

Jess was conflicted. Should they try and survive the winter in a cave? Could they actually *do* that? Or should they take their chances heading north again, knowing they could be heading straight into danger? A part of her was exhausted and heartsick. She missed home dreadfully, even though she knew that home might not even be there anymore.

Another part of her simply wanted to stop running and rest for a while. It was exhausting, constantly being afraid of every movement in front of you, behind you, and all around you. To stop and breathe, to sleep in one place each night sounded like heaven to her.

She made eye contact with David and even Tina. Tina was young, but she still had a vote. Both seemed eager to stay in the cave. The thought of heading north and encountering bodies, being caught in a firefight or encountering more like those at the farmhouse, was terrifying to them both. Although they said nothing out loud, the answer on their faces was clear. Jess asked, "So...what will we need to do to prepare for winter?"

Old Madge's face lit up and she pulled the small notebook out of her pocket and began to list off what they would need. It was an odd and varied list and she explained each item in detail. The next few weeks would be filled with frenzied activity, and a great deal of learning.

"You look around you and you see something from long ago. I look at the bones and the history and think of yesterday and tomorrow. What my people knew then, we must know now. Without that knowledge, we cannot survive. The memories of ancestors – how they lived, what they hunted with, even their rituals and legends hold great meaning to us, here and now. Never forget that. It may mean the difference between life and death." – **From the Journal of Dr. Madeleine Falling Water**

By mid-October the nights were quite chilly, but Jess had managed to bag a large buck with one clean shot with Madge's deer rifle, a 94 Winchester model. It was easy once she had thought about their habits. They were active at twilight and at first light.

Conveniently, Jacob was now sleeping a good portion of the night. He woke around 2 a.m. for a feeding and then slept until 8 a.m., sometimes even 9 a.m. Jess had fully recovered from his birth now and the extra time he was sleeping meant she wasn't as sleep-deprived as she had been. Thanks to better living conditions, and nutritious food, she felt energized, especially in this quiet, peaceful place.

Each morning she would get up carefully, nestle Jacob against Madge, and slip out of the cave and down to a stand of trees downwind from the water's edge. She had studied the deer tracks, and it appeared that several of them always came to the same place to drink from the lake.

The first day she headed out too late, and met a surprised buck heading back. The second day she moved at the wrong time, startling the small group of deer before they were in full range of her scope. The third day was success. One shot, into the shoulder as the young buck stood broadside 20 yards away, killed the great animal instantly.

She stood over its body, thankful at the magnificent creature's quick death. No suffering, and the animal was dead before it hit the ground. The hunting she and Erin had done at the cabin had not included deer. Not because they weren't around, and Erin had certainly wanted to try, but the .22 Rimfire was far too small of a caliber to be an effective and humane kill. Jess smiled sadly at the thought of her friend. Erin would have been so proud of her right now.

They had all quickly become familiar with the area and moved about the surrounding woods with assurance once Madge showed them other signs that would indicate the location of the cave if any of them got turned around or confused. There were notches on trees, rock piles, and rags tied to branches to help point them back to the rock shelter.

The cave was extensive. The back of the sleeping chamber led to three additional chambers – a section used to store dried foods was on the left and then the passage emptied onto a second small chamber which contained another dig site. Madge explained that it was a sacred burial site and asked them not to go any further than the food storage chamber. Beyond the burial chamber there was another chamber that had collapsed.

"The burial site and beyond are not only sacred, but also in danger of collapse," Madge explained, "We had to abandon efforts in that area until we could get it shored up better." She looked sad, "And, of course, I couldn't do it on my own."

The thought of the cave collapsing was frightening until Madge explained the architecture of the cave and showed them the supports that had already been put into place.

"As long as we don't get a major earthquake, like the New Madrid earthquake in 1811-1812, we'll be just fine here."

She smiled crookedly, "If an earthquake that size hits, well, let's just say it's the last thing any of us will have to worry about. Even outside wouldn't be safe. That 1811-1812 series toppled millions of acres of forest."

The rest of the cave traveled for miles. There was another large passage leading west from the back of the large inner chamber. David followed the stream with a lantern in hand for several hundred yards until it disappeared into a rock wall. The cave continued for miles, Madge informed them, but warned them of the dangers of becoming lost in the different passages and sub-chambers that branched off in different directions.

One night, not long after they had decided to stay for the winter, David had dreamed of Erin. It had been more of a memory really. He had never spoken of what had happened in the farmhouse and Jess had never asked. He awoke with a shout and it had startled Jacob enough that the baby began to wail.

It was early, the sun was barely peeking over the horizon and he slipped out past the campfires and through the small entrance to the outer chamber. He knelt near one of the pits and stared into it. The sections were neatly marked and he could see that one of the pits held a small skeleton. Next to it was a spear and what appeared to be the remains of woven grass moccasins. He stared at the hole and tried to forget the dream.

A few minutes later, Madge's bony hand on his shoulder caused him to flinch. Jacob had stopped crying; perhaps he had been lulled back to sleep.

"*Mind'se*, you are troubled by your dreams. A burden shared can be a burden halved. Will you share with me what yours is?"

David fought the tears welling up inside him. "It was just a dream." He wiped at his eyes with the back of his shirt. It smelled and was stiff with dirt. He needed to wash it soon.

"It was more than a dream, *Mind'se*, it was about what happened at the farmhouse and how Erin died, wasn't it?"

The old woman was persistent. She had watched David for weeks and knew that whatever had happened in that farmhouse was eating at him. He pushed himself so hard, helping out wherever needed and sinking into his cot each night exhausted from work that would have tired a full-grown man. It was as if he were trying to atone for something.

"I...yes...I." He couldn't even put the words to it, "It was my fault. Erin died and it was my fault."

Madge sighed and tugged at him until he turned and faced her. She met his eyes with her soft brown, liquid ones, "Do you trust me?"

"Uh, yeah, I mean, I guess so."

Her face was solemn, "Tell me what happened and I will tell you the truth of it. If you were responsible, then you must unburden yourself *Mind'se*. Do you trust me to be objective, to tell you honestly what I think?"

He had held it in his heart for far too long and it came spilling out then, the memory of that afternoon tearing from him in great gasps of pain and guilt.

"I wanted to explore the farmhouse. I had done it dozens of times in town, there in Clinton. I'd seen bodies, even found some houses where people were living and they'd just told me to go away or given me a can of food and told me to not come back. We were in the middle of nowhere, so I figured, 'why not?' right?"

The boy's tears poured forth as fast as his words. "Erin wasn't far behind me but she headed for the farmhouse and I headed for the barn. I had wanted to find a small shovel. I saw one, but it was mounted high and I was trying to find something to climb on. Before I could do that, I heard Erin scream."

David gulped; his cheeks wet with tears and wiped his nose on his shirt. Madge reached out and patted his shoulder, "Go on."

"I went in through the back, as quiet as I could and I was scared, real scared. I wanted to run, but I knew she didn't have a gun, nothing to fight back with. And I know those soldiers, the ones Jess and Erin got away from. They did bad things...they," he looked down at the ground, unable to even speak it out loud.

"They did terrible things. Yes." Madge's answer was soft and forthright. "You were brave to go in, *Mind'se.*"

"I killed one of them." He looked scared then, his eyes darting to her face and searching for any recrimination but there was none. "I'm not sorry I killed him. But it didn't matter 'cause Erin still died. She saw him aiming at me and ran towards him."

His voice rose in pitch, "She died trying to save *me.* What if all they were gonna do was take her back with them? If I had run back to Jess, warned her, we could have stopped them together."

"Oh, *Mind'se...David,* you are..." the old woman's eyes filled with tears, "You are not to blame, my brave one. You did what was right and what was brave. You did what a *warrior* would do."

She placed her thin, bony hands on each side of his head, stroking his tangled unkempt hair. How long had this child been without parents to love and protect him? And how had he risen to the occasion, willing to take so much on and expect so much from himself?

"You are not to blame," she repeated firmly, "They would have taken her to a place far worse. They would have done unspeakable things to her and they would have killed her in the end. Never blame yourself again for this."

Behind her, Jess had appeared at the rock entrance. She had heard it all, the details she had dreaded asking about and yet wished she had known. To hear how it had all played out was as much of a relief as it was painful. She knew she had blamed him, in some small corner of her heart, and been afraid to ask for fear she would truly hate him if she knew the truth of it. Instead, she found she was relieved. He had tried to protect Erin, just as she had given her life to protect him in return. Madge had said they were a family and she was right. They were. She placed her hand on David's shoulder, startling him. Madge looked up at her, her old face lined with wrinkles, a question in her eyes.

"Madge is right, David." She said, tears in her own eyes, her voice unsteady. "Family protects family. That's what you did for Erin and that is what she chose to do for you. We are a family. And I wouldn't have it any other way."

It was a healing moment for all of them. The days and weeks that followed slowly became happy ones as the odd, mismatched band grew to know each other better and make new, gentler memories.

One of the other anthropologists had been an avid bow hunter and Madge had his bow and arrows. They were composed of an ultra-modern, lightweight substance and she encouraged Jess and David to practice with targets daily.

After watching him practice, she clucked in approval to Jess, "*Min'-dse* is grown beyond his years, he knows when to be quiet and listen and watch. His aim improves each day."

By the end of their second week at the cave the boy insisted on carrying the bow and arrows with him everywhere. As Jess and Madge fished on the edge of the lake early one morning he moved quietly along the southern edge and disappeared into the forest. Quincy followed silently behind.

Tina watched him go, "He been practicin' walking so he don't make any sound at all." Madge just smiled and patted Tina's head, running her bony hands through the little girl's short, brown curls. The months the two children had spent alone had left the small child with a mane of filthy, matted, dreadlocked hair. They had finally given up on getting the worst of the mats out and cut it short the week before. Tina had cried during the entire ordeal. But at least now they could keep it under control.

Madge kept the little girl busy pulling grass and collecting plants while Jess fished. She had fashioned her own fur-lined sling for Jacob and cooed and sang to him. This gave Jess a relief from the constant care.

She was surprised, since up to this point, Jacob would tolerate no one holding him but Jess. He still screamed if David or Tina tried to pick him up, but with Madge he was content unless he needed to nurse.

Madge pointed at different plants and explained their uses to Tina, who despite her young age, listened and watched intently. Jess pulled out three good-sized small-mouthed bass and dumped them into a bucket of water. They kept a lid on it to prevent the fish from jumping back out. Jacob squawked in hunger and Madge had just handed him to Jess when they heard a loud 'whoop' and Quincy let out one sharp double-bark.

"I got one! I got one! Oh wow! *I got one*!" they could hear David's voice in the distance; he couldn't have been more than a hundred yards away. Jacob squalled in frustration as Jess paused and looked into the woods. A deer? With only a bow and arrow? No way. She looked at Madge, who smiled smugly, and waved her fingers at Jess to go ahead and feed the baby.

"Three is enough fish for now," she said, reeling in the line, "Besides, it's around ten, they'll be moving towards deeper waters now. You sit and feed *Mi'-da-in-ga* and I'll go help *Min'-dse*, who is living up to his name so well." She beckoned to Tina, "*Ni'-da-wi*, come, we will help your brother dress his first kill." She took the little girl's hand and they quickly disappeared into the trees.

It was past noon when all three of them re-appeared, Quincy leading the way. The little dog's tail wagged furiously, and from the blood on her muzzle, she had already had a fresh treat. David was strutting. His small chest jutted forward, his shoulders were high and his back straight, his eyes shining with pride. Madge was grinning too, proud as a mother hen. They had rigged a bower of sorts and they dragged the deer carcass behind them. It was partially dressed, and Jess blinked at the surreal scene. Before her were one old woman, two little kids, one dead deer, and one hell of a lot of blood caking them and the mutt running circles around their feet. The corners of her mouth curled up, damned if he hadn't gotten that deer after all. And with only a bow and arrow!

Lunch was an abbreviated observance. They ate quickly and got to work skinning and butchering the enormous buck. Jess's stomach roiled a bit, and David actually looked as if he were about to be sick.

He gulped hard and got back to work. That seemed to impress Madge even more than the kill. They set up the meat in a smoke hut just ten yards south of the cave. Madge's team member had built it two years ago and had supplemented their packaged food with fresh out of season deer during the past two dig seasons.

Little of the deer went to waste, and Madge even knew how to preserve the hide, which Jess paid special attention to. Later that winter it would come in handy during the cold nights. They were finally finished by late afternoon and David and Madge prepared the bass, stuffed with wood sorrel, wild carrot and other fresh edibles that Madge and Tina had gathered. They feasted on the succulent fish and as they finished Madge turned to David and made a small bow in his direction, with great formality, "*Min'-dse*, you have lived up to your name truly this day. The spirit of this great deer was sacrificed so that we might all live. Will you tell us now of how you accomplished this great deed?"

Story time, as Madge called it, had become a daily theme for the little group. Usually, Madge would tell them a story about her ancestors, other times she encouraged Jess or David to tell a story that they knew. Jess soon found herself remembering the tales from the Grimm's Brothers and Hans Christian Anderson. David would often share a portion of Harry Potter, especially the first three books. His mother had grown up with the series, attending the movies into her teens and been excited to share them with him. The nightly story time had begun to include props and theatrics, and everyone looked forward to what performance the evening would bring.

He grinned, "Okay, sure." He looked around, thought for a minute, and then stood before beginning, "I walked into the dark forest, quietly, without making a sound. I had seen the deer before and I had followed his tracks a few days ago. I knew if I walked quietly, he wouldn't know I was there and I'd have the best chance at a good, clean shot." He looked around at the small group, and Jess nodded to him encouragingly. "So, I walked about a hundred yards in and found a good place to keep a lookout, somewhere I knew the deer would come by if he wanted to go drink from the lake. I sat for a long time; I was about to give up when Quincy whined quietly. I looked down at her and she was pointing, with her foot, and when I looked at where she was pointing it was the deer! I had the bow and arrow ready in my hands and I raised it up, took aim, made sure, and then let the arrow fly!" He yelled then, "And THWACK! It hit him in his chest!"

Jacob woke with a fitful cry from the yell, nuzzled at Jess's breast, and fell back asleep. David looked sheepish until Jess grinned at him, "You did *great*, David, really, and you were amazing. I never thought an arrow could kill a big deer like that."

The boy lit up, glowing with pride. He went on to describe how Madge helped him send a prayer of thanks to the deer's spirit for giving its life for them. Night had fallen by now and the fire was a lone light in thick darkness. As they settled down for the night, dampening the fire and snuggling under blankets, Jess heard David yawn and comment, "I really think we need at least one more deer to get us through winter, though." The fire crackled quietly; Tina burrowed under the blanket in a small ball against her big brother. They were safe, well-fed, and happy.

Far, far away, guns cracked off shots and bullets tore through flesh and bone. But the little band heard none of this, only the crackle of the fire and the occasional hoot of a nearby owl.

Christmas Presents and Shotguns

"*All weddings, except those with shotguns in evidence, are wonderful.*" – *Liz Smith*

"Oh! Brr!" Carrie closed the door to the house behind her and handed Joseph the basket of eggs. "I hate the cold!" She rubbed her arms vigorously and pushed past Chris to get near the stove. Chris kept his distance. The last few weeks, Carrie had been a bit *off*. It felt as if she had drawn a perimeter which included a warning alarm in case anyone got too close. Snappy and tense, she had projected a clear warning to *stay away*.

The instant he let it slip he knew there would be trouble. It was just one small, tiny little snort. But out it came and he immediately regretted it. She turned on him, "Oh, and what are *you* laughing about?"

Man, oh man, women should come with early warning systems. Or a manual at least. How would it read?

The human female, as she enters the beginning of her monthly menstrual cycle is a dangerous and unpredictable creature. The utmost care and concern must be shown at this time towards the female. The employment of calming methods, such as the introduction of chocolate at moments of extreme duress, coupled with a shift in attitude toward a more submissive posture from the male of the species, will avoid conflict. Under no circumstances should you engage in an argument with a pre-menstrual female. Avoidance and flight are perfectly acceptable solutions enabling one to escape with all reproductive parts intact.

Chris saw that Carrie was now glaring...at him...and tapping her foot, expecting an answer. He realized two things at once. One, he had just stood there like an idiot for about a minute, fantasizing about a manual that unfortunately did not exist. And two, he had some stupid shit-eating grin on his face, which looked as if it was further adding to her anger.

"I...uh..."

"Yes?" The yes sounded like a hiss and he knew he was in deep kimchee. Hmmm, maybe the truth would be best.

"I just thought it was funny 'cause you and Liza and Joseph are from New York and it gets really cold there. Winter down here is a walk in the park, right?"

His brain tuned out the words, but not the vision of her angry face yelling at him. He just stood there, let her yell, and waited until she had stalked off. It was the same response you might see from a deer that freezes, dead in the sights of a hunter, hoping beyond all hope that the hunter will somehow not see him, or perhaps take pity on him and let him go. No such luck, at least, not for this human animal. God, how he wished there was a manual.

"Boy," Fenton snorted close by his ear, "Haven't you got a lick of sense?"

"Sir?"

"Never say what's on your mind to a woman in that state of mind. Might as well commit, what's that word…mahi mahi?"

Liza chimed in, "Mahi-mahi is a fish, Gramps. You mean hara-kiri, or seppuku, which was the ritual disembowelment reserved only for samurai…"

"Got it, Liz. Thanks." Chris interrupted, head hurting from another female voice. No matter that it was a friendly one. "Gramps, if this is PMS, she's been having it for *weeks*. It's like everything I say or do irritates her."

"Give it time, son, give it time. Only God knows the minds of women, and I gotta wonder if even he doesn't get confused off and on." Fenton thought of Molly, dead for more than thirty years, and smiled wryly, "I can remember bein' in hot water a time or two, myself." Seemed like after they took out all her reproductive parts, it wasn't regular at all, she'd get mad anytime anywhere, or be preternaturally calm, you never could tell.

They cooked lunch and sat down at the table together, even Carrie, who just sat and simmered at one end. Not much was said as they passed sandwich fixings around the table and enjoyed the rich flavor of the pulled pork. One of the largest pigs, Butt Roast, had been slaughtered, cleaned and cured a few weeks ago when the temperatures dipped down into the 40s.

It had been a toss-up between who would be slaughtered, Butt Roast or Applewood Bacon, until they weighed them. Butt Roast tipped the scales at 225 pounds and Applewood Bacon had only weighed 202. He was slated for an early spring slaughter. Chris had been amused to discover that they named the pigs after food. It made sense, though.

One of the other pig's name was Pork Chop and another Ham Hock. It kept the endgame in plain sight. These creatures weren't pets, they were food.

Chris kept stealing glances at Carrie and looking at just the wrong times. After the third glance she startled everyone by shouting, "What?!"

"Nothing!" Chris snapped back. God, he felt like an idiot. What in the hell was he doing wrong, anyway? Why was she so pissed at him?

Fenton cleared his throat, scowled at his eldest grandchild, and asked Chris, "You said something about going into town today?"

"Yes sir. I mean...Gramps." He usually got it right, but in moments of high stress, like he'd been having for the past *three* weeks, he fell back on the crisp and forceful "Sir!" he'd learned as a conscript. "I was planning on a little Christmas shopping and figured I'd get in some bartering with that hog."

Liza chimed in, "I'll go with you, Chris. I've got books to trade." She tried not to look too eager, but Chris knew she was hoping to visit Carl Owens, a friend from school and fellow book geek. They would trade books all right, and some gropes and kisses as well if he wasn't mistaken. Carl was two years older and he had been visiting often in the last few months. He had helped out on the farm during harvest. He was a nice kid.

"It's settled then," Chris said, "Liza and I will go, and..."

"What about me?" Carrie looked resentful, "Did you even think of asking what I want? I mean, I..."

"Carrie Lynn Perdue," Fenton stopped the beginning tirade dead in its tracks, "You have been a right large pain in the patoot recently. If you were Joseph's age, I'd send you to your room and tell you to come out when you had a new attitude. As it is, I don't know what to say to you, 'ceptin to shut it and get yourself away 'til you got a civil tongue in your mouth."

Carrie sat there, tears forming in her eyes, opened and shut her mouth like she was about to say something, then stood up, knocking her chair back with a crash, and bolted from the room down the hall to her bedroom. Everyone sat in shock for a moment, Joseph wide-eyed, and they stared down the now-empty hall.

"Gramps!" Liza looked devastated, "You made her cry!" Chris held himself back from pointing out that everything nowadays made her cry. She'd cried the last time they made love, she'd cried over burning bread, and she'd cried a river when they'd slaughtered Butt Roast even though that damned pig had bit her twice just the month before.

Fenton looked a bit chagrined, but said nothing as he finished his pork sandwich and licked the barbecue sauce off his fingers. He stood up, leaned over and picked up Carrie's chair and then took hold of her plate.

"I'll go talk to her. Joseph, you get the rest of the dishes to the sink. Liza, Chris, you best get on your way. Take the buggy it will be quicker and it gets dark 'bout five these days. Y'all want to get back before it's too dark to see anything."

Liza had a stack of books ready to go by the door. She pulled on a coat and shoved half of the stack into Chris's arms once he had finished zipping his coat. Outside they quickly loaded up the wrapped pieces of pork haunch they wanted to use for trade. They didn't need much in the way of staples right now, but Chris had a very specific present in mind for this visit.

He had seen the ring at the Trade Mart two weeks ago when they were there stocking up for the winter. It wasn't your typical wedding ring of diamonds and gold. Instead, what had struck him and drawn him in was the amazing color of green of the emerald set in the center. It was a square cut emerald, with four fair-sized diamonds, two on each side, set in a white gold band.

The emerald's color was a rich, forest green. He had gazed at it and felt as if he were staring into Carrie's eyes. Her eye color changed, depending on her mood, from an almost lime green when she was mad to the deep forest green of the emerald right after they made love.

It seemed that lately, all he had seen was the lime green, which snapped with lightning and fire.

When Liza broke the silence, he realized they had already left the farm far behind. "You're getting the ring today, right?" She was the only one he had confided in, mainly because she had seen him talking with the woman who owned it while Carrie was deep in bargaining for flour and sugar with one of the other town folk. The old woman had elicited the promise from him that he build her a new chicken coop and bring her ten pounds of pork and five laying hens in the spring in exchange for the ring. The coop would be easy, and she had agreed to wait for another month for that. But the 'deposit' on the ring was the pork and he aimed to deliver it in time to pick up the ring and give it to Carrie for Christmas.

"Yeah, I'm getting the ring."

He paused, thinking about Carrie's incredible mood swings lately. Well mainly they had swung between depressed to irritable, and sometimes plain insane.

"Liza, do you think something's wrong with Carrie? I mean, do you think she still wants to marry me?"

The teenager snorted, "Are you kidding? Carrie loves you. And you love her. If anything, I'll bet she's just wondering why you haven't gotten around to asking her yet."

"But I did. At the end of September. I asked her and she said yes." Liza's neck snapped towards him so quickly he was afraid she had whiplash.

"You asked Carrie to marry you?" Her hands had gone slack on the reins but the horse plodded on. They were almost to the site of the burned out Western Front trucks and not too far from town. Ichabod knew the way by heart.

"Well yeah. And she said yes, but I didn't have a ring then. I've been look-ing for one, and..." His voice faded weakly away in the face of yet another an-gry Perdue woman.

"Have you two, you know, *done* it?" Liza asked, looking angry and a tiny bit scared.

"Well...umm...yeah."

"When? How often? Did you use protection?" The questions came hard and fast and Chris felt like he was talking to his mother, not a fourteen-year-old girl. This was crazy, why had he even said anything?

Now she was going to be mad at him too and he didn't know what the hell he had done wrong this time either.

"Liza...I'm not...I shouldn't be talking about this with you."

"Christopher Michael Aaronson," now she sounded like Fenton, "Just answer the damned question."

Jesus, he seemed to be in for it again. "September, around harvest time. When your Gramps got hurt in the barn. And well, a couple times since," that was a terrible understatement, "and do you *see* any protection around here?"

He had even checked with the Trade Mart, carefully of course, to see if he could trade for condoms. No such luck and the pharmacy, what was left of the burned-out shell, was laughable.

"Shit."

"What?!" He was getting frustrated, and pissed. Both of them on his ass, ripping his head off and shitting down his neck, damn but...

"Carrie is pregnant." Chris's mind went blank. They passed the lookouts and Liza collected herself enough to wave at them and jostled Chris to do the same. He put up a hand and waved woodenly, his mind completely and totally overwhelmed. Pregnant? Pregnant! Oh God, *pregnant*.

Liza spoke again, "And worse yet, Gramps is talking to her right now. Sure as anything, it will come out and he'll just shoot you before he bothers askin' questions." She shook her head, "Damn Chris, I thought you were smarter than that." She patted his leg, "Been nice knowing you."

"Oh, thanks so much for the vote of confidence," he replied sarcastically, and his bowels twisted.

She grinned at him then, "Now when you see the shotgun, run, I'll try and buy you some time, maybe a few hundred yards, enough to make it to the tree line. And remember, avoid the lake, we know you don't do well out there." She was grinning now, obviously remembering how they had found him, laid up with a broken ankle after taking a fall in the bog they still insisted on calling a lake.

"Ha, ha, ha, geez Liza, you are just so damn funny." He glared at her, his mind still reeling. He sobered, "Do you really think she's pregnant?"

They were nearly in town and he said it quietly, under his breath in case anyone heard their conversation. There were a few folks walking, wrapped up like it was an arctic winter, rather than a cool thirty degrees out.

Liza nodded, with a smirk, "Oh yeah. I remember Mom getting that way when she got pregnant with Joseph. Had Dad running scared until they both figured out what the hell was going on. Dad had a vasectomy after I was born, so it didn't even *dawn* on them what was happening until she was a few months along. So much for a vasectomy being foolproof. Did you know that shit can grow back? Anyway, Carrie's never been what you'd call regular with her periods, so if she knows, she's just now figured it out."

"Why wouldn't she tell me, though?" Chris protested, "I mean, we love each other. I'm not going anywhere, I want to marry her, and I figured eventually that also meant having babies with her." He stopped then, imagining Carrie's stomach swelling full and round, thought of the child growing inside and months from now, the feel of a tiny baby nestled in his arms. Blond hair, and would her eyes be blue like his or green like Carrie's? For some reason he couldn't imagine a boy, only a girl. A girl who could wrap his heart around her little finger, and...

"Hell Chris, I don't know why she wouldn't tell you. Maybe she's scared. There aren't any hospitals nearby. I mean I know I've been studying, but I'm not a full-on doctor. Hell, I'm not even a midwife.

And maybe she's afraid you don't want kids, that you won't love her if she goes and gets fat."

"Pregnant isn't fat. Pregnant is beautiful." He said it forcefully, and a bit louder than he intended, one woman looked at them curiously as they passed.

"Oh Chris," Liza sighed. Chris made Carl look like such an idiot, and she *liked* Carl, a *lot*. Chris had a way of making everyone feel special, loved, and accepted. She smiled up at him.

"Just get the ring. We'll go back home and it will all work out, you'll see. She loves you and you love her. Despite all of Gramps' tough words, he approves of you. He knows you love Carrie as much as he does."

She pulled on the reins and stopped the horse. They were a block from the Trade Mart. "I'm going to Carl's; I'll meet you in an hour at the Trade Mart." She slipped down out of the seat after handing Chris the reins.

As the buggy pulled away, Liza called after him, "Don't get into trouble!" He just waved at her in dismissal. For only being fourteen years old, the girl was already a mother hen. It seemed to run in the family.

The Trade Mart was busy, and the street was full of town folk. There was barely room for Ichabod to be strapped to the bike rack, but he managed to find a spot that required a bit of a squeeze. The horse wasn't going anywhere until he was done.

Chris stopped by the hardware store and dropped off half of a sweet potato pie that Carrie and Liza had made the night before for Mr. Liles. The ancient man was close to entering his 106th year, which blew Chris's mind. Most of the old man's teeth were gone so sweet potato pie was right up his alley.

The bent and fragile old man had visited the farm twice in the summer, but the onset of winter slowed him down and confined him to town. He was a bit of a celebrity, considering his advanced age, and the rest of the town folk pitched in to keep him fed and warm in his little apartment above the hardware store. He spent a few minutes talking with the old man, relayed Fenton and the rest of the family's greetings and promised to bring chicken soup on his next visit. One of the chickens wasn't producing eggs as much as she used to, it was time to make way for other younger layers. Old Otis loved Carrie's homemade chicken noodle soup and asked about it whenever they visited, no matter the weather. He said his goodbyes and headed toward the Trade Mart.

As he walked in the door, he saw a familiar, unwelcome face – Wes Perkins. The man had added another knife to his collection, he was practically his own armory with two long hunting knives, a short tiny curved knife in a sheath, and today he was sporting what looked like a .44 Magnum *and* the ubiquitous rifle he carried with him everywhere.

At least this time Chris didn't feel so under-dressed for the occasion. Carrie had given him a ruggedly wicked hunting knife the month of their 'anniversary.' He had been embarrassed that he hadn't remembered and didn't have something to give her in return. It was probably the lack of gift or remembering that it had been exactly one month since they made love for the first time that had started the emotional roller coaster they had been on ever since. He also had begun carrying a M1911, a .45 caliber, well-maintained pistol that Fenton had used in Vietnam.

There had been reports of isolated attacks by deserters or small bands of men. They were usually in search of food or ammunition. They would sneak in, take what they wanted and usually leave without engaging the locals, but one girl had been raped and another older couple had been killed. Both attacks had occurred within the last month. Fenton had made sure everyone, except for Joseph, was armed at all times, around the farm or off the property.

Chris met Wes's unfriendly stare with an equally calm one. He would stand his ground, and fuck Wes if he didn't like it.

Wes began to move forward and intercept Chris. He probably wanted to stop him from entering the Trade Mart. But Mrs. Jennings had spied him at that moment and called across the store, gesturing for him to come and see her. She smiled at him and he ignored Wes and strode over.

"Christopher! How are you?"

Not everyone in the town was an asshole like Perkins. Alice Jennings was a widower, with no children. She was also Tiptonville's librarian.

She looked around, "Where's Liza? I have a book for her."

"She'll be here soon, Miz Jennings." He gave her a light hug, "She's visiting a friend."

Alice sighed, "I imagine it's that Owens boy. Ah, young love. A bit of a nerd, but then, so is Liza, bless that child. I found a book for her that will fill in her education nicely."

She reached back to a shelf and pulled out the book, "Here it is, 'Epidemiology: Beyond the Basics.'" She started to hand it to him.

"She'll be here soon, Miz Jennings, would you like to give it to her yourself?"

"Oh yes, dear, that will be fine. In fact," she nodded, shelving the book, "I really need to check if she is ready to move away from obstetrics or if she was interested in advanced surgical procedures next."

She stared at him for a moment, and he waited patiently, "Oh dear, I'm sorry, you want the ring, don't you dear?"

"Yes ma'am, I brought the piece you asked for," he handed the neatly wrapped pork section over to her. "And I can come by after Christmas and start on the coop."

Her eyes lit up, "Oh Christopher, it's far more meat then I had asked for! Are you sure?" She was thin, and Chris wondered if she ate much meat at all these days.

"Fenton wrapped it and sends his regards. He sure appreciates all you've been doing for Liza." The old man had been impressed with the large tomes of medical information that Liza was slowly absorbing and discussing. His forehead wound had been sutured so neatly that there was only a tiny reddish scar that remained.

"Oh, it is nice to have such an apt pupil. Liza is quite a brilliant young woman, you know." At that moment, Liza appeared at his elbow.

"Well thanks, Miz Jennings!" She immediately spied the book on epidemiology. Alice had partially shelved it, but it was sticking out prominently from the rest, "Oh my, you found the epidemiology book!"

Her eyes sparkled. Most girls would look like that over a new dress or shoes, but Liza was not like most girls. Alice handed her the book and the girl thumbed through the table of contents with intense interest, "Ooh, multiple regression techniques...and it has an appendix for the test of homogeneity of stratified estimates!" She looked up and grinned at Chris and Alice, "This is perfect! Thank you!"

"Careful there, Liza, your inner geek is showing."

Her grin turned to a glare. Alice finally remembering what Chris had been so patiently waiting for reached into her pockets and pulled out a small box.

"Christopher dear, I shined it up for you." She handed the box over. It was brown leather, worn in spots, "I tried to find a box to put it in, dear, and I'm sorry, this is the best I could find."

Liza gasped as he opened the box. The emerald and diamonds were blindingly brilliant. "A little toothpaste and water are all it took." Alice's voice sounded a bit misty, Chris was too distracted by the ring to notice the woman's tears, but Liza did, and put her hand on the old woman's arm. Larry Jennings had died nearly two years ago, and Alice still missed him terribly.

Chris stared at the ring, everything inside of him churning. God, he hoped she liked it. What if she didn't? What if she wanted something more traditional? Liza's voice reassured his fears, "Chris, it's beautiful. It matches her eyes exactly!" He looked over at the girl and relaxed. If Liza, a geeky, sci-fi and epidemiology textbook-loving non-girly girl thought it was beautiful, then it had to be special.

Chris knew a lot of things. He knew about war and fighting, he knew hard work and how to fix leaks and raise crops. He knew football. But he was absolutely sure of his own ignorance when it came to women's jewelry. He also had no idea that, if this part of the world had still run on cold hard cash, he would have had to fork over a lot of it. He was holding a ring worth nearly $5,000.

He didn't know that Alice Jennings had been given the ring by her mother. He didn't realize how special the ring was to the old woman or even that the emerald that was mounted in the ring was her birthstone.

Chris only knew that it had spoken to him, reminded him of Carrie's eyes after they made love or kissed or laughed. He desperately hoped Carrie would like it and that Fenton wouldn't shoot him before he had a chance to give it to her. He smiled at Alice Jennings, "Thank you ma'am, thank you so much."

She smiled in return and patted his cheek softly, "You are welcome, young Christopher. Do bring her in after you've given it to her, I would so like to see it on her hand."

"Yes, ma'am, I will." They said their goodbyes and headed towards the exit. Chris had snapped the box shut and put it away carefully in his jacket. He was in the process of zipping the coat when Wes Perkins stepped into his path.

"Maybe you should watch where you're going, *soldier*." Wes stood a good half of a head taller and smelled dangerous. It was a sharp, gunpowder and oil scent. He was close, purposely so, he stood inside Chris's personal space and it was an obvious challenge. Chris felt Liza's hand settle on his sleeve.

"We need to be getting back home now, Mr. Perkins." She said it with a level voice, but there was a slight tremor in her hand. She was afraid for Chris. Around them there was a lull in conversation. Chris could feel a dozen sets of eyes, watching and saying nothing.

Wes ignored Liza, he glared at Chris, tried to stare him down. Liza tugged on Chris's arm, "C'mon, Chris. Let's *go*." She tugged on his sleeve firmly. Chris allowed her to pull him to the right and around Perkins, keeping eye contact until Liza jerked him insistently through the door and down the street.

"All right, all right, you can stop walking me like a dog on a leash, now." He snapped at her irritably as she attempted to shove him up into the buggy. "I'm going already." Liza's face was pale.

"Let's just get out of here. Now." She was shaking.

"Okay, okay. Chill out. We're going, we're going." His good mood had vanished. What the fuck was up with that guy anyway? It was like Perkins *knew* he had been in the Western Front. And that wasn't possible, no one knew but the Perdue's and they sure as hell weren't going to say anything.

The ride out of town was uneventful, but it was tense and silent. They passed the lookouts and the awful burned wrecks of trucks. The burned and blackened skeletons still hung from the windows or lay crushed underneath. Chris's stomach turned every time he saw it. The town had left them there on purpose, as a warning, but it made him sick to see it. No matter what those men had done, they were people, they had been alive and breathing. It didn't seem right to leave their bodies out there, exposed to the elements and not given a proper burial. Then again, he had heard some of the stories, whispered to him by the girls when Fenton wasn't around. The Western Front had done terrible things to the citizens of Tiptonville. They had more than earned the hatred the townspeople felt towards them.

He glanced over at Liza and saw a tear trickle down her nose, then another and another. They were still over a mile from the farm. He pulled Ichabod to a stop, turned and looked at her. The girl was hunched over, arms crossed in front of her protectively, and as she noticed his gaze she began to sob hysterically.

"What the..." Chris sighed and closed his eyes; this was definitely not his day to deal with the Perdue women. "Look Liza, everything's fine, the guy is an asshole, don't worry about it."

"He knows."

"What? What does he know?"

"That you were in the Western Front."

He started to scoff, then stopped and tried to meet her eyes. They flicked up, saw his, and dropped to the buggy floor and she began to cry even harder. "Liza...what did you do?"

"It's what I didn't do. I mean I *tried* to burn the clothes. Oh God! Gramps is gonna kill me!"

"Liza..." he grabbed her shoulders, turned her towards him and forced her to meet his eyes, "*I'm* gonna kill you if you don't tell me what the heck you are talking about."

It rushed out in one large torrent, "I didn't burn the clothes! Your uniform. I mean, I *tried*, and they were burning and I heard someone coming so I ran away quick. They must have seen the fire, put it out and found the clothes. "

He gave her a small shake, "Must have?"

She cried harder, "When I went back the next day to check, the clothes were gone."

Chris closed his eyes. "Crap, crap, crap. Double crap. Triple crap...shit!"

"You hate me, don't you?" Liza sounded so tiny, so childlike and fearful. He opened his eyes and saw her wincing in his grasp.

"No Liza, I don't hate you." He struggled to explain his emotions, "I'm worried. I'm scared I've brought trouble to your door, to all of you, and I don't know what to do."

"I'll tell Gramps."

"We'll tell Fenton together. Right after I propose to Carrie and right before he shoots me for knocking up his eldest grandchild." He managed a small smile, "Like you said earlier, it will all work out." That earned him a weak laugh in return.

He set Ichabod to a nice trot and the last twenty minutes were spent with cracks about shotguns and ducking for cover. As they entered the private road that led straight through to the farmhouse Chris could see he wasn't too far from being right. Fenton had had enough time to not only clean the shotgun but reassemble it. It was resting across his folded arms and the old man looked pissed.

Liza took it all in and summed it up in one succinct word, which she muttered under her breath, "Shit."

"Elizabeth Molly Ann Perdue," Fenton barked, "you know I can read lips." Liza winced in response. "Boy, you have got some explaining to do." He caressed the barrel of the shotgun and adjusted it so that it aimed, ever so slightly, in Chris's direction.

"You better show him what you got, Chris, *now*." Liza whispered.

But Chris had a different idea about how this was all going to play out.

"No." He climbed down from the buggy, unbuckled the knife and pistol and set them up on the seat next to Liza. "Sir, I would like to speak with Carrie, please."

Fenton pursed his lips, reached over and yanked the door to the farmhouse open and bellowed for her. A moment later she appeared her eyes puffy and red. They widened when they saw Fenton's shotgun.

Chris wasted no time. He strode to the porch, knelt on his knee at the top step, and looked up into Carrie's eyes. "I'm sorry it took me this long to find it. I love you, Carrie Lynn Perdue. So...please," he fished the box out of his pocket and held it up to her, "Will you marry me before your grandfather goes and put me out of his misery?" This earned a choked laugh from Liza and Carrie and an angry grunt from Fenton.

Carrie reached out and took the box from his hand, opening it slowly, and gasping when she did. "Oh my God, it's beautiful!"

Chris sighed, partially in relief, and then in exasperation as she began to cry. Why did they always have to cry? She pulled him up to her and hugged him violently.

He could feel her tears soaking his neck and he struggled to breathe as she clung to him and cried harder, "Yes, yes, yes! I'll marry you!"

"Young woman, don't you have some news of your own?" Fenton *still* sounded pissed. Carrie jumped a little at his voice, and pulled away from Chris, looking a little scared.

"I'm uh," She struggled to utter the words, "I'm pretty sure I'm pregnant."

Her eyes searched his eyes for rejection or anger. She had been afraid to tell him; afraid he would leave or maybe not want to have kids. They had never talked about it and they were both so young, something that Gramps had repeated over and over until she had dissolved into tears and he had stomped away.

Chris reached down and placed a hand on her stomach. There was the tiniest of bulges there. It was firm, not soft or mushy, and he wondered at the miracle growing inside. His child...their child. He looked into her eyes, watched them turn that emerald green he loved to see.

"We need to get married soon, then. How does January sound to you?"

She laughed and hugged him again. Fenton snorted, but this time it was with less anger. He stomped down the stairs, grabbed Ichabod's reins and began to lead the buggy and Liza away to the barn.

"I'm bringing my shotgun to the wedding." Fenton said as he strode away.

"*Your intelligence is measured by those around you; if you spend your days with idiots you seal your own fate.[1]*" – *Author unknown*

"*The greater the loyalty of a group toward the group, the greater is the motivation among the members to achieve the goals of the group, and the greater the probability that the group will achieve its goals.*" – **Rensis Likert**

Captain Scott Cooper seethed as his second in command brought him the numbers. Three more missing, slipped away in the night. Two of them had been from the ragged remnants of Tent Five, the pretty blonde he'd broken in a couple of months ago and a recent tasty morsel that he hadn't quite finished with.

Of all of the whores he'd had, the newest one had reminded him the most of Tiffany. Or at least a young version of his sister before she'd filled out and started knowing her own mind and ran to Daddy to complain about him touching her. He'd gotten the beating of his life after that. Old Coop would have thrown his ass out then and there, but Mama was already sick and had begged her husband to show mercy on Scott. She always had been particularly fond of her son. She had ignored or explained away his dark deeds, saying only "boys will be boys." When Tiffany had gone to her mother first, she had been ignored and then punished for making up such awful lies.

By the time that pathetic, stupid woman had gotten around to dying, he'd left. The uneasy truce between him and Arno collapsed the moment his mother's body had cooled. He'd heard of the Western Front, listened to the whispers that they were now in Colorado and marching east and he'd set out to join up. It was his bravado in walking right up to the troops on those grass-filled plains of Kansas outside of Fort Riley and asking to join that had caught Granger's attention. And later, after their unit had been left as an out-

---

post outside of Springfield it was his intel that had provided the rewarding raids on nearby towns, including his own hometown.

His mind strayed for a moment as he remembered the girl's body under his, no real woman breasts on the new one, not even the beginnings of pubes. The rest had worked out just fine, though. Sex was what whores were for; no matter how old or young, that was all they were really good for anyway. His Mama had made that clear when she went tramping around, spreading her legs for that fool in town and getting knocked up with Tiffany.

An awkward cough brought his thoughts back to the present. He blinked, realized he'd been standing there lost in thought for far too long.

Evers looked nervous standing there, waiting for Cooper to either explode or start barking orders. He hadn't wanted this promotion, but the last guy who'd had this job had tried to leave three weeks ago. *Tried* being the operative word, for he hadn't gotten far at all. It still turned Evers bowels into Jell-O to think about how that guy had looked when Cooper had finished with him. He had wiped off his blade, ignoring the piece of dead meat at his feet that had screamed for mercy just moments before and returned the blade to its sheath. He had turned to Tom Evers and said, "You're 2nd Lieutenant now, Evers. Don't let me down."

It had been all Evers could do not to empty his bladder on the spot. Who wanted to be a second to a psychopath? The memory of it was still sharp as he cleared his throat, "There is one more thing, sir."

"Yes?"

"They sliced the tires on the last seven trucks. And we got no spares left."

"We had *eight* trucks yesterday." Cooper's eyes smoldered with fury, anticipating the next sentence that would come out of Evers mouth.

"Yes sir. They took that last one. They must've pushed it out a few hundred yards before starting it up and driving away 'cause the sentries didn't hear a peep. Well, except for Private Angelo, who they knocked out and tied up. We found him this morning and sounded the alarm."

"Yes," Cooper's voice was dry and cold, "I heard the alarm." It had woken him with a start, pulling him from a dream filled with blood and sex. He felt frustrated, sleep-deprived, and the darkness in him threatened to boil over.

He fought to contain it, and then smiled as he focused on a 'positive' outlet for his frustration. "Bring Angelo to see me after I've had some coffee."

Tom Evers saluted, Cooper barely bothered to return it, and the man hastened away. He winced as he imagined what would happen to Private Angelo. The poor kid would probably be better off dead after Cooper took out his frustration on him.

Cooper fought to control his fury. No more trucks, how would they move out without the vehicles? The areas surrounding had been picked clean and anyone still living was deep in hiding. They had crossed into what amounted to a no man's land a few days before inside the Mississippi side of border between Arkansas and Mississippi. The closest town was that of Lobdell, Mississippi, and it was dead quiet, any inhabitants who remained were deep in hiding.

The last two months had been one disaster after another. The unit had moved south into Arkansas and hadn't gotten far, only to a tiny town in the hinter boonies called Mountain Home, and promptly gotten their asses kicked. The small towns were wising up and either fleeing or, in odd cases such as this, arming themselves and fighting. He'd lost nearly five dozen men before they took the town. When Granger had been in charge, they'd had nearly two hundred and fifty men. Now the complement was down to a hundred, maybe less. Especially after a second ass-whipping in Forrest City, miles to the southeast.

The men were losing a taste for war and conquest and more deserted each day. Cooper couldn't understand it. This was his perfect world; it was all he had ever dreamed of after those years of being smothered by his fool whore of a mother and ignored by an indifferent father.

Old Coop had spent more of his time kowtowing to Tiffany, that little slut had the old man wrapped around her finger. What kind of man preferred the company of another man's child, a man who had cuckolded him no less, to his own son?

No matter, each and every day of the past six months he had gotten to have whatever woman he wanted, take what he wanted and go where he wanted. It wasn't just the power that got his rocks off, it was the freedom to say and do whatever he pleased. He liked to see the fear in the men's eyes. He'd earned every ounce of it and more.

Still, now they were without transportation of any kind. His sipped the steaming cup of atomic waste the cook had prepared. They had managed to grab several pounds of coffee when they blew through the border and into Scott, Mississippi. That had been what he called a 'grab and stab.' Scope out the town from a distance, find the weakest point, hit them at sunrise and grab what you could and kill anyone who tried to stop you. It was better than a frontal assault, especially now that the people who were left were the tougher ones, determined to survive, with the weapons to back themselves up. His thoughts spun like they were stuck in mud up to the axles. How in the devil were they going to keep moving?

The flap of the tent moved aside and a soldier walked in with Angelo, who was bleeding from a cut on his forehead. No one had bothered to patch him up. Ever since their medic team had up and disappeared halfway through Arkansas, first aid services were a tad scarce nowadays. The man looked terrified. His back was ramrod straight, and he saluted Cooper, a slight tremor in his hand as he did so. Scott nodded to the other soldier, excusing him from the tent and he left quickly.

A half hour later and Cooper stepped out of his tent. He calmly walked to a creek that ran by the edge of the camp and washed the blood and gore from his hands. His first in command, First Lieutenant Riley, stood a few feet away impassively.

"I'll be taking over your tent, Riley."

"Yes, sir. I'll clear that out for you, sir." Riley then motioned to two of the grunts standing nearby and looking rather pale and pointed them towards Cooper's tent. It would take them several hours, and two panicked runs outside to vomit before they finally managed to clean up the mess. The stains on the canvas walls of the tent, however, were permanent. Riley didn't much care one way or the other. Bloodstains notwithstanding, he liked having a bigger tent.

A unit that had once been nearly 200 men strong was now a very dangerous, violent gang of raiders. Cooper had many more moments of fury and frustration in the next two weeks. By the end of them, only twenty-five men remained of the one hundred plus who had crossed into Mississippi with him. Of that number, six were too terrified and cowed to leave, and twelve of the men were far too stupid to know when to cut and run. Another three were biding their time, hoping for a better opportunity that might include a set of wheels, and the last four, which included Riley and Cooper, were complete psychopaths bent on murder and mayhem. They had managed to hold on to three of the women. The rest of the women had escaped, or died while trying to escape.

Some simple-minded redneck named Brad Osterman, and the woman and girl he had taken with him, had broken the back of Western Front outpost while making their timely escape in late October. Disabling the vehicles had dealt a heavy and rather unrecoverable blow to the unit. In time, Cooper and his remaining men managed to scrounge enough useable tires from abandoned vehicles and surrounding terrain to return three vehicles to service. They headed up Highway 1 in mid-November and drove until the road dumped them on Highway 49. This they followed southeast until the road crossed the state line into Tennessee and moved towards Memphis. There were plenty of small towns to loot and burn along the way. The trucks moved inexorably north.

"*Grow old along with me, the best is yet to be.*" – **Robert Browning**

Chris pulled the edge of his jacket out of Mutton Chop's curious mouth. Tomorrow was Christmas and the week had flown by. It had been tense; Fenton was still perturbed that the 'natural' order of things had not been observed.

He finally confronted Chris in the barn after breakfast. Chris had just finished feeding the goats and was mucking out Ichabod's stall when Fenton came in.

"There's courtin', then askin' the father for the girl's hand in marriage," he glared at Chris, "Which would be me since her daddy is gone, marriage, the lovin' and *eventually*," he stressed the word and glared, "lil 'uns." His vernacular degenerated when his emotions ran high. "You seem to have your priorities ass backwards, young man."

He had said this after three long days of silence and brooding. Chris felt ashamed. The shock of realizing that Carrie was pregnant combined with his concern about her young age and his lack of control had lessened him in the old man's eyes. In the last few months, Fenton had become a unique combination of father, grandfather and mentor. He felt Fenton's disappointment keenly and wished he could change how it had all played out. He studied the ground, searched for the right words and felt the old man's gaze steady and unrelenting.

"Sir...I," What could he say to make this better? He had agonized over it, but if he couldn't make it better, at least he could apologize and ask forgiveness, "I'm sorry. I know I screwed up."

He looked up and met Fenton's eyes, struck by how old and sad the man looked, "You're right, there's an order to it all and I should've exercised control and waited."

Fenton pursed his lips and sighed. "Christopher, I know you love my granddaughter. I know you'll marry her and I know it coulda played out a lot worse than it did." He shook his head, "You disappointed me, son. But I'll get over it...'cause tomorrow you're gonna make this right."

"Sir?" Chris was confused, tomorrow was Christmas.

Fenton's eyes had lost their disappointment and sadness and now they twinkled with mischief. He reached over and clapped Chris hard on the shoulder. "You're getting married tomorrow, son." And with that he sauntered out of the barn, Chris staring after him, stunned.

In a daze he finished his chores, not sure what to think about Fenton's statement. It was as if his brain could simply not process what the old man had said. They were getting married tomorrow? On Christmas day? Did people actually do that? Wasn't there a rule or something against it? He shook his head, finished his chores and headed for the house. It was almost noon and usually there would be lunch in process, but when he opened the front door and walked in, he took in an amazing scene. Boxes of ornaments...everywhere. And an old trunk sat in the middle of the living room, lid open, and Carrie stood on a small stool beside it wearing the most amazing...

"Oh!" Liza ran from Carrie's side, neatly avoiding Joseph who was sprawled on the floor attaching hooks to tree decorations, "Get out! You aren't allowed to see her dress before the wedding!" She flipped Chris around and shoved him back towards the door, "Out, out, OUT!"

"But...I..." Chris was propelled out the door, which slammed closed behind him. To add insult to injury, the deadbolt turned in the lock. He was locked out of the house! Liza giggled and called through the door, "Hitch up the horse and go to town, you need to bring Mr. Liles back with you and ask Reverend Thomas, Carl and his family, and Mrs. Jennings to be here tomorrow morning for a wedding and then lunch." There was a pause, "Oh! And be sure to get a pound of sugar if you can." Chris started to walk away from the door, "Oh and..."

"For crying out loud, girl, give the boy a list." Fenton interceded.

"Wait there, son, I'll get you a sandwich for the road and Liza will get you a list." And a few minutes later the door opened wide enough to shove a small lunch sack through.

Liza grinned at Chris as he took the bag, "The list is inside. Don't come back until dark."

Chris just shook his head and took the bag, headed for the barn and hitched up the horse. The day was turning rather surreal and he didn't know what to make of it. As Ichabod moved briskly towards the town his state of shock persisted. Sure, they had talked about marriage and getting married for months. Now that it was here, now that it was apparently just a day away, it felt unreal and frightening and exciting all at once. He couldn't believe it was actually happening. He smiled suddenly. By this time next year, he would be holding their baby in his arms. He could see her now, a little girl, with blond hair and her mama's gorgeous green eyes. The vision of it moved him past the burned-out trucks and skeletons, past the lookouts with barely a thought to wave, and on into town.

He visited Mrs. Jennings first. Liza had written directions on the note on how to find the house and he figured it was right that she should hear the news of the wedding and get the first invitation since she had been so kind to give him the ring. She lived in a tiny little cottage. It was an exquisite little Victorian with carefully turned spindles and latticework. It would have been immaculate, inside and out, except for the huge piles of books. She seemed to having nothing but stacks of books in one of the bedrooms. No furniture, except for one lone chair, and a lamp surrounded by leaning stacks and walls of books.

"You *must* stay for lunch, my dear," she said, bustling away to the kitchen despite his protests that he had already eaten. After she filled Chris with soup and bread, they sat in the living room, surrounded by books and she served him hot mint tea. Liza visited Alice often after the library had been destroyed by fire. They had salvaged all of the books they could and set up shop in Alice's tiny house.

She laughed as he described the talk with Fenton and then being thrown out of the house and sent on errands. Her blue eyes sparkled, "Oh my dear, truly, I am happy for you. You and Carrie make a lovely couple." She wagged her finger at him, "And as for the baby, don't you be too hard on yourself, I know for a fact that Fenton may wish for things a certain way, but he knows the world doesn't always work that way." She smiled and sipped her tea.

"Did you know that his wife Molly and I were best friends?" Chris shook his head, "Well we were completely inseparable from kindergarten until our senior dance in high school." Her mouth turned down, her lips trembled, and "I wasn't as good of a friend as I should have been. We both saw him at the same moment, and he looked so handsome. An older man, you understand, three years older than Molly and me, Fenton was. He walked in, we both saw him at the same time and she called dibs." Chris laughed.

Alice smiled, "Laugh all you want, but remember, we were young once too, and silly girls do that. She had called dibs and we were best friends. So, she got him and I didn't. Oh, how jealous I was!" She took another sip of tea. "Here, have another cookie." She pushed the plate of cookies over and he took one out of politeness, despite his desperately full stomach.

"I met my Larry a year later. We married before Molly and Fenton and we were all so close in those early years. But Molly had Isaac. As for me...well, the babies just never came. I was so jealous, Christopher, so sad I could never have one."

Her eyes misted, her lip trembled, and "I wasn't a good friend. After all she went through having Isaac and I couldn't even stand to see that child, wondering year after year why she had had a baby and I didn't. And the years passed and we didn't speak and then she was gone, before I even knew she was sick." She looked at the carpet, looked back up at Chris, "I'm so sorry dear, I don't know why I told you all of this."

What was it with women? Chris was beginning to wonder if they were just *filled* with tears. And what was it with the subject of babies and marriage that set them off so? Sitting in the wing-backed chair, trying not to knock off the dainty doilies on each arm, he struggled to think of something to say.

"Mrs. Jennings, you uh, you seem very nice to me." He said it awkwardly, "I, uh, I really had better get going. I have to visit Carl's family and the reverend, and pick up Mr. Liles. If I don't, I doubt I'll get let back into the house tonight."

Alice laughed, wiped at her moist eyes and patted his hand, "You are a dear, young Christopher, listening to an old woman so patiently. Pass word, if you will, to the Carters I would like to share a ride with them if they wouldn't mind."

The Carters, Carl Owens' mom and his stepdad John, had converted their van to run on biofuel. It ran on a diesel made of corn. The van had plenty of seats and room to spare.

He promised that he would and set off to visit the different houses on his list. He lucked out at the Carter's and promised a dozen eggs in return for the pound of sugar. The Trade Mart was closed for the day, which was a relief, he didn't care to run into Wes Perkins and said as much to Abby. Abigail Carter was a tiny woman, and at age six, her daughter, Tabitha, had already grown past Abigail's shoulder. Her son, Carl, who was sixteen, towered over her and he was still a good head shorter than Chris. Abby gave a wry smile, "Wes has always been a bit of a jerk. Family or no, I don't much associate with him these days now that both our parents have passed."

Chris gave a start, "You're related?" Oh God, he'd put his foot in it this time. His face must have shown his dismay because Abby laughed then. She looked far too young to have a teenage son.

John, Abby's husband, laughed too. "They're first cousins, on Abby's mother's side. Wes's mother was the oldest of five, and Abby's mother was the youngest."

"Mama had me when she was nearly forty. I was quite a surprise, even more so since I was the first to give her a grandbaby." Abby grinned wryly, "Wes always was a jerk," she looked around and saw that Tabitha had gone back to her room and then leaned forward conspiratorially, "A real bastard, actually. Shoulda seen what he did to his wife after he came back from Iraq. Blackened both her eyes. PTSD, be damned, he's always been a prick." Abby shook her head, her short curls dancing, "Those kids were so damned cute. They played with Carl almost every day. Course that was over ten years ago.

He beat her up; she packed up the kids and left the next day. Can't blame her a bit for it, but I sure have wondered where they are now, especially now, with all that's happened out there in the world."

"Abby," John gently interrupted, "Chris needs to be heading home. It's getting late. And the man's getting hitched tomorrow."

Abby apologized and hugged Chris, "We'll be there tomorrow! Give my love to everyone and tell them we'll see them soon!"

And with that, his list of chores complete, Chris headed for home. John and Abby had assured him that there was room for Mrs. Jennings and Mr.

Liles in their van and even offered to give Reverend Thomas a lift if he didn't mind a cozy ride. He had the sugar Liza had demanded and everything was a go for a Christmas wedding.

It was pitch black out by the time he returned and Fenton had left a lantern out on the porch to guide his way. He unhitched Ichabod, set him to eating dinner and closed the barn up tight. The lantern shone brightly and he could see specks of snow beginning to fall. Just spits of snow, really, nothing exceptional, this was Tennessee after all. He took the steps two at a time and was at the front door before he remembered his reception earlier that day, and decided to knock.

He could hear Joseph's voice and running feet, "Chris is home! Chris is home!" The door opened and the little boy hugged him and peered around behind Chris, "Where's Mr. Liles?"

"He'll be here tomorrow, Joseph, riding in style with the Carter's."

"Oh." The little boy looked disappointed and then perked up, "Come see! Come see!" He tugged on Chris's arm and pulled him into the house. Chris shut the door behind him, turned, and took in the beautifully decorated rooms. Liza and Fenton were sitting on the sofa, looking exhausted, Carrie was nowhere in sight. The old trunk was gone, as was the wedding dress that Chris had had only the smallest of glimpses of. In place of the boxes was a tree decorated with all the trimmings, a few wrapped presents underneath, and a fire crackled merrily in the fireplace. Wreaths and garland adorned the walls, and a hand-carved Nativity scene was center-stage on the coffee table. The bookshelf, every one of the shelves normally filled with books, had one shelf cleared for a Christmas village.

Joseph bounded through the living room, skidding to a stop in front of the bookshelf. "Look Chris, look! I did the Christmas village. 'Ceptin we couldn't make the houses light up 'cause they run on 'tricity." His mouth turned down at the corners, mournfully. The little boy had no idea what television was like, and didn't miss it, but he missed making the village light up.

"You did great, Joseph." Chris smiled at the little boy. "Wow," he said, feigning surprise and wonder, "Is that real snow?" Chris pointed to the white folds of fabric the buildings rested on.

"No, silly, it's pretend snow!" the boy bounced up and down, pleased with Chris's response.

The sofa and Fenton's favorite chair had been moved back against one wall and there was now a large empty space in the middle of the living room. Liza didn't move, but she smiled and asked, "What do you think?"

"It looks beautiful," Chris answered honestly. He pointed to the open floor space, "Is that where..."

"Yup," Fenton looked exhausted, "That's where Liza and Carrie say the 'best spot' is for gettin' hitched. Good lord, I'm beat."

"Gramps slaughtered Drumstick today." Liza waved a tired finger towards the oven, which was beginning to emit the most luscious smell. Drumstick had been the largest of their eight turkeys and already slated for Christmas dinner. Chris had noticed the pile of feathers in the corner of the barn. His stomach gave a slow, audible growl. It had been a few hours since he had eaten at Mrs. Jennings. Liza snickered and pointed again towards the kitchen, "There's soup there on the stove." He didn't bother pouring it into a bowl. There was enough left in the pot for him and not much more. It was still warm too. He grabbed a spoon, an oven mitt and sat on the sofa and ate.

"Where's Carrie?" he asked, trying not to slurp. The soup was full of carrots and potatoes as well as cubes of pork, *yum*...Butt Roast sure had turned out to be one fine-tasting beast.

"Asleep," Fenton yawned, "*in her own bed* where she belongs until tomorrow."

"Remember, its bad luck to see your bride before the wedding," Liza grinned playfully, and wagged her finger, "Don't go sneaking a peek before tomorrow." The evening ended quietly. Chris excused himself at the same time as Fenton and lay down in his room, alone in the bed.

He stared into the dark, unable to sleep as the hours ticked by. He thought of Jess and his parents, all dead, their bodies' cold in the ground. If they had been lucky enough to be buried. He thought about Allen and Toby, even Easter and Burton, and all of the nameless others. Chris wished that Carrie was tucked close beside him and he thought of the child growing inside her. So much death, and yet right now, in the face of that death and pain, the promise of new life. How he missed Mom and Dad and Jess. How they would have loved Carrie and all the rest of the Perdue's. How he wished things had been different!

Without the war, and the Western Front, and all of the evil and pain he had seen, he would not be here. He would never have run into Fenton, met Carrie, or be getting married or expecting a child. To wish his parents, sister and friends to life, would mean the loss of all he had now. He wrestled with this, stuck in a loop of would have's and should have's. The clock chimed four a.m. before he finally drifted off to sleep.

Joseph pile-driving into his stomach was his early morning wake up call. As he struggled to recover from the assault of an overly excited four-year-old, Liza materialized holding a huge mug of chicory coffee. It was an acquired taste, meaning that they hadn't been able to acquire coffee and had been extending the stash by mixing it half and half with ground chicory, which grew on the roadsides and wild in fields. It didn't have quite the same kick as coffee, but it was hot and who needed the full caffeine boost anyway? He muttered his thanks and tried not to spill it on his bare chest as he sipped and Joseph bounced.

Liza took pity on him and grabbed Joseph in mid-bounce. "Come on Joseph, we have to get ready for the wedding." The boy protested he wanted to open presents. "No Joseph, we talked about this. *Tonight,* we'll open presents."

Before the little boy could begin wailing in earnest, Chris reached over and pulled out a small box from the bedside table. Mr. Liles had given it to him yesterday, instructing that it was a present for Joseph from Chris.

He'd winked at Chris, "Young man, you have enough on your plate with a little one on the way and a wedding tomorrow. Little Joseph will love these. And it'll keep him quiet 'til the ceremony is over." The box was handmade, crafted out of a soft wood. The top slid off to reveal tiny, hand-carved wooden cars with tiny button wheels that turned on tiny spokes held in place with cotter pins.

When Chris had looked over at Mr. Liles gnarled and twisted hands in surprise, the old man had laughed. "Oh my, no! My *grandson* made these years back when he still could manage to see all those details. He's blind as a bat nowadays, worse eyesight than me!"

Chris handed the box to Joseph, "Here Joseph, 'cause today's going to be crazy. I want to be sure and give this to you now." The boy looked took the box, and Chris helped him with the lid. He squealed then and ran off to show the rest of the family his prize.

"Good one, big brother." Liza grinned.

"I'm not your brother yet."

"All in good time." She jabbed her finger in the direction of the closet, "Gramps found you a suit to wear. It belonged to Dad. But you'd best wash first. And hurry up about it, 'cause, Carrie's gotta get ready and that takes time."

"Say no more." He headed to the garage, which shared a wall with the kitchen. No water pressure meant that all of their water was from the old well. Thankfully, this was close to the house and could be pumped directly into the kitchen via an old-fashioned pump. However, it did not extend to the bathroom.

Earlier that year, Chris and Fenton had figured a way to run a mount a small sink high up on the shared wall and then run a pipe through the wall to the garage which then emptied into a barrel mounted on concrete blocks five feet off of the ground. By slightly crouching under the spigot a person could take a rather Spartan shower.

To be able to shower, one would load up the rain barrel by pouring buckets of cold water into the sink straight from the tap and alternating with water boiled in a pan. It took about a half hour to prepare all of the water needed for one short shower, and at this time of year it was freezing cold in the garage. The summer wasn't so bad, but winter sucked and it meant that everyone, with the exception of Joseph who still got to bathe in the large kitchen sink, usually waited a week or so before bathing. In between full baths they would just wash their hair in the sink. It worked out well enough. Chris stepped into the frigid garage, washed down quickly and, teeth chattering wrapped the towel around his waist and sprinted back in.

"Now go in your room and stay there until we tell you to come out," Liza ordered. Chris rolled his eyes at this. He'd seen Carrie every day and night since he'd arrived here, it seemed like a silly ritual. But he let Liza push him into the room and promised he wouldn't peek. The room was dimly lit and it looked as if it was beginning to snow in earnest. Big fat flakes were drifting down steadily.

Carrie's dad must have been slightly smaller than Chris. The pants fit fine, but the shirt was tight, especially around his shoulders and biceps. Outside of his room he could hear Liza and Carrie run past his door giggling like giddy schoolgirls. He combed his hair back and looked in dismay at the tie. *How in the heck do you tie one of these things?*

He settled it around his collar, flipping it this way and that way while peering at his reflection in the mirror. The last time he had worn a tie was his senior graduation. That had been silly when you realize that his suit and tie were both covered by his graduation gown. His mother had put it on him, her hands moving with calm assurance as she made a perfect knot. He could see her face now, eyes shining with pride. College had been out of the question, what with the instability of the entire country and the dominoes of the collapse already beginning to fall. She had cried though, and then whooped and hollered with the rest of them as the caps had flown into the air.

He yanked at the tie. It was no use; he was hopeless at this. A soft knock at the door and Fenton's voice, "Boy? You decent?"

"Yes, sir." The door opened and Fenton sidled in, closing the door as one or both of the girls ran past again, giggling madly. He sighed and shook his head.

"Well son, the food is cookin' and the girls are primpin' and," he took in Chris's suit, looked it up and down slowly, "Oh son...oh." He stopped and looked down at his shoes, Chris was alarmed.

"Sir? Is something wrong? Does the shirt look too small? I can't figure out this tie to save my life." His words tumbled out, climbing over each other, revealing his growing panic. Oh God, he was getting *married* today.

The old man looked up and smiled, his eyes turned misty, "You look fine, son. You do. I was just..." he inhaled, let it out slow, "I was just remembering when I bought that suit for Isaac for his first job interview in the big city. Straight out of college and he was going all the way to the Big Apple."

He shook his head, "Shouldn't be sad about it. My boy landed that job. Workin' there, he met the sweetest girl in the world to marry." He smiled wistfully, "And those two lovebirds made three fine grandchildren to comfort me when he was gone. I just miss him, even now."

He reached out and took the tie from Chris, looped it around his neck and tied it with practiced hands. "There," he smoothed the tie and turned

Chris towards the mirror, thumping him firmly on the back. They stood there silent for a moment, examining Chris's reflection.

Outside the snow fell harder and the two men could hear Joseph running down the hall shouting that the van was there. "It's nearly time. You take a moment, then come on out and greet our guests. Will you be all right son?"

Chris gulped, "Yes sir." One final thump, and the old man took his leave to go and greet the reverend and the wedding guests. Chris realized he hadn't eaten anything for breakfast, which was probably a good thing. Right now, he felt downright nauseous. He closed his eyes, thought of his parents and Jess. *Deep breath.* Then he turned and walked out to greet everyone.

Days later he would swear that Christmas morning had moved at the speed of light. Looking back on it he remembered waking up, washing, dressing, greeting guests and the ceremony all flashing past in a blur.

The only true clarity to the memory was the beautiful stranger he had found kissing him back that morning. Carrie's straight blond hair had been a mass of curls that ran from twists on the top of her head to ribbons of gold that danced on her shoulders. Her dress had been an ivory satin, a family heirloom, and it had clung to her hips and cascaded down to the floor. Peeking out from the hem were a pair of Liza's hand-knitted rainbow socks and blue Converse tennis shoes.

"Something borrowed *and* something blue," she had whispered to him, eyes twinkling.

Until she had spoken, he had wondered if he were dreaming. She was beyond beautiful, beyond his ability to describe in words, a sweet promise of the years to come. The butterflies in his stomach were gone and he stood and they exchanged vows. He slipped the brilliant emerald and diamond ring onto her finger and kissed his bride.

Everyone applauded, Joseph and Tabitha bounced in and around them, and the snow fell thick and heavy.

It was Christmas Day. It was snowing. It was a white wedding. And Fenton even put his shotgun down long enough to give away the bride.

"You must plan for every contingency – enough greens, meat, grains, blankets, wood, even access to clean water. Without all of these, and more, you will find yourself in deep trouble mid-winter. Assume nothing, prepare for everything to go wrong, and you just might survive to see spring." **– Author unknown**

They packaged the smoked deer meat in waterproof baggies and submerged them in the water. The stream was fed by an underground aquifer which produced ice-cold, clean water for drinking. This eliminated the need for boiling and kept the stored meat at an acceptably cold level. David had been right; they would need at least one more buck to ensure their survival through the winter.

Jess and Tina had gathered large amounts of grass and bulrush for mats as well as absorbent material for Jacob. The supply of diapers had long since run out. Jess watched her son closely, observed his habits and quickly recognized a pattern of elimination. This allowed her to fashion a handful of strips of deer hide for the outer layer of the diaper, with plenty of grass lining the inside and absorbing any waste at the times he was most likely to need it.

Throughout the weeks Madge urged cup after cup of milk thistle tea on Jess until she finally asked the old woman why. "It promotes lactation. You need all the milk you can make for *Mi'-da-in-ga*." She cupped the baby's head and cooed at him lovingly as she explained this. The infant stared back; his deep blue eyes intent on watching the old woman speak. "It also increases your circulation and builds your strength. He is growing well, *Mi'-na*, a healthy and strong boy child. He will make a brave warrior one day."

Tina watched the old woman intently. She asked Madge about every plant they encountered outside of the cave until she could recite as many as David could. "Why you call her Meena, Grandmother? Her name Yess, not Meena."

Madge smiled at the girl, "For the same reason I call you, *Ni'-da-wi*, my little fairy child. You with your pretty brown hair, when I see you, I think of a garden fairy. I call Jess *Mi'-na*, which means oldest daughter, for she reminds me of my oldest girl when she was young." For the old woman, naming the children made them family, showed her love for them. For a long time, Tina insisted her name was Ni'-da-wi and would stubbornly refuse to answer to any other.

By the end of October, they had accumulated a large store of fish, which they smoked and then stored in the back of the cave. A small mountain of grass had been gathered, washed and dried. They used it to stuff bedding and also for absorbing Jacob's waste. David had whittled several bowls out of a fallen log and they no longer had to share bowls. Jess and Tina had learned to weave baskets out of the reeds they had collected from the lake shore. Madge showed them where wild onions grew and they harvested basketfuls of nuts, and armfuls of sump weed and plantain.

The first week of November, David bagged another deer with his bow and he sent a prayer of thanks to its dead spirit. He wasn't Osage, but if Grandmother Madge thought it was a good idea then he was all for it. It seemed respectful somehow, to give thanks to this enormous creature. Its meat and hide would help keep them alive through the winter.

Quincy had been with him again on this hunt, although she typically preferred to stay by Jess's or Jacob's side. In the evenings or during the day when Jess had to help climb a nut tree and shake the limbs for more nuts, the dog would stay glued to the infant's side, whining softly moments before he stirred. At night Quincy's soft whine helped Jess to wake and put a breast to little Jacob's mouth before he was even fully awake. That way there was far less wailing to disturb the small group's slumber.

Quincy was young, but she was an intelligent pup. David looked at the carcass of the giant deer and knew he needed help. He turned back to Quincy, busy sniffing the ground around the deer and said, "Go Quincy, go find Jess and Madge." The pup looked up at him, gave one short bark, and plunged into the forest in the direction of the cave. He began the process of field-dressing the buck. He had just begun on the guts when the rest of their band arrived, Quincy leading the way. Their help made short work of it and soon the deer had joined the newest batch of fish in the smoke hut. "I said the words you taught me, Grandmother." David said as they laid out the last deer haunch in the hut, "I talked to the deer's spirit and thanked him for giving his life so we can eat this winter."

The old woman stopped, it was the first time David had ever called her that, and hugged him close. "Thank you *Min'-dse*," She turned and looked at the others, misty-eyed, "I am proud to call each of you my family. You honor the old ways and make me so happy." She hugged each of them in turn and kissed Jacob's forehead gently. "Come, come, we have dinner to prepare for our mighty hunter!"

In November the temperatures fell dramatically. Madge taught the children how to weave screens of saplings and evergreens to act as a shield across the opening of the cave and reduce the chilly drafts. They built and maintained several fires to deter rodent invaders and increase heat in the living portion of the cave and kept large stacks of firewood near the cave entrance. If anyone wandered close, they would instantly see that the cave was occupied, but in the long winter months no one ever did. Madge reminded them that the cave was far from any established trails, and it wasn't marked on any public maps. The chances of discovery were unlikely. "Only members of my team know of this location," her expression turned grim, "I fear that none of them survived to return."

For the children it felt as if the world outside their cave had ceased to exist. A new world, full of family, simple food, learning, stories and laughter filled their days. The snow fell deep that year, further insulating their tiny cave beneath the drifts. Jacob rolled over for the first time around Thanksgiving and David improved his whittling skills. Soon they had wooden bowls, spoons of their own and even several two-tined forks. Jess learned how to sew deerskin hides and Madge taught Tina her letters and told the ancient stories of her people.

They celebrated Christmas with a feast and an exchange of presents. Jess and Madge had collaborated to create a small doll for Tina. Madge fashioned the body out of stiff cattail reed and Jess sewed on a tiny dress out of buckskin and then pierced tiny berries on a string to drape around the doll's neck for a necklace. Tina was enchanted with it and created a sling for her doll similar to Jess's and Madge's so that she too could carry her 'baby' around.

David had whittled a small piece of wood into a round disk, engraved a rough 'J' onto it and pierced a hole near the top that he threaded cord through, turning it into a necklace and giving it to Jess. She hugged the boy and immediately put it around her neck.

Madge received a fur muff made of rabbit pelts (mainly from Quincy's kills) and roughly sewn together by Jess. "To keep your hands warm, Grandmother," Jess said, and hugged the old woman. Madge ran her hands over the fur, commenting on its softness, and managed a weak smile. She hadn't been sleeping or eating well in the past week, Jess worried that the old woman was falling ill.

The old woman slowly stood, walked to the back of the cave and retrieved a hide-wrapped bundle and handed it with great ceremony to David. "*Min'dse*, you have proven yourself an able hunter. My people valued this ability highly. A hunter ensured his people's survival in the darkest of times. Someday you will be a fierce warrior as well, and protect your family from harm. Listen, learn, and grow strong. Protect the ones you love at all cost."

The boy's spine straightened and he opened the bundle, examined each of the objects inside with awe. Madge had given him several of the dig artifacts – a spear tip, a stone knife, and an atlatl. The last object brought a gasp from Jess, for she knew how valuable these artifacts, especially the atlatl, were to Madge and the archaeological world. This was her work, part of the ancient history of her people, and she would not give these things away without long contemplation and deep regard for the boy.

It seemed strange though, the thought that the old woman would give such valuable artifacts to a child. It bothered Jess a little, as if there were some part of the story she didn't know. For all Jess knew, the old woman might have the beginnings of dementia or Alzheimer's. She said nothing; however, because she was distracted by the last gift to be handed out.

It was a field journal. Unlined paper, soft tan leather binding, and Jess saw that Madge had carefully written "Jacob" and then "Misae" was written under it and accompanied by a pictograph of a sun. Jess opened and recognized that the first few pages of the journal were filled with tiny writing. They were journal entries, the first one was dated September 19th, 2016, the day they had met Madge.

Jess looked up and locked eyes with Madge, who said, "I had a dream one day. In it, I saw a group of people walking west. There were adults, some children, even a small baby. Leading them was a handsome young warrior, smooth-chested, barely a man. When I looked upon his face it was like looking at the sun, blinding, hot. The rays reached out and lit the land before them with a blinding white light. I was not with this group, but I could see them and move among them."

She paused, "I saw you, *Mi'-na*, but you were older than you are now, fully a woman. You cradled a tiny baby in your arms and a tall young man walked by your side. There were others, a handful of others, all of you walking through the plains. All of you connected by blood, by commitment, by love. A voice came then and said, 'Old woman, stop your dreaming, go to the shore of the lake.' And so, I did."

She smiled at Jess and the others, "And I met you that day. I had just begun this journal, and I have written in it as often as I could in the days since. Someday, you will give it to *Mi'-da-in-ga*, when he becomes a man. He is the white sun that I saw in my dream, *Mi'-na*. You will know the right time to give it to him."

Jess took the journal silently. The leather was butter-soft, the papers rough and irregular. She realized that it had to have been made by hand. Madge added, "My daughter Penelope made that and gave it to me two years ago. It was the last time I saw her."

Such a gift! She did the only thing she could think to do. Jess reached out and hugged the old woman close, tears leaking down her cheeks, and said in a whisper, "Thank you Grandmother, I will treasure it always." Their embrace was interrupted by a squirming inside of Jess's sling and temperamental wail from the youngest member of their group.

While Jess fed Jacob, Madge and Tina prepared the food for their long-anticipated Christmas feast. Venison stew, brimming with the greens they had gathered, and the corms of a cattail filled their bellies.

Before the weather had turned too cold, the entire group had hiked southwest several miles from the cave to a grove of hickory trees.

They had spent a day trekking there, gathering as many nuts as they could carry, and then trekking back. Jess marveled at the old woman's cooking skills as they ate not just roasted hickory nuts, but also a type of bread, heavy and dense, made from the nuts and some kind of sweet/tart berries. A prized jar of wild violet jam, which Madge had made in her home in Kansas City and then brought with her to the cave, topped the bread. The sweet finish came in the form of hot chocolate, one cup for each of them, the last of the instant hot chocolate packets that Madge had squirreled away for a 'special' day.

"Grandmother, tell us a story." Tina asked, drowsily nestled against her brother.

Madge smiled, closed her eyes for a minute to think, and then said, "I will tell you the story of the first moccasins." She reached for Jacob and Jess handed him to her carefully. He was asleep and his eyes didn't even flutter as he was passed from one set of arms to the next.

"There was a great Chief of the Plains who had tender, sensitive feet. Other chiefs laughed at him; the people of the tribe also laughed at the chief's discomfort. The medicine man, an advisor to Chief-of-the- Tender-Feet was afraid and troubled. Each time he was called before the chief he was asked, 'What are you going to do about it?' The 'it' meant the chief's tender feet.

Forced by fear, the medicine man at last hit upon a plan. Though he knew that it was not the real answer to the chief's foot problem, it would work. The medicine man had the women weave a long, narrow mat of reeds, and when the chief had to go anywhere, four braves unrolled the mat in front of him. One day, the braves were worn out. They carelessly unrolled the mat over a place where flint arrowheads had been chipped. The arrowheads had long ago taken flight, but the needle-sharp chips remained. When the big chief's tender feet were wounded by these chips, he uttered a series of whoops which made the nearby aspen tree leaves shake so hard that they have been trembling ever since.

That night the medicine man was given an impossible task by the angry chief: 'Cover the whole earth with mats so thick that my feet will not suffer. If you fail, you will die when the moon is round.'

The frightened medicine man crept back to his lodge. He didn't want to die on the night of the full moon, but he could think of no way to avoid it. Looking down, he saw the hide of an elk pegged to the ground, with two women busily scraping the hair from the hide, and an idea flashed into his head. He sent out many hunters. Many women were busy for many days. The braves cut with hunting knives, and women sewed with bone needles.

On the day before the moon was round, the medicine man went to the chief and told him that he had covered as much of the earth as possible. When the chief looked from the door of his lodge, he saw many paths of skin stretching as far as he could see. Long strips which could be moved from place to place connected the main leather paths. Even the chief thought that this time the magic of the medicine man had solved tenderfoot transportation for all time.

One day, as the big chief was walking along one of his smooth, tough leather paths, he saw a pretty maiden of the tribe gliding ahead of him, walking on the hard earth on one side of the chief's pathway. She glanced back when she heard his feet on the elk-hide pathway and smiled. The chief set off at a run to catch up with her, his eyes fixed on the back of She-Who-Smiled, and so his feet strayed from the narrow path and landed in a bunch of needle-sharp thorns! The girl ran for her life when she heard the hideous howls of the chief.

Two suns later, when the chief was calm enough to speak, he had his medicine man brought before him. He told the man that the next day, when the sun was high in the sky he would be killed for his failures.

That night, the medicine man climbed to the top of a high hill in search of advice from friendly spirits on how to cover the entire earth with leather. He slept. In a dream vision he was shown the answer to his problem. Amid flashes of lightning, he tore down the steep hillside, howling louder than the big chief at times, as jagged rocks wounded his bare feet and legs. He did not stop until he was safely inside his lodge. He worked all night. The warriors who were to send him on the shadow trail came for him just before noon the next day. He was surrounded by the war-club armed guards and he was clutching something rolled in a piece of deerskin tightly to his heart. His cheerful smile surprised those who saw him pass. 'He is brave!' said the men. 'Yes, he is very brave!' said the women.

The chief was waiting just outside his lodge. Before the medicine man could be led away, he asked if he could say a few words to the chief. 'Speak!' said the chief, sorry to lose a clever medicine man that was very good at most kinds of magic.

The medicine man quickly knelt beside the chief. He unrolled two strange objects and slipped one of them on each foot of the chief. The chief seemed to be wearing a pair of bear's hairless feet, instead of bare feet. He was puzzled at first as he looked at the elk-hide handcraft of his medicine man. 'Great chief,' the medicine man exclaimed joyfully, 'I have found a way to cover the earth with leather! For you, O chief, from now on the earth will always be covered with leather.' And so it was."

The cave was quiet. From the dark, David said sleepily, "I like that story." No one said anything more and the fire burned low as they all slipped into dreams of moccasins and Christmas. Outside, a light snow began to fall.

The Death of Falling Water

*"To say goodbye to her was almost more than I could bear. She taught us so much, gave us such hope and loved us so deeply in those few short months. She renewed my trust in others and imbued a sense of joy in the simple act of living. After all that we had seen, life was a challenge, enjoying the process seemed impossible, but Madge saw things differently. She lived her life on her terms. She was kind, down to earth, and loved us well. If I live to be a hundred, I doubt I could be as special and as wonderful as that old woman was to us. In the end, I can say only this, she became Grandmother Falling Water, and we honor her memory to this day. She reminded us that the world was not all death and hate and violence. She taught us, she loved us, and we will carry her stories and lessons with us forever." – **Jess's Journal**

One evening, in late January, they gathered around for a story and Madge sat silent for several moments. She had been tired that day, sleeping longer into the morning than usual in the past few weeks and eating less each day. As she sat there silently, Jess was struck by how old Madge looked. When they had arrived, she had not wanted to ask the old woman's age. It would be rude, so she held her tongue. Tina had not been held to the same social norm and had asked her loudly one day if she were a hundred years old. Madge had laughed and shook her head, never answering the little girl. As they sat there waiting for Madge to begin her story, Jess thought that Madge looked older that evening than she had ever seen her look before. The moment passed, and the old woman looked around, smiled at the children surrounding her and the tiny baby in her arms, cleared her throat and began to speak…

"What is the meaning of life? Why is it that people grow old and die?

Although he was young, those questions troubled the mind of Little One. He asked the elders about them, but their answers did not satisfy him. Eventually, after asking and asking, he knew there was only one thing to do. He would have to seek the answers in his dreams.

Little One rose early in the morning and prayed to Wah-Kon-Tah for help. Then he walked away from the village, across the prairie and toward the hills. He took nothing with him, no food and no water. He was looking for a place where none of his people would see him, a place where a vision could come to him.

Little One walked a long way. Each night he camped in a different place, hoping that it would be the right one to give him a dream that could answer his questions. But no such dream came to him.

At last he came to a hill that rose above the land like the breast of a young maiden. A spring burst from the rocks near the base of a great elm tree. It was a beautiful place that seemed to be filled with the power of Wah-Kon-Tah. Little One sat down by the base of that elm tree and waited as the sun set. But though he slept, again no sign was given to him.

When he woke the next morning, he was weak with hunger. "I must go back home," he thought. He was filled with despair, but his thoughts were of his parents. He had been gone a long time. Even though it was expected that a young man would seek guidance alone in this fashion, Little One knew they would be worried. "If I do not return while I still have the strength to walk," he said, "I will die here and my family may never find my body."

Little One began to follow a small stream that was fed by a spring. It flowed out of the hills in the direction of his village, and he trusted it to lead him home. He walked and walked until he was not far from his village. But as he walked along that stream, he stumbled and fell among the roots of an old willow tree. Little One clung to the roots of the willow tree. Although he tried to rise, his legs were too weak.

"Grandfather," he said to the willow tree, "It is not possible for me to go on."

Then the ancient willow spoke to him. "Little One," it said, "all the Little Ones always cling to me for support as they walk along the great path of life. See the base of my trunk, which sends forth roots that hold me firm in the earth. They are the sign of my old age. They are darkened and wrinkled with age, but they are still strong. Their strength comes from relying on the earth. When the Little Ones use me as a symbol, they will not fail to see old age as they travel along the path of life."

Those words gave strength to Little One's spirit. He stood again and began to walk. Soon his own village was in sight, and as he sat down to rest for a moment in the grass of the prairie, looking at his village, another vision came to him. He saw before him the figure of an old man. The old man was strangely familiar, even though Little One had never seen him before.

"Look upon me," the old man said. "What do you see?"

"I see an old man whose face is wrinkled with age," Little One said.

"Look upon me again," the old man said.

Then Little One looked, and as he looked, the lesson shown him by the willow tree filled his heart. "I see an aged man in sacred clothing," Little One said, "The white down of the eagle adorns his head. I see an aged man with the stem of the pipe between his lips. You are firm and rooted to the earth like the ancient willow. I see you standing among the days that are peaceful and beautiful. I see you standing as you will stand in your lodge, my grandfather."

The ancient man smiled. Little One had seen truly. "My young brother," the old man said, "your mind is fixed upon the days that are peaceful and beautiful." And then he was gone.

Now Little One's heart was filled with peace, and as he walked into the village, his mind was troubled no longer with those questions about the meaning of life. For he knew that the old man he had seen was himself. The ancient man was Little One as he would be when he became an elder, filled with that great peace and wisdom which would give strength to all of the people.

From that day on, Little One began to spend more time listening to the words his elders spoke, and of all the young men in the village, he was the happiest and the most content.

This was one of the longest stories Madge had ever shared and she looked exhausted at the end. Usually her stories were short or often funny. As she finished, she looked down at the ground and tears formed in her eyes. "I have not been entirely honest with you, Little Ones. I told you I came back here to this cave to continue my work, but that isn't the full truth." She paused and stroked Jacob's sleeping face as he lay cuddled in her arms. "In the weeks before fighting broke out in the city I was not feeling well. I'd lost a lot of weight. No matter how much I tried, I could barely bring myself to eat.

I underwent a series of tests and the doctors found cancer. They said it was just a matter of time. They told me it was too advanced, and that it had metastasized throughout my organs and they could do nothing for me. They gave me six months, and told me to call my children. Then things turned bad in the world, and," she shrugged, "I came here. I tried several herbal remedies and things improved. I felt better, my appetite returned and I felt younger than I had in years."

She smiled at them, taking in the young, worried faces looking at her in the crackling firelight. "I came out here to die, not to continue my work. Then all of you came and you made me feel so alive. You have made these past few months a joy and a gift at the end of an old woman's life."

Jess's voice broke as she choked the words out, "You're dying?"

Madge laughed, clear and clean, and the sound bounced and rolled through the cave magnifying and expanding, "Oh *Mi'-na*, from the moment we are born we begin to die. My moment will come soon, far sooner than yours, and it will be on my terms and through my choice. I could have stayed there, gotten the treatments that would have robbed me of my hair, turned the food I ate to dust in my mouth. I could have survived with a few less organs than I currently have. But I have lived a long time and I am satisfied with how I have lived it. I have loved, and been loved. Given birth and raised my children. Taught and learned much about my people and my history."

She smiled at them again, tears flowing freely down her lined cheeks, "I thought I had seen everything and done everything I wanted to do, and then you came. And these weeks and months have been a beautiful finish to a well-lived life." Tina crept close, nestled against her right arm, and Madge hugged her close. "But I can feel it in my body, eating away at me, killing me with each day that passes. I don't think it will be much longer, a month, maybe two. Forgive me children, for I asked you to stay not just for your safety, but for my own selfish needs. I did not want to die alone, even here, in the home of my ancestors. I wanted someone to be here at the end. You have seen far too much death, and I ask too much of you, I know I do."

They were all in tears and Jess reached out and held the old woman's hand. "We won't leave you Grandmother. We won't leave you alone, I promise." She said it with conviction and David nodded nearby, looking at the ground as he tried to hide his tears.

Madge had not been far off when she said the end would come soon. After that night in January her condition worsened quickly. They had all made such progress in storing food and supplies in the months before winter that one less hand in chores was not missed. However, Jacob had grown used to hours in Madge's wizened arms. He looked for her, even from the wraps of Jess's sling and whimpered fretfully.

He was teething, and this did not help his mood. Jess solved this by moving her cot right next to Madge's, so the baby lay between them at night and close to Madge during the day. This brightened his mood and Madge's as well. She would smile with joy when she opened her eyes and saw him there just inches from her.

Madge would sleep all night, wake for breakfast, then nap again until lunch, and often again until dinner. She touched very little of the food and only smiled and shook her head when Jess or David attempted to feed her more. Slowly she shrank in size until her bones jutted prominently. She now looked every inch of her Osage heritage with the hawkish nose, high cheekbones and long limbs. David stayed by her side constantly, as did Tina, and they listened to her stories now told at a mere whisper. It was as if she was attempting to fill their heads with every piece of knowledge she had and they were just as intent on memorizing it.

Jess sat by her side one day and wrote down the names of Madge's children, along with birth dates (as well as Madge's failing memory could remember them), last known locations and promised to do her best to contact them. They deserved to know what had happened to their mother and the good that she had done for others in the last months of her life.

January slipped into February and as that month drew to a close, it became obvious that the old woman would soon be gone. Her skin was pale and mottled, clammy to the touch. Her breath came in short gasps, and no food or water had passed her lips in over two days. The children had seen heartache and pain and the ugliness of death. Far too much for their short lives, but somehow, this ending was different.

Madge had said she wanted to die on her terms, and she did, surrounded by people who had come to love her and care for her deeply. They stayed awake through the long night and as the rays of the sun pierced through the woven hangings at the front of the cave, Dr. Madeleine Falling Water gave one last, soft gasp and left the world, with all of them by her side, their hands holding hers, tears streaking their faces. Quincy howled mournfully.

That afternoon, Jess and David wrapped the old woman's body in deerskin, sewed it shut, and laid her on the ground a few feet away from the thong tree. The ground was still frozen, and there was no way they could dig a deep enough hole, so they gathered stones and made a cairn. When it was done and the sun was slipping down through the trees, the group gathered and stood at the heap of stones, silently for a few moments. Jess spoke first, reciting a poem Madge had taught her just days before.

"The Track of the sun
across the Sky
leaves its shining message,
Illuminating,
Strengthening,
Warming,
us who are here,
showing us we are not alone,
we are yet alive!
And this fire......
Our fire....
Shall never die"

Tina had discovered some tiny yellow flowers poking up from the snow and she solemnly placed them on the pile of stones. David cleared his throat and began to recite the last story Madge had ever told him...

"A young man wanted to become a respected elder, so he went to an elder and the elder told him, 'You must learn to count to 100.' Simple enough, the young man thought.

One day a homeless and dirty old woman limped into town. Some people looked at her and turned away. Others stared and whispered behind their hands.

The young man felt sorry for the old woman. He approached her and said, 'Grandmother, come in, rest.' He put his arm around her shoulders and took her into his home. He welcomed her, offered her water, and when she had rested and drank some water, he gave her soup.

He called to his mother and sisters, 'Help Grandmother wash and change. Put her in one of your buckskin dress and give her those new moccasins.' The mother and sisters bathed the old woman, washed her hair and braided it, dressed her in new clothes.

Then the family invited her to live with them, to join the family.

Later the young man brought her to the elder and introduced her saying, 'Grandmother has a new family.'

The elder asked, 'Is that the old homeless woman? You did this?' When the young man nodded the elder said, 'That is one.'"

"Thank you, Grandmother, for the lesson and the reminder that there is good in this world." David said clearly, despite the tears slipping down his face, "Look for the day that I learn to count to one hundred."

They could think of nothing more to say. Returning to the cave felt surreal, the heart of this place was gone without old Madge. They ate dinner quietly and Tina fell asleep huddled in David's lap. She had cried off and on throughout the day and was worn out. Jess had wrapped Jacob up and laid him on her cot where he would probably stay until the sun rose. She looked over at David, his face was morose and he stared off in the direction of the cave entrance. It struck Jess that he looked older, more grown up. "When's your birthday?"

"Huh?" He seemed startled to hear her speak.

"When's your birthday?"

"April 4th, I'll be twelve." He seemed a little surprised at the thought. His thoughts drifted to his parents, dead for nearly a year now. He had turned eleven and not even really thought about it. They hadn't exactly been paying attention to calendars at the time it had rolled by last year.

He thought a minute more, "Tina turned four in January. The 11th, I think." He looked embarrassed and somewhat guilty, "I didn't remember her birthday."

Jess stirred the coals of the fire, "I guess I never really asked or thought about it before, myself. I turned sixteen exactly two weeks after Jacob was born. I was so damn tired those first few weeks it's entirely possible that I slept right through it."

She paused, let the silence deepen and then said, "Adults would say you and I are both still kids, y'know. But we aren't. We've seen too much awful shit to be kids anymore." She spoke to him as an equal, more than she ever had before.

David nodded slowly, watching her; he wondered where this was heading. Then it dawned on him and he knew. "You think it might be safe now."

"Huh?" Jess looked confused for a moment, "Oh. Hell, I don't know. It's been nearly six months, that's one heck of a cold trail. They've probably forgotten all about us by now. Besides," She gave a smoldering log a sharp, angry shove, "It isn't two teenage girls anymore, so we don't fit the description on that paper."

"You still do." It was a fact; her hair was beautiful. Long, deep curls and golden blond, – it was hard to forget hair like that.

"I could cut it short. And then I'll dye it with some of those damn walnut shells that made our fingers black for a week." She grinned, "Can't do much about my eyes, but lots of people have blue eyes."

David grinned back, "Can I help cut it?" The look of horror in her eyes at the thought of him cutting her hair made him laugh for the first time in days.

"T*he battleline between good and evil runs through the heart of every man."*- **Alexander Solzhenitsyn**

Scott Cooper stretched out on the comfortable bed. At the corner of the bed on the floor, handcuffed to the bedpost, was a girl.

Occasionally he would hear her sniffle or sob. For the moment he simply ignored her. They had been traveling for days, hitting farms but not staying long due to the local militias. Damn, but he was tired. He hadn't been sleeping well and they'd been on the road way too long.

Most of the area seemed to have wised up and organized themselves. Memphis had a particularly strong militia in place, which would have been effective except they were also dealing with a nasty case of cholera.

Just north of Dyersburg they had managed to get a truck. It was a broken-down rust bucket. The engine ran rough, and none of the men knew much about maintenance, so they kept nursing it along, hoping for something better.

After they had pushed their way into Tennessee, in late November, two men left under the cover of night, while on sentry duty. Two more had died in skirmishes with locals as they navigated through a warren of tiny towns and backwoods hillbillies who were armed to the teeth.

By the time Cooper's band entered Memphis he was down to nineteen men. At that point the women they had had with them in Mississippi were all dead and six of the men who had been too scared to leave now realized they would die no matter what. Four of them managed to escape into the sprawling ruins of the city; and the other two were shot in the back as they ran. Four more men, a buddy of Riley's and three more grunts were shot by the Memphis militia. This left him with nine men. He turned and hightailed it out of Memphis heading northeast up Highway 70. Arlington and Stanton that took two more of his men, and another was lost on the outskirts of

Brownsville. They turned northwest then, passed through Ripley without incident before losing one more on the outskirts to Dyersburg. This left Cooper with Riley, Kimmel and Eckhardt. All of them were bad, all of them tough as nails.

They weren't an army any longer. But that was okay in several ways. None of the remaining men were stupid. They were all experienced fighters. And with only four men, there wasn't much advertisement to their presence. Try moving 200+ people through an area and see if someone doesn't notice. Four men, however, were easily hidden. And it was just the right amount for hitting the isolated farms along the way.

The girl gave another hiccupping sob. That annoying sound and the accompanying rumble from his stomach, made him sit up. He stood up and pulled his pants on and reached over to the girl. She cowered from him. Her shirt was ripped and bloody, her mouth cut and the rest of her clothes were gone. Bruises ran up and down her legs. Cooper unlocked the handcuff attached to the bedpost and yanked the girl to her feet.

"Come on, you're going to fix us something to eat.

He dragged her past the other bedrooms, where Riley and Kimmel were still busy with the girl's mother, and down the stairs and into the kitchen. The kitchen was all done up in red and white checked curtains, red cabinets, and matching accessories. Above a small table in the kitchen was a plaque that read "Home Sweet Home" and under that, "Welcome to the Austin's."

They had taken the house in the evening, shortly after dinner that evening. Under cover of darkness they had stormed both doors, two through the front and two in through the back, and the family had been taken unawares, without a shot fired, while sitting in the living room. The blood of the menfolk had splashed the floor and the walls and left dark, rust-colored drag marks out the front door and down the steps. They had put all the bodies in the old farmhouse, out of sight.

Eckhardt didn't seem to mind the blood and gore at all. He was snoring contentedly on the couch, his pants off. Apparently, he'd gotten first dibs on the mother. Cooper hadn't bothered asking, the others knew the girl was his and his alone until such time as he tired of her. This time might come soon if she didn't stop her damned whining.

He kicked Eckhardt as he passed him and the man jumped awake, a sharp hunting knife materializing in his hand. Disconcerted and still in the throes of his dream, he snarled at Cooper.

Scott just laughed. "Find me a chain for her."

He ordered, pointing to the girl. Eckhardt sheathed his knife and walked away muttering under his breath. A few minutes later a cold, rusty chain had been attached to the handcuff. The other end of the chain had been wrapped around a column that stood between the kitchen and dining room and locked in place with a padlock. Cooper slid the key into his khakis and sat down in the living room. Morning was dawning, he had worked up an appetite, and after he ate, he wanted to sleep.

The area was remote. They were two miles or so out of town and there was plenty of cover of trees. He set his feet up on the couch, motioned to Eckhardt to keep an eye on the girl in the kitchen and settled back. Cooper closed his eyes and smiled, they could afford to take a break for a few days, maybe even a couple of weeks. By now they had learned the trick of it. It had actually become rather easy to take the locals by surprise. Just hit them at dusk when their defenses are down and it's too dark to go running through the woods when you couldn't see where you were going.

From the kitchen he could hear the girl cry out as Eckhardt moved in and pressed her against the countertop. His hands groped her.

"Leave her be, Saul," Scott called out without opening his eyes, "I want some good old Southern cooking in me. You'll get a turn at that before too long anyway."

He ignored the man's mutterings as the sounds in the kitchen turned back to cooking.

An hour later as he gulped down the biscuits and gravy the girl had served up, he smiled. Maybe they'd stay for a while.

"Because I could not stop for Death—
    He kindly stopped for me—
The Carriage held but just Ourselves—
And Immortality." – Emily Dickinson

Liza pulled her prized stethoscope down to her neck and stared thoughtfully at Carrie's stomach. "I wish we had Doppler to listen to the baby's heartbeat. You just don't seem to be gaining much weight."

Carrie rolled her eyes at her little sister, "I've only been able to keep down food for the past month, sis, give it time."

Liza sighed, "I just wish I had more sophisticated equipment. At least we got some prenatal vitamins for you to take. Try eating just a little more at meals for a while, okay?"

She stared at her sister's belly speculatively and Carrie grew impatient, pulled her shirt down and sat up. It was true, she was barely showing anything at all, and she figured it had to have been four months by now, or near enough. As skinny as she was, it was weird that she didn't have much of a baby bump.

"All right, all right, I'll try and eat more. You're such a worry-wort! C'mon, I promised Chris this would be quick and then we could ride the buggy into town and look for parts for the windmill he's hoping to build."

Liza snorted and headed for the door, "What the heck do we need a windmill for, anyway?"

"Electricity!"

Liza scoffed, "No way!"

"Yeah way."

"Whatever."

"Also, he can build one that pumps water straight into the house...including the toilet and bathtub. Maybe we could even get the regulator on the hot water heater going if there's electricity."

"Really?" Liza closed her eyes and imagined the luxury of a long hot bath. Sponge baths and scrubbing their hair in the sink were the norm, despite the jury-rigged shower in the garage.

"Really. I'm taking him to Dorian's Junkyard to see if we can rustle up some parts."

Liza looked starry-eyed at the thought of having running water in the hall bathroom. Not having to hunch under the spigot in the freezing cold garage would be such an unbelievable luxury...and no more flushing the toilet with a bucket each time? Sweet!

Then her thoughts turned to town and visiting Carl, "Wait, let me get some books, and I'll take them in to...uh...trade."

Carrie smirked at her little sister, "Trade, huh? Trade kisses, maybe trade some gropes," she would have said more but Fenton limped down the hall headed for the bathroom.

His right knee had been bothering him for weeks and their grandfather was a wretched old grump when in pain. He fluttered his fingers in front of him in a shooing motion.

"Carrie-girl, take that sister and brother of yours away to town with you. Joseph keeps wantin' to dive into my lap sayin' he's Superman and Liza's bout to drive me up the wall with all her wantin' to poke and prod on me. And this damn leg is aching till I'm fit to be tied. You all go and get out of my hair for a while. I want me a nice, peaceful nap in my easy chair."

He shuffled past them and closed the bathroom door firmly.

Carrie winked at Liza, "Well, it looks like we're all going into town. Best get those books to *trade* and I'll round up Joseph." Liza grinned and dashed towards her room to put on a touch of makeup and run a brush through her tangled hair. She pulled it up in a ponytail, shrugged into her warmest coat and was at the front door waiting, books in hand, before Carrie could corral 'Superman' and shove him in a coat. Carrie eyed her sister sternly, "But you have to take him with you."

At Liza's horrified expression, Carrie amended it, "He can play with Tabitha."

"Jeez, sis, and I *thought* you were cool!" Liza complained. Carrie just laughed.

It was early February and Christmas had been the one and only snowfall that year. It wasn't too cold, the thermometer on the side of the barn registered in the mid-40s, but everything around them was barren and dead except for the random patch of green grass. Winter had them in its grip for at least one more month, possibly two.

The girls and Joseph pitched in and helped Chris finish with the morning chores. They hitched up the wagon, snuggled Joseph and Liza in the back under a thick lap quilt and Chris and Carrie shared another on the front seat of the wagon. Carrie had pieced the quilts together in the past few weeks, using her great-great-grandmother's treadle-operated sewing machine to finish each quilt. It had been a surprising find. The sewing cabinet had sat in the guest room, served as a table covered with knickknacks. The sewing machine was intact and usable inside, and it had only taken some oil and a new belt to put it back into service. The quilts kept them toasty warm on the drive into town.

Chris had never been to the junkyard. Jim Dorian was a collector, mainly of junk, but if you were looking for the odd or the innovative, then Dorian Junkyard was the place to go. When school had still been in session, the Tiptonville high school kids were taken on an annual trip to the junkyard. Here they learned to re-purpose old items into art, or cobble together eclectic furniture, and more. You never knew what you might find. After they dropped off Liza and Joseph, and made sure it was okay for them to visit, Chris and Carrie headed for the junkyard. Jim Dorian peered out of his double-wide, which was parked at the entrance of the fenced-in junkyard and grinned at Carrie.

"Well, I'll be. If it ain't Miss Carrie Lynn Perdue." He grinned at Carrie, "You made a lovely little charm bracelet, as I recall. Wore a sparkly blue tank top." Carrie had tried to prepare Chris as they drove over.

"Gramps says that Jim Dorian is some kind of savant. But he's odd, I'm warning you of that right now. He's got this amazing memory.

Once he has been introduced to someone, he never forgets their names and he remembers the strangest details. It usually weirds people out, but Gramps says he's harmless."

"Morning, Mr. Dorian. This is my husband, Chris." Carrie still loved saying that, "My last name is Aaronson now." The disheveled man did not tell them congratulations as others had; he simply turned his attention to Chris.

"Chris Aaronson, husband of Carrie Lynn Aaronson. Yes. I've heard of you. Wes says you were with the Western Front. He says you should go and not come back to these here parts." Carrie gasped and Chris bristled. Dorian did not pause at their reactions, "One, two, three names, four if you count the old one, Carrie." His hands fluttered, creating shapes, first a triangle, then a square and finally a ball-shape. He looked down at the ground for a long moment.

"Sixteen, seventeen, eighteen, nineteen, twenty. Grandma always said don't let more than twenty seconds go by without making polite conversation." He looked up and smiled pleasantly, "The weather is nice today, don't you think?"

Chris didn't know how to react, but Carrie recovered quickly, "Lovely weather Mr. Dorian, the sun is shining. And it feels warmer than yesterday. We're here to see if we can find the parts to make a windmill."

Jim Dorian's eyes lit up, "A windmill! Yes. For water or for electricity. A majority of windmills have four sails, but really six or eight is best."

He began walking rapidly into the heart of the junkyard, "Come this way, twenty-three paces straight, then five paces to the left."

He strode away, counting out loud and snapping his fingers at each step. They quickly followed him, exchanging glances, with Carrie shrugging her shoulders in an "I told you" fashion. Dorian was one odd bird.

An hour later they had filled the back of the buggy with metal sheets, poles, struts, and what seemed like a million little components. "What can I give in trade, Mr. Dorian?" Carrie asked.

Dorian's eyes fell on her gleaming emerald and diamond wedding ring, "Five stones. One, two, three, four round ones, one square, that makes five. Em-er-ald and di-a-mond. Pretty."

Carrie smiled, "It is very pretty, Mr. Dorian, but I can't offer it in trade. It was a gift and it's my wedding ring."

She said it gently but firmly, making sure there was no misunderstanding. His face was blank in response.

"Perhaps some food to trade, Mr. Dorian? Eggs through until spring? Two of our goats will be birthing soon, would you like a goat in the spring?"

Dorian looked thin and a tad malnourished. His hair was dull, and his eyes were sunken with dark circles underneath. Not particularly surprising.

His grandmother had died five years ago. In good times, everyone pitched in to help keep him fed. In a small town like this, everyone knew everyone else's business. But it was winter now, and the good times were certainly absent. Most people were struggling to make it through the winter. The residents of Tiptonville weren't bad people, maybe a tad neglectful, but Dorian never asked for help.

Nelda Dorian, Jim's grandmother had raised him since his parents died in a car accident when he wasn't yet out of diapers. A hard-working, proud woman, she had instilled in him the basics – politeness, hard work, and an independent spirit despite his disabilities.

Jim Dorian smiled in his peculiar way, one side of his mouth curled up, while the other stayed level. He always looked decidedly lopsided. "Pickled eggs, Miz Carrie?"

Carrie smiled back, "Mr. Dorian, I will bring you all the pickled eggs you care to eat!" She was determined to slip in some jars of green beans and some fresh potatoes. They still had plenty of the russets left.

A haunch of meat would do him good as well. She promised that one of them would bring it to him next visit into town which was sure to be soon, what with Liza liking to visit Carl. A sharp cramping in her abdomen halted her step up into the buggy.

Chris had been helping her up, when she doubled over in agony.

"What is it? What's wrong?" he asked, panicked. In the past few months their relationship had changed as her pregnancy progressed. Despite the fact she was barely showing, their lovemaking, once so frequent (as evidenced by the child growing inside of her) had vanished. He insisted that he was 'just too tired' and treated her like a fragile little china doll, handling all of the chores that required any lifting and bending. All of the chores, really, except for feeding the chickens and goats which Joseph was able to do.

"I'm fine, I...ooh!" It felt like she was being stabbed, "Let's just get Liza and Joseph and get out of here okay? Help me up in the buggy and we'll get on our way." But before he could even help her up, trouble arrived.

"What the hell are you doing here, soldier?" Chris felt his anger rise. It was, of course, Wes Perkins. He stood there, his hands holding Ichabod's reins. The horse shifted slightly, uneasy. Even Ichabod could tell Wes was bad news.

"Good day, Wesley Perkins," Dorian piped up, "Two names, no middle name, no middle name, none. Went to Iraq in oh-three and returned in oh-five. Two years gone; eleven years returned. Eleven is a good number. Very good, will be twelve soon." He nodded, examining the ground. "They're gonna make a windmill. Electricity, water, windmill, yes. Six blades, not four."

Wes took this in. He might have been a prick to everyone else, but for some reason he was always kind to Jim Dorian.

"That's good Jim, very good." He handed the man a small sack, "I brought you some of that food I promised you last week. Why don't you go put it away?"

Dorian nodded to Carrie and Chris and walked away, peering into the bag and muttering as he did. He climbed the steps to the front door of his decrepit double-wide and went inside without another word.

Wes's eyes narrowed, "Building you a communications array there, soldier?"

Carrie gripped her husband's shoulder, trying not to scream as another horrible twisting pain hit.

"Give me a hand into the buggy, Chris." He helped her up, keeping eye contact with Wes the entire time.

Chris sounded calmer than he felt, "I've told you. I'm a friend of the family, well more than that, now that Carrie and I are married. And you heard yourself what we need the parts for, so why don't you just back the hell off, Wes? What is your beef with me, exactly?"

That was all the challenge Wes needed. The man closed the space between them with one fluid stride. His face was inches away from Chris's.

His words were low and menacing, "I know a soldier when I see one. You've seen action. I know about that uniform you tried to burn and I am watching you, *every day*." His breath stank and he obviously didn't bathe often.

"Chris," Carrie tried to keep the fear and the pain out of her voice as another horrible twisting pain hit. What was this? Could she be having contractions? "We need to go...*now*."

The men did not move or speak. It looked as if they were locked in a staring contest, daring the other to move first. It was Carrie's moan of pain that ended it. Chris looked up and realized how white she was, her lips were thin and her entire body was hunched. He jumped up into the buggy, pulled hard on the reins and turned Ichabod and the buggy towards the Carters' house. He didn't bother to look back at Wes Perkins who wisely didn't try to stop them. In the two blocks to the Carter's, Carrie's pain seemed to subside. When Chris pulled her close and asked her if she was okay, she nodded.

"I think I'm getting that stomach flu that's going around." She looked up at his concerned face and smiled, "I'm sure I'm fine."

She insisted on waiting in the buggy as Chris jumped down, made room for Liza and Joseph to sit in the back and everyone loaded up.

She said little on the drive home while Joseph and Liza chattered on and on about how Abigail was pretty sure she was pregnant. "She might be about two months along," Liza chattered, "So Little Christopher," she was sure Carrie and Chris were having a boy, "will have someone to play with."

Carrie didn't respond, just leaned in closer to Chris.

He pulled the buggy to a stop directly at the steps of the farmhouse. The fact that Carrie had been so quiet scared him more than anything.

Liza jumped out making a comment about valet service and turned to go inside. "Liza," Chris called to her, "Could you please have a look at Carrie? I'll be there as soon as I get Ichabod settled in." He helped Carrie down from the buggy gently, and smiled at her with concern. "Go lay down, I'll be there in a minute."

It was in the barn that he saw the blood. Why hadn't he noticed it before? He had to have been blind. It was bright red. A large circle of it spread on the quilt, drips of blood down the side of the buggy where he had helped Carrie down. How had he not seen it? He ran then, leaving the horse still hitched to the buggy. He ran full out, despite the sharp pain from his weak ankle. He ran through the open barn doors, across the wide yard and up the stairs, barely touching them as he barreled through the door.

Fenton had barely opened one eye, still half asleep in his favorite recliner when Chris flew through the door. He passed Joseph, who was sitting at the counter in the kitchen sipping from a cup of hot chocolate left over from breakfast, "What in Hades is going on?"

Fenton bellowed as he stood up, wincing visibly as he put his weight on his bad leg. Chris did not answer; he was too busy flinging open the door as Carrie began to scream and Liza called out frantically for towels.

No one ate dinner that night and Ichabod spent most of the afternoon and evening standing in the barn without being unhitched from the buggy or fed.

At nearly ten o'clock that evening Fenton and Joseph went out and cared for the horse, which had stood patiently waiting while tears and loss unfolded within the farmhouse walls. The old man moved slowly, as if he could feel the entire weight of the world on his shoulders.

"Gramps?"

"Yes, Joseph?"

"Will Carrie be okay?"

The little boy looked up at his grandfather. He didn't remember either of his parents. His father Isaac had died before he was born and his mother when he was still an infant. Carrie and Liza were his mothers, and Gramps and Chris, were his dads. The fear of losing any of them had suddenly been made very real.

Fenton didn't bother to wipe away the tears that still fell all these hours later.

"Yes, Joseph, Carrie will be okay...in time. But she's awful sad right now."

"And the baby? Is the baby okay?"

"No Joseph." The old man couldn't bear to say anything more. He sat down on the rough plank bench, pulled his grandson close and cried.

Inside their bedroom, sheets changed and the small body wrapped, Carrie sobbed, her heart breaking. Amy Lynn Aaronson had lived for five brief minutes, each breath a struggle, before her chest had risen no more and her body had stilled and then cooled in their arms. She had been tiny, not a single hair on her head, her skin bright red.

Chris held his wife and cried with her long into the night.

"*F unny to think of a cave as home, but it was, for just that little while. Despite the drafts and the invading rodents, we healed there, again. It seems that, up to that point our lives had been a cycle of trauma and recovery. I think it was the tipping point, the path to something better. Where the next few weeks would take us would eventually be a place I have come to think of as home. Each step, from Clinton, to the cave, to the moment we stepped into that house in Belton...no matter how terrible some of those memories are...I think I would not be who I am now if not for the steps I took to get here.*" – **David's Journal**

Madge's passing had changed everything. The cave was different, less full of life. Jacob whined constantly, looking at each of them in turn as if he were searching for the old woman.

Two days later, Jess reluctantly asked David to help her cut her hair. There were no mirrors, other than a tiny handheld one. Without his help it would have been by feel. It was a rough job, but her long, wavy hair turned into tight little curls which hid much of the unevenness. They then gathered all of the black walnut shells and boiled them in water on the stove. After the water had cooled, Jess hunkered over the pot and dunked her cropped hair into it repeatedly, holding her hair in the water as long as possible.

The result, after her hair dried, was a mass of muddy brown curls, a marked difference from the long-haired blond she had been that morning. They both had stained fingers from the walnut shells. It turned their hands an odd shade of brown that did not go away for several weeks, no matter how many times they washed them.

They didn't discuss leaving, other than to begin making a pile on one side of the cave of things they wanted to take with them. The pile grew and shrank, then grew again as Jess and David tried to decide what was worth taking and what would be too much. They also experimented with expansions onto their original backpacks, adding loops that could hold tools and

Jess sewed the buckskins into cot lengths that could be rolled up and tied, then hooked onto their knapsacks.

Tina went out daily with Quincy by her side and picked the fresh greens that were just emerging...she brought back oxalis, wild violet, fresh new plantain, and handfuls of fiddlehead ferns. The greens were a welcome break from their stores of preserved meat and the last few packages of ramen noodles. The little dog acted as a guide and a hunter. Three times they returned with fresh rabbit as well as plenty of greens.

David had improved even further with the bow and arrow, whooping in excitement the first time Quincy pointed at a bird and he successfully brought it down. It was a scrawny pheasant, but Jess and Tina had both been excited to eat something other than squirrel or dried venison and encouraged him to continue trying.

Food on the trail would be scarce since it was still early in the year, each of the packs included as much dried meat and fish as it could comfortably hold. The dog would help them catch food too, but that would only help if it was safe enough to build a fire and cook whatever she killed and brought back to them.

Jess wedged the beautiful leather book into her pack. She had read through the entries over and over the past few days, seeking the comfort of Madge's scribbled words. What she had read had brought tears to her eyes. The old woman had loved them so much, felt so thankful for their arrival, and Jess felt her loss keenly. She had become a mother to them all in the short time they were together. The other journals, mostly specifics around the work she was doing, were sealed inside a metal box and placed in the off-limits section of the cave. Jess added a note to the top of the stack before sealing the box. In the note she explained who she was, how they had wintered with Madge in the cave, and their eventual destination.

Jess figured that anyone who knew where the cave was would be able to find the box and make their way to Belton and find her. She hoped it would be one of Madge's children and that she could meet them and someday share with them her special memories of their mother.

She kept one other notebook out and stuffed it in her jacket pocket. Madge had sketched many plants, some here at the cave, many not, and listed by each sketch the name and uses for each plant, along with notes on what part of the plant should be used. Madge had filled Jess's ears with more information than she could easily remember, but the little notebook helped with the tiniest of details.

She also had the names and last known contact information for Madge's family within the journal in her pack, for whatever good that would do her. How in the world would she find them when there wasn't mail service?

On the fifth day after Madge's death they looked around and realized there was nothing left to pack. There was plenty of things, but nothing more than they could fit comfortably in their bags or via the travois they had rigged to pull behind them. It was time to go. They ate breakfast, washing their meal down with bitter hot boiled chicory and doused the fire.

Before the trees closed behind them the little band stopped and looked at the cave opening, almost fully hidden unless you knew what to look for, and it felt like they were leaving home. They trekked down the trail to the rock cairn and thong tree, stood for a few moments, and then silently turned north and began to follow the waterline of the lake.

What little discussion they did have had come last night. Until given a reason to avoid them, they would try to find the nearest highway and begin the journey back to Belton that way. It would cut time off of their journey and kept the travelers near any remnants of civilization and possible food sources. It meant returning to Clinton, following Highway 7 into Harrisonville and then up 71 to Belton.

The air was cool and the sky clear. According to the pocket calendar they had kept in the cave, it was March 5th. This time last year Jess had been planning her and Erin's escape from the camp.

"God willing and the creek don't rise, we'll be in Belton within two weeks. We'll head north until we meet up with YY and take it to Highway 7 'till it turns into Highway 71," she pointed on the map to David each step along the way. "If the fighting has died down, we might even hitch a ride and make it in days or even hours."

She glanced at his worried face, "Don't worry, we've got ammo and you are a great shot. You're our backup. Things get bad, they aren't going to expect a teenager with a baby and two little kids to haul off and start shooting."

His worried look turned into a smirk, "Who 'ya calling little?" He waved in his sister's direction, "She's the short one...I've grown two inches over the winter!" That earned him a laugh from the teenager. From the way his pants were riding high, he'd put on more inches the past summer as well, the 'kid' was growing up fast.

They took pains to hide their weapons. Jess was right, what they had on their side was their youth and the element of surprise. It might just come in handy along the way. Madge had shown them a trail when they had first arrived and told them if they followed it, it would put them on a relatively straight course to Clinton. They followed this, thereby avoiding backtracking their path to the cave and avoiding the bodies to the north as well as the old farmhouse where Erin had died.

The first two days they made good progress, winding their way back up to Route YY and then heading west back into Clinton. The town was deserted, and it looked as though there had been more fighting, as well as an extensive fire. It took some doing to find their old house. It looked as if there had been a fire.

Nothing was left, just blackened ruins and a flooded basement. Tina made a beeline for their parent's grave, plucked an armful of tulips and jonquils that poked out of the patchy grass of their old yard and laid it on the mound. The cross that David had set there had disappeared.

Jess saw that the children needed a little time. "We can camp here tonight, that shed where Jacob was born is still relatively intact." No one argued. One edge of the shed had been blackened by fire and a large tree limb had fallen and gouged a divot in the roof, but it looked better than camping out in the cold. The days were cool and the nights often dipped below freezing.

The previous night they had curled up together for warmth. Jess on one side and David on the other, with Tina and Jacob sandwiched in between. The two on the outside had spent far too much of the night awake and shivering. The walls of the small shed would provide a break from the wind and contact with the cold earth.

David found a piece of limestone rock and scraped a cross and his parent's initials into it. Jess helped him pull it into position and, as had become their custom, they spent a few moments the next morning remembering who they had lost. She had never met them, but Jess knew David and Tina well, so she talked about how proud their parents would have been to see them and know they were doing well and learning and growing. Before moving on they tried sifting through the blackened ruin of the house, but there was nothing left to salvage.

By noon they were on Route 7, the road was clear, but bodies in advanced stages of decay appeared at intervals in the ditches that ran parallel on each side. It made them all nervous, but none of these bodies were recent. They were dressed in an unfamiliar uniform. None of the group was willing to get close enough to the corpses to find out which army they were from. Quincy was their barometer. The dog was smart, more attentive than ever since they had set out, and she stuck close by their side at all times.

"Still think we should be using main roads?" David asked, in mid-afternoon when the dog began to first whine, then growl deep in her throat. The day had begun sunny but near noon the clouds had rolled in and the sky was gloomy and overcast. The wind had picked up, and they were walking into it, which made it harder. It was possible they could get snow; it was only March and snow this late in the season wasn't unheard of.

Quincy had begun to whine after they crossed over the South Grand River. They looked around, but nothing appeared out of place. Still, the little dog knew her stuff, something was up.

"Let's get off the road and into that stand of trees over there." Jess pointed to a small patch of forest on the other side of a marshy section of land. It wasn't the best cover, the trees were still bare of leaves, but it was better than walking down the middle of the highway. They kept a sharp lookout, headed for the trees, and soaked their shoes walking through the marshy area. This was a problem, especially for Tina and David, who had barely usable shoes, having grown over the winter.

Their toes rested firmly against the ends of their shoes, straining against the fabric. The water was icy cold, and they were relieved to get out of the open as the wind continued to increase. Jess quickly began to realize the depth of the danger they were in. They did not have good shoes, there was still a strong possibility of snow and freezing weather, and they had no idea where to find shelter for the night. *What in the hell was I thinking wanting to leave the cave so early?*

The small group plunged into the tree line, pushing on until the road was difficult to see. Quincy had stopped growling and was now only whining, as if she was picking up the scent of something familiar, but something that bothered her nonetheless. The escape to the trees had only taken a couple of minutes and none of them were surprised to see several camouflage Army trucks motor down the now deserted road, full of soldiers and weapons. They were heading into Clinton, not out of it, so for now the band was safe. If Quincy hadn't warned them, they would have never made it off the road and into hiding in time. Jess reached down and scratched behind the pup's ears with stiff, half-frozen fingers. "Good work, Quince. Now if you only knew how to find us some shelter for the night, we'd be set." The dog gave a little whine and licked Jess's fingers. Then she sprang away, nose to the ground, leading them west.

"It will take longer if we stick to the trees," David said as they followed the little dog, "But if we keep the road in sight, we'll have cover and some safety and still be following the main roads." Jess just nodded, it sounded like a good plan to her. An hour, perhaps far later, her stomach rumbled painfully. It had to be mid-afternoon by now and they hadn't stopped to eat any lunch. Tina was stumbling along listlessly to the rear, even David looked worn out. Trekking through woods was far more difficult than the road.

Jacob sealed the deal by waking and crying fitfully. At nearly six months of age, he wasn't as impatient as he had been a few months ago. Then it had been a cycle of wake, scream for food, eliminate, scream to be changed, rinse and repeat. Now at least he gave her time to get settled, and would reach his arm up out of the sling to touch her face. He loved the necklace David had made for her and played with it for hours on end. She reached in, caressed his head, and put the disk of the pendant in his tiny hand. That would distract him for a while, but he would need to eat soon.

The sky was gray and ominous through the trees. It held an almost certain promise of freezing rain or even snow within the dark clouds. And although it was only mid-afternoon, the light was fading. David looked up at the sky as well, "We need to find shelter, Jess, shelter and food, and soon." As if to emphasize the point, Jacob whined again, kicking his legs against Jess's stomach in displeasure.

At that moment, Quincy, who had been heading west with her little nose to the ground, gave a short bark and dashed south, to the left, disappearing within the trees. "Squirrel? Rabbit?" Jess asked, looking in the direction that the little dog had gone. David shook his head, and turned south. They could hear the dog give two sharp barks a few hundred feet away. Five minutes later, deep in the woods now, they found Quincy at a small clearing. The smell of wood smoke had made them nervous, but as they approached, they saw a small family and relaxed a little. There were four of them, a man and a woman and two small children, a boy and a girl.

" **G** *ive sorrow words. The grief that does not speak whispers the o'er-fraught heart, and bids it break. -* **Shakespeare**

It was mid-March and Chris had been working hard, preparing the beds for planting. The last frost date was a month or so away, not much different than it was in Chris's hometown, but there was much to do beforehand. He had climbed onto the roof of the barn and fixed the areas torn loose in a winter storm. It had, for a period of time, rendered one of the stalls unusable and they had moved Ichabod to a smaller stall until the hole could be mended. Chris had thrown himself into his work, stopping only for a bite of bread and cheese at lunch. These days he barely ate at all, and usually fell asleep early, holding Carrie close in his arms through the night.

A fog of grief had descended upon the Perdue farm. They had buried the baby as soon as Carrie was well enough to be carried to the small cemetery on the farm's southeast corner. The Perdue farm had been in the family for five generations and consequently it had its own private plot 100 yards due south of the original homestead.

Mrs. Jennings attended, along with the Carter-Owens family, and John Carter gently took the small coffin from Fenton. Fenton looked as if he hadn't slept a wink in three days and his eyes were rimmed in red. Chris insisted on lifting Carrie, still weak and listless, and he refused all offers of help as he held his wife close and carried her to the family cemetery.

The plot was of decent size, perhaps twenty feet by thirty. Along the south fence were the Fenton's grandparents and parents. In the middle of the plot were the graves of his great-grandparents. There were also three small headstones next to his great-grandmother's headstone that were obviously those babies who had not survived to adulthood. Chris remembered Fenton mentioning that his grandfather had been the only child to survive, just as Fenton had been an only child, and Isaac after him.

On the north fence was Molly, with an open spot in the northwest corner for Fenton. Beside Molly's grave rested Isaac's. Isaac's wife Amy was the most recent addition. John had come early that morning to help dig the hole for the baby while Abigail made breakfast. She had given her son Carl a light push in Liza's direction and motioned for him to take her for a walk. In the small cemetery, Chris had pointed to where the other children's markers were and asked Fenton if it would be all right to bury her there. It seemed right somehow, that she should be close to other children, even if their little girl hadn't gotten a chance to be a child. The old man had just nodded and walked away, moving slow and looking as if every step, every breath was an agony.

The past few days had aged him.

Reverend Thomas, along with a small group of Tiptonville residents that Chris knew only in passing showed up by mid-morning and the funeral was subdued. Carrie made no sound, didn't cry at all, until the coffin was placed in the ground and the dirt began to be shoveled over it. She had insisted on standing as Reverend Thomas read the benediction and the Lord's Prayer and when they had begun to cover the tiny coffin she had collapsed on the ground, sobbing. Those who hadn't had tears in their eyes did at the sight of her sobbing, heartbroken, in Chris's arms.

In the weeks since, the cohesiveness of the family had been tested. Fenton had always insisted that the family gather for every meal. But Carrie stayed in bed and often refused to eat. She had grown gaunt and hollow-eyed. Liza was subdued, a stark contrast from her ebullient, energetic self, and she would disappear into the forest alone and walk to the old homestead or to the cemetery. Sometimes she would be gone for most of the day, slipping in only when the sun had set and the night shadows had stolen across the farm. Lunch as a family was nearly non-existent and breakfast and dinner were dismal, silent affairs.

The breaking point came at breakfast on a cool, crisp Sunday morning. Liza had slipped out before dawn and had not returned to make breakfast, a responsibility that she and Carrie shared, but one which she had shouldered entirely in recent weeks. Without his coffee, which was really a mix of chicory and coffee (heavy on the chicory), Fenton was not one to be trifled with. In fact, he was looking rather ticked off. Chris had been making the morning rounds of the livestock and had seen Liza slipping around the pond, heading towards the old homestead.

She'd taken the loss of the baby as hard as he and Carrie had. He suspected she felt responsible somehow, although he couldn't imagine how. Sometimes babies came early. If it was anyone's fault, it was his.

He shouldn't have gotten Carrie pregnant. She was too young to be having a baby. He remembered the 'family planning' classes in high school that had preached abstinence as their main theme. His teacher had explained that a woman's body wasn't fully developed until she is around twenty, and that carrying a child puts a lot of strain on any woman's body. She had even explained that teens had an increased chance of a premature birth and a host of other problems.

Dad had sat him down long before that class and explained to him in detail what sex meant. He had squirmed and wished he could shut off his ears. It is one thing to look at a pretty girl and let your imagination run wild. It is another to hear your parent remind you that sex is how you came into existence. The thought of his parents doing *that* still made him a bit nauseous and that was an image he *didn't* need.

Michael Aaronson had laughed at the expression on his son's face and said, "Just think of it like this, son – every time you think of actually having sex, imagine that you will be making a baby with that girl. If you just 'sort of' like her, what's having a baby and having to raise a child for the next twenty years with her going to be like?"

Michael Aaronson had been pretty laid back. The only son of two hippies who had met and fell in love while attending college at UC Berkeley, he had spent the early years of his life in East Wind, an 'intentional community' located in a remote area of Missouri.

He and his parents had left there and moved to Kansas City after an upheaval within the membership when he was twelve. His memories of the place had been rich and he had shared many stories of growing up on the property – canoeing, exploring caves, and running through the fields and extensive gardens.

Fenton's bellow shook Chris from his reverie, "Where the Sam Hill is that girl?" He had been so lost in his thoughts that Fenton had called out twice before bellowing in frustration.

Chris snapped to attention, "Sir?"

Fenton frowned at him, looking irritated, "Stop callin' me that, boy."

"Yes, sir," Chris winced, "I mean...Gramps."

Fenton just rolled his eyes in exasperation and asked again, "Where's Liza?"

"I saw her heading around the pond a few minutes ago," Chris answered.

At that moment a scream came echoing from the trees. Both men reacted instantly, Chris dropped the bucket of water and began running through the open barn door. Fenton was right on his heels as he hung a sharp right and began to run along the path at the pond's edge. Some geese had nested for the evening by the pond edge and began to scatter as the men ran through them, honking loudly as they took to the air or waddled out of range flapping their wings in distress.

There was one more scream, which added wings to Chris's feet. Already Fenton was dropping behind, struggling to move his old bones faster.

Ahead of him a shot cracked off and Fenton bellowed and fell to the ground. Chris twisted in the air and threw himself to the ground as another shot came whistling by. It had been so close he had felt it zip by him in the air.

Here by the pond was cover of sorts, the dead grass and weeds were still tall, undisturbed. He turned and crawled on his belly back to Fenton, trying to move the old man off of the clear path and into the weeds. He quickly examined Fenton's left shoulder, which now had a hole punched in it. He'd been lucky, a few more inches down and it would have hit his left lung, but it looked as if the projectile had passed straight through. He was bleeding and wheezing in pain. Holding on to Chris with his right hand he crawled into the brush as another bullet whizzed by overhead.

"You armed, son?" Fenton whispered behind clenched teeth; his shoulder was on fire.

"Yes sir, always." Chris had not forgotten the chaos of Belton. It had haunted him how easily the town had been taken; how easy it had been for the soldiers to round so many up. "I've got the .45, but just one clip. You?"

Fenton winced as Chris bumped his shoulder and pulled the gun out and into ready position, "I forgot mine. We're in a bad spot here and we got Carrie and Joseph in the house." His mind was spinning, working strategy.

Chris took the safety off and handed the .45 to Fenton. "I can crawl back, go 'round the barn and use the yard for cover and get back to the house and get more firepower. I'm just scared one of us will hit Liza if we shoot blind."

Fenton shook his head, "You need to get us some help. Get back to the barn, saddle the horse and ride to town."

"Sir, you're hurt. You go into shock and they've got Liza and an open shot at the house and our livestock with nothing to stop them." Chris knew Carrie and Joseph had heard the screams and shots. It was quiet out here, sound carried well. Right now, Carrie was probably arming herself to the teeth and keeping a close eye on Joseph. Another shot whizzed by and they could hear muted sounds of a struggle. Liza was fighting them tooth and nail, from the sound of it. But she was a slip of a thing compared to a full-grown man. There was no way she would be able to win a fight like that. He thought about Jess and burned inside.

What had it been like for her in that awful place? How long had she fought before being kicked and punched into submission? They had to get her back and defend the farm. If those raiders moved in, they would strip their stores bare, kill Chris, Fenton and Joseph, and then kill Carrie and Liza after violating them in terrible ways.

There had been months of silence since the raids in late fall. Were these men new to the area? Or were they the same ones, returned for more looting and murder?

"Send Joseph," The old man's voice was unsteady, probably shock.

"Send Joseph on Ichabod and get us some help. The Austin's must be dead, 'cause that stand of trees backs up to their property and we hadn't heard a peep all winter. Town is our only hope of getting extra firepower."

Time was of the essence. Chris knew Fenton would hold on as long as he could, but the man was no spring chicken and he was going into shock. Chris turned and began to crawl through the grass, moving as quickly as he could and ignoring the mass of goose crap that decorated the ground and oozed between his fingers. Several large ganders were still in the vicinity and they honked menacingly as he moved through.

He froze as one approached, its head low and wings spread, ready to attack. The shot that hit the gander was undoubtedly meant for him. With that shot, and the strangled squawk the goose gave out as it died, the rest of the flock rose into the air, honking and cartwheeling through the sky. Chris used the distraction to jump to his feet and race the final few yards to the shelter of the barn.

He could hear Fenton fire off one shot and a second as he raced to saddle Ichabod, the horse snorting and pawing the ground nervously. Chris figured it would be easier to ride out himself, and get help and get back here as quick as he could. He was so involved in getting Ichabod ready to go that he nearly jumped out of his shoes when a tiny hand tugged on his pant legs. "Jesus Christ on a stick!" Joseph jumped and cowered and Chris grabbed him and pulled him close, "Joseph, what are you doing out here?"

"I followed Gramps, and I was standin' there when Liza screamed," the boy looked scared and Chris realized Joseph thought he was in trouble. He hugged the boy.

"Joseph, you are going to get help for us. Can you do that for me, Joseph?" The boy nodded eagerly and Chris lifted him up to Ichabod as a third shot rang out from the pond and two shots sounded back.

"I'm going to send you out the back way. You stay down, keep close to the horse and go to the sentry towers. Tell them we need help right away. Can you do that, Joseph?"

The boy nodded again, looking scared and determined and Chris led the horse to the back end of the barn. The raiders would be watching the entrance and not expecting the barn had a back exit. He slapped Ichabod hard on the rump and the horse whinnied and bolted forward down the drive, Joseph flattened against the horse, past the house and into the distance. Chris dashed to the house.

It was a straight shot for him, just fifty feet and much of that obscured by the barn, and a line of fruit trees that lined the west edge of the garden. He flew up the steps, safe now from view and crashed into the front door. Seconds later, Carrie undid the bolt and pulled him inside, her delicate fingers running over him, checking him for bullet holes.

"Fenton's still out there. He's been hit and we need to get back to him." Chris's words tumbled out as he reached for the rifle Carrie had in her hand. He had to try and come up with a plan to get back to Fenton, rescue Liza, and stop the raiders in their tracks.

Carrie had already pulled every weapon she could find from the gun safe and other locations. She was half-dressed, just jeans pulled on under her pajama top and a windbreaker over that. Her hair was tangled and she was barefoot. There hadn't been any more gunshots since he had run for the barn. Silence had fallen, except for the occasional outraged honk of the geese. Chris ran and peered out of one of the windows. He could just barely make out Fenton's boot sticking out of the tall weeds. "I've got to get out there. I sent Joseph for help and they should be here soon. You stay in the house."

"The hell I will! That's my Gramps and sister out there!" Carrie snarled as she loaded Fenton's prize shotgun, grabbed some extra shells and shoved them in her pockets. Her face was gaunt and there were circles under her eyes. But to Chris she looked more alive than she had in weeks. She headed for the door, turned and looked at him, "Well?"

"Shoes," he said pointing to her feet, "And we need Liza's med kit." Carrie glared at him, and ran down the hall to get the kit and shoes.

Chris listened carefully, peering out of the windows towards the stand of trees and trying desperately to see something, anything of the men who had been firing on the farm. Seconds later, Carrie re-appeared, shoes on her feet and the medical kit in one hand.

"I can't carry the kit and still shoot," she said, tossing it towards him.

"And I'm the better shot, so, here you go."

It was true; she was dead accurate in her aim. It was a fact he had been made painfully aware of a few months back when the raids had been making everyone twitchy and Fenton had insisted that everyone except for Joseph improve their aim with a little bit of target practice. Carrie had been a crack shot and he'd been horribly jealous of the ease in which she handled everything from a revolver to shotgun.

His parents hadn't owned guns and he was never trusted with one as a conscript. Carrie had better aim than him with her eyes blindfolded.

"Back of the garden, around the barn."

"Yeah, that's the way you need to go." She buckled a revolver on her holster. "I'm heading around to the north. I'll use the cornfield as cover and come in from that direction."

"Shit. At least wait for the militia to arrive!" Why, oh why, had they not had a plan in place for this?

"Get Gramps fixed up. Stop the bleeding and make sure he's okay." Chris started to object but the look on Carrie's face stopped him,

"Please Chris, help Gramps. I've got to get to Liza before they hurt her." She pulled him close and kissed him. "Please, Chris?" All objections melted in the face of her pained face.

As they exited the front door, each diving in opposite directions and running as fast as their legs could carry, there was silence except for their own feet running. Chris ran full out, behind the raised beds and cover of trees and to the edge of the barn. He peered around it, saw nothing and dropped to a crouch and ran the rest of the way, sliding to a stop on his belly next to Fenton who was still watching the tree line, his face chalk white and sweating. "I think they've taken off. I heard a truck start up, some ways off. That there engine don't sound too good, sounded rough." Fenton winced as Chris pushed a fold of thick gauze against the bleeding wound. "Damn that hurts!" He pushed at Chris,

"Why the dickens you're worryin' over an old codger like me, I'll never know. Y'all need to be taking off after Liza and those men. I'll be fine."

Chris put his hand back against the wound earning a bark of pain from the old man. "Carrie's headin' their way, armed to the teeth."

"What?! Why in the Sam Hill would you let her do that?"

Chris eyed him, his mouth tipping into a lopsided grin.

"She's a Perdue, there wasn't any *letting* on my part. Besides, she's a better shot and even more stubborn than you. There wasn't any asking, there was only telling. She told me and that was that." He grabbed at the wound and the old man let out a sharp bark of pain. "Now if you would stop fighting me, I might be able to stop this bleeding!"

Behind them came the sound of horses. Behind the horses came the welcome sound of a truck. The truck screeched to a halt on the far side of the truck and Chris heard the door slam. Men on horseback were out of sight, but definitely there, he could hear the whoofing of the horses who'd just been ridden a half mile in a hot hurry.

"Fenton!" A voice called out, Chris waved his hand up out of the grass and sat up. He felt a flash of anger. Well, didn't it just figure it would be Wes Perkins come to the rescue? The man barely spared him a glance as he ran up at a crouch, keeping his eyes fixed in the direction of the old homestead.

"They've got Liza. I heard 'em take off maybe three minutes ago." The old man swayed dizzily as they pulled him to his feet. "Chris says Carrie's headin' round the other side so's don't you shoot her when she pops out of the corn-field. They ain't gotten much of a head start, so if you's think you can catch them in that rickety old truck,"

Wes cocked an eyebrow at the old man, unsure how to respond to his 2012 F150 Dodge Ram with reinforced steel and cattle bar on its front being referred to as 'rickety.'

"You'd best take this young man here." He waved a bloody finger at Chris, "He sure ain't any good at doctorin.'"

"On it." Was Wes's clipped answer. He nodded brusquely at Chris, "Let's go, soldier."

Two other men had arrived by now. One man covered the trees while the other put an arm around Fenton, turned him and slowly headed back towards the house. Wes spun on his heel, Chris close behind him and they sprinted towards the truck.

"We'll head south on Mooring Road and try and catch up to them."

Wes started up the engine with a roar, put in gear and spun out of the gravel road.

"And then what?" Chris asked.

"What do you mean, and then what?" Wes sneered at him, "We shoot the bastards."

"Yeah? Hey, I'm all for that except for one small detail. They've got Liza and how do we keep her out of the crossfire?"

"Anything's better than what those assholes will do to her."

"Damn it, Wes! We want her back alive! Why do you have to be such a..." Chris was cut short as Wes slammed on the brakes and Chris hit the dash hard enough to make his vision fill with stars.

"So, what do you really care, soldier? Aren't them raiders *your* people?" Wes fingered the Bowie strapped to his leg, "Why do you give a shit about some little girl who you ain't even fucking? Or are you tapping that too?"

His lip curled and Chris could see he was begging for a chance to fight, it didn't really matter who he fought with.

"I'm not a soldier."

"Really?"

"They killed my family, raped and murdered my little sister, and when I wouldn't join them, I got to dig latrines and graves." Chris yelled at the man, "Now do we really need to have this discussion now? Or can we figure out a way to save Liza so I don't have to tell my wife and Fenton that I failed them too?"

Wes's lip curled up and his face held a strange mixture of smugness and approval. He unbuckled the leg holster, handed the Bowie and the strap to Chris and resumed driving. "You'll need that."

As he drove, he explained that when Joseph had ridden up to the sentry towers, Wes had been running down all the 'check-ins.' "We've been having all the outliers check in monthly. Most, like you and the Perdues, show up in town at the Trade Mart and I tick you off our list.

The Austin's, over to the south of you, haven't been into town in over five weeks. I was just about to send Jeremy Black over that ways when little Joseph came riding in like the devil himself were after him. So that's where we're headin.'" He shook his head in grim satisfaction, "I *knew* you were caught up in that shit from the west, I just *knew* it."

"You don't know shit, Wes." Chris was still pissed. He strapped the Bowie on his leg.

"Yeah? Well, I know this. We'd be better waiting until after dark. They'll think they've made a clean break. It'll be an element of surprise on our side. That and the dark."

"No way. We got at most an hour before they..." Chris closed his eyes, Liza looked so much like Jess, there was no way he'd let that happen to her. "We have to get her away from those animals and do it *now*."

Wes sighed and shook his head, and turned onto Upper Wynnburg Road and then made another quick left, pulling off of pavement and heading up a bare rut of a road. It was nothing more than packed earth with grass and weeds sprouting up.

"I can take you in a ways, but you'll have to go on foot for about a half mile. They'll hear the truck if I get any closer." He stared out at the road and saw faint tracks. "Shit. This is how they got in and got the slip on the Austin's, guaranteed." He stopped the truck.

"What are you thinking we should do?" Chris asked, his beef with Wes fading fast in the face of this shared enemy.

"I'm thinking we're screwed to be walking into this in daylight is what I'm thinking." Wes shrugged, "They didn't get what they wanted, which was your farm and all its food and livestock. They're probably already taking it out on her." He shook his head again, "Shit. Okay, let's think here. Jeremy will have secured the Perdue house and then followed through the woods behind Carrie. They definitely had to have taken the old access road. It runs up past the back of Perdue land and then heads northeast. I know the Wilkes family is fine, 'cause I saw Tommy two days ago, so they probably backtracked to the Austin's. The question is, are they in the new place or the old one?"

Chris was itching to get moving, but most of what Wes had just said was a mystery. "Map?"

Wes opened his door, grabbed a rifle from the rack and quietly closed the door. He looked around for a moment and grabbed a stick and began to trace in a patch of muddy soil. "Their old house is here, the new one is here, and then there's outbuilding, garage, outbuilding."

He drew and pointed. "Here's us and Carrie should come this way and be in position behind the new house. Now if Jeremy's caught up with her than we've got radio and can coordinate."

He checked his radio and there were a series of responses back and forth. In all, they had Carrie and Jeremy to the east, Chris and Wes coming in from the southwest, and two more men were on their way from town on horseback. Wes directed the men on horseback to head up the main drive to the house, which was further east on Upper Wynnburg.

"Now here is the north field, smack dab in between the old house and barn and the new one." He pointed with the stick at a stand of trees, "We stick to the trees and we'll have cover up until the last ten yards. I'm betting they are in the old place. Not everyone knows about it. It's been years since it was occupied."

After a bit of planning and an update from Jeremy when he caught up to Carrie they slowly closed in on the property. Chris and Wes approached the old Austin homestead from the south and Carrie and Jeremy approached the new farmhouse from the east. It was silent and there was no truck or men in sight. By the time they reached the old farmhouse, the smell hit them. There was definitely no one left alive in there. Wes double checked, pulling his shirt up over his nose, he went inside. A moment later he emerged, hard lines forming on his forehead, his brown eyes almost black with rage and pain.

Wes stopped outside of the old farmhouse and tried to calm his breathing. He spoke then, quietly, and Chris strained to hear his words, "They're all dead. It looks like they killed Lyle and the boys right away. They've been dead a while, maybe more than two weeks.

But Katherine and Maddie, those bastards kept them alive for a long time." His voice caught, "It looks like a couple of days ago for Katherine and Maddie...well, maybe last night at most."

Chris's heart hurt in his chest. The raiders had been close, too close, and he and the Perdue's had never suspected, never thought to check, while an innocent family was slaughtered.

Wes pulled a rough hand over his eyes and Chris was sure he had seen moisture, even a tear run down the man's cheek. His view of Wes changed, altered, as he came to realize how deeply the older man cared for the residents of his tiny town. No wonder he had been such a dick, Wes had known how dangerous the Western Front was, and the thought of having even a deserter come moving in must have been disconcerting.

Wes looked up, focused on the new house in the distance, "Come on, we gotta meet up with the others." Ten tense minutes later, all parties converged in front of the Austin house.

Carrie looked pale, "The main house is empty. They must have killed everyone in the house, dragged them to the old place and been living in the main house for the past two weeks. There's blood everywhere in there." Indeed, Chris could see a long wide brown track leading from the front door onto the porch and down the steps.

Even Jeremy, a tough, greasy-haired man in his mid-30's looked sick, "Must have been at least five or six of them. The Austin's had two grown sons along with a teenage daughter. And I know Lyle Austin didn't go anywhere without at least a gun and a knife on him. It'd be hard for just one or two of them to get the jump on the rest."

Chris gripped Wes's arm, "You said something about the Wilkes being up that outer access road? Well if the truck didn't head this way, then it could have headed back in that direction instead."

Wes turned without a word and ran for his truck. If the Wilkes family was still alive, they were fighting for their lives right now. A few minutes later, the entire group was careening along the rough access road, headed for the Wilkes farm.

"I tried to talk Serena and Brad out of heading for Clinton. There was noth-ing left of the town, no supplies, no people. I had hoped they would come with us, more safety in numbers, but Brad seemed determined to return to his hometown. I warned him that we had seen troops moving that way and Serena got pale and worried, but she must have felt she owed him somehow for saving her from the camp. We parted ways the next day. She was pretty, a completely different person that the broken woman that came to town less than one year later." **– Jess's Journal**

"Hello!" Jess called out and the man tensed, then relaxed when he saw Jess with Jacob's tiny head peeking out from the wraps. They had a large tent, a fire, and several small pieces of meat roasting on sticks over the campfire. Probably rabbit, from the shape of them. Quincy energetically licked the youngest child's face, a boy, who looked to be the same age as Tina and who was giggling in glee at the pup's attack. The girl beside him looked somber, she did not smile at the puppy. Jess figured she was about ten, maybe eleven years old.

"Hello to you!" the woman called. She looked young, a few years older than Jess perhaps, but certainly not old enough to be the mother of the two children. She stood up then, slowly, and Jess saw she was heavily pregnant. Then the young man stood and Jess stepped back quickly in alarm, he was wearing a Western Front uniform. David looked back behind him in terror, seeking an exit or quick escape in the woods behind them.

"Wait!" the young man spoke urgently, "It isn't what you think. I was forced to join them, and Serena here, well, we got out together, about four months ago." His arms were out at his sides. He stared apprehensively at the revolver that had appeared in Jess's hand without her even thinking about it. David and Tina were still as statues, ready to run.

"I'm Brad, Brad Osterman, I'm from Clinton." He put an arm around the woman, "This here is Serena, and she hails from Springfield. We found the boy, Max, about twenty miles south of here, just wandering in the road. The girl was in the camp, she doesn't talk, so we just made up a name. We call her Annie."

Annie stood there frozen, staring at Jess's gun. Her hair was a golden blond and her eyes were cornflower blue. She was a pretty girl but Jess could see the look of deep, dark trauma in her eyes. Her breath caught in her throat as she replayed Brad's words, *the girl was in the camp*. It couldn't be, surely, they wouldn't have had her in Tent 5, and she was so terribly *young*.

Silence followed. Quincy had stopped playing with the boy and moved closer to the young man, sniffing his outstretched hand and then licking it. Jess slowly lowered her gun. The dog trusted him, and Quincy was a good judge of character. If the pup thought they were okay, well then, they probably were, she hadn't been wrong yet. After all, she and Erin had been clothed in Western Front uniforms when they escaped and that didn't make them the enemy either.

Serena spoke then, "It looks like the weather is turning bad. We have some food we could share, and there's room in our tent if you need shelter." She was pretty, with blond hair and blue eyes. She smiled at Tina and David and gave Max a little push towards them. "Max, say hello to the little girl. What is your name, sweetie?"

The question jogged them out of their silence and the band began to talk at once, sharing names, setting down packs and pulling out dried meat and greens to share for dinner. Jacob once again made a loud, uncompromising demand for food and Jess adjusted layers and put him to her breast to nurse while Serena kept stealing glances. "How old is your baby, Jess?"

"Nearly six months now. He was born last August. His name is Jacob." She rubbed her son's head, petted his tiny button nose, avoiding Serena's steady gaze and the question that remained unspoken.

Serena rubbed her belly, "I think it's been about seven months now, maybe eight. I'm not totally sure." She leaned close so that no one else could hear, "Brad's not the daddy. Leastwise, I don't think he is. I sure wish he was. But he got me out of there. That's better than most. The bastard in charge, he has the women killed when they start to show."

Annie had moved away from them and Serena pointed to her and leaned close to Jess. "She's twelve. What kind of monster would rape a twelve-year-old?"

Jess felt a cold chill. "Where was the camp when you escaped?"

Serena shivered, "Arkansas, near the Mississippi border. They were heading southeast, so we went northwest. We stole a truck, drove it as far as we could before the transmission gave out. Brad's mechanically inclined, but we just didn't have the parts to fix it. Highway 13 was taken out just north of Collins so we took Route 54 west to Nevada.

We holed up there for most of the bad part of the winter, after the truck crapped out on us just outside of town. After that we followed the railroad 'til we hit Montrose. When we got there everything opened up onto fields then and, well, it seemed like a better idea to stick to some kind of cover." She shrugged, "Harder going in the woods, but we feel safer."

Jess switched Jacob to the other breast; he patted her free breast, and gently tugged on her necklace. "My friend and I escaped right outside of Springfield a year ago," she winced as Jacob sucked harder, almost gnawing her boob; she wondered if he was teething. "She died a few months later. It happened last fall, just two day's walk east of here."

Serena's expression tensed, "Was she pregnant? Did she," she gulped and looked pale; "Did she die in childbirth?"

"No! Oh, no," Jess felt bad, obviously the woman was scared about giving birth without a doctor and a hospital, "Soldiers found us and I didn't get to her in time. They shot her." She realized it was the first time she had talked about Erin since a few days after the farmhouse, when she had told Madge their story. It was less painful this time, still a wound, but not as painful as those first few days.

"But you...I mean..." Serena looked uncomfortable, and looked down at her belly, "At least, well, *you* know what happened to me." She stole a glance at Brad who was admiring David's compound bow and arrow a short distance away. "They weren't all bad. Brad came to see me often, and he got us both out of there when I told him I was pregnant." She shuddered, "That bastard Cooper, he..."

Jess interrupted, it felt like all of her blood had turned to ice, and "Did you say *Cooper*?"

"Yeah, *Scott Cooper*, I'll remember that sonuvabitch name till the day I die," Serena practically spat. "He raped me over and over the first night after I was taken. I could barely walk for most of a week. And little Lucy Abernathy, oh God, poor Lucy." Her body tensed, "Lucy was up on his roster the next night. He hurt her so bad she killed herself two days later." Tears welled up, "She was only fourteen, I mean *shit*, and I used to *babysit* her on Tuesday nights when her mom bowled in the league." Serena's hands were shaking. "I pray every day that this baby is Brad's. But I know it isn't. It's that bastards." She looked up, gazed hard into Jess's eyes, "Y'think I'll be able to love it? Even if it is from *him*?"

A thousand memories flitted through her mind, but through the fog of pain and fear Jess remembered the moment she had first held her son. The love she had felt, the strange and deep sense of healing. She stole a glance at Jacob, quietly nursing at her breast, his eyes locked on her necklace. His hair was jet black, but he had her eyes.

Jess's reply was simple and direct, "Yes."

Quincy's muffled bark disturbed their intense exchange. In her mouth she held a jackrabbit, the animal's long legs kicking futilely. "Damn! I like this dog!" was the only comment Brad made.

As the first flakes of snow began to fall, they had it skinned, gutted and roasting over the fire. A can of green beans was opened and passed around, along with a small bag of smoked venison and berries. Tina sat next to the boy, chattering away, the older girl Annie watching silently.

At their feet Quincy gnawed contentedly on a handful of bones and the remains of a half-rotten squirrel she had dug up from somewhere. There wasn't much, but the meal took the edge off of everyone's hunger. The flakes began to swirl with intensity as dinner ended, and the light faded. They doused the fire to avoid any unwelcome notice and everyone piled into the tent. It was a tight fit, but the combined body heat soon made the tent toasty warm. When in doubt, sleep, and that is just what the group did, except for Jess.

The sounds of the others stilled and were replaced by relaxed, slow breathing, and the occasional soft snore from Tina who had what sounded like the beginnings of a head cold. Jess lay awake on the hard ground, eyes wide open and staring into the dark.

Scott Cooper. Old Coop had said his son's name was Scott. But lots of people had that name, right? Cooper was a common name. It didn't mean that Old Coop's son was the same sonuvabitch that had raped Serena, Erin, Jess and countless others. It could be anyone, right?

Jess's dad had once said that life was like a giant jigsaw and there were moments when, after trying to fit piece after piece together, two pieces slide together like butter and you know, for sure, that they are a perfect fit. "The pieces meld together, they become one, and you know, that this is the way it was meant to be. This is it." He had said to her, "You'll know it, beyond a shadow of a doubt what the truth is, just by the way it *feels*."

Scott Cooper was Arno Cooper's son. He was also Jacob's father, and most likely, the father of Serena's unborn baby. She cupped her son's sleeping head in her hand. His hair was silky-smooth and he smelled so damned good. She loved him so much. All that he was, all that he would grow up to be...would be of her and by her. His dark hair was the only suggestion of his father so far. Jess suspected Jacob would also be handsome, maybe have the same high cheekbones and dashing good looks. The devil himself couldn't be better looking than Scott Cooper. But she knew, deep in her heart, that was where the resemblance would end. Jacob would be good and kind, she would make sure of that. She would raise her son to be the antithesis of his father.

And what of Scott Cooper? The father of her son? The father of Serena's baby? She didn't love her son any less, but she swore to herself, on that night, that she would find him someday. She would find Scott Cooper, maybe she'd even have to stand in line for the chance, but she would do her best to *kill* him. The thought made her smile. It was a good thing she was the only one awake, and that it was dark. The smile would have scared the shit out of the rest of the tent's inhabitants. And with that vow firmly in place, she allowed sleep to steal her away.

"*We said our goodbyes, though I pleaded with them to change their minds. I thought of how they had sent soldiers in search of Erin and me. We hadn't even stolen a truck and they had hunted us. We warned them, but they didn't listen, I really wish they had.*" – **Jess's Journal**

"Don't go to Clinton. There's nothing left there but bones and ash." Her voice faltered, she liked Serena a lot. The kids got along great, and even Brad was an okay guy. "Come with us to Belton, I know if my home is there, we could make a go of it. We have a little land; we're even set up for raising crops and small feed animals."

Serena looked interested, real interested, but Brad shook his head. "My family is here. They weren't in the camp, so I figure they kept their heads low, they'll be there. We'll be fine and my Ma will be awful excited about a grand-baby." He looked over at Serena and ran his hand down her back. "I hoping we have a boy. I want t'name him after my Gramps."

Jess sighed. She'd done her best; they weren't going to budge in their plans. She closed her eyes, willing away the certainty that these two would die. She wanted so much for things to go well for them. The cup of dandelion and chicory tea had gone cold. She emptied it onto the ground.

The snowstorm had been intense. During the night it had dumped six inches onto the ground and then continued to snow heavily through the morning. David gathered wood and they restarted the campfire so they could cook the two squirrels Quincy had managed to flush from their lairs. Because snow meant tracks, and tracks could mean problems for either party, they agreed to stay until it melted, which would probably be the next day considering how warm it had become after the snow stopped.

When Brad busied himself with gathering wood for the fire, and enlisted the help of the kids, Jess took the opportunity to talk more with Serena. She shared more of her own experiences, and begged Serena to change her mind and head towards Belton. "It's the opposite direction of those soldiers and any fighting."

Serena just shook her head, "You don't know that it's any better off than Clinton. You said yourself you haven't been there in over a year and a half. For all you know, the entire town could be occupied by the Western Front or in ruins." She grabbed Jess's hand, "Stay with us, we're stronger if we stay together, and I'm scared of being alone when the time comes to have my baby. You've been through it, and now you know all that herb stuff that you learned from the old Indian lady. Stay with us." She looked so desperate that Jess nearly said yes, but stopped short.

"I can't. I have to go home. I have to know if my parents are alive or dead." Jess hugged the woman to her, "You will be okay, you know. No matter what..." She took a deep breath, steeling herself for the words she had to say, "I think Jacob and your baby have the same father." She stared at the ground rather than meet Serena's shocked gaze. "I look at Jacob and I'm sure of it. From what you've said about the timing of yours, I think maybe it's the same way for you." Serena wrenched her hand from Jess's and started to turn away.

"Serena, wait, listen to me. I know this isn't something you want to hear right now, but...an old man told me something I didn't want to hear either, just a few weeks before Jacob was born. He said that Jacob was innocent, a child of God, and that he deserved my love. And he did, Serena, he did. I love him so much. I wanted him dead, *I* wanted to be dead rather than have him growing inside of me, but it all changed when he was born. I love him, completely, irrevocably, and I will until I die. It will be the same for you, Serena. No matter what, this baby is a part of *you*. Never forget that."

Tears were welling in Serena's eyes, "Oh Jess...I..." She searched for the words, as the tears slipped down her cheeks, took a deep breath and said bravely, "I'll remember what you said. And if things don't work out in Clinton, I'll tell Brad I want to head for Belton. I don't want our first hello to be a forever goodbye."

The next morning, bright and early, the two groups parted ways. Both Serena and Jess waved goodbye with tears in their eyes. Then one group turned and headed east towards an empty, burnt town while the other headed west and then north towards the unknown.

"*We achieve inner health only through forgiveness - the forgiveness not only of others but also of ourselves*" – **Joshua Liebman**

Grace Wilkes was looking forward to turning thirteen. Just three weeks more to the day. She secretly hoped for a surprise party but she knew how unlikely that was. Just Mom and Dad and Tommy and Vic. Mom had promised she could have a sweet sixteen party in a few years and it seemed that was the best she could hope for.

She slipped outside the house with Danny, a still feisty twelve-year-old border collie and headed for the creek. Tommy was on her these days to stay close to the house and always within sight. Mom and Dad too, after hearing some whispered accounts of goings on recently. Tommy had come home several times sick and scared, and would say nothing to her, just go straight to Dad and tell him quietly about what he'd seen when out with the militia.

Two weeks ago, Mom had taken Grace aside and explained that sometimes bad men did things to girls, things she would understand when she was older. Grace knew what she was talking about immediately – on trips into town to the Trade Mart she had heard it from the other girls – rape, murder. She had walked carefully for days, spooking at the slightest sound, panicking if Danny ran too far from her. But everything was quiet, no one lurked in the woods, and her fears faded quickly.

She was just about to cross the outer road and see if the beavers were up and out of their den. She loved watching them and had even gotten Danny to stay silently by her side instead of barking and chasing after them. As she stepped out onto the road, she could hear a truck gunning its way through. It was running loud and rough.

As it came into view from around the bend, Danny began to bark. It was not his "who goes there" bark, but instead was loud and defensive. A ridge had formed along his back and his teeth were bared as he growled and barked furiously. Grace was surprised by his ferocity. The only one who came this way was Maddie Austin or sometimes Thomas or James, come to visit her brothers. Maddie was two years older than Grace, but she was crazy for Tommy even though he had nearly eight years on her. There had been a time when Maddie and Grace had been closer, but lately, with no one going to school in town any longer and things still being in such upheaval, it had been weeks since Maddie had visited or Grace had been allowed to visit the Austin's.

The truck was slowing and she tried to see inside the mud-streaked windows, wondering if James or Thomas had bought a fixer-upper. The truck stopped, its engine running loud and rough. Danny was in a complete frenzy by now, and Grace saw that there were two men inside the cab and two more in the back with a blond-haired girl. She was struggling when one of them, a dark-haired gorgeous looking one backhanded her, sending her head thumping solidly against the truck bed. He looked up, took in Grace and Danny, who was still barking frantically, and smiled. It was a terrifying smile. She stood rooted in place as Danny's bark was cut short by the dark-haired man's knife.

He threw it almost casually and it arced through the air, burying itself deep into Danny's chest. One of the men from the cab grabbed her, throwing her in the cab, sliding in after her and closing the door before she could even think of fighting. A knife at her throat and she shrank against the man holding her. He smelled bad. Danny was on the ground yelping and thrashing, a knife buried deep in his chest, blood pooled from his fur.

"How many?" The man holding her asked.

"How many what?" she whispered, shaking so hard her teeth chattered. Danny had stopped making any noise, he jerked once more, then lay still.

"How many people at your house?" Riley gave her a shake to help her along.

"Just...just...my parents and my...my brothers." Grace faltered, too terrified to lie. The man squeezed one of her small breasts painfully tight. "My two brothers, but...but...Vic is just ten."

"Good girl." He nodded to the man in the back, "We can take them." At this, Eckhardt gunned the motor and the truck started back down the Outer Access road heading straight for the Wilkes farm.

It wasn't far to go. When they stopped a few yards from the house, all four men jumped out, pulling the half-conscious girl from the back and Riley kept a tight and painful grip on Grace. There was no point in struggling, he was far too strong. Grace got a good look at the girl and realized it was Liza Perdue. She was the same age as Maddie Austin, but the two had never been close. Maddie was very much a girly girl and Liza was a tomboy who hung out with the boys and read science fiction.

Liza's mouth was swollen and her nose was bleeding. On cue, she began to resist the good-lucking, dark-haired man holding her. He cuffed her again, pulled her close and whispered in her ear something that made her glance over at Grace and turn white as a ghost. Her resistance faded.

The group was mere feet away from the front door when it opened to the sight of Anthony Wilkes and a large shotgun in his hands. "You are going to put that down right now," the dark-haired man holding Liza said." He nodded to Riley, who put the knife back to Grace's throat. "He won't hesitate and you'll lose your little girl."

Anthony Wilkes didn't move, and Cooper barked, "Riley, slit that girl's throat if this stupid sonuvabitch doesn't put down his shotgun in five seconds." He paused for one heartbeat, "One...Two...Three."

"Okay, okay, just don't hurt her." Anthony lowered his shotgun and placed it on the ground. At that very moment a shot rang out from the south. None of them had noticed Tommy Wilkes peering around the barn. He had been milking the cows when he heard the truck approach. The gunshot entered Oliver Riley's right ear and blasted a chunk of bone and scalp into Scott Cooper's face cutting him deep, and disrupting his hold on Liza. That first shot was followed quickly by a second that caught Derek Kimmel, standing directly behind Riley, square in his body mass and dropped him to the hard-packed earth instantly.

Liza twisted away from Cooper and grabbed Grace's hand pulling her away, towards the left. There was nowhere to take cover, no shelter of any kind. Eckhardt took aim and shot Anthony center mass, dropping him in the doorway. Inside the house Grace could hear her mother scream.

Eckhardt turned towards the barn, firing off a shot randomly, and grabbing Cooper who was bleeding profusely from a deep cut in the side of his face. Cooper also shot blindly in the direction of the barn.

Tommy ducked back into the barn. Liza and Grace ran then, full out back towards the woods that Grace had been walking in only moments ago. Behind them, Cooper and Eckhardt stumbled back to the truck, intent on retreating.

It was Karen Wilkes who fired the fatal shot into Eckhardt's back as he ran toward the truck. As Eckhardt slumped to the ground a second shot grazed Cooper's side and neatly severed his right pinkie, effectively disarming him. He ran, started up the truck and whipped it around back the way they had come. A third shot shattered the back windshield, sending glass spraying in all directions. He gunned it and disappeared around the bend in the road.

Wes's F150 screamed with power down the rough and bumpy road. To the right Chris could see flashing glimpses of Reelfoot Lake through the trees. Carrie was tucked in tight in the middle seat and Jeremy held on white-knuckled in the open back as they flew down the dirt and gravel road. They could hear gunfire ahead and to the right.

Sometimes time can move so slowly. The next few minutes, time went from flashes of light and gunshots ringing in ears to a slow protracted growl. Chris would remember that moment for a long time afterwards.

He remembered seeing the battered old truck come around the corner racing away from the Wilkes farm. He remembered turning and seeing the look on Wes's face as he struggled to turn the wheel in time. What stood out most for Chris, the thing that haunted him for nights afterward, was the sight of the face of the man driving toward them.

Despite the injuries and the blood, he knew him. He knew just who he was.

In the half-second before impact, Chris Aaronson locked eyes with the man who had raped and killed his sister and brutalized countless other women. And then there was nothing, but glass and noise and pain.

It would be days before he woke up. And it would be months before he could walk without excruciating pain. His left ankle, which had healed relatively well since last spring, broke again, along with his lower left leg. Several ribs had cracked and he'd suffered a significant concussion. Wes and Carrie had sustained relatively small injuries as well and poor Jeremy had broken both legs in the resulting crash. It had taken all the medical know-how that Liza could sum up to ensure that the man ever walked again.

It had taken nearly half an hour for Liza, aided by Tommy Wilkes and his grieving stepmother, Karen Wilkes to reach the crash site on foot.

By the time they had arrived, Scott Cooper had disappeared.

March had come and gone and the land was beginning to warm again. Already Carrie and Liza had been out preparing the raised garden beds for planting. Chris sat on the porch in a comfortable rocking chair, his leg wrapped in a splint, one of Fenton's walking sticks propped against the rocker. He jumped when Liza's voice sounded next to his ear.

"Wow, you were really lost in thought. I said your name twice!" She smiled at him. Her face had healed quickly, the bruises from the beating she had taken faded from purple to green to yellow and then they were gone. She was still twitchy though, and jumped at sudden noise. She hadn't gone for any walks alone either.

But Liza was tough, despite her youth, and she had only been punched and slapped. They hadn't had time for anything else. Chris had worried about that and finally asked Carrie to make sure. Somehow the reassurance that there had not been any sexual violation of Liza or Grace made him feel a tiny bit better.

"You doing okay, Chris?" Liza's smile faltered a bit. She put on a brave front, but it was just that, a brave front. It had been a close call, and she had survived, but Cooper was still out there. That stuck in the Perdue's thoughts day after day.

Chris smiled back at his sister-in-law, "Yeah, I'm okay." He reached out and squeezed her hand. "When do I get to take this damn splint off?"

"Give it another week."

She turned to go and Chris held onto her hand, "Are you okay, Liza?" He'd heard her cry out in the night several times in the past few weeks.

Liza stopped, looked at him, and smiled, "Yeah. I'm going to go see Grace Wilkes on Friday. Carl's gonna come pick me up and drive me over there. Her mom has had a bad time of it, losing Mr. Wilkes like she did. I told her we'd help her and Tommy and Vic get the ground ready for planting. If we all stick together..."

Chris smiled, "We'll all be better off."

The sun was setting. Carrie and Joseph made their way from the barn, both armed. Carrie and Liza had spent several weeks with Joseph making sure he understood gun safety and proper stance as well as accuracy. As for Cooper, if he was smart, he had gone far, far from here. The militia was still keeping a sharp eye out and had recruited double the members it had had prior to the raiding party. But in case Cooper decided to come back for a visit or to get revenge, the Perdues, and the Aaronson's were ready for him.

Miles to the east, Scott Cooper walked. He was no longer handsome.

The bone shards from Riley's skull had torn through his right cheek, shredding the skin. Then the impact from the collision had broken his nose and his jaw in two places. The fact that Cooper had survived the crash, ran away, and managed to get by with such injuries testified to his own dark will to live.

For now, Chris and Carrie, the Perdues and all of Tiptonville were safe.

*"**My** dad used to say, 'Jess, never underestimate the power of the mind to delude itself.' I never thought it could happen to me. I was "tough" and I was a "survivor" and all that. But really, that chick Pollyanna? She has nothing on me. I managed to delude myself for over a year. Maybe it kept me alive, maybe it gave me a purpose, but still, the truth, when I was finally faced with it, was devastating."* – **Jess's Journal**

Thurman Banks watched the ragged group approach town. They came up Y, which was littered with burned out shells of homes. When the Western Front had torn through, the homes to the south had been obliterated. There were still one or two farms on the outskirts of town that were holdouts, but they were on their own, too spread out for the Belton Militia to protect. Until Y intersected with Main Street, there was practically nothing and no one to sound the alarm. Thurman dialed in the zoom on the high-powered binoculars, Farley had insisted that all of the police surveillance binoculars be assigned to militia members. They were mighty powerful; he'd been able to see the group clear as day for well over a mile and count their fingernails from a good half mile.

The tallest, a teenage girl with what looked to be a baby wrapped in a sling across her chest, looked somewhat familiar, but the two younger kids weren't ones he recognized. Damned if they didn't have some floppy-eared mutt leading the way. The dog trotted a yard ahead of the teenager, nose to the ground, ears cocked forward.

Belton wasn't a large town, but it wasn't that small either, and he couldn't see them well enough from the sights of the gun. They looked relatively harmless; certainly not any of those damned Western Front soldiers come to prey on the remains of his beloved town and home. He lowered the rifle, slowly slung it over his shoulders and stood up, stiff from sitting so long in one position. At least the weather was warm, today was only the first day of

April, but already the days were in the mid-70s. It was about time to start planting.

Since the invasion, those who were spared had formed an informal militia. They did what they could to watch the entry points to the small town and report in if they saw anything of interest coming their way. He pulled out a sheet of paper, scribbled on it a short message, and reached his hand out to the German Shepherd lying quiet at his feet.

Isa was at his side instantly, perfectly quiet, but her fur raised and stiff. These were strangers, but they were small, similar to the little ones who used to play in the nearby houses each day. Those children were all gone. Isa had smelled some of them, their fear scent, sometimes even the painful death scent, in the days back in the cold time, when they had been taken by the bad men. She missed the little ones. She sniffed the air, smelled the woman-girl and the tiny one cuddled against her, the sharp fun smell of a boy (they were the best for playing with), and a small girl-child beside him. The pup galloped in front of them and the sight of it drew a small territorial growl from the older dog's throat. Despite the distraction, her attention was still closely focused on her master. Isa knew her place, knew her part in the pack, and waited for orders from the old man she loved so much.

He spoke softly to her as he tucked the note into a small film canister that dangled from her collar, "Isa, go to Farley. Go!" The dog sprang forward, ran down the steep stairs along the side of the building and disappeared around the corner heading west towards the old courthouse.

Thurman followed the dog to the stairs, moving far slower, joints creaking. The nights were still cold and his knees ached fiercely until midafternoon. He slowly moved down the stairs and off of the roof of the old grocery store. On street level you could still see most of the sign, B—ks Grocers. Thurman had inherited the store from his father, bequeathed it to his son Mark and he guessed he owned it still, though it was bare to the bones now. The shelves were empty, had been half empty that fateful day when the Western Front had blown through. Now both windows were broken and nothing remained within to sell or steal—not even the shelves or cash register. He had washed the blood of his son from the walls and floor and buried him in the cemetery, next to his mother and Mark's wife Annette. Thurman thanked God and fate and all the rest each day since that his Mary had been gone and buried before that terrible day. It would have killed her to know her only son and daughter-in-law were dead and her precious grandson missing and most likely lost to them as well.

He headed south towards the small group coming in. Farley would be along soon with backup if it was needed. Thurman doubted they were a threat, but Farley was mayor now, and he could make up his mind on that.

Jess was nervous, scared to death, actually. The endless miles they had walked, the dangers, the hunger, just so she could 'come home' suddenly seemed so ridiculous and foolhardy. How could she possibly know if Belton had been spared? What if her home was gone and enemy soldiers occupied the town? Serena's words echoed in her head and David and Tina both looked at her expectantly, even a little frightened. They too wondered quietly, what if this town was no better than the others they had traveled through?

She saw the old man approaching them and recognized him. Thurman Banks lived two blocks to the north of her parent's home. Old Thurman was Allen's grandfather and he used to mow the lawn for granddad in the summer then head down to Jess's house to see his buddy Chris. That old Thurman was alive and here in Belton brought a whoosh of air back into her lungs. She smiled in relief. "Mr. Banks! Oh, Mr. Banks! Do you remember me? I'm Jess Aaronson, Michael and Julie's daughter."

"*Jessie*? My God, Jessica Aaronson," Thurman was amazed, none of those taken in the first wave had returned, he had written off the children and their parents as dead long ago.

"Where is Chris? Your parents?" He took hold of her and hugged her to him, and then pulled back, "Have you word of my grandson, Allen?"

All of Jess's hopes crashed and died in that moment. The past seventeen months had been filled with horror, struggle, and even success. My God, she was alive, so were David and Tina and little Jacob. The miracle of that had not escaped her notice. But all along, in the back of Jess's mind she had clung to the belief that her mom and dad had made it through. They hadn't been in the camp, but then again, she had never seen Chris, although Allen told her he was there.

She didn't know when she had decided it, with such Pollyanna certainty, that Mom and Dad were still home in Belton. But she had.

And now it felt as if she had been shot in the chest.

"My parents aren't here? And Chris and Allen, they didn't make it back?" Her mind began to spin. She had been so sure, so absolutely sure that Mom and Dad would be here, waiting for her. She had imagined their reunion over and over. Their joy at seeing her, the love they would show Jacob and the surety that she would be safe again, for good, in their arms.

She had imagined too, that Allen and Chris had made it out that night like Allen said they would. Surely, they had made it out. Guilt at not helping them, at not having a plan that included them and her and Erin together, it all exploded like fireworks in her head. Her legs felt like rubber and she slowly knelt down on the ground, her brain and heart spinning faster and faster. No Mom. No Dad. No Chris. Erin was gone, her blood spilled in an abandoned farmhouse so far from here.

She remembered vomiting what little food she had in her stomach before the world turned to black, first at the edges and then all over. From far away she could hear Tina scream her name and David yell for help as she slumped to the ground.

She was finally home, but those who had made it a home to return to were no longer here. Farley and several others arrived in time to see her pass out on the hard ground.

Author Note

Thanks for reading! Please take a moment and write a review of this book on your favorite book buying website.

Put simply, reviews indicate that someone has a) read the book and b) thought enough of it (either way) to post a review of it. Positive or negative, your opinion does matter and I would be deeply appreciative.

Sign up for my newsletter below or by visiting my author website: https://christineshuck.com

You don't ever have to spend a dime.

My monthly newsletter provides:

- An occasional short story (*exclusive for subscribers*)
- A summary of all of my blog posts
- Advance notice of giveaways and promotions

I promise to *never:*

- Sell/share your email address
- Avoid greasy used car salesman tactics (I apologize if you are a used car salesman, obviously, I'm talking about the *other* guy)
- Make unsubscribing as easy as pushing a button.

Interested? Great! Join the newsletter list here: https://mailchi.mp/c05ceb84e66a/subscribe-me

A Café on Main Street

"*We overstayed our welcome. We bullied, we pushed, we invaded...and when we were done, when the world had felt our presence in every corner of it, felt our hand on their backs, shoving our way into every aspect of their lives, faiths, even their very existence...we were hated. God, were we hated. In retrospect I can feel no real surprise for what happened next. Our time had come. For our hypocrisy, for our crimes, we each paid such a terribly high price. The world we had known, the nation that our parents had been told to be proud of, a place of fast food and 'freedom fries', home of the consumer, center of capitalism, world leader, it all ceased to exist. It was a slow, painful end, an extended death rattle, as we slowly tore ourselves apart, and then allowed others to finish off what remained. What was left in the wreckage of the world that was? We were. And this is our story, my story, and the story of us all. We have survived. We have found a way to live on...in a world where ghosts haunt us and memories whisper in our ears. Life goes on, one day at a time, and by the skin of our teeth and the force of our will, we will continue. What else can we do?*" – Jess's Journal

"Drink it slow," an unfamiliar face in the crowd swam into focus.

The woman's face was prematurely aged, her brown hair streaked liberally with gray. Her brown eyes crinkled at the edges as she smiled at Jess. Jess blinked and accepted the steaming mug offered. She was sitting in a café, at a battered little table right across the street from Banks Grocers. It had been the last place she had stood before being ripped from Belton some seventeen months earlier. She couldn't see it right now; too many people were blocking the way, staring in through the window, staring at her. Some looked vaguely familiar, but most were strangers. The café, dimly lit, and packed full of the mayor, Mr. Banks, and far too many others, was charged with excitement. Jess's fingers nervously traced the cracked Formica top of the table and tried to will away the rising anxiety. She hadn't seen this many people in a long time. God, they were close, so close; she could barely breathe.

Tina had scrambled under a table and buried her face in David's leg as he stood awkwardly. The little girl was shaking like a leaf. It had been a very long time since Tina had seen this many people in one place. David, his dark hair disheveled, a smudge of dirt on his cheek, wasn't doing much better. He kept attempting to move closer to Jess, seeking some amount of space between this overwhelming mass of strangers and him. Quincy stood at attention, glued to Jess's side, eyeing the crowd warily.

Another mug appeared before David, who sat down awkwardly, his sister wrapped around his leg, clinging to him with a tenacity that would rival that of a lamprey eel.

The same woman who had spoken to Jess lightly touched his shoulder, "Would the little girl like anything? I might have a packet of hot chocolate here somewhere."

David shook his head, "No thank you, ma'am. I'll just try and get her to drink out of my cup in a minute or two."

The woman nodded and smiled again before slipping back behind the counter, giving up the space to Todd Stevens, the militia leader, Mayor Farley, and old Mr. Banks, who had, after all, been the one to discover them in the first place.

Jacob mouthed a hard, dense biscuit.

Madge had shown Jess how to make them, pointing out their uses, saying, "They are good for traveling, since they never go bad, and when Mi'-da-in-ga begins teething, they will give him something to chew on." She had winked at Jess, "Believe me, Mi'-na, they are worth the trouble to make."

As with everything else she had taught them along the way, she had been right about this. The biscuits had provided countless boosts of energy, propelling Jess, David, and Tina down miles of road and kept Jacob from fussing. One tooth nub was finally poking through his little gums, with a second not far behind, and the edge of the sling was now dingy and encrusted with biscuit slime.

Mayor Farley and Mr. Banks had sat down in chairs around the small table. Jess thought that Mr. Banks looked much older than she remembered him. His hair was a shock of white and hadn't been cut in a while. The mayor, who had once been obese and shaped like a big round ball with skinny legs and possessing an overly large red nose, was now rather lanky, the extra skin hung in folds, but his nose was as red and large as ever. As she looked around the room, Jess couldn't see anyone who was overly large. The mayor spoke first.

"Now, you are, hmm, Angelica?"

Jess shook her head and Thurman Banks spoke up, "This here is Jessie, Michael and Julie's daughter." He said, correcting Mayor Farley's mistake, "You remember Julie baked bread, taught classes, and helped organize the farmer's market. Before the..." He looked distinctly uncomfortable, "Well...you know."

Jess could see by the slightly blank look on the mayor's face, who she still thought of as the president of Congress Bank, where Mom and Dad had had all of their accounts, that he didn't remember her mother at all.

"Of course, Ang...err...Jessie," he smiled at her broadly, before turning his attention to David and Tina, "But who are these children? And this baby there?"

"This is my son, Jacob," Jess answered without any further explanation on that topic, "This is David and Tina Farnsworth. They are from Clinton."

"*Your son*?" The mayor blinked, looking scandalized. "And the father of the child?"

Jess felt a quiver of anger run through her, "He has none."

"I see." The mayor's voice definitely held a tone of disapproval now.

Mr. Banks, who understood far better than Mayor Farley put a hand on Jess's thin shoulder. He could feel her bones sticking sharply through the fabric and he suppressed a surge of fury at the mayor's lack of tact. Here was one of their lost children, who had gone through God knows what, returning to find only disappointment and misunderstanding.

"One of our own, everyone, Jessica and her family have traveled a long way to return home again." He said it loudly, so it would carry to the crowd outside, and he emphasized the words "family" and "home." He had long suspected the mayor was an officious, small-minded fool, and Farley was proving him right by leaps and bounds.

"What Jess and the kids need right now are food, a safe place to rest, and some time to settle in."

He ignored the mayor, who was trying to hush him and muttering something about the two younger kids not belonging.

He looked around at the crowd expectantly, "I think we can give them a good home-cooked meal while Todd goes and scouts out the Aaronson house to see what shape it's in."

Todd Stevens, who had been watching this whole exchange, nodded and stood up.

"I'll go and do that right now. What's the address?"

Jess found herself stumped at such a simple request. Her address? When was the last time someone had asked for that? She closed her eyes at the memory of those tents, the group of men sorting the prisoners.

Name? Family?

But even they hadn't asked for an address. It seemed so immensely mundane, so *normal*, that her mind just went blank for several long seconds before memory kicked in. She rattled it off to him and he nodded, gave her a small encouraging smile, and slipped away through the crowd.

They could hear Sarah, the woman who had given Jess and David the steaming mugs of tea, talking in the kitchen of the small café, issuing directions to a young woman a year or two younger than Jess. Wonderful, mouth-watering smells began to waft their way and the kids' stomachs began to rumble painfully. Jess was so grateful for old Mr. Banks's intercession that she could barely speak. And then, of course, she remembered Allen, and his visit to Tent Five, the first and last time she had ever seen him since she had left Belton.

She turned to the old man, leaning close so that the others could not hear, and said, "About Allen, Mr. Banks."

He set a large, callused hand over hers and shook his grizzled head, "Not now, Jessie. Later. You tell me later, all right?"

He could see from the look on her face that it was unlikely his grandson would ever return home. Despite wanting to know, even if the details hurt, he couldn't bear it in front of such a large crowd. Better to keep his grief close and to care for the living. The girl had obviously been through terrible trauma. And from the wary look on the boy's face, he and his sister had as well.

"Right now, we need to get you all fed and a place set up to sleep for the night. I'm assuming you all want to stay together?" Jess and David nodded.

"Okay, I'll see what I can do."

Farley, who had been quiet far too long, felt the need to intercede.

"Now Ang...I mean Jessica, where exactly have you been all this time? In Clinton?"

"No sir, Clinton is in ruins, although there continues to be a lot of fighting and different troops moving through there," Jess answered. "I was held by the Western Front until a year ago. I escaped with Erin McGowen, discovered David and Tina in Clinton, where Jacob was born, and we over-wintered in a cave near Truman Lake before heading back through Clinton and up Highway 71."

"A *cave*? You lived in a *cave*?" The mayor looked incredulous.

He would have said more, but at that moment the food arrived. Two large plates were set in front of Jess and David. There were eggs, thick slices of homemade bread with butter and a dollop of homemade jam, and slices of bacon still sizzling.

Jess winced as her empty stomach rolled ominously, reminding her of how she had just been sick not an hour before, and also that she hadn't had such rich food in a long while. Sarah Turner stood near her, her brown eyes soft and kind.

"Is the food too much for you, dear? Do you need something simpler?" David had already inhaled nearly half of the plate before remembering to offer a slice of bacon to his sister, who had folded herself neatly under his chair.

"I, um," Jess didn't want to be rude, but she felt exhausted. From hunger, from stress, and from the fear that her stomach would not be able to hold down anything she put into it right now.

Sarah patted Jess on the shoulder, "Don't you worry, honey. I'll scrounge up some oatmeal for you that should settle your stomach."

She bustled off and Jess slid her plate toward David and Tina. The offer of a slice of bacon had been enough to lure the little girl from under her brother's chair and a grubby set of fingers snatched at a piece of the toast while David eagerly cut into the eggs. Quincy whined once, licking Jess's fingers, and she offered the dog a piece of her bacon.

Quincy pulled it gently from her fingers and gratefully swallowed the delectable meat, staring at her mistress with a hopeful look, hoping for more.

She wasn't disappointed. David slipped a triangle of toast under the table to the hungry hound.

Farley looked even more disapproving. Jess was surprised this was even possible.

"Dogs use up limited resources."

Her spine straightened and Jess stared the mayor square in the eye and said, "Quincy hunts for her own meals. Squirrels, rodents, sometimes a bird." She broke a piece of bacon in half and handed it to her dog, "She's helped feed us and she's protected us too."

Mr. Banks interceded again; he was sitting nearest to the dog, "Sounds like a fine hound, well worth keeping."

The corners of Mayor Farley's mouth turned down, but he said nothing.

After all, he thought, *if the girl was fool enough to get herself knocked up, and take on more mouths to feed along her journey home, there really wasn't much point in talking sense to her. Was there?*

A bowl of oatmeal was set down in front of Jess and Mr. Banks introduced Sarah to Jess.

"Jessie, this here is Sarah Turner, one of our newest residents. She hails from back east, here with her two young 'uns for goin' on a year now. They were caught in a tussle between the Western Front and the Washington Guard; barely made it out of St. Louis. And Sarah makes the best lemon meringue pie I've had since my wife passed on. God rest her soul."

Sarah beamed with pride. "Not that we see many lemons these days, but I do manage to make a few each time we see a trader come from the Southern routes." She turned her warm brown eyes on Jess, who had managed a bite of the oatmeal. "Is that better, dear?"

Jess swallowed, her stomach settling some and said, "Yes ma'am, thank you."

"Call me Sarah." She reached out and petted the top of Jacob's head and then turned to look at David and Tina, both of whom had finished the food before them and were now running fingers along the plate to catch the last of the egg. Not a crumb had gone to waste.

"I would give you more, but that's a lot of food to eat after not eating much for so long. You take it easy, now." David nodded and thanked her.

Between bites of oatmeal, several in the crowd asked Jess questions about missing friends and loved ones. She shook her head no too many times to count. No, there was no one else she remembered seeing. Only Allen and Erin, but Erin and her family were dead, and she wasn't going to speak of Allen publicly. That would wait for a private moment with Mr. Banks. He deserved to know what little she knew—but in private, away from all of these eyes and questions. Jess found herself wondering if coming here was a good idea. No Mom, no Dad, no Chris. And the way that stuffed shirt, that bank president turned mayor, Jonathan Farley kept eyeing Jacob—it made her angry. As if she had *asked* to have a baby. As if she could have stopped it.

Jacob began to fuss then, turning and nuzzling her shirt, picking up on her emotions and wanting reassurance, wanting food. He was just a baby, innocent and sweet. As her body responded to his need, the milk rushing into her breasts, she was filled with love for him. Never mind how he had been conceived, or the dark thoughts she had had about him while pregnant, walking those long miles with Erin. He was hers, and she loved him deeply. And wasn't that as it should be?

Jacob pulled at her shirt, more insistent now, and Jess looked for an exit. She wasn't going to breastfeed here, near this officious stuffed shirt and dozens of prying eyes. Her eyes met those of Sarah, who had seen the baby nuzzle at Jess's shirt. Sarah slipped out from behind the counter and made a beeline for her.

"I think that Jess needs to rest a little, away from everyone," she said diplomatically, "after such a difficult morning. There is a couch in the back, dear, why don't you and the baby go in there and relax for a few minutes?"

Jess nodded gratefully, stood up, and let Sarah lead the way, the crowd opening for them.

Mayor Farley looked decidedly out of sorts. He had been in the middle of pressing for details on Erin and wasn't satisfied with Jess's short answer that she had died outside of Clinton. Jess suppressed a wave of anger; he hadn't even remembered Erin either, only Erin's brother Toby, who had been an Eagle Scout and the valedictorian of his graduating class. The mayor looked as if he wanted to follow Jess out of the room. He was the type who wasn't used to being told "no"—and his recent elevation to mayor had made him even more pigheaded than normal. Sarah Turner had quelled him with a stern look as he began to stand up and follow and Farley had suppressed a desire to physically push her out of the way. She wasn't even *from* Belton. But at that moment one of the townspeople had tugged on his sleeve and suggested he update the crowd outside. The mayor's attention was successfully diverted to one of his favorite tasks: speaking authoritatively to crowds.

The back room was quite obviously where Sarah and her family lived. There was a large living and sleeping area and a candle gave them a dim light. Jacob was fussing, pulling at Jess's shirt, insisting on being fed, *now*. Jess sat down on the couch, eased her shirt up and allowed the hungry infant to latch on. He made satisfied little grunts as he greedily sucked.

"Thank you, Sarah," Jess said. "How did you know?"

Sarah just smiled, moving a small box with the letters SAP carved into it, and put it out of view.

"How did I know the crowd was too much, or that you needed to nurse? Women's intuition, I guess." She busied herself clearing a chair free of books before adding, "That Mayor Farley is a real butthead. Don't you worry one second about what he thinks. He treated me the same when I showed up with two kids and 'no man to care for me,' is how he put it." She rolled her eyes, "As I hear it, they let him be mayor just to shut him up. He was carrying on so about how we needed 'structure and organization in this time of chaos.'" She grimaced. "I think it was because he just wanted to be able to tell others what to do." She winked at Jess, "*And* get out of serving on regular patrol in the town militia, like the rest of us have to do. They even look to me to participate in the patrols, now that I've been here long enough to be trusted."

Jess smiled in return, and relaxed for the first time since returning to her hometown. Belton was the same cozy little town she remembered, yet different. But then again, wasn't everything? Everything had changed. Jess wondered if her home still stood, and whether they could go there, right away, because she wasn't used to this, the people, the questions, the judgment. Not from everyone, obviously. Sarah was nice, and so was Mr. Banks. The militia leader, Todd Stevens, was young, maybe in his mid-20s, and he had seemed okay. Belton was organized, well-defended now, which was more than she could say for any of the other towns she had traveled near since this whole conflict began. Jess sighed. Perhaps, just perhaps, they were truly home and safe.

She closed her eyes and melted back into the couch, switched Jacob to the other breast, and barely cracked an eyelid open when Sarah led David and Tina in. They had been walking since daybreak, in the cold, with nothing but the hard biscuits to eat. But that wasn't what pushed Jess into an exhausted sleep. It was all of the people, the questions, and the prying looks. There was that and the black disappointment—after all this, all the running, all the struggles—her dream of returning to her family, to her Mom, Dad, and Chris—to learn they had never returned was overwhelming. If they weren't here, if they hadn't made it back by now, then they really were all gone. That was the last thought she had as she succumbed to sleep, and it would be the first thought she had when she woke up two hours later.

Acknowledgments

To Kate, Rachel, and Dori—my teachers at Independent Learning School who gave in to my endless complaints about the dreadfully boring Warriner's grammar books and just let me *write*. You saved my life and gave me a chance to fly.

To Dad who kept asking just "when in the hell" I was going to finish this book – well Dad, here it is.

To Mom who inspired the gardener in me and also passed on many thrifty tips that I have used to make ends meet during the 'starving artist' phase of this book. Love you, Mom!

To my girls, the eldest who helped shape the woman and mother that I have become and my youngest who remind me that life, love and happiness are found in the simple act of living and interacting with others. I love both of you and always will.

To Baby Bean – I mourn what could have been.

To Pat Whelan of the Anita B. Gorman Conservation Discovery Center in Kansas City for his amazing knowledge of wild, edible plants, the topography of Missouri, and his time and patience.

To Roger Renner, Firearms Consultant, who provided valuable advice in the manner of weaponry, ammunition and hunting strategy. You can learn more about Roger's expertise by visiting his blog at www.underhammers.blogspot.com[1].

And finally, to my husband David, who found me half a lifetime after high school and reminded me that hearts can and should heal. You have appeared in more of my little stories then I ever realized and you have encouraged me to write in those dark moments when I doubted myself.

---

1.   http://www.underhammers.blogspot.com

About the Author

Fueled by homemade coffee ice cream, a lifelong love of words, and armed with strong female (and male) characters I cross genres like the Ghostbusters crossed the streams in pursuit of the question.

"What is the question?" you ask.

The question is simple. It asks, "What would you do, if..."

What would you do if you were fifteen years old and the world as you knew it fell apart? Would you run? Would you fight? Would you survive? – Meet Jess and her brother Chris in War's End[1].

What would you do if you had a chance to live your life over? Not just once, but twice? – Meet Dean Edmonds in Fate's Highway[2].

What would you do if everyone you loved was lost to a terrible virus and you faced the real possibility of the extinction of the human race in the dark void of space? – Meet Daniel Medry in G581: The Departure[3]

What would you do if hitmen were after you and you had no idea why? – Meet Lila and Shane in Hired Gun[4]

If I don't keep you turning pages late into the night, desperate to know what happens next, then I have failed at my job. I'm a Taurus and born in Missouri. That makes me bull-headed and stubborn to boot. I don't believe in failure or mistakes, only learning opportunities and clever conversation. There's not much I won't do to make you burn the midnight oil reading my words while you suffer sleep-deprivation the following day. It's my secret superpower.

Born in flyover country, I've also lived in Arizona and northern California. I am an eclectic mix of snark and oddball humor. My colorful metaphors would make a fishwife blush. I'm an incompetent gardener, a dreamer and doer, in love with old houses and shooting pool, and chief organizer of all thing's household and financial. Feed me tiramisu and I'm yours forever.

---

1. https://books2read.com/u/bwYNpY

2. https://books2read.com/u/bPJG5Y

3. https://books2read.com/u/4jDgPl

4. https://books2read.com/u/bP0dOj

Join my Facebook group at General Malcontent's Grumbles and Scribbles: http://bit.ly/3jo0MVU

You can also find the latest updates on my writing adventures at: http://christineshuck.com.

Sign up for my newsletter at: https://mailchi.mp/c05ceb84e66a/subscribe-me

Follow me at:

Twitter: @christineshuck

Facebook: Christine.D.Shuck

Instagram: christinedshuck

All Published Works

Christine writes cross-genre and her books can be found in e-book and in paperback through most book distributors.

<u>Non-Fiction</u>:

Get Organized, Stay Organized

The War on Drugs: An Old Wives Tale

<u>Fiction Series</u>:

<u>War's End</u>

The Storm

A Brave New World

Tales of the Collapse

<u>Gliese 581g</u>

G581: The Departure

G581: Mars

G581: Earth (Summer 2021)

G581: Zarmina's World (Spring 2022)

<u>Chronicles of Liv Rowan</u>

Fate's Highway a.k.a. Schicksal Turnpike

<u>Benton Security Services</u>

Hired Gun

Smoke and Steel

Broken Code (Fall 2021)

www.ingramcontent.com/pod-product-compliance
Lightning Source LLC
Chambersburg PA
CBHW071209210726
48293CB00002B/347